A GALEBORNE RESOLVE

BOOK 3 OF THE DELIBERIA CHRONICLES

S. LYNN HELTON

ISBN (Paperback): 978-1-7348581-6-7
ISBN (eBook): 978-1-7348581-7-4

Scripturio Books
www.ScripturioBooks.com
24.04.03

Dedication & Acknowledgments

For my first and beta readers, and fellow authors who have been early readers. Thank you for all your input and for helping me continue to improve my stories.

CHAPTER 1

FROM ALORSHA'S JOURNAL

"Everything happens for a reason.... Some things are destined." At least so some people say. I don't know that I hold with all that. All I can say is that Jarthan and I had been together almost since birth.

Our families lived in the same village, Avorth, in the land of Varoia, one of several smallish kingdoms and countries on the large island of Deasa. A small village, so of course everyone knew each other and each other's business. There were several children, of all ages, but just a year separated my age from Jarthan's, with him the elder of us two. Both of us had older brothers and sisters, but none close to our ages, so it seemed natural that we worked and played together.

Mama gave me my first journal the day Jarthan left for school. I still have it. It's mostly filled with silly things: talk of the butterflies I saw one day, how much I missed Jarthan, village celebrations, some truly awful attempts at writing songs, and too many complaints about my ongoing struggles with fancy sewing. To which Mama would say to me, "Alorsha, keep at it. None of your siblings managed it right away either. Your eldest sister never managed more than the basic stitches for repair work."

I do miss Mama.

But, of course, that journal doesn't tell our whole tale, Jarthan's and mine.

And Devrand's.

My apprentice Gyasi has frequently asked about how this whole magical hunt came about, this strange worlds-crossing chase in which we find ourselves. I've told him in bits and pieces, trying to explain and describe what happened without taking an entire day, or more, to tell it all. Finally, he suggested I collect the whole story together, write it down to make better sense of it and preserve it. And write about the ship's travels, too. Ship's Captain Mikolus and Ship's Master Saevalde agreed with him. Saevalde even gifted me a new leather-bound journal she found during one stop in a sizeable coastal city in one of the worlds we passed through.

Odd to think of my younger self. Sometimes it feels like I couldn't ever have been her.

Anyway, to remember…. To tell what happened with the magic. How it all came about. What went wrong.

~ ~ ~

The girl perched in a warm beam of sunshine on one of the rails of the wood fence that ran around the village green. She kicked her feet back and forth in irritation and directed her frown toward one house in particular. *He's late.*

A slender girl, not too thin, with golden-brown skin and dark eyes, Alorsha had just seen her ninth spring. Her straight black hair hung long, but most of the time Mama made her braid it or otherwise tie it out of the way for chores. Like most of the children in the village, she wore a loose shirt and trousers that had been dyed in muted colors. Unlike most of the other children, Alorsha's shirt had delicate flowers embroidered at the neckline. Mama had done that and was teaching her how to. But she was not very good at it. Sometimes she wondered if she would ever be good at it.

But she was done with chores for the day. She and Mama had baked many loaves of bread earlier and Mama was off trading them with the neighbors for other things the family needed. Papa was out in the fields with other adults from the village. They would all be home soon for the evening meal. But, for now, Alorsha had some time to herself, and she and Jarthan had planned to meet. She had something wonderful to show him.

She jumped off the fence and headed around the green toward Jarthan's house. *He probably has extra chores.*

He often had extra chores.

As she lifted her hand to knock on his door, it swung open and he rushed out, almost running her over.

"Alorsha! C'mon," he said without further greeting. "I've got something to show you."

He ran along the village's one street, the one that made an oval around the green with an extension at either end that led out of the village. The villagers' houses lined the side of the street opposite the green: all constructed of sturdy stone walls—most of them light in color and many in need of some repair work—with dark roofs that sloped down to both sides to let the rain and melted snow run off.

Alorsha followed at Jarthan's heels, at first, then caught up to him and paced him at his side. She had always been a little faster than him, although he had the longer legs.

"Jarthan, I want to show you something, too."

"When we get to the meadow. Good?"

"Good."

They ran to their favorite place, simply called the meadow by everyone in the village. All the children played there from time to time, but Alorsha and Jarthan the most.

They dashed to the center and tumbled to the ground on their backs, their breath faster than if they had walked, but not at all winded. For a time, they gazed at the clouds and pointed out to each other the ones that resembled fantastic creatures from the storyteller's tales of olden times and faraway places.

After they enjoyed this favorite pastime until they could discover no new shapes, Alorsha sat up. She tapped Jarthan on the arm.

"So, what is it? What do you have to show me?"

Jarthan sat up and wriggled around to face her, their knees touching. He cupped his hands on his knees. From beneath his pale, shaggy hair, he gave her a serious look, uncommon for him.

Alorsha looked in his hands then back to his face. "What? I don't see anything."

"Give me a minute. I've not done this more than a couple of times so far."

Jarthan closed his eyes and breathed out lightly into his hands.

Alorsha watched. At first nothing.… *Was that a spot of color in his hands?* It had not been there before. She held her breath. *Could it be?*

As she watched, the spot brightened into a brilliant blue that morphed to purple followed by a swirled mix. A shape formed, stretched, parts of it flattened, flapped wings.

When Jarthan looked at her again, he held in his hands a small, perfect butterfly, in colors they had never seen on a real one.

Alorsha looked at him in awe. "Is it real?"

He grinned. "It *looks* real. Try to touch it."

"I don't want to ruin it."

"You won't."

Alorsha reached toward the butterfly, one finger extended and tried to touch a wing. Her finger passed through. She jumped back with a cry, but the butterfly was undamaged.

She looked at Jarthan's eyes and saw a faint glow in their green depths. "You did it!"

If anything, his grin widened. He threw up his hands and the illusion of the butterfly dissolved into hundreds of small bright sparks that rained down over Alorsha and vanished.

She laughed in delight. "Does this mean you'll be accepted to the mage school?"

"I think so. But I wanted to show you first."

They shared smiles.

"Now, what did you want to show me?" Jarthan said.

"Oh...." Alorsha looked away from his enthusiasm. "It's not as good as that."

Jarthan laid a hand on her shoulder. "Don't say that. I want to see."

"Very well." She looked around the meadow and spotted what she needed on the side furthest from village.

"Come over here."

Jarthan followed her to a small patch of yellow flowers that bloomed in the tall grasses. A few of the flowers had buds that had not opened yet. Alorsha knelt by one of the buds and cupped her hands around it, with gentle pressure on the stem beneath it.

Jarthan leaned in to see better and watched with a smile as the bud—oh, so slowly—opened.

Alorsha looked up with a question in her expression.

"That's brilliant!" Jarthan said. "Imagine us both discovering at the same time that we *do* have magic. Just as we've always hoped."

He grabbed her hands and jumped to his feet, pulling her with him. "This is the best! Now we can both go."

"I don't know about that." Alorsha hung her head.

"What do you mean? We've both got the magic. It'll mean good things for the village to have two of us at the mage school. It'll make the village important. Us, too."

Alorsha shook her head. "Jarthan, think."

He stopped bounding around and took a long look at her. "What is it? Alorsha?"

"Think for a minute. You created something that wasn't there. That's the type of magic that'll get you into the school. I just made something move. It's magic, but not at that level. Yours is so much more powerful than mine."

"Maybe that's just where you're starting from. You're younger than me. By this time next year, I'm sure you'll make illusions as good as mine. Maybe better."

Alorsha smiled at his enthusiasm. "Maybe." But she expected otherwise. Her magic was still a good thing. Just not of the level that the school would take to teach.

Jarthan noted her serious expression and draped an arm around her shoulders. "Hey. Even if not... if I go away to learn and you don't, I'll always come back here. You know that."

She nodded. "I know. 'Cause if you didn't, your grandmama would come get you and drag you home by your ear." She grinned at him.

Jarthan laughed and rubbed his ear at the memory. "Don't remind me."

Alorsha laughed too. "Race you to the green?"

"Later. When we have to go back. For now, let's work more magic."

So, they made more illusions of butterflies and sparks and opened more buds and curled leaves of flowers.

When they tired of working the magic, they climbed a favorite tree at the edge of the clearing and scooted out onto a strong branch. They rested there as twilight spread across the sky. Until their families called them home, they swung their legs back and forth and chatted about all the wonderful, amazing things they would learn to do with magic.

CHAPTER 2

Alorsha frowned in concentration as she poured the small bits of leaves into the potion in a steady stream. This was a new concoction to her, more complicated than any she had yet tried in the years since she and Jarthan had shown their parents the magic they could do, and their lives had changed. During those years, while she and Jarthan still had chores, they had spent increasing amounts of time learning from Izmireva, the village's coppice-mage. They played with their magic on their own, too. They spent most of every day in each other's company as they learned and explored their magics' potential.

Hard to believe it's been two years.

Alorsha poured the last of the leaf bits into the potion and stirred it to blend everything. *Hope Jarthan's got the next ingredients ready.* She glanced at him and frowned.

He lay stretched out on a low bench and watched her. He had been doing that sort of thing a lot in recent months. Could it be that he just liked to look at her?

Alorsha turned away as odd flutters and tingles pattered inside her and her face warmed at the thought.

She stole another peek at him as she continued to stir and considered that idea.

They made an odd pair, she and Jarthan. When younger, Jarthan's hair had been almost white. It had grown darker as he grew older, but never anywhere near as dark as Alorsha's. His light skin freckled something fierce in the sun, while Alorsha's just got a little browner.

Although they did not speak of it, they both knew that soon the mages from the school would come and test him. They might even already be on their way. If he passed, something Alorsha never doubted, he would leave their village for several years, at least. With only short visits home.

The idea of going away from the village to the school in the city frightened the wits out of Alorsha. *Perhaps a good thing my magic likely won't get me into the mage school.*

When Jarthan had first discovered his magic, he had been thrilled at the thought that he would travel and see other places. He had shared that delight with everyone, at every opportunity, it seemed.

But lately he had not spoken of it at all.

"Jarthan, you're supposed to be helping," Alorsha said.

He jumped to his feet. "Right, sorry."

While Alorsha mixed the next ingredient into the water over the small fire, Jarthan prepared the rest for her, in the proper amount. He had each herb chopped or crushed and ready when she needed it.

A knock at the door interrupted their focus. Izmireva rose from her padded chair in the corner and opened the door.

"I'm sorry to interrupt," Jarthan's papa said from just beyond the door.

Alorsha and Jarthan froze.

"The mages are here. For the testing," Jarthan's papa continued.

Heedless of the herbs in his distraction, Jarthan hurried to the door. "I didn't think they'd come so soon. I don't feel ready. I need more time to practice."

"I understand, son, but they're here now and ready to see both of you right away."

Alorsha looked from the half-completed concoction to the ingredients that sat on the table. "But we're in the middle—"

"Both of us?" Jarthan interrupted.

Izmireva nudged Jarthan to move him out of her way and eased the spoon from Alorsha's grip. "Yes, both of you. Now go, children. I'll clean up here and get everything set for when you return to show them what you can do."

Alorsha and Jarthan wiped their hands on one of the spare cloths kept for that purpose—spreading magical plant bits around would not do—and ran out the door.

Outside, they found the rest of the villagers gathering on the green. Off to one side stood three formidable-looking people, a man and two women, who all wore the deep blue robes that marked them as masters in the mage school.

The man stood a little taller than his two companions. He wore his black hair—as black as Alorsha's—tied at the nape of his neck in a short queue. His skin was a darker brown than hers, while his companions both had lighter skin. The woman with brown hair had light brown skin like Jarthan's and wore her hair pulled back and piled atop her head. The third mage, a slight woman with even lighter skin and white hair, wore her hair in a queue like the man's, but with many loose strands framing her face.

Alorsha caught a strand of her own hair that the light breeze blew into her eyes and tucked it behind her ear. She smoothed her hands down the front of her plain dress. *Would've liked time to change.*

"Do I look mussed?" she whispered to Jarthan.

"No, you look wonderful. Well, except for...." He brushed his hand across her cheek to remove a smudge.

She smiled at him, and his cheeks and the tips of his

ears turned pink.

"C'mon." She took his arm to urge him to walk with her.

Tingling prickles danced along her skin, as if everyone stared at them as they circled the green and approached the mages. Since the village had never before had anyone test to go to the school, probably everyone *did* look at them. She kept her gaze straight ahead, leery of looking back at all those staring faces.

Someone started to clap and soon all the villagers clapped for Alorsha and Jarthan. Even if the two did not qualify to study at The Gramaire, just testing as mages brough a great honor to them and the village.

Alorsha's face grew warm, and she saw that Jarthan blushed again. *Poor guy.* At least her blushes were harder to see on her summer-darkened skin.

The two children stopped in front of the mages, stood straight and still, and waited for them to speak first, as they had been instructed.

The mages conferred with each other, and the man stepped forward. He gave Alorsha and Jarthan a kind smile.

"Try to relax, if you can," he said in a low voice.

The village headwoman held up her hands and called for silence from the villagers. She got it without trouble. "My friends. Today marks a historic day for Avorth. Today, not one, but two of our own stand to be tested, stand poised to be recognized as mages."

She waited for the cheers to quiet and continued. "We're honored to welcome three distinguished guests from The Gramaire: Mages Zhivko, Nijole, and Raska." She waved a hand toward each mage as she named them.

The mage she had indicated as Mage Nijole—the woman with the brown hair—stepped forward. A stout woman, she seemed to be about the same age as the headwoman and looked much like her.

"Citizens of Avorth, thank you for your hospitality this

day," she said. "As you've just heard, we're here to test two of your own for admittance to The Gramaire, the school of magic. I imagine you're all eager to support your two candidates. At the moment, you can best do that by continuing with your regular activities while we speak with them and see what they have to show us."

She waved a hand toward a small cart that stood nearby. "We've brought food for the feast this evening, and a few of our own people to take the burden of the preparations. If you're willing, we'd ask that you help them ready the feast while I and my colleagues meet with your candidates."

As people from the village called out how they could help, and suggestions, the mages drew Alorsha and Jarthan to the side.

The mage with the white hair smiled at them. "That'll make it a little easier on you two. Keeping your folk occupied and not peering over your shoulders."

Jarthan and Alorsha each gave her tentative smile.

"Before we get to the real matter of why we're here, however," said the man, "we've a few minor details to attend to."

Alorsha and Jarthan exchanged looks.

"First, direct introductions," the man said. "I'm Mage Zhivko. This is Mage Nijole," he indicated the woman who had spoken to the crowd of villagers. "And this is Mage Raska." He indicated the woman with the white hair.

Mage Raska pulled a small book and quill pen from a pocket, while at the same time trying to tuck behind her ears several strands of her wispy hair that the breeze had caught. "You are Alorsha Tavaros, is that correct?" she said to Alorsha, who nodded.

She abandoned her attempts to catch the strands of her hair and wrote in the book—using ink from the bottle Mage Zhivko held for her—then turned to Jarthan. "And *you* are Jarthan Ilyevano."

"Yes, ma'am."

She wrote again. "Good, good. Now, is it true that neither of your families have evinced magical abilities previously?"

Alorsha and Jarthan exchanged glances.

"If that means that no one else has the magic, then yes, that's right," Alorsha said. "At least as much as any of us know, as far back as we know."

The mage wrote again in her book.

"Good. Ages, please."

"I've just seen my eleventh spring," Alorsha said.

"And I, my twelfth," Jarthan said.

The three mages exchanged glances.

"Older than usual," Mage Zhivko said. "Although not by too much."

"Sir, our parents decided we both needed to learn a couple of years with Izmireva," Jarthan said. "To make sure, they said."

Mage Zhivko nodded his head. "None better than Izmireva. Uncommonly prudent. Too many want to rush you youngsters in—"

Mage Nijole broke in. "We're ready for you to show us what you've learned from Izmireva, and what you can do with it. Please. I'd imagine that Izmireva has everything set out for you."

Jarthan bowed, a little wobbly, and Alorsha followed his example. They then led the three to Izmireva's workshop.

Izmireva awaited them at the door. After she greeted the three mages like old friends, she bowed to them and clasped Alorsha and Jarthan each on a shoulder.

"You both can do this. Just show them." With a wave, she strode toward the green.

Alorsha and Jarthan led the way inside and looked to the three mages who followed for direction.

The mages found spots to sit around the edges of the work area.

"So, which of you will go first?" Mage Zhivko asked.

"We usually work together," Alorsha said.

"I'm certain you work well together," Mage Nijole said. "But we need to see your individual abilities right now."

"I'll go first, if that's fine with you Alorsha?" Jarthan said.

Alorsha smiled and nodded. "It's fine with me." *He probably wants to go first because I'm better than him at the "plant stuff" as he likes to call it and they can't compare his actions to mine if he's first.*

She found a seat near Mage Zhivko, settled back, and hoped that Jarthan's nerves would not get the better of him. Otherwise, some impressive, but unwelcome things could occur. *I've seen that enough times!*

Jarthan perused the supplies Izmireva had laid out for him.

Alorsha did likewise from her spot at the side. *Looks like Izmireva recommends he do Blueness, a challenging potion, but within his skills. As long as he concentrates.*

Jarthan hung the small pot above the low fire to warm the water within and set about crushing and chopping the herbs. Alorsha felt him brush them with his own magic to draw out their magical properties and nodded.

She smiled as he double-checked the quantities and their degree of readiness before he stirred each one into the hot water in the correct order.

After the last ingredient, bluebark that he had shredded into finger-long threads, he sat back for a count of one hundred.

Alorsha caught his eye while he counted under his breath and gave him a nod. *No mistakes.*

He smiled briefly and grabbed a small bowl.

He poured his concoction into the bowl, holding it to let the mages see the absolute colorlessness and clarity of the liquid. He set the pot aside to cool and looked around. "What shall I prove the potion on?"

"Here." Mage Zhivko held out a small glass cup. "If you've worked your potion correctly, this will show us.

Please pour two fingers of the potion into the bottom and set the cup on the table."

Jarthan did as instructed and watched the glass.

Alorsha watched as intently as he did, uncertain what to expect. She held her breath. *This had to work.*

At first the glass, and the liquid inside, remained colorless. Then a hint of blue appeared on the cup at the edge of the liquid inside. The color deepened as it crept up the sides of the cup to the rim and became the dark blue of a twilight sky.

Jarthan watched the mages, his expression nervous. He glanced at Alorsha and away.

The mages finished writing in their small books and looked up at him.

"Excellent work," Mage Zhivko said. "Well done. But this type of magic isn't your strength, is it?"

Jarthan looked at the ground and mumbled, "No, sir."

He jumped when Mage Raska clapped her hands. "Then young sir, please show us your delight, your passion, your strength in the magic."

Jarthan's gaze slid to Alorsha when Mage Raska said 'delight'. He drew his attention back to the mages who waited on him with expectant expressions.

"Um, anything?" he said.

Mage Nijole laughed. "Please, nothing destructive. There will be a place for that at another time if that's one of your strengths."

"Oh, well, of course. I mean, I don't know about destroying stuff." He shuffled his feet.

"Jarthan," Alorsha muttered.

"Oh, right."

He moved back to the far wall to give himself plenty of room. With half-lidded eyes he spun the magic as he had played with it these past two years, drawing extra to himself from the air around him and the sunlight that streamed in the room's single window.

He cupped his hands and formed the blue-purple

butterfly. As it fluttered around the room, he formed several small brown birds, and a few more butterflies of other colors, and sent them flying about. He glanced at the mages and smiled at their delighted expressions.

Alorsha nodded at him. *It's going well.*

After he had filled the room with little birds and butterflies, he closed his eyes to block out distractions. Faint at first, but growing clearer and louder, birdsong filled the room. When he had that set, Jarthan opened his eyes again. He grinned at Alorsha, and she grinned back.

He spread his arms wide and sent all the fliers to hover near the ceiling. When they all fluttered there, he dissolved them into a shower of multicolored sparks that rained down and disappeared before they touched anyone. He watched the mages for their reactions.

For their part, the three mages exchanged glances then leaned together and chatted, with animated gestures. Jarthan gave Alorsha a questioning look and she leaned toward the mages. She shrugged at Jarthan, unable to hear what the mages talked about.

After several tense minutes for Jarthan, the mages looked back at him and clapped.

"First-rate control," Mage Zhivko said.

"Well done," Mage Raska said. "And you're able to produce sounds, too."

Mage Nijole just smiled.

With squeak of joy, Alorsha jumped up, ran to him, and wrapped her arms around him. Jarthan froze in surprise before he hugged her too.

At the sound of Mage Zhivko clearing his throat, the two jumped apart and stared at the floor.

"Congratulations, Jarthan," Mage Zhivko said. "It's clear that the mage school will be the right place for you." The mage held up a finger to his lips. "But you two hold that information close for now. We'll officially announce it at the feast."

"Come sit, Jarthan," Mage Raska said. "Now, Alorsha,

please show us your strengths."

"But I'll not go to the school," Alorsha objected. "My magic isn't like Jarthan's."

The mages exchanged a look. "That decision about who attends the school is ours to make," Mage Nijole said. "But whether you do or don't learn there, wouldn't you like to have official acknowledgement of your magic, which includes the status of mage?"

Alorsha's eyes grew wide. "You'd do that? If I'm good enough?"

"Of course. Not all mages study at the school. Not all mages have strengths in the same types of magic. Now, please...."

"Of course."

Alorsha found that Izmireva had set out supplies for her, as she had for Jarthan. *How'd I miss seeing them before?* She stepped over to her worktable and scanned what Izmireva had left for her.

Could it be? Does Izmireva really *recommend I do that one?*

Alorsha double-checked what Izmireva had set out and saw that she had not assumed incorrectly. By the ingredients there, Izmireva indicated she should work the Blue-Vanishing magic. A demanding magic, it represented a true test for someone not yet an apprentice mage. But she *had* been able to make it work before. *Hope I can do it now.*

So, like Jarthan, she began by warming a small pot of water over the fire. But, right away, she tipped four drops of moonshine into the water before it grew warm. She looked up to surprised expressions on the mages' faces. *Must be that few hopefuls do this one for their testing.*

Alorsha worked her way through the preparations of the herbs, flowers, and barks that the concoction needed, and dropped each into the water at the right time. As with Jarthan's concoction, threads of bluebark came last. For a hundred-count, she whisked the mixture while it still hung over the fire.

When she had finished that part, she took the pot from the fire and let it cool for another hundred-count. Mage Zhivko handed her a glass cup, just like the one the mages had given Jarthan.

"Two fingers?" Alorsha asked.

Mage Zhivko nodded.

Alorsha poured her concoction into the cup and held both that and the pot to show the mages the liquid as she poured, to show them the absolute clarity and the faint blue tint.

She set aside the pot with the rest of the potion and watched the cup.

As with Jarthan's creation, at first the glass remained colorless. Faster than Jarthan's, the hint of blue appeared at the top of the liquid inside, deepened, and swept up the sides of the cup to the rim. The color deepened further to become the dark blue of a twilight sky. Then it turned black. With a small pop, the black portion of the cup vanished.

Alorsha gazed at the mages. Almost as one, they approached the table and each one reached out and tapped the invisible portion of the cup. Three times the glass rang. They all looked up at her and she stepped back. She clasped her hands together to hide their trembling.

"I've not seen the like before," Mage Nijole said.

Mage Raska nodded. "Indeed. Excellent work, child. Superior."

"The Gramaire's potion-masters couldn't have done better," Mage Zhivko added.

Alorsha relaxed and could not stop smiling.

"One last thing," Mage Zhivko reminded her.

"Of course, sir." Alorsha looked around the room and spotted the pot of dirt that Izmireva had prepared for her. Several seeds lay next to it.

She cleared her worktable and brought the pot to the mages, holding the seeds in one hand. "Would you please pick the seed? Or do you have a different one you'd like me to use?"

Mage Zhivko smiled at her and pulled his hand from his pocket.

"It seems we do." He opened his hand to reveal four different seeds. While Alorsha scrutinized them without yet touching any, Mage Nijole took the seeds she held and pocketed them.

"We'll return these after," she said.

Alorsha nodded, absorbed in trying to figure out the seeds Mage Zhivko held out to her. She had never seen their like before and had no idea what kind of plants they would grow into. She smiled to herself. *Must be the point. So how do I pick?*

Finally, she pointed to a narrow, reddish seed, about half the length of her longest finger, which resembled a curled-up, dried petal.

"You may take it," Mage Zhivko said. "But why that one? Do you recognize any of these? Have you heard of the chervynai before?"

Alorsha shrugged and shuffled her feet. "No, sir. I've never seen any of them before. And I've never heard of the chervynai. I-I just like red."

The mages chuckled, but not unkindly.

"As good a reason as any for this," Mage Raska said.

Alorsha took the red seed back to her table. With her fingers, she created a hole in the dirt in her pot. "Does it prefer shallow or deeper?"

"This one prefers shallow and damp," Mage Zhivko said, while the other mages wrote something.

Alorsha nodded and returned some of the dirt to the hole. She placed the seed in the hole and covered it with loose dirt. She breathed out over the pot and drew the moisture from her breath into droplets of water that she let fall on the dirt. She repeated this until the soil grew moist. Then she cupped her hands around the pot and reached out to the magic in the seed. She concentrated, closed her eyes to better focus, and encouraged it.

It began to grow.

Two little leaves poked through the dirt, stretched upward, and grew more leaves. The plant filled out into a small bush about a hand's length tall. From the midst of the bush a single stalk grew. It stretched upward, and a single large bud formed at the top.

Alorsha paused and peeked at the plant. She still had no idea what it was, beyond its name, but it was taking a lot out of her. *Still, I have to finish.*

When one of the mages began to stand, Alorsha closed her eyes again and immersed herself in the plant's magic. *Ah, there.*

Less concentration, and more just a kind of tickling, she coaxed the bud into flower. She opened her eyes and dropped into a chair as the strength drained from her legs.

Atop the stalk perched a flower much the same size as the bush, with deep red, scalloped petals, each edged with gold. If she thought such a thing possible, Alorsha would have said real gold.

She watched as the mages conferred. Jarthan smiled at her.

When they finished talking, as for Jarthan, the mages clapped for her.

"Most impressive," Mage Raska said.

"Excellent control," Mage Nijole said. "Most others falter at the bud."

"Others?" Mage Zhivko said. "Hah. Few others even have a chance to grow this flower, let alone such a perfect specimen. Congratulations!"

"I-I'm to go to the mage school, too?"

"Oh, no, my dear," Mage Raska said.

Jarthan's hopeful expression wilted and something inside Alorsha matched the sentiment. She reminded herself that she had not particularly *wanted* to go to the school. *But still....*

Mage Raska stood and clasped one of Alorsha's hands. "The mage school wouldn't suit your strengths at all," she said. "It might even ruin you."

"You'll apprentice with Izmireva and learn all you can from her," Mage Zhivko said. "She's our best coppice-mage. The best in all the lands, even. You cannot do better for a teacher."

"And you'll be recorded as a mage in the official scrolls," Mage Nijole said.

This time Jarthan clasped Alorsha in a hug. "Brilliant, Alorsha!"

"We'll make all the announcements at the feast tonight, but you can tell Izmireva after you clean up in here. I'm sure she's eager to learn how it went."

After the three mages clasped hands with Alorsha and Jarthan, they left the two to their clean-up.

CHAPTER 3

After Alorsha and Jarthan passed the mage test, he left within the week to study magic at The Gramaire. Alorsha had been listed, as Jarthan had, in the official annals as a mage apprentice, so her time since then had been filled with all sorts of things to do, all sorts of things that helped distract her, at least for a time, from how much she missed him.

Izmireva had taught her more than just how to take plants and draw upon their magical essences for potions, elixirs, and tinctures. There were all sorts of creams and oils, too, and some inks. Also, every day, Alorsha had practiced sensing the strengths within a plant's magic by mere touch, whether the leaves of one would help strengthen other magics, or the stem of another held healing magic.

But her lessons concerned more than the magic. Izmireva taught her about the lands around them. Alorsha learned that their village was just one of many in the demesne of Baron Horic and that his demesne was one of several in the kingdom of Varoia. Before those lessons, she had not even known they had a king.

"As a mage, you can be called upon by King Lovain and the court to travel to other parts of the kingdom, and even to other nearby countries," Izmireva told her. "You should at least have a basic knowledge of those places."

So, Alorsha spent long hours bent over maps that Izmireva rolled out on the largest worktable. She traced roads, trails, and rivers, learned the names of the rulers of each demesne of Varoia, and learned of the demesne's nearest neighbors Pirkuo, Wolshor, and Cothria, and how the people there lived.

Alorsha enjoyed learning about the maps so much that she even copied them, drawing them repeatedly until she could draw them from memory alone, at first in the dirt, then on parchment, when Izmireva got some for her.

The months had piled up into four years as she learned and grew in her magic. She saw Jarthan a mere handful of times during those years.

~ ~ ~

It had been close to six months since Jarthan's last, brief visit home. A visit only long enough, it seemed, to exchange quick stories about what they each had learned. Then he returned to The Gramaire, and not a word since, until the letter. This day, Jarthan would be returning, and could stay for longer than before. His letter had said so. But it had not told her why.

This would make his second visit this year, when in past years he had come once each year. *Hope this visit is for a good reason, and not something bad.*

Alorsha had dressed in new clothes for this day. She wore a long-tunic that reached her ankles, blue and of a medium-weight fabric for the cooler weather. She had embroidered the flowers and leaves at the neckline herself.

Pausing from time to time to glare down the empty road, Alorsha paced at the edge of the village. *Where is he?*

She squinted in the hope of catching sight of him at last and played with the ring on her right middle finger. The gray metal ring with its sliver of the red-tinted dark stone called erythros—used in all mage rings—signified she was a student mage. The placement meant she was still an apprentice.

Is that dust? Alorsha took a few steps away from the village and squinted again in the late afternoon light. It looked like a lot of dust for one rider.

She waited, shifting back and forth, and wrapped her arms around herself as the late autumn air turned chill.

There. Just coming around the bend atop the last hill before the village. Two horses. *Who's Jarthan bringing with him?*

She waited until Jarthan pulled his horse to a stop and slid off. They hugged and stepped apart to look at each other. The other horse stopped behind Jarthan's and Alorsha glanced at the rider: another boy. He looked to be about Jarthan's age.

She turned her attention back to Jarthan. He had grown, of course, as had she. The top of her head now came to the bridge of his nose. His hair had darkened to a gold-brown color, but with lighter streaks in it. His green eyes looked much the same, crinkling at the corners with his smile.

He reached out and touched her hair. "You cut it."

She laughed. "Yes, silly." She ran her hands through her shoulder-length hair and swished it around. "This way it stays out of whatever I work on. It's still long enough to tie back, if I choose, but I don't have to do those silly braids."

"Isn't your mama irked with you over that?"

"She was. But now she says she likes it like this."

Then Alorsha squealed—and winced that she would make such a sound—when she saw that Jarthan wore his ring on the first finger of his right hand.

"You made craft-mage?" She hugged him again.

23

"Brilliant! Congratulations!"

Jarthan grinned. "You must be close."

Alorsha nodded. "I think I'll test for it next month."

"Great. We'll probably still be here. New craft-mages get a long visit home before they take up their new studies."

"Speaking of 'we'...." Alorsha looked over her friend's shoulder at the other boy.

"Oh, right." Jarthan waved the other boy closer.

Alorsha studied the newcomer as he dismounted and joined them. He stood of a height with Jarthan, with thick auburn hair and eyes an unusual blue-green color. He was slender to Jarthan's stockiness, his skin a brown lighter than Alorsha's, with a hint of freckles on his cheeks. The ring on the first finger of his right hand declared that he was also a craft-mage. He reached out and clasped her hand and bowed over it.

"I'm Devrand Charnov," he said as he straightened and smiled at her. "I'm a reprobate, and I'm pleased to meet you."

Alorsha's face grew warm.

Jarthan punched him in the shoulder. "Incorrigible is what you are."

Devrand released Alorsha's hand. "Right. That's the word." He grinned at Alorsha, and she could not help but grin back.

"I just wanted to give this pretty lady a proper greeting and leave her with no delusions about myself."

"Ah, true enough." Jarthan gazed at Alorsha. "And you *are* pretty, Alorsha. But *I* should have been the first to say so." He punched Devrand in the arm again.

Alorsha tilted her head to hide behind her hair. "My thanks."

Jarthan reached out and brushed her hair back. He draped an arm around her shoulders as he turned to Devrand. "This is Alorsha Tavaros, my best friend. I've mentioned her—"

"Several score times," Devrand broke in.

"Well, yes. Anyway, my best friend, and a right amazing coppice-mage in her own right."

Devrand nodded. "I'm horrible at that type of magic. I'd love to see some if you'd be willing to show me."

Alorsha smiled. "Uh, sure."

Mama called her from across the green.

"We'd better get you two settled," Alorsha said. "Everyone's been eager to see you and wondering why the second visit this year, Jarthan. They'll be thrilled at your advancement."

Jarthan's cheeks reddened. "I had to get there at some point." He grabbed his horse's reins and headed toward the blacksmith's – the one place in the village with room to stable horses, although the villagers kept no horses of their own. Devrand followed and Alorsha paced them.

"Are you from a small village, too?" Alorsha asked Devrand.

He shrugged. "Sometimes."

At Alorsha's questioning look, he grinned, although the expression was half a grimace.

"In my family, and where I'm from, off to the southwest, it's not always the parents who raise the kids. A lot of the time, the kids live with one relative or another for a while. Along with the other kids who were within a couple of years of my age, I spent each year with a different relative's family. So, while I've spent several years total in various small villages, I've also lived in some of the cities, even the king's seat for a time."

"Wow, that sounds… well, strange, I'll admit," Alorsha said. They both laughed. "But incredible, too. So, you've already seen a lot of the kingdom. What made you decide to come here? Why not spend the time with your family? Or one of them?"

Devrand gave her a long look. "My family's not people to spend time with. Besides, Jarthan's always talking about his village and the great friend he has here. Since we're good friends at school, I wanted to meet others who are important to him."

"C'mon, you two," Jarthan called from the blacksmith's doorway. "Hurry up. I'm hungry."

The three settled the horses and hauled the boys' packs to Jarthan's house.

After she waited through lengthy greetings for the boys and helped get Jarthan and Devrand settled, Alorsha headed back home, with promises to meet the two the next day.

When Alorsha told Izmireva about Jarthan making craft-mage, Izmireva let her have a couple of days free from her lessons to spend with her friend in honor of the achievement.

That first free day, Alorsha and Jarthan took Devrand around the village. They told him where everyone lived and little fun stories about them, and they wandered out to their village meadow. Since it was autumn, Alorsha had no buds to make bloom, but the three enjoyed playing with their magics and showing off for each other.

Alorsha learned that Devrand had just passed his sixteenth spring, which made him the same age as Jarthan, a year older than her.

After the first couple of days, Alorsha needed to return to her studies. Often, Jarthan and Devrand joined her, with Izmireva's permission.

It became clear that Devrand had not exaggerated his lack of ability with Alorsha's type of magic. While Jarthan managed a few simple things, not much more than he had been able to work the day of his testing for The Gramaire, Devrand could not even manage the beginner tasks.

He laughed at himself but kept trying. "It's been this way all along," he told them. "But, who knows, if I try enough times, maybe someday I'll be able to manage to chop leaves rather than mangling them."

Izmireva frequently had the three of them work together. "Mages need to learn how to mesh their magics with other types," she told them. "While we're at peace now with neighboring lands, that hasn't always been the case. And even if not to defend the kingdom, meshing can help accomplish other tasks faster, and even better at times."

Under Izmireva's guidance, the three practiced working their magics with and around each other's. They discovered that they could mesh their magics as effectively as Jarthan and Alorsha had ever been able to.

Their strengths became apparent as they did this. Alorsha could draw to the surface and enhance the magics from any plant they found. She needed to hold, or at least touch them to do so.

Jarthan could create exact, elaborate illusions, which included sight and sound, and he was learning to make them affect real things, such as an illusion of a person who left tracks in the dust. The tracks did not linger long, but he told her he was working on that. He had also better learned to draw magic from his surroundings, needing less to greater effect, to supplement his own.

Devrand had the ability to bolster the others' magics, although he had talents with neither of their types. But his touch vastly enhanced their own magics. The magic flowed easier and stronger, although not for long.

So, the days passed. Alorsha, Jarthan, and Devrand spent all their free time together and, in jest, some of the villagers called them 'The Triplets'. Izmireva delayed Alorsha's test, saying the boys distracted her too much. But she promised the disappointed girl that she would test soon after the boys returned to The Gramaire.

Too quickly, they reached the last day of the boys' visit.

Around midday, the three grabbed some food from Alorsha's house and perched on the fence that circled the village green to eat.

"You've lived here all your life?" Devrand asked Alorsha around a bite of fresh bread.

Alorsha nodded. "So far. But Izmireva says I could

begin traveling soon. 'It benefits a craft-mage to journey to practice her arts and learn from other mages,' she told me."

"Absolutely," Devrand said. "Maybe you can come to The Gramaire and visit us."

"I'd like that," Alorsha said.

"Me, too," Jarthan said.

"Let's make a Concord," Devrand said.

"We're not supposed to work such magics until we're done with our crafter years," Alorsha said with a frown. Concords were a magic that required at least two mages and served to ensure that parties to an agreement adhered to the terms, like in a treaty between warring groups. Or a marriage between feuding families, according to some stories.

Devrand shrugged. "We're supposed to push our magics, learn to do more. I'd think we should already be testing if we can do it."

Alorsha looked to Jarthan, who grinned. "Devrand's always finding ways to stretch the magic. Besides, it'll only be a small Concord. I think we can do this."

Alorsha looked from one to the other as she considered their words. "That's fine, I guess. After we've been able to work together so well these past days, I suppose we can work such magic."

Jarthan and Devrand nodded.

"But not here." Devrand gave Izmireva's house a significant glance.

They gulped the rest of their meal and ran to the meadow. Clouds had built throughout the day, which made the usually cheery place gray and cold.

"Here?" Alorsha asked.

"Looks good," Devrand said.

"So, we have to get the wording right," Jarthan said. "And bind it with a touch of our own magic."

"You do know how to do that, right?" Devrand said to Alorsha. "Izmireva has shown you?"

"Some," Alorsha said.

"Good," Devrand said. "So, let's say this: 'we shall meet again within the year at The Gramaire'. How's that sound? Nothing there to trip us up?"

The others considered the words.

"Maybe 'within a year from now, we three shall meet again at The Gramaire'?" Alorsha said.

After further consideration, they agreed that phrasing would work.

That decided, the three stood together in the middle of the field, close enough that their shoulders touched. Devrand held out his right hand and nodded to Alorsha. She placed her right hand atop his and made sure her mage ring touched his. Jarthan placed his right hand atop hers and his ring touched hers. Alorsha's hand warmed between the boys' hands.

"Ready?" Devrand said.

Alorsha and Jarthan nodded. Alorsha shivered, whether from nerves or just the chill air, she did not know. Devrand gave her a reassuring smile.

In unison, following the formula that they had all heard that mages used for Concords, they said, "We three gathered here do make a Concord. Within a year from now, we three shall meet again at The Gramaire."

They each reached within to that spark of magic that they carried and drew the tiniest amount to their rings. A bright flash blinded them.

"And that should be that." Devrand pulled his hand back.

"How can we be sure it worked?" Alorsha asked.

"Concentrate on your ring," Devrand said. "You should be able to feel it there."

She did as he directed and after a moment felt the Concord lurking within the ring. As she noticed it, her ring gave off a faint glow.

"Hope it doesn't do that where anyone can see," Alorsha said.

"Should only be when you touch it with your magic," Devrand said. "And something pretty incredible... I've heard a mage can carry more than one Concord, and can learn to read them somehow, to tell what each is."

"Mages can hold Concords for others, too," Jarthan said. "That's supposed to be one of the things the court mage does."

Properly impressed, Alorsha said, "So, some rather advanced magic."

"And we did it." Devrand said. He grabbed their hands and pulled them with him to dance around the meadow. "*We* did it! Who knows what else we'll be able to accomplish together."

"Together!" Jarthan shouted.

"Together!" Alorsha mimicked and tried to ignore the small sliver of worry that crept through her.

CHAPTER 4

Alorsha cursed under her breath when her knife slipped and she ruined the stem she was trying to peel. That marked the second time that day she had ruined her ingredients.

Izmireva stepped close to look over her shoulder. "You seem distracted. Is something wrong? Your sister and the baby are doing well?"

Alorsha glanced at her teacher. The past months, she had grown so that she stood eye-to-eye with Izmireva.

"They're doing fine," she said. "Evka has the weakness from the illness, always tired, but the baby is well now."

"Good to hear. So, what troubles you?"

Alorsha threw up her hands, aware of how overly dramatic the motion was. But she needed some gesture like that. "I don't know. I can't concentrate. I can't seem to do things that came to me so easily even a month ago. Things I should practically be able to do asleep.... What?"

She squirmed under Izmireva's narrow-eyed scrutiny.

"Hold out your hands," Izmireva ordered.

Fear washed over Alorsha. *Something must be exceedingly*

wrong. But she did as Izmireva directed.

She watched as Izmireva leaned over to examine her shaky hands from a mere finger-length away. The more Alorsha tried to get them to stop, the worse they shook. Without looking, Izmireva reached back and plucked two petals from Alorsha's chervynai plant. Izmireva placed one in each of Alorsha's palms. The petals curled into tiny balls.

"Magic amiss," Izmireva muttered.

Alorsha's ring—now on her right-hand first finger as befit a craft-mage—glowed just a little.

Izmireva gazed at her, her features drawn into an anger that Alorsha had never seen from her before. "What have you done, Alorsha?"

Alorsha could not meet Izmireva's gaze, and she shook uncontrollably. She backed up and sank into a chair. "I... we...."

Izmireva turned away. "Is it a Concord?"

"Y-yes."

Izmireva nodded but did not turn around. "I see. You'd better tell me about it."

So Alorsha told her everything, how Devrand had suggested it, but they *all* decided to try it, how they had worded it. Everything.

Izmireva stood a moment longer turned away, then she turned back to Alorsha, the anger gone.

"At least you three took some care. This was over a ten-month ago?"

Alorsha nodded. "More like eleven."

"All of this," Izmireva waved a hand at Alorsha and the worktable, "is because you haven't fulfilled the Concord. And it'll get worse. We must get you to The Gramaire to meet your fellow miscreants. With the weather this year, I hope we have the time."

She turned away again and opened cabinets to pull things from them as well as from the shelves.

"Go," she said when she saw that Alorsha sat in a daze.

"Go pack for long travel and cold weather. Be sure to bring your best clothes, too." The mage turned back to her own preparations.

"I could've wished for a better time of year," she muttered as Alorsha opened the door and headed outside.

~ ~ ~

As Izmireva had anticipated, the journey was long and cold. Since the village had no horses, she and Alorsha walked. At times, they received rides from people driving carts along the road, but otherwise they were on their own. While they stayed at inns sometimes, or at some friendly person's house, they also camped several nights in the cold. At least the snow stayed moderate to light.

By the time they arrived at Thienas, the city which held The Gramaire, Alorsha was jumpy and unable to concentrate on anything for any length of time. Izmireva took her directly to the entrance to The Gramaire compound.

There Alorsha paused and stared.

"Not what you expected?" Izmireva smiled at her young charge.

"Uh, no. Not really. I'd pictured a large building."

"Somewhat like a castle?" Izmireva smiled. "Yes, most of us anticipated that sort of thing when we first came here."

Alorsha looked around the walled compound. Every building stood a single story tall, built of a light gray stone that had silvery sparkles in it, with roofs of red slate. The same gray sparkly stone comprised the wall that enclosed the compound. It stood about half a pace high and looked to be there more to separate The Gramaire grounds from the rest of the city than for any kind of protection or defense.

"But they're beautiful," Alorsha added.

"Yes, that they are," Izmireva said in a soft voice. "I've

always loved this stone." She brushed a hand across the wall next to her.

"Uh, Izmireva?" Alorsha interrupted her reverie.

"Yes?"

"Why are those people staring at me?" Alorsha glanced down at herself. *No, I didn't spill something on my clothes. Although they* are *wrinkled from the journey.*

Izmireva chuckled. "My dear, to them, you're new. So, I'd imagine they're wondering about you, perhaps speculating how you'd be coming here mid-year. And I suspect that those boys, young men really, just appreciate a pretty woman about their age who they haven't seen before."

"Pretty wo—oh."

Izmireva smiled. "Yes. With your seventeenth spring close, that would be you. I see that you feel rather better."

"Oh, yes. I don't feel like my skin is itchy-twitchy anymore. But I *do* want to see Devrand and Jarthan. I *really* want to see them."

Izmireva nodded. "Some of that's from that Concord. Which, young lady, I'll discuss with you three after we get you all together."

Then she smiled at the approach of one of the young men.

He bowed when Izmireva looked at him. "May I be of assistance, ma'am."

He looked at Alorsha the whole time he obviously spoke to Izmireva. Alorsha gave him a tentative smile.

"Indeed, Craft-mage…." Izmireva said.

"Zan Riovan," he said when she trailed off.

"Craft-mage Zan, we need to see the dean right away. Is he still in the axial building?"

"Yes, ma'am. Can I take your things to a guest house while you speak with him?"

"Thank you, but please put everything in Khagjayan House."

The craft-mage's eyes widened. He peered at Izmireva

and bowed deeply, this time his attention completely on the older woman. "Of course, Khagja." He called some of his friends over and they relieved Alorsha and Izmireva of their packs.

"Come, Alorsha." Izmireva took her arm and guided her the opposite direction the young men had headed.

"Khagja?" Alorsha repeated. "*You're* the Khagja?" Her voice squeaked during her second question. "You cured the entire ruling council and their families in Cothria when that mystery illness threatened them all! Are you from Cothria?"

Izmireva only smiled. "Yes, that's me, although that was a long time ago. And no, I come from much further away. You know me as I am now and, I'd imagine, don't think of the life I had before you came along. I remember I was that way when your age. Now hurry. If I've figured the dates right, we're short on time."

"So, what does 'Khagja' mean?" Alorsha asked as she followed Izmireva along a variety of paths through and around the buildings.

"It's Old High Cothrian for the concept of something unlooked for and impossible to anticipate that staves off disaster. The grateful council made it into an honorific for me and spread the story." Izmireva opened the door to a building much like all the others, except perhaps twice as large, and situated in the center of the compound.

Within, Izmireva led the way to the third door on the right and knocked. A tall, white-haired man dressed in a faded tunic and trousers opened the door. His solemn expression disappeared when he saw Izmireva, and he grabbed her in a hug.

"Izmireva! I hadn't expected you. You look wonderful."

Izmireva laughed. "Ravnajor, it's good to see you again, you big oaf. Now let go. We have something important to deal with and little time in which to do it."

Reluctantly—so it seemed to Alorsha—the man

released Izmireva. He looked at Alorsha with his bushy eyebrows raised.

"This is Craft-mage Alorsha Tavaros, my student," Izmireva said. "Alorsha, this is Ravnajor, current Dean of The Gramaire."

Alorsha bowed. "I'm pleased to meet you."

He returned her bow. "And I, you."

"Alorsha, please wait out here." Izmireva indicated a bench along the wall a pace from the dean's door. She followed Dean Ravnajor inside and closed the door behind her.

Alorsha sat on the bench then jumped up again to pace. She avoided going too near the dean's door. She did not want to look like she eavesdropped. She did not want to accidentally eavesdrop, either. *Although it* is *tempting.*

"Psst."

Alorsha pulled her gaze from her feet and looked around for the source of the sound.

"Here."

She looked at the double doors that led outside and saw Zan peeking around the edge of one.

"Hello again," she said.

"Hello again to you, too. Stuck outside the dean's, huh?" Zan stepped just inside the door and Alorsha had a better chance to study him. He wore dark blue trousers and a matching tunic that looked like some sort of uniform. The others he had been with had dressed similarly, she remembered, with maybe a slight variation in the shades of blue. Zan stood a little taller than she did and had dark brown skin and darker hair and eyes. He wore his curly hair short, and he had the hints of the beginnings of a beard and mustache.

"Seems so," Alorsha said.

He grinned. "Been there a time or two, myself. Will you study here, now? Don't mistake me, the Khagja's absolutely brilliant. We learn about a lot of her methods and discoveries, but pretty much everyone eventually ends up here, even if just for their last year or two."

"Oh. I didn't know that. Any of it. Hard to believe that Izmireva's really the Khagja."

He grinned. "She never said anything?"

Alorsha shook her head. "Not a word."

"Well, we've been told that she exemplifies the modesty that great mages should show. But to not tell her own student...."

Alorsha grinned. "The subject never came up before today."

"I'd wager a lot of other subjects came up, though."

"Oh, yes." The two settled on the bench to compare what they had studied and learned so far.

Alorsha lost track of time in the enjoyment of talking with another craft-mage. She jumped when the dean's door opened. Izmireva came out alone.

"Oh, good, you're here Zan. I need you to find two of the other craft-mages. This instant. Jarthan Ilyevano and Devrand Charnov."

"Yes, ma'am." With a slight smile for Alorsha, he ran off.

When he returned, Jarthan and Devrand followed at his heels. All three panted from the run.

Jarthan and Devrand halted when they spotted Alorsha. The guilty expressions on their faces told Izmireva all she needed.

"You may go, Zan." The boy left, with a grin over his shoulder for Alorsha, who saw both of her friends' expressions darken when they saw that.

"Well, Alorsha?" Izmireva asked.

Alorsha greeted her two friends with quick hugs and turned back to Izmireva. "Some better, but still not gone."

She avoided looking at the two boys. They, in turn, shifted their feet and stared at the floor as if it were the most interesting thing they had ever seen. None of the three could hold still.

Izmireva scrutinized them each in turn.

"Quickly, each of you, tell me what sort of place first comes to mind when I say 'The Gramaire'."

"A large building," Alorsha said.

"Yes," Jarthan agreed.

"Someplace crowded with knowledge," Devrand said.

Izmireva nodded. She called through the dean's door. "The Archives, I believe."

"On it." His faint voice drifted out to them. "Go."

"Come with me." Izmireva led the way back out the double doors and across the compound, not bothering to sidestep the various patches of snow that lingered on the ground.

"What time of day did you three make the Concord?"

"Around midday," Jarthan said. "Maybe a little after."

Izmireva looked from one to other of them. "You're all holding up remarkably well, then. We're likely past the time, but only just."

She increased her pace, until she jogged. They matched her.

"What do you mean?" Devrand asked.

"The year of your Concord has ended. Yes, Alorsha told me all the details when I figured out you three had done something you shouldn't have. After the time in a Concord has ended without the Concord being fulfilled, the parties involved should be in much worse shape than you three. Some would even be dead."

"B-but we were very careful about the wording," Devrand said. He gave Alorsha a stricken look.

"We were," Alorsha said.

"You took care with the words you included, but the Concord must also always specify the consequences if it remains unfulfilled. When that's not done, the magic has an alarming tendency to produce extreme results."

"Oh, no," Devrand muttered.

"Here we are," Izmireva said. "This should finish the Concord. Stay close." She opened the door to a small building and indicated they should enter.

Jarthan looked around. "But this doesn't fit—"

"Hush and follow," Izmireva instructed.

She led them into the building, through a second door inside and down some spiral stairs.

They descended the stairs in silence, for what seemed like a quarter hour or more. Sconces at even intervals along the way lit as they approached and went out after the next one lit. At random times, a strange tickle danced across Alorsha's skin and vanished after another step or two.

When they reached the landing at the bottom and faced the closed door there, all three craft-mages struggled to stand, their legs shook so from the descent. In contrast, Izmireva breathed only a little faster than normal.

"Craft-mages aren't normally allowed in here," she said, "but I expect this is needed to fulfill your Concord. To meet the unconscious requirements of what you each meant by 'The Gramaire'. Touch nothing unless I say you can."

The three nodded.

Izmireva held up her left hand, where she wore her mage ring on the last finger as all master-level mages did. "Ravnajor," she said in a soft voice.

The door swung open toward them and crowded them all on the landing as the three tried to avoid touching it.

"The touch of the door won't harm you now," Izmireva said. "But touch nothing else, except the floor with your feet. Follow me."

She led them into a room that smelled musty and dusty. Devrand stifled a sneeze. Izmireva lifted both hands high and the light from scores of candlesticks that stood along the walls flared, with flames that were not real fire, banishing the darkness. The light revealed row upon row of shelves that reached to the ceiling, crammed with books and scrolls.

The craft-mages looked around, awe written clearly in their expressions.

"Come in. We're going to the center," Izmireva said.

"I don't feel right," Devrand said.

The others studied his face. His skin looked pale, and he was sweating.

"Hurry," Izmireva said.

She led them through the stacks at a run. The three stumbled behind her but managed to keep pace with her.

Alorsha started to feel sick, too. And weak. *Might not be able to stay upright much longer.* She looked at Jarthan. He looked ill, too.

"Here," Izmireva called from further in the room.

The three emerged from the close shelves into a large area with scores of tables and chairs. Izmireva stood in their midst, in the middle of some elaborate design in the floor.

"Here, in the center," she instructed and stepped off the design. "Take the places you used to form the Concord. Now."

The three stumbled onto the design and again stood shoulder to shoulder. Alorsha felt marginally better just from the support of her friends. They held out their hands as they had when they made the Concord. Alorsha placed her right hand atop Devrand's and Jarthan placed his atop Alorsha's, all with rings touching. Their rings flashed a brilliant red, then went dark, as normal.

And Alorsha felt well again.

She looked at her friends. They looked much better, too.

"And that fulfills your Concord," Izmireva said. "Come sit."

She took a chair at a nearby circular table and waited for them to join her.

"I'll tell you that you three are powerful together," she said. "Your magics mesh well and give you strength that you might not have with just two of you, or alone. This means you can do some extraordinary things. Some dangerous things. I remember my learning years. Always the desire to experience more, to do the amazing things I saw older students doing. Or full mages. That *will* come. But you...." She pointed a finger at each of them in turn. "Each of you must live to reach that level. Do *not* do anything like this again before you are full mages. Am I clear?"

They all nodded.

"Do I need to make it a Concord?" Izmireva demanded. "Be assured that mine will be both more effective and, while not a threat to your health, far more uncomfortable for you."

They all assured her that she need not do such a thing. They gave their word that they would do as she said.

Izmireva nodded in satisfaction. "Good. In addition, don't speak of this with anyone who isn't a full mage, nothing about these Archives, nothing about the Concord."

They nodded again.

"Excellent. Now let's get back upstairs. You three will very soon be famished after this ordeal, and I'd rather not be stuck here with a trio of ravenous young craft-mages."

They chuckled at her quip and headed back to the long climb upstairs.

CHAPTER 5

FROM ALORSHA'S JOURNAL

I was relieved to return to our village after my precipitous first visit to The Gramaire. I never did study there. Izmireva, the Khagja, could teach me more than any of the mages at the school, at least for my type of magic. Although I *did* visit some other villages and towns to learn different techniques from other coppice-mages. In the aftermath of our Concord, I tired more easily than usual for about a month before I felt normal again.

When Devrand and Jarthan visited the village, we still practiced together. And Devrand spoke often of advanced magics he had heard of or seen. We speculated how they would work, talked about possibilities, but did not try any of the ones reserved to full mages.

We did try all the more-advanced craft-mage magics that we learned about, and many times ended up quenching random fires in the meadow. Sometimes I'd spot Izmireva watching me with a slight smile. I had the feeling she knew of our exploits but let us be as long as we didn't push it too much.

~ ~ ~

On a rare winter visit, Jarthan and Devrand brought Alorsha a surprise. When they hauled the heavy bag off Devrand's horse, Alorsha gave it a suspicious look. *Not like the little gifts they've brought on their other visits.*

It had started with a couple of ridiculously large hair bows that Jarthan and Devrand had brought her. Apology gifts for getting her involved in the Concord, they had told her. After that they each brought something with them every time they visited, apparently attempting to outdo each other with the pretty, impractical little gifts.

"No Zan this time?" Alorsha said as she followed the others toward Izmireva's workshop. Zan had visited the village in company with Jarthan and Devrand a few times.

Matching frowns crossed both boys' faces at the mention of the other boy's name.

"He was busy," Jarthan said.

"It's too bad, but he couldn't make it this visit," Devrand added, an odd tone in his voice.

Alorsha peered at him but could read nothing further in his expression. *Probably happy Zan hadn't come.*

She *had* noticed the two of them, he and Jarthan, seemed to do all they could to draw her attention away from Zan when he came with them. It would have been funny, if it had not been so annoying. Zan had taken to visiting at times when the other two would not be there – something she felt uninclined to share with the two boys. The attention from all three was sweet, but she was *not* looking to pick someone to spend her life with. *They're all charming and great friends; don't want that to be ruined.*

"So, what's this?" she asked after they retreated inside.

The boys grinned.

"Open it," Devrand urged her.

She untied the rope that secured the bag shut and peeked inside.

"You didn't!"

Both boys almost danced in their excitement.

"We did," Jarthan said. "But with permission. Dean Ravnajor allowed us to bring you ten of the books from the craft-mages' library to go along with all that Izmireva is teaching you. I hope we picked good ones."

Alorsha smiled as she removed the books one by one and read their titles before she placed them on her worktable. "These look great! My thanks."

Devrand and Jarthan beamed at her obvious delight.

With a flourish, Devrand pulled a small, thin book out of his tunic. "I brought a special one for the three of us. This has a magic we have to try."

Alorsha eyed the untitled book. "That's not full-mage level magic, is it? We promised, you remember."

"I found it tucked away in the craft-mages' library, so don't fret."

Jarthan took it from his friend and flipped through it. "Just the one magic?"

"Yes, but look at it closely. This is what we've been after. This will make our magics even stronger together."

"Let me see." Alorsha grabbed the book and skimmed through it, focusing on any materials they would need. "A couple of these plants are pretty rare."

"But you have them here," Devrand said. "Don't you?"

Alorsha grinned. "Well, yes. I just hope there's enough. These candles have very precise instructions. How long are you two here this time?"

"We have two weeks before we have to go back," Jarthan said. "Then it's the final push to full mage status."

Alorsha grinned. "I think we'll have enough time, then. But you'll both have to help."

The boys nodded.

The next several days, the three gathered and prepared the materials they would need. Izmireva let them use the rare ingredients they needed after they assured her that they were not working any magic of full-mage level.

They finished gathering and preparing everything the day before Devrand and Jarthan were to return to The Gramaire. Because the boys were due to leave in the morning, the three decided to meet after the evening meal to work the magic.

The villagers had created a special feast to send the boys off, so the three worked their magic much later than they had planned. Well after dark and bundled in coats against the cold, they headed to the meadow with bags of their supplies.

Alorsha supervised the set-up in one of their burnt areas. At least they would not need to worry that they might set any more of the meadow afire this time.

With Devrand's help to make sure the lines were straight and one corner pointed north, Alorsha marked out a square in the dirt. Jarthan placed the special candles they had made on the points, while Devrand drew a second square rotated from the first to form a star shape. Alorsha placed the rest of the candles on the points of that square.

She pulled out the three special potions that they had made working in tandem. Each of them took one and splashed it into the star, taking care not to splash on the lines. After Devrand reviewed the final instructions in the book, the three stepped into the star and formed a small triangle with their shoulders touching.

"The book says four is best for this," Devrand said. "But with the way we can work together, I'm sure that we three can manage it."

Alorsha fought a shiver. Whether from the frigid air, or misgivings about the magic, she did not know.

"Hands," Devrand said.

They clasped hands with each other and raised their arms above their heads.

"Draw on your magic," Devrand said. "Bring it to our clasped hands. I can guide it from there. Oh, and avoid your rings. We don't need the magic to get stuck there."

Alorsha did as he directed and felt the others do the

same. Devrand took control of the magic. He wove it into a fascinating, beautiful, diaphanous symbol that hung in the air with a golden glow. When he completed the shape, he sent it out from them, expanding every direction.

It rushed out of sight, then surged back toward them and slammed into them. They fought to maintain their grip on each other's hands. Alorsha wobbled as dizziness engulfed her and she gasped against a pressure on her chest much like having the breath knocked out of her. For a moment, her vision turned gray around the edges. Then warmth flooded through her, and the glow of magic filled her. She smiled in delight. The others reacted the same way.

"Hold. Hold for a bit," Devrand said. "Draw it in, like when you pull your own magic back to yourself. That should be enough to make it your own."

They did. And it worked.

With deep breaths and relieved sighs, they reversed their motions, let go of each other, and relaxed their stances. As Alorsha let go of Devrand's hand, motion at the corner of her eye caught her attention. A dark gray wisp lifted out of the ground at Devrand's feet, much like a tendril of smoke in appearance. It rose into the air and flew off. The others did not react, did not seem to have seen anything, so Alorsha said nothing.

They snuffed the candles, crushed them together into one big lump of wax, as the book directed, and wiped away all traces of the drawn squares, to leave the meadow much as it had been before the magic.

"At least we didn't set any fires this time," Jarthan said with a laugh.

"I feel all warm," Alorsha said.

"I'd say you're glowing, but not from the magic," Devrand said.

Jarthan frowned at the other boy. The expression morphed into a silly grin. "I can sort of feel you two!"

Devrand nodded. "It's to be expected from this kind of

magic. That sensation's supposed to fade pretty quickly. And notice that your own magic is greater now? Pretty amazing, right?"

The others nodded.

"I believe we can work the magic again, but after a year at least, to increase our own magic even more," Devrand said.

Jarthan gave him a slight smile. "Maybe. We'll see."

Devrand grinned back.

Alorsha shivered. *Was that a gray-black wisp that just flew overhead?*

"Let's go back," she said. "It's late and you two have to leave early tomorrow."

CHAPTER 6

"Alorsha, you have to come see," Alorsha's older sister Olzanka—the sister closest to her in age—called to her. Alorsha sighed when the interruption caused her to lose the magic.

"What is it, Olza?"

"Just come," Olzanka yelled. "To Mama and Papa's house. You won't believe it!"

Alorsha sighed again and dusted off her hands. A glance at her worktable told her that it could await her return. Izmireva had gone out for the day to find some early spring plants, so Alorsha had the day to herself. She would rather continue to prepare for her final testing for full mage status, but Olzanka would continue to bother her if she did not go see what caused the fuss.

She opened the door to her parents' house – a dwelling she still shared. "What is it?" she repeated.

Then she stopped dead.

Mama and Papa gave her eager smiles, and Olzanka bounced like she had when much younger, but the three luminous spheres that sat on Mama's table captured

Alorsha's attention.

"They all just appeared on the table," Olzanka said. "We're sure they're for you."

Alorsha nodded. She had not heard of such things, but they were clearly magical. Three different shades of blue, each sphere was small enough to hold in one hand. She reached out toward the one to her right, and hesitated. She hoped these were not what she suspected they might be.

Their last visit, the boys, as she still thought of them, had seemed a bit too attentive, rather too eager to win her favor for their antics. True, she had reached her nineteenth spring, and they their twentieth, and so such things might be strong in their thoughts. But Alorsha had not yet reached full mage status. She did not want to consider a life-partner before she had at least achieved that. She was not ready to ask one of them, or for any of them to ask her.

She took a deep, steadying breath and lifted the first sphere, hoping it was not going to ask the question she dreaded.

It warmed in her hand. Zan's features took shape before her. He spoke, his message an announcement of his attainment of full mage status and an invitation to the ceremonies. When the message finished and his face faded away, Alorsha saw by her family's expressions that they had neither seen nor heard any of what she had. So she relayed the message.

She set Zan's sphere back on the table and lifted the next one. From Devrand, it contained much the same message. The last sphere came from Jarthan, with a similar message. Although at the end of his message he told her he missed her, and he looked forward to seeing her again. She shared their messages with her family, except for the last bit from Jarthan.

Alorsha studied the spheres a few minutes longer before she looked back at her family.

"I'll need to pack," she said.

"Of course," Papa said. "Let us know how we can help."

"My thanks."

"So?" Olzanka said after their parents had left the room. "Which one are you going to pick?"

"Olza! I'm not going to pick anyone—as you put it—until after I've finished my time as a craft-mage, at least."

"But you're almost done. Then you'll pick one, right?"

Alorsha sighed. "We'll see. But I promise I'll let you know first."

"Better be second." Olzanka grinned at her. "You should tell the fortunate young man first."

"Oh, you." Alorsha threw a towel at her sister and left to find Izmireva to tell her about the ceremony.

~ ~ ~

Their journey to The Gramaire was much more pleasant than the previous trip. As Alorsha and Izmireva approached Thienas, they found more and more travelers headed the same way.

"Looks like a number of craft-mages are advancing," Izmireva said. She leaned close to Alorsha. "We should have time to complete your testing after we arrive and before the ceremony. So you can advance with your friends."

"Really?"

Izmireva smiled at Alorsha's hopeful expression. "Really."

"Oh, thank you. Thank you!" Alorsha flung her arms around Izmireva, to the amusement of the other travelers.

"Can we hurry, please?" Alorsha said when she let go.

Izmireva chuckled. "Why do you suppose I've pushed our pace these last few days. You needn't worry. There'll be time."

~ ~ ~

So Alorsha stood with Devrand and Jarthan and Zan to advance to the status of artisan-mage, the lower of the two levels of full mage. Several others, about a score, Alorsha estimated, had also finished their studies, and waited for the final acknowledgement of their status as full mages.

The ceremony passed in a blur for Alorsha. Mages she did not know talked at length about honor and the hard work the craft-mage students had done. Alorsha managed to smile at the appropriate times. *Hard to believe I'm finally here.*

The dean announced the names of the students, one by one, and each climbed the steps onto the raised area where the speech-givers had been earlier. The craft-mages bowed to several older mages and received new rings, which they placed on the thumbs of their left hands. They were also given a chain to wear their student rings at their necks, if they chose. At least for that day, everyone chose to do so.

When it came to Alorsha's turn, she froze. All those people, more than in her entire village. How could she go up in front of them all? *I'll make a fool of myself somehow, probably trip.* Especially considering the way her legs trembled.

Jarthan squeezed her hand and shared his sweet smile with her.

"You can do it. You've been Izmireva's first apprentice in more than two-score years. You can do anything."

Alorsha smiled back and her jitters slipped away.

So, yes, she walked onto the platform, bowed properly, and received her new mage ring, which she placed on her left thumb to signify her new status as an artisan-mage. Trying to act with appropriate dignity, she strung her student ring on the chain they gave her and slipped it over her head. Then she took the small book one of the mages handed her and bowed to all the people who watched the ceremony, who cheered for her accomplishment. She spotted her parents, and Jarthan's parents and his grandmama, in the crowd. They must have come sometime after she and Izmireva had arrived.

And she spotted Izmireva near the front of the crowd. Her teacher waved, with a big smile for her. Then she bowed. Alorsha returned the bow with a smile and hurried back to her friends.

~ ~ ~

The celebrations that night lasted long and late, with several different parties happening both on The Gramaire grounds and out in the city. Alorsha stayed with Jarthan and Devrand as they visited with Alorsha's and Jarthan's parents and Jarthan's grandmama first, then as many parties as they could. Jarthan and Devrand introduced her to far too many people to remember which names belonged to which faces.

When the parties dwindled, the new mages returned to The Gramaire for breakfast. Most were subdued, tired but not yet ready to sleep and close out their big day.

Alorsha spotted Zan across the hall in which The Gramaire served breakfast and waved. He waved back and beckoned her over.

She excused herself from Devrand and Jarthan's company and noticed their frowns in passing.

"Alorsha!" Zan clasped her hands in greeting. "Let me offer my congratulations again."

"My thanks. And to you, too."

"And… there's something I've been meaning to say…." He looked at their clasped hands.

Alorsha wanted to pull away. She had hoped to avoid this yet for a while. *Please, please, don't let him ask me now.*

"Alorsha, I *do* like you. I expect I always will. But my family has arranged a life-partner for me. I should have told you sooner, but I kept losing my nerve. I've met her and she's nice enough. But for both our families, it's more of a business arrangement than anything else. It'll keep our families from ruin. It's what we do in my home demesne."

This was not what she had expected to hear. A pang shot through her, but it hurt less than she had anticipated at his words.

"Zan, I thank you for telling me. We'll always be good friends. And I wish you happiness. Perhaps you and she will come to love each other."

"She said something like that, too." He hesitated then, with a small smile for her. "I'm sorry if I led you to think we might be more than friends. I once had thought maybe…."

Alorsha smiled. "I had once thought maybe, too. But you have a duty to your family."

"And you still have your two suitors to choose between." Zan nodded in Devrand and Jarthan's direction. Alorsha glanced back at their stormy expressions and her face grew warm.

Zan grinned at her. "Have fun with that," he said. "I have to go now. I've a long journey home."

Alorsha gave him a quick kiss on his cheek. "Take care. And watch for us. We just might descend on you sometime for a visit."

He laughed. "I'll look forward to that. You also take care of yourself."

Alorsha watched him leave the hall before she turned back to her two boys. As she crossed the hall, she purposefully looked at them, rather than just the quick looks good friends give each other.

Both stood about the same height, which put them about half a head taller than her, each handsome in his own way, although lately Devrand's brows had seemed drawn down too often. She should make a choice soon, if she was going to. They deserved that.

"What's all that?" Devrand asked when she returned to finish her breakfast.

"Zan's going back home. His family has a life-partner waiting there for him."

She watched, amused, as their frowns changed into expressions of relief.

"Oh, that's great," Jarthan said. "I mean, great for him. Ah... that *is* great, right?"

Alorsha nodded. "Yes, that's great." Her gaze lingered on him for a moment. She turned to Devrand in time to see his expression of relief turn somber. A shiver ran down her spine.

"So, what's next?" she said.

Devrand's eyes flicked to Jarthan and away again.

"We have lots of options," Jarthan said. "That little book they handed you lists places that would welcome artisan-mages of various types all over the kingdom. We can ask around here, too. We don't have to make way for new apprentices for a couple of months, at least, so we can stay here at The Gramaire and learn more and figure out what's next."

Devrand leaned close. "We have access to the Archives, now."

They all exchanged looks.

"Staying here and exploring the Archives, it is," Alorsha said.

~ ~ ~

The first week of freedom from studies, the three artisan-mages spent their time learning, in general anyway, what the Archives held. After that, between odd jobs to help support themselves, they separated in the Archives to look for areas of personal interest. They each found a section that appealed to them and spent most of their time there.

Alorsha discovered writings of past coppice-mages, along with some old reference books about various plants. Some of what she found had since been disproven, but it made for interesting reading and provided some new ideas for her to try.

Jarthan found some books about elaborate illusions of the past and devoured all they had to tell him of techniques and possibilities. But one book he prized above all the others. He found a book that claimed to be able to instruct illusion mages in techniques that allowed them to make the illusions real. He buried himself in that book after he found it, and Alorsha and Devrand saw little of him for days after.

Devrand, to Jarthan and Alorsha's surprise, spent his time in the section of ancient and dead languages. He claimed, when they asked about it, that he had a talent for languages.

"Besides, who knows how soon it'll be that one of you finds an ancient book that you need to have translated." He grinned.

~ ~ ~

The months spent at leisure to explore the Archives flew by – almost three, as it happened. During what they anticipated to be their last couple of weeks there, they scrambled to make copious notes of information from the books that they would not be able to borrow. Others that they could return to borrow any time, they set aside for the future. And they hunted in the city for lodgings nearby. They had decided to stay in the vicinity, at least for a while longer.

Alorsha was packing her belongings to leave the room she had used the past months at The Gramaire when Jarthan and Devrand burst into her room.

"Open this." Devrand held out a folded parchment with Alorsha's name on it.

"What is it? Where did you get this?" She accepted it and turned it over. She found a small plain wax seal on the back.

"One of the compound's messengers brought us each one, and when we saw that he had one for you, too, we told him we'd bring it to you." Jarthan shifted his feet and grinned at her. "Open it!"

She did and skimmed the contents. "They're offering us a place here?" She glanced at the boys' grinning faces and reread the letter.

"All of us," Jarthan said. "For a full year, at least."

"To help the instructors, assist with master-mages' personal studies…" Alorsha read key parts aloud. "This is great! But why us?"

"Why not?" Devrand said. "We're here already." His expression turned serious. "There've been some rumors of oddities around the kingdom, magical troubles maybe. I've not found anyone who knows what exactly's going on. Or at least who'll say. But some are saying that it might be something preparatory to an attack."

"Nothing's happened near The Gramaire," Jarthan added. "Some of the mages here have packed kits and headed out to various parts of the kingdom. At the king's request, so the rumors say. So, they need the help here for the new apprentices. It would also give us more time to decide what we want to do now that our official studies are complete."

"It gives us another year of easy access to the Archives," Devrand said. "And will pay better than the odd short-term jobs we've all had so far. It might even let us get better access to whatever we need to create our masterworks to become master-mages."

Alorsha looked from one of them to the other and grinned. "Sounds good."

Devrand clapped Jarthan on the shoulder. "Told you she'd be interested." He grabbed Alorsha's hand and tugged her out the door. Jarthan followed. "We need to tell them we'll do it. Before any others sneak ahead of us and take *our* places."

CHAPTER 7

FROM ALORSHA'S JOURNAL

I relished our months of exploration in The Gramaire's Archives. So much there to learn and some information hinted at other knowledge, just enough to intrigue. I lost myself in all the wonders of the collection.

Helping the master-mages at The Gramaire for what became two years was an incredible opportunity. We all continued to learn and expand our magic and had plenty of time to spend in the Archives still.

During that time, I learned that while I liked Devrand well enough, Jarthan was the one who drew me. I reveled in his company. I loved the way his expression lit up when he found a new magic. I loved his smiles, especially the one whenever we caught each other's eyes. A touch from his hand made me feel appreciated, special.

Just because everyone in our village had assumed all along that we belonged together didn't mean they were wrong.

At the end of our extra years at the Gramaire, Jarthan and I returned to our village for the simple ceremony that recognized us as life-partners. Devrand accompanied us there and stood with us for the ceremony. He seemed happy for us. But sometimes I caught a dark look in his eyes that sent a shiver through me.

Jarthan and I followed our village's custom and combined our second names into our new family name: Tavano. Mama and Papa and Jarthan's parents gifted us with four plain rings made of a lovely pink-gold metal, two for each of us to mark us as life-partners. We placed one on the third finger of each hand – another of our village's customs.

We later found a goldsmith in Thienas to decorate them with sculptural relief embellishments of a fanciful swirl design with a hint of butterflies. Her work made the rings beautiful and unique.

~ ~ ~

The door to the herbalist's shop flew open, banged against the wall, and startled Alorsha.

"You've got to come see what Devrand's up to now," Jarthan said. With a quick kiss on one cheek, he grabbed her hand.

"That's all I get?" Alorsha demanded as she set the plants she had been working with on a nearby table.

Jarthan grinned and gave her a kiss worthy of the word.

"Better." Alorsha grinned at him. "I'm getting hungry anyway. Let me just tell Sutoth that I need to take a long lunch. He won't mind."

She and Jarthan and Devrand had found positions in Thienas and settled into life in the city. All of them also taught some and otherwise helped out at The Gramaire. And Devrand pursued several different projects on his own, secretive activities about which he spoke little.

Alorsha followed Jarthan along the street and toward the city harbor. "Are you going to give me a hint?"

"It involves a ship. That's all I know for certain."

Alorsha groaned. "He's not trying to improve them again, is he?"

"Not sure. That's why we're going to see."

At the city harbor, they stopped and looked for their friend. The harbor was busy, with more boats than Alorsha had ever seen before, most of them large. Although they had lived in the city a couple of years already, and The Gramaire a couple of years before that, she had not visited the harbor, rather had just passed by on her way elsewhere. Scores of people all hurried about on some business or other. She scanned the bustle of activity.

"See him?" she asked Jarthan.

"No. Maybe he's at the shipyards instead. That's where they build new ones. Since he seems bent on trying to improve them somehow."

"That makes sense."

So, they turned south to make their way roughly parallel to the coast. The shipyards sat at the edge of the city that direction.

The approach to the shipyards from the city put them higher than the coastline at that point, so they had an unobstructed view as they got closer. Five ships sat there in various stages of construction. Again, a lot of people bustled about, and a lot of wood lay around, some in large stacks.

One ship caught Alorsha's eye. Its wood was much darker than that being used for the other ships, a dark brown close to black, with a reddish tint to it. The ship also seemed longer and sleeker than the others.

"There," Jarthan said and pointed.

Devrand waved at them. Alorsha and Jarthan clasped hands and made their way down to where Devrand waited near the dark ship.

He gave them a smug smile as they approached.

"Isn't she a beauty?" He waved an arm back toward the incomplete ship.

Alorsha tilted her head and inspected the ship, or rather

the skeleton of the ship. "I suppose."

Devrand laughed. "She'll get better. And she's all ours!"

"What do you mean?" Jarthan asked.

"She's ours. It's all arranged."

Alorsha and Jarthan exchanged looks.

"Nothing underhanded," Devrand assured them. "Not this time." He grinned.

"When she's ready, we can travel wherever we want, find new magics and work our magics elsewhere for even better pay than here," he added. "She's still at least two years out from being seaworthy, so we'll have plenty of time to get ready and get a crew and all that."

"Do you know anything about getting a crew?" Alorsha asked.

Devrand grinned. "One uncle I lived with for a couple of years was first mate on a merchant ship. I learned a thing or two. But come, Alorsha, you need to take a close look at the wood. It's something special."

Alorsha followed Devrand through the tumult of the busy workers to a stack of the same wood as that which formed the ship so far.

Devrand nodded to the wood.

Alorsha took a tentative step closer and stopped as she sensed something. Another step and she touched a piece of the wood with the tip of a finger. She did not even have to concentrate to discover what Devrand meant.

Magic filled the wood, more than she had ever encountered in any plant before, save perhaps her chervynai. *Something else to study more, but another time.* The wood felt perfect for holding that magic, indefinitely. She looked at Devrand.

"Amazing, isn't it?" he said.

"Very. Where'd you get it? And so much. I'd guess something like this would be rare and valuable."

Devrand nodded with a secretive smile.

"What is it?" Jarthan looked from Alorsha to Devrand.

"It holds magic," Alorsha said. "That seems to be its

only magical property, from what I can sense. I think a person could add more to it, too."

Devrand nodded again. "It's called taiawood. Ours to use for this."

"Oh," Alorsha said. "I'll have to tell Sutoth, then, that it'll be longer than we had expected before I'll be able to buy the shop from him. And we'll need to get started on preparations."

"Sounds like there's plenty of time yet," Jarthan said.

"We need to work that magic again, too," Devrand said in a low voice. "I expect we're all going to want to be as strong in magic as we can get."

"I'm not sure about that particular magic," Alorsha said. "Let's walk."

When they reached a spot far away from anyone who might overhear, Alorsha told them about the gray wisp she had seen when they worked the magic before.

The two men exchanged glances.

Jarthan shrugged. "I didn't see that. And the spell said nothing about anything like that. Have you seen it since?"

"No," Alorsha said. "But I have this sense that it was something not quite right. What if the magic isn't properly set up? What if we did something wrong?"

"We reviewed the instructions many times," Devrand said. "We all took extra care in the preparations and working. And we succeeded! I've been stronger in my magic than before. You have, too, right?"

Alorsha nodded. "Yes. But still, something about it makes me uneasy."

Devrand waved a hand in the air. "I'd wager that's just lingering from our nervousness that night. I know I worried we'd be interrupted. We'll be fine working the magic again. We're even better with our magic now, and we won't have to worry about interruptions. We can use one of the practice rooms at The Gramaire. It'll be perfect. And if your smoky wisp appears again, it won't be able to escape us. We'll have it trapped in the room and we can catch it and figure out what it is." He gave them both a confident grin.

Jarthan nodded and matched his grin.

After a moment, Alorsha nodded, too.

~ ~ ~

They took their time to work through the preparations for the spell and took care to address every detail. Each of them reread the small book Devrand had found years earlier to make sure they would not miss anything by trying to work the magic from memory.

They met in a small workroom at The Gramaire to work on the elixirs and the candles, as often as possible, with much of Devrand's time taken helping other mages with their magics. A couple of weeks after they had first learned of their pending journey, Alorsha spotted a problem.

"The floor in the practice room is brick," she told the two men. "We're going to have to use something to make the star that won't create a permanent mark in the floor, don't you think?"

Jarthan looked up from the herbs he was methodically crushing. "Maybe something like this? Maybe some plant that we can powder and use to make the star?"

"Some spells use chalk to draw magical symbols," Devrand commented from where he lounged near the door. "But that sort of thing is more your magic, Alorsha. I'm just the enhancer."

Alorsha gave him a sharp look. That last had sounded bitter, but his expression belied the timbre. She considered the men's suggestions.

"I believe we'll do better with something powdered, or maybe an elixir. Let me check the books and see what I can find that'll work well with the spell."

"Maybe you don't have to," Devrand said as he sat upright. "What about some of the taiawood? It wouldn't take much, and its magic should fit with what we're doing."

Alorsha stared at the floor as she considered potential ramifications. "Perhaps if we mix the taiawood in an elixir. That way we wouldn't have to use as much of the wood."

"Great! I'll go grab a few of the scraps from the ship. I've been setting them aside; in case we need them for anything else. They're too valuable to throw away or burn. I'll bring them tomorrow. After I'm done with my duties." Devrand jumped up and ran out the door.

Alorsha stared after him. His tone had seemed dour when he spoke of duties. "Is Dev all right?" Alorsha said when she was certain their friend had gone.

"In what way?"

"I haven't seen him with anyone in a while. He doesn't seem to ever relax. Does he still spend time with Lorai?"

"I think so. You know he's got a lot of women friends."

Alorsha grinned. "I'd noticed. But just now, he seemed... I don't know... off somehow. When he spoke of duties and being an enhancer. He's great at it and much in demand. Seems that everyone requires his help."

Jarthan shrugged. "A few years ago, he mentioned that he wished he could do what I do. Make things from the magic. Like this."

Jarthan grinned and used a spark of his magic to create a beautiful red flower. He handed it to Alorsha with a bow.

She smiled and accepted the flower. "So sweet." She pulled him close for a lingering kiss.

"Are we almost done here?" Jarthan gestured at the tables and herbs around them when they separated, his voice breathless.

Alorsha smiled. "Done enough for now."

~ ~ ~

The taiawood turned out to be both a delight and an

annoyance to work with. Its magic entangled Alorsha whenever she touched it. But trying to chop and crush the dried wood while wearing gloves was not something she wanted to even consider. So, every time she worked to prepare it for the new elixir she was creating, she had to force herself several times to drag her attention back to what she was doing.

The touch of the wood was intoxicating and the magic within seemed eager to leap to her bidding. Glorious, and yet perhaps concerning. She shared her thoughts with Jarthan and Devrand.

"Just a new, stranger-than-usual magic," Devrand said and waved a dismissive hand. "You'll figure it out and get used to it, I'm sure."

Jarthan gave her hand a quick squeeze. "I know you can do it."

Alorsha smiled but did not share their optimism. Still, she loved the feel of the wood, even chopped and crushed.

Weeks passed and they gathered all their supplies one by one for the spell. They also figured out supplies and other things needed for their journey. Finally, they were ready for the spell.

Again, they set up after dark, this time inside, in a small practice room just large enough for the star drawing. After Alorsha drew the star, the taiawood elixir gave off a faint glow. She exchanged looks with Jarthan. He nodded.

"I see it, too," he said. "And I can sense it. Somewhat." He looked at Devrand. "The taiawood's a good choice."

Devrand smiled. "Wait until you hear about all the ideas I have for the ship. But later."

As they had done years earlier, the three stepped into the star drawn on the floor and stood with shoulders touching and hands clasped. They called on the magic as they had the previous time, but this time the star around them burst into flames that gave off no heat.

"Feel that strength," Devrand said. "Now!"

Devrand took control of the magic and wove it into a

symbol of a different shape from the one he had made before. It still glowed golden but carried a grayish tint around the edges. Devrand just grinned at Alorsha's disconcerted expression.

"This design will be more effective," he said. He sent the symbol out from them, expanding all around them, right through the walls.

A moment later, it rushed back and slammed into them. They held their grip on each other's hands, and this time Alorsha felt less dizzy and sick, but again like her breath had been knocked out of her.

The expected warmth flooded through her, and the glow of magic filled her.

"Hold, hold," Devrand reminded them. "Now draw it in."

They did. The flames along the taiawood elixir dwindled and vanished. The glow disappeared, as well.

Alorsha turned to look at the section of the darkened star that lay behind her. "That—"

An unseen force threw them back, out of the star, and slammed them into the walls of the room. From there they slid to the floor. A large gray-black wisp, which resembled the smoke from a large campfire, rose from the center of the floor, swept around the room once, and charged through the ceiling.

"Did you see that?" Alorsha squeaked, fear making her voice strange.

"Yes," Jarthan said.

"Was that like what you saw before?" Devrand said.

"Much bigger." Alorsha picked herself up off the floor, cautious of her hurts. Tomorrow she would probably be in a lot of pain. "What could it be?"

The two men also stood. They moved like they hurt, too.

"No idea," Jarthan said.

"Interesting," Devrand said. He leaned against a wall and flipped through the book that contained the spell.

"Nothing like that mentioned here. But it felt strong."

"Could it be alive?" Alorsha asked.

Devrand shrugged.

~ ~ ~

They did not speak of the wisp again. They kept so busy that they scarcely noticed the time it took to complete the ship. They spent every spare minute they could in the Archives, taking notes about anything they thought might be useful. Alorsha also hoped to learn more about the gray wisps, but she found nothing concerning them.

The day the workers completed the ship, close to three years after Devrand had first shown it to them, Devrand cajoled Jarthan and Alorsha out of their preparations and down to the harbor to look her over.

He paused at the bottom of the ramp and, with a grin, held out a letter. "Take a look at this."

Alorsha and Jarthan both read it while Devrand held it.

"The dean wants us to look into the oddities?" Alorsha said.

Devrand nodded. "Who better? We're the best coordinating mages alive. And none of the others have been able to make any progress determining what the oddities are, or what to do about them. They've grown more numerous, over the last couple of years or so." He dropped his voice to just above a whisper. "I hear the king has offered something extraordinary to those who solve the problem. And with the ship, we're in the perfect position to do that."

He all but pushed them up the ramp in his enthusiasm. At the top, they paused and looked around.

Largest of any in the harbor, the ship boasted four masts, a single raised deck at the bow, and two raised decks, tiered, in the stern. On the raised deck at the bow, and on the highest deck at the stern, sat two large contraptions that looked somewhat like crossbows, but much larger.

"Ballistae," Devrand said when he noticed what had caught Alorsha's attention. "Bolt throwers. To defend the ship in case we run into any trouble."

Alorsha nodded. "Makes sense. So have you decided on a name for the ship?"

"I've a few ideas but have yet to settle on one," Devrand said.

"Bad luck to go out without the name first," a passing crewmember mumbled just loud enough for them to hear.

Devrand scowled and turned toward the crewmember. He subsided, though, when Alorsha laid a calming hand on his arm.

"Show us the rest," she said.

Devrand nodded and regained his good spirits as he led them through the entire ship, even to the lower decks and the rowing benches.

"And here is for you," he announced when they returned above. He opened a door off the lowest raised deck at the stern to a large area divided into two rooms, one behind the other. He led them into the first room and opened a small door to one side to reveal a cupboard that looked bigger than it should. "We'll store all the magic materials here."

"Aren't these rooms supposed to be for the Ship's Master?" Jarthan asked.

"Normally," Devrand said. "But we three are the owners of record, and so we displace the Ship's Master. Don't worry, there's a spacious room on the floor beneath this one for them." Devrand waved a hand that direction in a vague gesture.

"What of you?" Alorsha asked.

"My room's also on the floor beneath this one and is just as nice as the Ship's Master's," Devrand said.

"I figure we'll have a large table in this front room," Devrand continued. "A place to work on your potions, Alorsha. Or to look over maps or whatever and meet to make any plans we need to. Back there will be your bed." He waved toward the second room just visible through the door in front of them, with an exaggerated wink for both Jarthan and Alorsha. They smiled back.

"How are you, or we, paying for all of this?" Alorsha said.

"Per that letter, we work for the crown now, although somewhat unofficially," Devrand said. "Well, irregularly, might be a better word. So, we have no worries about paying for whatever we need. Or about paying the ship's crew. It's all taken care of. Which reminds me...."

He pulled three pendants from a pocket and handed them out.

"These are for us, if we venture to our neighboring kingdoms and need to prove we aren't pirates or some such."

Alorsha looked at her pendant. A metal disk hung from a chain long enough to slip over her head. A stylized copy of the king's personal seal—a striking hawk—decorated the front of the disk, made of a carved, amber-colored stone. On the back, what looked like the king's signature had been etched into the metal. The metal was goldish in color, but harder than gold would have been.

She put it on, as did the two men.

Devrand tucked his into the neck of his tunic. "It's not a big secret, but if we don't need to show them around, we probably shouldn't."

Alorsha and Jarthan imitated him and tucked their pendants away too.

"Oh, and something else..." Devrand said. He placed a hand behind him on the wall of the room, made of taiawood, like the rest of the ship.

"Alorsha, would you please get the best materials you need, whatever you need, and start working on the wood, on the ship?"

"Doing what?"

Devrand gave her a steady look. "Whatever can

improve it, enhance it, make it better or stronger. Make it capable of storing as much magic as possible. I'll enhance what I can while you work, of course. The ship needs to be unlike any other out there and capable of amazing things once we're done with it."

He grinned. "Of course, it also needs to hold up to the winter storms that we'll encounter as we sail around the island. Wouldn't do to have this great ship flounder."

"What of a name for the ship?" Jarthan said. "What are the ideas you have?"

Devrand shrugged. "Not important now – I've decided. I've been looking in the Archives and found some of the ancient languages that used to be spoken in Varoia and the other lands on the island. A word from one of those will be best, I believe."

Alorsha planted her hands on her hips, with an exasperated look for him. "And?"

"The ship will be the *Aiokta*. It means magical in one of those ancient tongues."

~ ~ ~

Another couple of months passed as they finished gathering everything they could think of to take along. Devrand seemed engrossed in the preparations but made himself available whenever Alorsha needed to work with the taiawood's magic.

Although mostly absorbed in all the preparations, Alorsha stayed aware of any word about the oddities they were supposed to investigate.

Most of what she heard truly fit the word oddities; things like a family that went to sleep in their home one night and woke the next morning to a house of a different color, like purple. She also heard about places where overnight new, unheard-of plants grew, or spots on the ground appeared and looked like they had burned, but with no flames sighted. That last caught her attention particularly. It reminded her of the burned spots she and Jarthan and Devrand had been responsible for in Avorth.

One afternoon, she cornered Devrand away from the ship.

"We need to talk," she told him.

"Fine. Here?" They stood in a small square of shops in Thienas.

Alorsha looked around. "Better back at The Gramaire."

They found an empty classroom in the compound and sat on the hard chairs there.

"What is it?" Devrand asked. "You're not having a change of heart about coming along, are you? Or are you leery of sailing?"

"It's not that. I can learn that. It's the oddities. Do you know when they started up?"

Devrand gave that some thought. "A few years ago?"

Alorsha shook her head. "Before that. Best I can tell, they first showed up not too long after we worked that magic to increase our strength. The first time. And they've grown more numerous since we worked the magic the second time. I think they might be connected to what we did."

Devrand laughed. "How could they be? The magic only came to us."

"But the wisps. The symbol that flowed out from us...."

Devrand placed an arm around Alorsha's shoulders. "There's been nothing about the smoky wisp. No one has said anything about seeing anything like that. As for the symbol... it didn't send the magic out. It felt like it went out to find some to bring to us. Didn't you feel that?"

Alorsha shook her head again. "I didn't feel much of anything until the time when we needed to hold."

"Oh. Well, that's what it did."

He turned her to face him. "We've done nothing wrong with the magic. Pushed its limits, yes. That's what we're supposed to do. What we're still doing, and why they picked us to go out and deal with the oddities, I think. The timing's just a coincidence. But even if the wisp is involved, who better to get it? Right?"

Alorsha studied his expression as she weighed his words. "Get it?"

"Yes. Capture it. Examine it. Whatever's needed."

"What if it's going to need to be sent back wherever it came from? Or maybe destroyed, if it's that much of a danger."

"Oh. Sure. We'll just do that." Devrand waved one hand in the air. "I'm glad we had a chance to talk this over. Feel better, now?"

Alorsha gave him a noncommittal grunt that he took for agreement.

"See you at the ship to stow the rest of the taiawood scraps." He sauntered out the door.

Alorsha stared after him a long time as she tried to squelch the uneasy feeling that had washed over her at his words.

What does he plan to do with the wisp after he captures it? Why did the idea make her all shivery?

CHAPTER 8

Carrying the last of the plants she planned to bring with her, Alorsha boarded the ship. She paused to observe all the activity, all the crew doing things with ropes and such. They all ran barefoot. *What's that about?*

She shook her head at herself. No doubt she would learn before too long.

The ship held provisions to last about a month, if they needed. But they planned to follow the coast as much as possible, to allow them to spend time on land, to investigate the oddities mainly, but also to give the crew frequent breaks from the work of sailing.

Alorsha turned to go to her room, 'cabin' she reminded herself she should call it, and almost ran into the Ship's Master.

The stocky woman put out a hand to steady her, then bowed. She stood just Alorsha's height. Strands of her brown wavy hair that had escaped from the short braid at the back of her head waved in the light breeze. Her skin was browned and weathered, and her light blue eyes sharp. Alorsha guessed she might have seen two score years so far, as compared to her own score and six years. The woman wore a simple tunic and trousers, no different from the rest of the crew, except hers looked a little less worn.

"Welcome aboard, Mage Alorsha," she greeted her.

"My thanks."

"Your fellows arrived a few minutes ago," she continued, "and are seeing to their matters. I'm Master Saevalde Eztevo. Very pleased I am to be sailing with you, and such a fine ship you've given me to work with."

"I'm honored to be able to help out with this," she added. "Dean Ravnajor told me the purpose of this journey, and anything I can do to help, let me know. These oddities are worrisome, and increasing, so it seems."

Alorsha nodded.

Together, the two women watched two crewmembers board, each carrying a lidded basket woven so the sides contained multiple holes. The second crew member also carried a large bag over one shoulder, filled with jars distinctive in both shape and their blue color.

As the crewmembers passed Alorsha, the lids of the baskets popped up and half-grown cats peered out. One basket held two black and white cats while the other held a tricolor white, black, and orange cat and a white cat.

"Cats?" Alorsha said.

"From two different ships' litters," Master Eztevo said. "The black and white cats are Stormy and Knots. Knots is the one with just that little patch of white. The white cat is Catnap, and the tricolored cat is Catapult. They'll keep rats away from our food stores. Also, they're good company when a sailor's tired of all the people about."

She waved a hand at the bag of jars. "And the powder there works just as well for the cats as it does for any of the crew who feel frisky. A bit in a drink keeps the ship from being swarmed in a few months with kittens and babies." The Ship's Master laughed.

Alorsha smiled, her expression more polite than

appreciative of the other woman's humor. She noticed then that Master Eztevo also wore no shoes.

"Aye, barefoot," Master Eztevo said with a grin as she saw the direction of Alorsha's gaze. "Shoes are for in port. Toughen up your feet and you'll be happier barefoot on deck. Good for climbing the rigging, too, if you're of a mind to be doing that."

Alorsha looked up. "Maybe after I've learned a bit more." She grinned at the Ship's Master. "Before I came to Thienas, I went barefoot much of the time."

"So, you'll be running with us in no time." Master Eztevo grinned. "Well, off to finish the last duties and we'll be heading out. Might want to find a tunic and trousers instead of that pretty dress," she told Alorsha over her shoulder. "You'll be happier on board, I expect."

Alorsha hurried to her cabin and tucked her plants among the others that already lined the top of low cabinets under the windows before she changed into her work tunic and trousers. They had become quite worn, but that did not matter here. They were comfortable. After some consideration, she left her shoes and stockings behind, and returned to the deck to watch all the activity.

Master Eztevo muttered something about the tide and bellowed orders. The crew scrambled to carry them out.

Then the ship headed out of the harbor and into the deeper water not too far from the coast.

Jarthan joined Alorsha. He snaked an arm around her waist and gave her neck a quick nuzzle.

"Who'd have thought it," he said.

She gave his cheek a quick kiss. "Yes."

"North or south?" Master Eztevo called to them.

"We'll head north," Devrand answered from behind them, his voice growing closer as he spoke. "Check out the oddities in our own kingdom before we see if the southern lands have any oddities of their own. Maybe get through before the winter storms set in."

"Aye, north it is."

Devrand stopped next to Alorsha and Jarthan. "It sounds like we'll sail a few days before our first stop," he told them. "The oddities haven't happened much close to Thienas, so we have to go a bit to reach the nearest."

Alorsha nodded. "Did you get all those books I'd asked about?"

Devrand nodded. "The dean was reluctant to let some of them come with us. I guess some of the coppice-magics in them are... somewhat extreme. But I managed to talk him into it."

"Great. I think there might be some magics in there that I can adapt to add to the taiawood magics."

"Wonderful."

The three stood for a time and watched the crew and the Ship's Master, watched the harbor recede behind them and the coast go past. Alorsha saw nothing of much interest yet along the coast. *Expect I won't until we're at least several days further away from Thienas.*

"Place more magics now?" Jarthan said after the harbor was no longer visible.

Alorsha shook her head. "Not yet. I want to read some in those books."

"They're tucked in one of the cabinets in your cabin," Devrand said.

"My thanks. I plan to treat them to endure the spray without damage before I'll bring any out here. What are you two going to do?"

"I think I'll see if Master Eztevo has some time to explain some of the workings of the ship to me," Jarthan said.

"I'll see if one of the crew has some time for me," Devrand said, with a toothy grin.

"What's her name?" Jarthan asked.

Devrand's grin widened.

"Just don't interfere with her duties," Alorsha called over her shoulder on the way to cabin. With a sloppy imitation of the salutes they had all seen the city guards use from time to time, Devrand strolled the other direction.

~ ~ ~

To her surprise, Alorsha found she had little trouble adjusting to the life on the ship. She stayed out of everyone's way and spent a lot of time reading. She and Jarthan often stood with Master Eztevo to learn about the ship and crew. Alorsha never once fell sick from the motion of the ship, although Jarthan suffered a couple of days before he recovered.

"How long will it take us to round the north shore of the island?" Alorsha asked Master Eztevo their fifth day out.

"Depends on how many times we must stop. Like tomorrow. And how long you three need to stay to take care of those oddities. I *think* we'll be heading back south before the winter sets in. But we could be seeing a few storms."

It was then early summer, and the winter storms came to the northern shore sometimes as early as the beginning of autumn.

"That long?" Alorsha said. "So many months."

"Well, we're not pushing her." Master Eztevo gestured at the ship. "We want to allow plenty of time for you mages to be working your magics. Could be we'll be around the north much quicker. All depends."

"I see."

"Don't worry, lass. Between the way she's built and the magics you lot are sinking into her, your *Aiokta* will weather any winter storm we might get." She grinned at Alorsha. "You might not enjoy it, but she'll get you through it."

Alorsha grinned back.

CHAPTER 9

Close to midday the following day, they dropped anchor in a small cove.

"This is as close as the *Aiokta* goes," Master Eztevo told the three mages. She had the crew lower one of the tenders, small boats the ship carried, and a crewmember rowed them to shore.

The crewmember settled himself next to a nearby tree with a bottle, a packet of food, and some mending from the ship. "I'll wait here for your return," he said. "Also, Master Eztevo said you need only go an hour or so inland to find the oddity."

So, shod once again, since they were on land, the three mages set out.

As the Ship's Master had estimated, an hour's walk brought them to a strange spot at the edge of the woods. From where they stood, they saw a small village not too far off. But between them and the village a strip of plants grew, different from those in the surroundings, with spikey leaves and colored a dull brownish green.

Alorsha exchanged looks with Jarthan and Devrand,

and edged closer to the strange plants, one hand extended to brush the closest. The two men watched, on the alert for danger.

Alorsha touched the plant and reached for its magic to learn about it.

With a flash, the entire section of strange plants burst into flame. But the flame burned gray, rather than the normal oranges and golds of a regular fire. Jarthan knocked Alorsha back and away as Devrand jumped away too.

"Are you injured?" Jarthan asked her.

"No. The fire didn't catch me."

As they watched, the fire burned swiftly, and only burned the strange plants. After it consumed all its fuel and burned itself out, blackened land lay smoking between them and the village.

"Did you learn anything about the plant?" Devrand asked.

Alorsha shook her head. "It was strange. I couldn't touch the spark of magic within. I could barely feel it. It felt... I don't know, out of place?"

Raised voices reached them as several people ran from the village and stopped on the other side of the burned area.

"Honored Mages are you unharmed?" shouted an older man.

"We are," Jarthan shouted back. "Stay there. We'll come to you."

"Begging your pardon but is that wise?" a woman shouted to them. "To walk across on that?"

The three exchanged glances. "Why should we be wise now?" Alorsha muttered for them alone and the two men chuckled. "Devrand, I think this is for us. Let's link and see what we can sense."

"Oh, certainly, let me help," Devrand muttered, his tone sullen.

However, his expression was anything but, when

Alorsha looked at him sidelong. She held out a hand and Devrand took it. They stepped to the edge of the burned area and paused. Bolstered by Devrand's magic, Alorsha managed to reach deep into the ashes that littered the smoky ground, into a faint magic that was strange to her. She took the time to explore it and even poked the ashes with a stick to try to learn about the magic.

When she returned to herself, she became aware that everyone there stared at her. She blinked a few times to clear her head and released Devrand's hand.

"Did you catch any of that?" Alorsha's voice sounding rough to her own ears.

Devrand nodded. "Some. That magic felt off somehow. Different."

Alorsha turned her attention to the villagers on the other side of the marred land. "It's safe to walk on. There's nothing there now that will cause any harm." She crossed the smoky ground toward the villagers to demonstrate the truth of her words, Jarthan at her side.

Devrand paused to hold a hand above the ashes. "Cooled already," he muttered and scooped up a handful. He dumped them into a belt pouch and joined Jarthan and Alorsha.

"I recommend you don't plant anything there come next spring," Alorsha told the villagers. "And keep an eye on what grows there, if anything."

They nodded and the man who had first shouted to them spoke. "Then the king sent you to help us?"

Alorsha and Jarthan nodded.

"That'll be all we can do for now, though," Devrand said.

"Perhaps yet one more thing," the man said. "If you've the time to take a look at one of the boys who wandered into that patch a couple of days ago—"

"None of us are healers," Devrand broke in.

The man nodded. "We had a healer out from the next town over, but it's not that. There's something... maybe it's the magic."

The three exchanged looks.

"We can't promise that we can help," Jarthan said. "Our abilities might not lie in the proper types. But we're happy to see what we might be able to do."

The man bowed. "My thanks. This way."

~ ~ ~

At the village, the man led them to a small house and knocked on the door. An older man opened it and talked in a low voice with the first man, then opened the door wide and bowed.

"Please come in, Honored Mages," the second man said. "I welcome anything you can do to help."

The first man said, "I'll leave you here. Borysk can see to anything you might need."

The three entered the house and, after Borysk gestured that direction, headed to the chair that sat in front of the low fire. In it a boy of about eight years hunkered and stared into the flames.

Borysk closed the door and joined them.

"Grigry, the mages would like to see you," he said to the boy.

Ever so slowly, the boy drew his gaze from the fire and turned toward the newcomers. He seemed to focus on them but said nothing. His expression remained blank.

"He talks, sometimes, but he's never the chattiest around strangers, even before."

Alorsha frowned. "I'm not sure—"

"I've an idea," Devrand broke in. "Let me take the lead on this one. I've learned a new way, I believe, with the magic and it might help us here."

Alorsha and Jarthan exchanged looks, and Alorsha turned to Borysk. She gestured toward Grigry.

"With your permission?"

"Yes, yes, of course. If your magics can help, please,

whatever's needed." He bowed again and backed away to give them room.

They gathered around the boy, and each laid a hand on one of his shoulders. Their other hands they clasped together.

"This might feel a little weird," Devrand warned them. He knelt to look into the boy's eyes.

Alorsha felt something, a hint of the magic from the ashes, and a gentle tug on her own magic. She glanced at Jarthan. Eyes wide, he nodded.

"Devrand?" she said in a low voice.

"A minute," he murmured.

The tug on Alorsha's magic came again, stronger this time, and a small sliver of her magic slid to Devrand's hand where it clasped hers. For a moment, she sensed Jarthan's magic there, too. Then she felt a magic from the boy similar to that in the ashes from the plants that had just burned.

Devrand did something, and the other magic flowed to his hand that gripped the boy's shoulder. Alorsha blinked. *Did the other magic flow into Devrand?*

No one was supposed to be able to pull magic from another person. Even what she did with all the plants did not pull the magic, but rather drew it throughout the plant to make it as strong as possible for the intended purpose.

Devrand dropped his hand from the boy's shoulder and released Alorsha and Jarthan. "Did you two sense any of that?"

"Did you pull the magic from him?" Jarthan said.

"I think… possibly. Look."

They watched the boy blink several times, and his gaze truly focused on them for the first time.

"Hello," he said, with a tentative smile, his voice no more than a whisper.

"Hello," Jarthan replied, as Borysk grabbed the boy in a tight hug.

"Oh, my boy, my Grigry! We were that worried."

"One moment," Devrand said.

"Is something wrong?" Borysk asked. He did not release the boy although the youngster had started to squirm.

"I don't think so," Devrand said. "I just want to check one more thing, something I noticed. Could we have him sit again?"

"I'm hungry," Grigry said.

"One more thing to take a look at before you can go eat," Devrand said. "Did a plant poke you, maybe you got one of those spiny seeds stuck in your skin, when you went in the area with the strange plants?"

The boy scrunched his eyes and nose while he considered that. "I-I… maybe. I don't remember…." He looked at Alorsha. "But my ankle hurts."

Alorsha nodded as Devrand knelt and rolled up the boy's trousers to reveal the source of the pain.

The mages all leaned close and got somewhat in each other's ways to see what it was. The boy giggled at them and Jarthan grinned back at him.

Alorsha inspected what looked like a long, green splinter under the skin of the boy's left leg, near his ankle.

"I don't believe we should touch that with bare skin," Alorsha said.

"On it," Jarthan said.

Alorsha watched him work his magic to form a small box. The boy watched too, wide-eyed.

"I'll seal a lid to the box once the splinter's inside," Jarthan said.

Alorsha nodded and looked back to the splinter. *Had it moved up the boy's leg?*

"Cut it out?" Jarthan said in low voice.

"I can't think of another way to get it," Alorsha said, also keeping her voice low. She did not want to alarm the boy.

"I might have an idea," Devrand said. "Maybe I can call it, like with the magic in the boy."

"So that *is* what you did?" Alorsha said.

"Later," Devrand said. "This, now. I think it's moving."

Alorsha nodded, certain this time that it had moved. She looked up at the boy.

"This is probably going to hurt," she told him. "We'll be quick. Can you do this?"

Grigry looked at Borysk, who nodded.

"I think so," Grigry said. "Hurry? It already hurts more."

Jarthan set the box on the floor beneath the boy's foot, in a good position for the splinter to drop into it after they got it out. He placed a hand on Devrand's shoulder and Devrand placed a hand on Alorsha's shoulder.

"Steady the box, please?" Devrand said.

She nodded and felt the pull on her magic again, this time less hesitant on Devrand's part than before. She watched as the splinter moved back down the boy's leg to his ankle, punctured the skin, and began to slide out. The boy whimpered but held himself still.

"There's a good lad," Borysk murmured.

Alorsha adjusted the box to make sure the splinter would not touch her hands on its way inside.

"Ready?" Devrand looked to her. After she nodded, he looked to Jarthan.

"Ready." Jarthan held the lid he had formed close to the box, prepared to pop it on after the splinter was inside.

"Now," Devrand said.

He slid the splinter the rest of the way out of the boy's skin and dropped it toward the box.

In midair, the thing twisted and lunged for Alorsha's hand. She flinched, but raised the box to catch it, and Jarthan dropped the lid on top. He grabbed the box, and sealed it closed with his magic. Alorsha sat back with a sigh, which Devrand echoed.

"Ow," Grigry said, and grinned. "My thanks. It feels better already."

A trickle of blood oozed from the puncture wound that the splinter had made. Alorsha grabbed a small bottle from her belt pouch and dribbled a tiny bit of the contents on the wound. Grigry gasped, then smiled.

"What was that?" he asked.

"A potion that I make," she said. She handed the bottle to Borysk. "I'm not a healer, but that will help keep the puncture from getting fevered. If you don't need it all, save the rest for the next time someone in the village gets injured."

Borysk's eyes widened as he took the bottle. "You're a coppice-mage?"

Alorsha nodded.

"Oh, my thanks, Honored Mage. We'll use this well." He clasped the bottle to his chest.

"We should be going," Devrand said.

Alorsha nodded as Jarthan helped her to her feet.

"Is there anything I can give you in thanks?" Borysk asked as they headed to the door. "Do you need more herbs, Honored Mage? Anything at all?"

Devrand frowned and slipped out the door as Alorsha shook her head. "Your thanks is enough," she told Borysk. "Truly. We need nothing more."

Outside the house, the scene repeated with the gathered villagers. The three mages at last got away with no more than several loaves of fresh-baked bread.

"At least we can share these with the crew," Jarthan said. "Although we're not long into the journey, fresh bread should be welcome."

"Indeed," Devrand said.

~ ~ ~

Back aboard ship, Alorsha grabbed Devrand's arm, pulled him into their front room and sat him at the table. She took a seat across from him. Jarthan sat to one side.

"Talk," she told Devrand.

He smiled at her and Jarthan. "For a while now, I've been able to sense the magics in people, and sometimes animals, and touch people's magic. I can usually tell which type they have, and somewhat get a feel for how strong they are."

"How long?" Alorsha said.

"Uh, since I was about eighteen."

"Nine years…" Alorsha said.

"That long?" Jarthan said. "Why didn't you say something before now."

Devrand shrugged. "For the longest time, I thought I must be imagining it. When I decided I wasn't, I still didn't see what use it was, even less than my usual type." He frowned.

"When did you learn to pull the magic from someone?" Alorsha said.

"Well, I've turned the idea around in my mind for a while. Considering it possible. But again, what use would it be?" He looked away from them. "Just here, it seemed like a good way to get that magic out of the boy." He waved a hand in the general direction of the box, which sat on the table.

"That magic doesn't feel like the usual magic I've encountered from various mages I've worked with." He pulled off his belt pouch, the one that held the ashes, and set it next to the box. "It doesn't feel like it belongs. So, I figured it'd be best if I pulled it from the boy."

"Did you notice if he had any magic of his own?" Alorsha said.

Devrand shook his head. "It felt like he's got that little bit that you find in most people. But he's not even apprentice qualified."

"Did you pull his magic, too?" Alorsha asked.

Devrand gave her a long look. "No. Just the other magic."

"What do you mean when you say it doesn't feel like it belongs?" Jarthan said. "I didn't feel anything like that about it, one way or the other."

Devrand shrugged. "I don't know how to describe it. Foreign, maybe?"

Alorsha leaned toward him. "Foreign? Like from another kingdom? Do you suspect another kingdom is secretly engaged in magic-based attacks on us and we're only now figuring it out?"

Devrand shook his head. "Not another kingdom. Or at least I don't think so. Hear me out. I've noticed that all the magics I've ever sensed share a certain feel to them. A sort of flavor, I guess you could call it. Although that doesn't really describe it. Anyway, all the magics share that sense to them: yours, Jarthan's, everyone's at The Gramaire, even the plants' magics that I've sensed through you, Alorsha. This just feels… different."

He looked at the box and pouch. "I can't say what it is. Where it comes from. I'm hoping those can help us figure something out."

"Hope so," Alorsha agreed. "What did you do with the magic, the strange one, that you pulled from the boy?"

Devrand shrugged and looked at the box again. "Nothing. It helped me pull that splinter."

"If you pull this strange magic from someone else again, maybe we should try to contain it somehow and study it, too. Do the plants create it? Or are they caused by it? Or something else?" Jarthan said.

They pondered that.

"Can you make a container that can hold magic?" Devrand asked Jarthan.

"Hm, maybe. I haven't tried anything like that. But we know taiawood can hold magic. Why not use that?"

Alorsha shook her head. "I'd rather not try that. Or at least not unless we have no other option. The taiawood is highly attuned to magic. I worry what that strange magic might do in it. Or *to* it."

The men nodded.

~ ~ ~

The crew appreciated the fresh bread, and Master Eztevo told the three mages that it would be more than a week to their next stop. In that time, the three concentrated their efforts on the ashes, to try to see what they could learn. They left the splinter locked in its box and tucked into the cabinet where they kept Alorsha's magic components. To calm their concerns about what the splinter might do, Jarthan created a second box around the first before they tucked it away for the time being.

By the time the ship dropped anchor again, the three mages had only determined that the ashes still held some magic, and that the magic was what they now labeled 'other-magic'. With practice, both Alorsha and Jarthan learned to sense the difference between the other-magic and all the magics that surrounded them regularly, the ones they were used to. So, they counted that as progress, although less than they had hoped for.

Jarthan struggled to create a container to hold magic, but not react to it. He managed to form something he told them should work, but they had no way yet to test it.

Their visit to the shore resembled the previous one. They found another area affected by the other-magic located near another small settlement. This time, the other-magic had changed plants in a random, wavy path that circled through a forest and out into a grassy area. No one seemed to have suffered any ill effects from the plants. When Alorsha tried to reach into their magics, these plants did not burst into flame, but she could not touch their spark to learn anything about their magic.

No one in the village could tell them anything about the strange plants, not even when they had first noticed them, at least not with any certainty.

"The sheep don't seem to want to go anywhere near those plants," one shepherd told them.

With care, and wearing gloves, Alorsha took small

cuttings of each of the various altered plants that they found. When she finished, she had gathered more than a dozen of them. Jarthan crafted individual containers for each one and sealed each inside. With help from the other two, Devrand reached out to pull the other-magic from the plants.

At first, it seemed that it would not work. But he tugged on Alorsha's magic, and he then pulled the other-magic.

Jarthan's container proved its worth as it held the magic that Devrand pulled. Just before Jarthan sealed it, Alorsha caught a glimpse of a dark gray vapor that swirled inside. A brief sense of that magic brushed her, but not from the wisp. From somewhere else. But before she determined even a general direction, it was gone.

After Devrand pulled the other-magic from the plants and slid it into Jarthan's container, the plants looked wilted and did not revert to what they had been before. So, Alorsha traveled back around the wavy path and gathered new snippets, to study them more while the ship sailed to the next oddity.

CHAPTER 10

Devrand, Jarthan, and Alorsha fell into a pattern in their travels where they studied the strange plants or ashes or other remnants that they gathered of the oddities while the ship sailed to the next oddity. The investigations progressed much slower than any of them wished and they often stormed out of the Tavanos' front room in frustration to stand on the deck to clear their heads while they gazed off across the water.

They learned little enough.

Alorsha could not encourage the other-magic to strengthen in any of the plant pieces they had gathered. She could not even sense what strengths the other-magic might have, whether for healing or protection or something else. She also could not make the altered plants grow or flower, as she could with all the plants she had worked with before. Chopping or crushing the altered plants to try to make potions or balms only resulted in inert, smelly liquid or goo.

Jarthan discovered that the other-magic seemed to eat away at his created containers, and so made new ones every few days.

Devrand could move the other-magic wisps about, with no apparent difficulty, so he moved them from old containers to new. But he could not seem to do anything else with them.

They compared notes and learned that they all had felt a sense of the other-magic from time to time that came from somewhere, not the wisps. Always fleeting and more a hint than anything they could grasp or locate.

After a time, after a cursory look to see if they sensed anything different from before, they simply bundled plant samples found at any particular oddity together and set them aside to return to The Gramaire. Maybe someone there would have new ideas.

At the oddities themselves, they found a little more success. They treated anyone who had been injured by any altered plants just as they had the first boy, with the same promising results.

Devrand became adept at calling the other-magic out of any people they found who had been infected by it. Sometimes the other-magic formed a wisp, which they caught in one of Jarthan's containers. Other times it seemed to get away, although Alorsha never saw any wisps fly from them. They never encountered any animals who needed other-plant splinters removed from their skins, nor did they see any animals changed by the other-magic.

They did notice a trend in the oddities themselves. As they encountered more of the oddities, they discovered that any that had existed for a longer time stretched over a larger area – whenever anyone had some idea when they first appeared.

So they journeyed through the warm months and into autumn, with little change in their travels.

~ ~ ~

Alorsha rolled over and hitched herself on her stomach

toward the head of the bed to look out the window there. The sea looked calm, and by the light, she judged that it was near dawn. They had rounded the northern coast of Deasa and sailed along the eastern shoreline as the weather cooled, having visited many of the small towns and villages of the far northern parts of the kingdom of Varoia. Master Eztevo had told them that she wanted to make a stop the next day to take on fresh provisions and give everyone a week or so of rest in the town of Kaimas, before they continued their journey, headed further along the kingdom's eastern coast and toward the coastlines of the kingdom's neighbors to the south. Alorsha looked forward to a visit home, although still a month or two of travel away at their current pace. Fortunately, there had been few reports of any oddities in the area, so there was little there that they needed to check into.

As Alorsha peered out the window, her thoughts wandered. *Do the other kingdoms on the island also have the oddities? Maybe, if they do, they'll share anything they've learned of them. Perhaps they've learned more than we have.*

She shot a quick glance toward the front room, toward the closet where they stored the other-magic wisps. She did *not* look forward to that afternoon. They had agreed to see what a wisp would do when brought to a small piece of taiawood. They had already tried the other-plants and the ashes, neither of which had reacted at all with the magic wood.

Alorsha shuddered, and not just from the cool air in the room. *Somehow doing what we plan seems significant. But how? Or why?* She dreaded it, for some reason.

Jarthan flung an arm across her waist. She looked that direction to see him peek out from beneath the covers, with that particular look in his eye.

"Come back over here," he murmured.

She smiled and set aside her concerns for a time. She had in mind something far better to do.

~ ~ ~

That afternoon, the three mages gathered at their worktable. Devrand had informed Master Eztevo that they needed to be undisturbed. The Ship's Master had given him a dubious look, before she wished them luck.

Jarthan retrieved one of the smaller containers that held an other-magic wisp. He set it in the middle of the table and sat. He created a plate with his magic and placed it next to the box.

Alorsha placed a scrap piece of the taiawood, about the size of her hand, on the plate. She and Devrand took seats at the table as well, equally spaced from each other and from Jarthan. They all stared at the box.

"Ready?" Jarthan asked.

"I wish we could put one of those defensive shells around us," Alorsha said. "Like Zan could make."

Devrand shrugged. "That's not a strength that any of our magics has. No point worrying about it. I won't let the wisp get away," he assured Alorsha and nodded to Jarthan.

Jarthan placed his hand atop the box. A line spread all around the top edge where he split it, to make a lid. He pulled his hand back and nodded to Devrand.

Devrand held one hand poised above the lid. With a glance to the other two, he grabbed the lid, tossed it to Jarthan, and put his other hand above the opening.

The wisp flowed out of the box and headed toward Devrand's hand. Then it stopped in midair and formed into a round shape.

"Devrand?" Alorsha reached out toward him in case he could use some of her magic.

"Wait."

The wispy ball spun in midair and plunged into the piece of taiawood. The wood glowed a red-orange and the glow spread out from the point of contact. The glow vanished and the three stared at the piece of wood. Alorsha reached a tentative hand toward it. *Is it redder than before?*

Devrand caught her hand. "Better together."

Alorsha nodded, reached out with Devrand, and they grabbed the taiawood at the same time.

Red lights exploded in front of Alorsha's eyes, and she lurched back, still holding the piece of wood. From what seemed a long way away, she heard someone call her name.

The lights swirled around and drew her into the taiawood in a way she had never been drawn into a plant's magic before. She sensed the normal magic of the wood, sensed its potential to enhance other magics, and sensed the other-magic blending with it, expanding it, infusing the piece of wood with enormous potential for some great magic, but she could not tell what.

She reached toward the magic, much like she had done so many times before to strengthen a plant's magic for use. This magic seemed to reach back, toward her. She felt a hint of yearning from it.

She sensed Devrand, there with her. The magic reached toward him, and she sensed he reached out to it. Sensed also that a wisp of other-magic wrapped itself around his own magic, merged with it.

Something pulled her back. She opened her eyes. *When did I close them?*

Jarthan's worried face was a finger's length in front of her. She looked past him to find Devrand slumped on the table.

"I'm fine," she assured Jarthan, who nodded and turned to Devrand.

He leaned the other man back in his chair and peered at him.

"He's breathing," Jarthan said. "But out, otherwise, as far as I can tell."

Alorsha started to stand. When fatigue swept through her, she leaned on the table instead.

"Alorsha?"

She waved a hand at him. "I'm fine. Truly. Just exhausted. Like that time I made potions all day without stopping. Drained."

She noticed the plate and box no longer sat on the table.

"The wisp?" she said.

Jarthan indicated Devrand, who still clutched the taiawood in one hand. After a moment's hesitation, she reached for it. To her surprise, she was able to take it easily.

When she touched it, she again felt the great potential magic within. But it did not reach for her.

"Box, please," she told Jarthan, and dropped it in as soon as he made one. He sealed it.

Devrand began to stir. He opened his eyes and looked around, without at first seeming to focus. Then his wandering gaze found them.

"What?"

"That's what I'd like to know," Jarthan snapped. Alorsha looked at him in surprise. She had not heard that tone from him before. "What exactly are you playing at, Devrand?"

Devrand shook his head. "What? Nothing."

Alorsha placed a hand on Jarthan's arm. He looked at it, then met her gaze. He returned to his chair.

"Tell me," he said. "I sensed the other-magic but couldn't tell anything else."

Alorsha related what she had experienced and sensed.

Devrand shook his head when she finished. "I didn't reach out to it. It pulled me. But I pushed back. It's all in the piece of wood, now."

"None of it wrapped around your magic?" Alorsha said.

Devrand's eyes took on that distant look that mages got when they assessed their own magics. "No. None of it," he said after a moment.

"So, it's in the wood," Jarthan said. "Now what?"

"It felt like it strengthened the wood's magic and its potential for magic," Alorsha said. "But I'm too drained to figure out anything else about it right now."

"My head's pounding," Devrand said.

Jarthan looked from one to the other. "Yes, you two look awful."

"Thanks for mentioning it," Devrand muttered.

"I'll go grab some food," Jarthan said. He put the box back into their storage cabinet. He paused at the door. "After we eat something, you both are going to rest until we go into town tomorrow."

"Yes, papa," Devrand said with a hint of a grin.

Jarthan shook his head and left to get the food.

~ ~ ~

"Alorsha?"

Alorsha pulled herself from strange dreams of bizarre-looking places.

"Hm?"

"We've dropped anchor," Jarthan said. "Do you feel well enough to go ashore for breakfast. Master Eztevo's sent some of the crew over already."

Alorsha sat up, shivered in the chilly air, and pulled the covers around her.

Jarthan chuckled. "There's snow over on the town. We're that close to full winter now."

Alorsha looked over the edge of the covers and across the room to the tangle of their few clothes that spilled from a small chair onto the floor.

"Grab me something not too shabby to wear," she said. "Then yes. Maybe we can see about some warmer clothes, too, since the season's changing."

Jarthan nodded and handed over a handful of her clothes for her to pick from.

"Shall I help you dress?" he said with a glint in his eye.

She answered him with a flirtatious look over one

shoulder. "As enjoyable as that would become, we'd lose a lot of time. And I'm hungry." Her stomach growled at the thought of food and Jarthan chuckled.

"Later, then," he promised.

Alorsha shooed him away and hurried into her warmest dress. *Not nearly warm enough.* She layered one of her tunics over it. *Not the best look, but warmer.*

She grabbed her cloak and joined Jarthan on the deck. Devrand and Master Eztevo met them there.

"Are you joining us for breakfast?" Alorsha asked the Ship's Master.

"If it's agreeable to you three. I need to be seeing about more provisions for us as soon as I can this morning, anyway, before that lot gets to the merchants."

She waved a hand toward the sea, where three ships sailed into the bay.

"King's ships?" Jarthan said.

"Aye," Master Eztevo said. "Unusual to see three together, but not unheard of. Might be a good idea to get any news from them, too." She grinned. "After I beat them to the best provisions."

"Then let's go." Devrand led the way to one of the ship's small tenders that a crewmember held ready to lower into the water.

~ ~ ~

Ashore, the four enjoyed a hot breakfast in one of the town's inns. The town boasted four. Master Eztevo gulped her meal and left them to see to her tasks.

The three mages lingered over the last of their meal and savored the warmth of the common room. It was easy to tell when the King's ships dropped anchor: the room filled with his people. One, who seemed to be in a position of authority, approached their table.

"Mages Devrand, Alorsha, and Jarthan?" the woman inquired.

The three nodded.

"Forgive my caution, but may I see your proof?"

For a moment Alorsha wondered what she meant, but she figured it out. Along with the two men, she pulled out the king's-seal pendant they had been given months earlier and extended her hand to show the mage ring she wore.

The woman took her time. She scrutinized each pendant and each of their mage rings and nodded. She pulled a roll of parchment from her pouch and laid it on the table.

"This is for you, then. I'm glad I encountered you here and didn't have to continue further north to find you." She gave them a low bow. "Good day, mages."

She returned to her fellows, and they all settled in at tables to await their own breakfasts.

Devrand tucked his king's-seal pendant away again. He gazed at the other two with raised eyebrows and watched as they also tucked away their pendants. "Shall I?"

Alorsha nodded and Jarthan waved a hand in the general direction of the parchment. "Go ahead."

Devrand unrolled the parchment, revealing that it was several rolled together. He scanned the top of each page. "Looks like they've got a copy for each of us." He separated them out and handed them over.

Alorsha looked at hers.

She held an official-looking letter from his majesty, via some clerk, which authorized the three of them to visit the other kingdoms on the island and confer with officials there regarding the oddities that had spread to plague the whole island. The other sheets seemed to be notes from various other mages with information about the oddities. *Something to read through later, back on the ship.*

She looked up at Jarthan and Devrand.

"So, we're to sail the rest of the way around the island, it seems," she said.

"It'll be interesting to visit the southern lands," Jarthan said. "Although I wish it was for a less concerning reason."

Alorsha and Devrand nodded. Devrand held out one of the parchments.

"This writ will help us get ready," he said. "Anything we need, and the king's coffers will cover it." He held out his hand to display the small, metal chits he held. They looked like miniature versions of their pendants. "We just give these to any merchant we deal with."

He shared them out. "I'll catch Master Eztevo and give her some, too."

Devrand headed out.

Jarthan finished his drink. "Shall we walk about town a bit? Are you recovered from yesterday?"

Alorsha set aside her own empty cup and took his extended hand. "I think so." Then she grinned at him. "Besides… a chance to visit new shops."

He chuckled.

By midafternoon, all the provisions and warmer clothes, and some new plants and herbs that Alorsha had found, had been purchased and stowed aboard the ship. The ship again set sail, and followed the coast south, drawing closer to home with each day.

CHAPTER 11

Alorsha woke sometime in the night. She lay there and listened to the normal ship noises. Why was she awake? Fatigue from dealing with the increasing number of oddities they had been finding weighed on her. *But there's something....*

She sat up and looked around. Faint light from the two small moons came in through the room's windows, but shadows mostly filled the room. She turned toward the door. *Is that a faint glow coming underneath?* It did not look like lantern light.

She slipped out of bed and grabbed a cloak that lay draped across a chair. The cold floor chilled her bare feet, but she ignored the sensation.

She padded to the door, opened it a crack and peered through.

No one was in the outer room. But the faint glow lit the room. From two sources.

The top of the table glowed red, but not the red of heated metal. More as if a light within the wood shone through the surface.

The second glow came from around the door to the storage cabinet.

Alorsha stepped into the room, closed the door behind her, and circled the table to the cabinet. She eased open the cabinet door. One shelf within glowed much like the table: the shelf that held the box into which they had placed the taiawood with the other-magic nearly three months previously. A brighter glow came from beneath the box.

Alorsha lifted the box and jumped when the piece of taiawood fell out the bottom. It, too, glowed.

She turned the box over and inspected the wood-shaped hole in it. She shook her head, set the box aside, and reached toward the taiawood scrap.

Her face scrunched in apprehension, she brushed the wood with a finger.

Nothing.

She glanced at the luminous tabletop and pressed her finger on the taiawood scrap.

Still nothing.

She tried to ignore her lingering weariness as she reached within the taiawood to seek contact with its magic.

It felt no different from earlier, stronger in the magic, with a hint of the other-magic. And it held a great potential for... something.

Next Alorsha checked the shelf, then the tabletop. The same thing.

She frowned. *Maybe we shouldn't have used the taiawood everywhere throughout the ship.*

She grabbed the box, set the taiawood scrap back inside, and placed it on a shelf with the open side up this time, so the scrap no longer touched the shelf. *That should hold it until we can all look at it in the morning.*

Did the shelf's glow already look dimmer? *Perhaps.*

She closed the cabinet door and returned to her and Jarthan's room. He had not stirred in the short time she had been gone. She glanced out the window. All looked peaceful.

She shed the cloak, climbed back into bed, and told herself she would wake early to share this with Jarthan.

In his sleep, Jarthan flung an arm over her. She snuggled into his warmth and drifted off.

~ ~ ~

The next morning, after Alorsha pulled herself from bed, she hurried into her clothes, and pushed a grumbling Jarthan to get ready. Within an hour, the ship would drop anchor at the small coastal town from which Avorth was a couple days' ride inland, assuming they found horses to borrow.

A passing thought disturbed her. *Something I'd wanted to....* But it was gone.

When she opened the storage closet to grab some of her herbs, she saw the box with the other-magic taiawood sat on a different shelf. With a shrug, she grabbed the herbs she wanted and closed the door. *One of the others must have moved it.*

An hour later, Alorsha and Jarthan waited while Devrand finalized the arrangements with a small stable in town for horses and provisions for them. It would take another hour to prepare everything, so the three headed to the town's single inn to get breakfast out of the late-winter cold. After, when their mounts and provisions were ready, they headed inland toward Avorth.

Snow the first night of their travels on horseback delayed them, so the afternoon of the second day of their journey found them still crossing the highlands that lay half a day away from Avorth, if one rode under ideal riding conditions. As they crested the last hill before the start of the descent, Alorsha's attention was drawn to the valley where her village sat.

"What's that?" Jarthan also peered in the direction of the village.

"Looks like… smoke," Alorsha said in a soft voice. She turned to her life-partner. "Oh, Jarthan! It looks like a lot of smoke."

Jarthan gave her hand a reassuring squeeze even as his expression grew worried. He glanced at Devrand. "How fast can we get there?"

Devrand studied the horses. "If we push them hard, I expect we can get there this night. It'll be sometime after dark, though."

"Let's go then," Jarthan said, with a decisive nod.

~ ~ ~

The rest of that afternoon and through the evening hours, they pushed the horses as much as they dared. Alorsha tried to reach out to any plant along the way that she could brush with her fingertips without slowing, to see if she sensed anything. Unlikely, but she had to try. Her efforts produced no results.

At times, Devrand or Jarthan stared into the distance, gaze unfocused for a brief time. *Must also be trying to sense something through the magic.*

But no one said anything.

More than an hour after sunset, the three rode their weary horses across the bridge over the stream below Avorth. They rode up the last little hill before the village.

Alorsha pulled herself from the doze she had fallen into. "Where are the buildings?"

The two men started out of their own dazes.

Alorsha slid off her horse and ran to the site of the village. Devrand and Jarthan followed on her heels. The weary horses stayed where they stopped and lowered their heads to munch on some scraggly grass that poked through the snow at the side of the road.

Alorsha stopped in the center of what had been the green. Bare, scorched land surrounded her, and nothing else. No sign of any of the houses, the smithy, the fence that had stood around the green. No sign of the villagers, her family, her friends. Heavy gray coils of smoke rose from the blackened ground. Alorsha coughed and ran off again.

She ran to the meadow. Another scorched area with nothing left. She ran to the pond where all the village children had learned to swim. Gone, the depression scorched like everywhere else. She ran back to the site of the village. She screamed for her parents, her brothers and sisters, for Izmireva. Only silence answered her.

Jarthan caught up to her there and wrapped her in his arms. His own tears mingled with hers as he held her close. Devrand came to stand next to them and stared at the ground.

"What happened?" Alorsha said many long minutes later. "How can there be nothing left? Not even a part of a wall?"

Devrand knelt in the ashes and pressed one hand flat on the ground. He looked up a moment later.

"You'd better check on this," he said.

"Can't it wait?" Jarthan demanded.

"Maybe," Devrand said. "But I'm not sure that it should."

Alorsha wiped her eyes on her sleeve. "It's fine," she told Jarthan. She imitated Devrand's stance on the ground.

"Go with caution," he said. "Just reach out a little."

Alorsha gasped as she touched the magic in the ground, in the ashes. The other-magic saturated whole area. It lunged for her. She yanked her bare hand from contact with the ground and jumped back.

She stumbled a couple of steps and turned a stricken gaze to Jarthan. "This is on us. We… we're the death of our village."

"Alorsha." Jarthan stepped toward her and reached for her, his expression as anguished as hers. Devrand watched from his crouch, one hand still flat on the ground.

Alorsha shook her head and backed away. "How could

we?"

Jarthan stepped toward her again. "We were children."

"I feel like we're *still* children. Playing with something we don't understand."

"But we're getting there," Devrand said in a soft voice. "We know so much more."

"At what cost?" Alorsha said. "Too high a cost. And it could be doing this elsewhere, too!"

"We'll find a way to clear it away," Jarthan said. "We can't...." His voice caught. "We can't bring them back. But we can find a way to get this other-magic out of here."

"How?" Alorsha shouted at him. "You can't make a box big enough for this." She waved her arms at the devastation around them.

Jarthan shook his head.

"I believe I can guide us," Devrand said.

The others looked at him. Alorsha's gaze dropped to his hand on the ground. He followed the direction of her gaze, snatched his hand away, and stood.

"It'll be much like when I've pulled the other-magic from those people," Devrand said as he approached Alorsha and Jarthan. "This I can do."

Alorsha took a step back, uncertain what bothered her about Devrand's assertion. "But where will you put the other-magic?"

Devrand smiled, and Alorsha shivered at the sight of it. "I've thought on this. If it truly came from our spell to strengthen our magics, a variation of that spell should work, should send it back where it came from."

"You know that it came from somewhere else?" Alorsha said.

Devrand nodded and looked from her to Jarthan. "Haven't you two also had the dreams of other places, strange places? I'm sure you must have. I wonder if we're seeing other... worlds, if you want to call them that. Real places that aren't here, where we live."

"I've had some strange dreams," Jarthan said. Alorsha

nodded agreement.

"But," Jarthan continued, "you're talking about the places in those stories we all heard as little children? The places where the nisse dwell, the fairies, the brownies?"

Devrand shook his head. He laid a hand on Jarthan's shoulder and touched the side of the other man's neck with his fingertips. "Only as a rough description, I suppose. I think real people live in these other places. I think this other-magic came to us from one when we worked our magic."

Jarthan seemed to relax under the touch of Devrand's fingers.

"I see," he said. "So, we'll send them their magic back."

Alorsha gave him a sharp look. His voice sounded strange, but she could not pinpoint how.

Devrand placed his other hand on her shoulder. His fingers brushed the side of her neck as he squeezed her shoulder. A sense of assurance washed over her. "This I can do," he repeated. "With you two, of course."

Alorsha nodded, feeling inexplicably soothed. They had all studied the other-magic for months now. They had worked together so long that they had a special bond that most other mages never created with their fellows.

"I haven't made any of the special candles in a long while," Alorsha said.

Devrand smiled. "I've a feeling that we'll have no need for them." He nudged Jarthan and Alorsha. "Let's go back to the meadow."

Alorsha and Jarthan both nodded.

"Makes sense to do this where we inadvertently set it off," Alorsha said.

"Indeed," Devrand said.

~ ~ ~

On the way back to the meadow, Devrand gathered three sticks, which they used to draw the square star in the ashes and dirt.

Devrand pulled the wisp-containing scrap piece of taiawood from his pocket.

"Why'd you—" Devrand's raised finger hushed her.

"Had a hunch that I should bring it," Devrand said. "Let's powder it and use it in the lines of the star."

He led the way to a small rock outcropping and placed the wood atop it. The wood glowed, the light faint.

With another rock, Devrand broke the wood into three pieces. Alorsha wondered briefly at that. *The wood shouldn't have broken that easily.* Then they each pounded a piece until they reduced all the wood to a red-black powder, which gave off a faint glow. Devrand swept it all into his hands, portioned some out to Jarthan and Alorsha, and led them in dropping the powder into the lines they had made.

When they finished, Jarthan and Alorsha stood and gazed at the glowing star on the ground. Slowly, Alorsha turned to look at Jarthan. *Something isn't as it should be.* She felt strange.

Devrand took their hands and pulled them into the center of the star. "You both know how this part goes."

Alorsha felt his touch on her magic even before they stood with shoulders touching and hands clasped. A soothing lassitude came from Devrand's touch, and he tugged on her magic to pull it to him.

"Devrand..." Alorsha said in a soft voice. He looked at her, then away. She sensed that he had pulled some other-magic into his own magic and twined them together, probably back at the green earlier.

He smiled. "I'll finally get the magic I should have had. I'll no longer be the support mage, secondary to others and worthwhile only to augment *their* workings. We'll be able to do anything!"

Devrand tilted his head to the sky and Alorsha felt him send out a call to the other-magic. It came, called to the other-magic he already held.

He welcomed it.

The magic came from the ground beneath their feet, gray wisps that spun around Devrand, plunged through him, and shook him with each strike. Larger wisps came too, from the direction of the village, and from other directions. They swirled around the three of them and joined together into larger and larger wisps, until just one circled them. Alorsha tried to pull back her magic, but Devrand's grip on it was too firm, his link to her too strong.

She looked to Jarthan and saw from his expression that he realized what Devrand was doing, and also could not do anything to interfere. But Jarthan gave her hand a squeeze. They would figure out something when they could.

The wisp circled and dove through Devrand each time it passed him, diminishing each time. Some of the other-magic tried to come to Alorsha from where she touched Devrand. She fought it back and away, experienced as a coppice-mage at keeping other magics separate from her own. *But did some get through to Jarthan?*

He shuddered.

The last of the wisp plunged through Devrand again and he howled, "All of it!"

The wisp circled again. It plunged back through him and up in the air behind him. It hovered there, then seemed to split apart. It flattened and opened into an oval-shaped hole. Within the hole, Alorsha saw a daytime cloudy sky above a field of orange flowers unlike any she had ever seen before.

Devrand turned toward the hole, stepped toward it, and pulled Jarthan and Alorsha along with him. Alorsha fought, with all her strength and magic, not that her magic was suited to such a thing. A thin other-magic wisp floated into her ring from Devrand's hand before she broke his hold on her. She helped Jarthan fight then as they together pulled against Devrand's hold.

At the brink of the hole, the passage someplace else—

maybe some other world—Devrand looked back at Alorsha with a sad smile.

"I'm sorry. I'd have liked to combine your magic, too. Although ill-suited to me, I'm sure I could've found a way to make it work."

He held out the hand that had been on her shoulder and a blast of air from it tore her away from Jarthan. She jumped to her feet and ran back as the two men tumbled into the hole. She lunged for it.

"Jarthan!"

The passage closed in her face, and she fell to the ground.

Alorsha muttered curses Mama would have cringed at and slammed both hands on the ground, raising puffs of ash, as she reached for the other-magic. *Have to open that hole!*

She called the other-magic to her. From the ground. From the air. But the plain dirt beneath her no longer held any other-magic. No other-magic came to her call.

She felt a faint sense of Devrand and Jarthan from her mage ring, and a faint spark of magic. And other-magic. *From that wisp that slipped into it?*

She reached again for the magic, through her ring this time, and fought to recreate the hole. But she did not have enough magic.

Fighting tears, head aching so much she could not see straight, she slumped on the ashy dirt, heedless of the mess it made of her clothes and skin.

A possibility came to her in her misery, and she lifted her head to gaze into the distance. *The ship, the taiawood, might have enough magic.*

CHAPTER 12

Three days of hard travel, punctuated by light snow and many tears, brought Alorsha back to the coastal town, where she returned the horses, and the unused portion of the provisions, to the stable there. She stumbled to the harbor, clumsy with fatigue and grief. When her eyes burned with more tears, she blinked against them. *Enough tears. Need to get to work. Hope Master Eztevo has one of the small tenders waiting.* She did, and sat with it herself.

Master Eztevo scrambled to her feet when she spotted Alorsha and hurried to her.

"Lass... Alorsha. What's happened?"

Alorsha shook her head, her expression listless as she met Master Eztevo's gaze. "Back on the ship," she said. "Get me back there and I'll tell you."

"But where are—"

"Not coming. I'll tell you all of it," Alorsha interrupted. "On the ship."

~ ~ ~

Aboard, Alorsha slumped at the table in her outer room. The Ship's Master sat across from her, and two untouched mugs of wine sat between them.

"So, they're now in this other place," Master Eztevo said. "Can you get to them there?"

Alorsha shrugged. "I don't know. Maybe. Somehow." She looked at the cabinet and pictured the boxes of wisps stored there. Boxes that might fail with Jarthan gone.

Jarthan....

She gave herself a shake, reached for her mug, and downed the contents in a few gulps.

"Maybe," she repeated. "But I *am* going after Jarthan. I do have an idea, but it'll take time. I can feel the faintest link to him. Devrand too, although I'm not sure I now care what happens to him. Anyway, I can feel a link, so I expect I can follow that."

"We," Master Eztevo said. "I'd not see you go alone into who knows what."

Alorsha smiled. "My heartfelt thanks, Master Eztevo. That eases my mind. Your help will be most welcome, too, as what I'm thinking will involve taking this ship with us."

Master Eztevo's eyes widened at that bit of news. "That hole you just told me about went from a meadow to a field of flowers, aye?"

Alorsha nodded.

"I'd not be having this lovely ship go through one of those holes to end up landbound in the middle of someone's field," Master Eztevo said.

"Oh. I hadn't thought of that. Of course not." Alorsha looked down at the table and idly traced the woodgrain with a finger. "I don't have the magic alone to open a passage like that. I think it's going to need the ship's magic." She sipped her wine as she considered the problem.

The Ship's Master also sipped her wine, and waited.

"I'll just have to imbue the magic with not only the purpose of travel but *safe* travel through the passage. Safe as in not dropping the ship on the land somewhere. And then I suppose we'll just have to find our way to Devrand and Jarthan."

Master Eztevo nodded. "Seems like a good plan to be starting out with."

"I hope it'll work. Are we fully provisioned?"

The Ship's Master nodded and added, "Although there are a few additional things that we should bring on such a strange voyage."

Alorsha nodded. "Get whatever you can think of." She poured the last of the King's chits into Master Eztevo's hand. "Then please return whatever's left of these to the King's people. They do have a presence at this harbor, don't they?"

"Aye."

"Return any remaining chits after you make your final purchases, along with a letter I'll have for you. I'm going to tell them I can no longer pursue this investigation, and also pass along notes to help whoever they decide to send to the southern lands. Assuming that what we did didn't take care of the oddities. If it did, all the better."

Alorsha gulped as sadness washed over her, then she straightened against it.

"After we're free of the King's directive, I'll need to work some magic preparations on the ship. Please release from service, and replace, if possible, any of the crew who don't want to go with us to who knows where and for who knows how long."

Master Eztevo nodded. "I'll take care of all that. And anything else I can help you with."

"My thanks." Alorsha turned toward the cabinet. "I'll have the letter and notes ready for you when you return with the last of the provisions."

Master Eztevo nodded and left, closing the door behind her. Alorsha opened the cabinet and surveyed the boxes within. *So far, so good.* No signs yet of the wisps breaking through. *But it'll probably happen soon.*

She pushed her worries, fears, and the deep hole of sorrow into a corner of her thoughts to deal with later as she gathered her notes and double checked that all her copies were complete. She had expected at some point to turn notes over to the King and other mages, and so had made duplicates as they went along.

She rolled the notes to send to the King and tied them securely. They made a thick bundle. She placed them in a pack with the plants and bits of plants she and the others had gathered from the oddities, although she held back some of each kind for herself.

A quick glance on deck showed her the crew busy with whatever they did in port, and the Ship's Master had not yet returned. She should have time for a small test of her idea.

That last link with Devrand had allowed her to assess his magic and watch how he worked with the other-magic. So, she had little worry that what she had in mind would fail. But before she made her split from the King's directive official, she had to determine if there was truly a chance.

She pulled out one of the boxes that contained a wisp, deliberately choosing the smallest of the boxes most likely to disintegrate first.

She sat on the floor and placed it in front of her. And stared at it. *Without Jarthan (Oh, Jarthan!), how to open it?*

She frowned at the box, and decided on something that might work. She set the box on the taiawood floor, cupped her hands around it, and reached out to the other-magic that had settled in her ring. She reached into it, much like when she reached into a plant's magic, and worked to strengthen it with the purpose of calling to other-magic, in this case that within the box.

Long minutes she concentrated as she tried to duplicate the feel of Devrand's call to the other-magic that she had felt back in her village.

With a small pop, a hole broke open in the side of the

box and the wisp flowed out. Eyes narrowed in concentration, Alorsha called the wisp to her ring first, where it forged a slight link with the other-magic there. Next, she nudged the wisp to the floor next to the box. She spread the wisp out there much like smoothing a sheet on a bed. Then she nudged again, and the wisp sank into the wood.

She placed her hands on the floor and touched the magic in the wood, as she had done many times before to enhance it. But this time, she blended the other-magic with it and fixed the purpose of safe travel in the blend, specifically safe shipboard travel to another place, tied to the link she felt to Jarthan and Devrand.

Hope this works.

She held in her mind the image she had seen in the hole above the meadow and delved into the other-magic wisp. It responded and grew stronger.

And that's a use for it.

She sensed the taiawood take on the purpose as well, not strong enough yet for what she would need. But it would be, once she blended the other wisps they had caught.

She sank back to lean against the wall and watched the glow in the floor fade away.

"I'm coming, Jarthan," she whispered. "And I'm coming for *you*, Devrand."

CHAPTER 13

Alorsha sighed and slipped the last of the other-magic wisps into the taiawood ship. She grimaced with distaste as she wiped her hands on her trousers, although she had not touched the magic with them. She disliked working with the other-magic. *Feels slimy, and slippery. Foul.* Although it sank into the ship's taiawood readily enough. Probably because some had already merged with the taiawood's magic. *That must've called to the rest.*

She had taken one long uninterrupted afternoon of effort to move all the other-magic wisps from their boxes into the ship. When each wisp left its box, each box began to crumble away. *More of Jarthan gone.* Two days later, none of the boxes remained.

Those two days, while the changing crew occupied Master Eztevo's attention, Alorsha kept herself busy packing away Jarthan's things, clothes mostly, in a small chest in the corner of their room. She placed her chervynai atop the chest. She had kept it with her all this time. *And it'll go with me now. A reminder of the better times.*

She also packed Devrand's belongings and sent them

overland to The Gramaire with a trader who planned to head that direction. She wrote a letter to the dean that told all of what had happened and her plans to follow the two men. She sent that with the trader as well.

While the Ship's Master worked the new crewmembers into the ship's routine during subsequent days, Alorsha locked herself away in her rooms and fought with the magics, as she tried to open a passage like the one back at the village, tried to recreate the feel of the magic when that passage opened and infuse that into her efforts. After many long days of this fight, still unsuccessful, she emerged to meet the King's representatives when they arrived aboard.

The same woman she had met before led the way, and two men followed her. The two men carried a small chest that was obviously heavy, needing both of them as it did.

The woman approached Alorsha and Master Eztevo where they awaited her on deck and saluted them both. She held out a scroll to Alorsha.

"His majesty offers his sincerest commiseration at what has happened," the woman said. "While your request to be released from his directive to investigate the oddities saddens him, he understands your need to pursue your fellows. So, he releases you from his directive, all of you," she waved a hand to indicate the entire ship, "and wishes you luck and success in your new task."

She nodded at the rolled scroll Alorsha held. "All of that's in there. He also sent this along for you."

She nodded at the two men behind her, who set the chest on the deck, with expressions of relief. They lifted the lid just enough to reveal the gold coins inside to Alorsha and the Ship's Master. Alorsha and Master Eztevo exchanged glances. That gold would no doubt be useful.

They both thanked the woman. She bowed to each of them and left. Her companions followed her example.

"That's best kept in your cabin," Master Eztevo told Alorsha and called over two of the long-time crewmembers to take it there.

"If you think so," Alorsha said and watched them carry the heavy chest through the door to her cabin. Then she turned a circle and surveyed the ship. A few more people bustled around than she had seen before, all busy with various shipboard tasks.

The ship itself had changed subtly. Its wood had darkened from the other-magic that she had fused with it and turned almost black. It retained the red sheen, although a much deeper red than before.

"I've been thinking about the ship's name," Alorsha said.

Master Eztevo made a noncommittal sound.

"I don't want any remnant of Devrand's presence lingering here, even the name he gave the ship," Alorsha continued. "I don't dislike the name. I just think we should change it."

Master Eztevo nodded. "You have a new name in mind?"

Alorsha nodded. "Assuming it meets with your approval." She glanced at the other woman to gauge her reaction. "I found a word from an ancient language. Yes, even as Devrand did, but it seems somehow appropriate to imitate his actions in this anyway. The word I found fits. To signify my resolve, our resolve, I'd like to rename the ship the—"

"Hold the name until we officially rename her. There's a certain way to be doing these sorts of things."

"But don't you want to know what I've thought of. Approve it?"

The Ship's Master shook her head. "I trust you to pick the best name. To tell me before we're holding the renaming ceremony could mean ill luck."

"Ceremony?"

"Aye, lass. There's an old tradition behind renaming a ship. Some say it used to be magic to help keep the ship from harm. Maybe it still *is* a magic of sorts." Master

Eztevo shrugged. "I'm no mage, as you know, but I'll not go against the tradition. Just in case there's something to it. We'll hold the ceremony before we sail."

"How soon can that be?" Alorsha said. "Now that the king has released us from his directive, do we need to stay here any longer?"

"We can leave on the morrow. Have you the means to follow Devrand yet?"

Alorsha shook her head. "No, not yet. But I'll keep at it and hope it'll come to me as we sail."

Master Eztevo gave her a curt nod. "Tonight, we'll rename the ship. I'll prepare the ceremony. And tomorrow we'll take her out."

~ ~ ~

That evening the entire crew gathered on the deck, with Alorsha and Master Eztevo and two crewmembers with cups and jugs of wine on the raised foredeck.

The Ship's Master showed Alorsha a small strip of metal upon which she had written *Aiokta*, then she raised the strip for the crew to see and waited for them to quiet.

"Oh, ye seas and oceans, we implore you in your graciousness to expunge for all time from your recollection and from the Ledger of the Deep the name *Aiokta*, which has ceased to be an entity in your kingdom. We submit this ingot that bears her name, to be corrupted through your powers and forever be purged from the sea." Master Eztevo tossed the metal strip from the bow and she and Alorsha watched it fall into the water.

Master Eztevo gestured to one of the nearby crewmembers, who handed her a jug of wine.

"Acknowledging your munificence and dispensation, we offer these libations." She leaned over the rail and poured the wine into the water as she moved from east to west around the bow.

Master Eztevo spoke again. "Oh, ye seas and oceans,

we implore you in your graciousness to take unto your recollection and the Ledger of the Deep this worthy vessel, hereafter to be known as...." She nodded to Alorsha.

"The *Deliberia*," Alorsha said.

"Guarding her," the Ship's Master continued, "and ensuring her of safe and rapid passage throughout her journeys within your realm." She lifted another jug and poured the wine into the water as she moved this time from west to east. "Acknowledging your munificence and in honor of your greatness, we offer these libations."

The two crewmembers brought Alorsha and Master Eztevo each one of the cups and hovered at their sides, each holding another jug of wine.

"Oh, ye mighty winds, through whose power our frail vessel traverses the wild and faceless deep, we implore you to grant this worthy vessel the *Deliberia* the benefits and pleasures of your bounty." Master Eztevo moved to the north side of the ship and faced that direction. Her crewmember followed and poured wine into her cup when she gestured for it.

"Great North Wind, permit us to use your mighty powers, ever sparing us the overwhelming scourge of your frigid breath." She tossed the wine from her cup to the north and nodded to Alorsha, who led the way to the west side of the ship. When she stopped and faced west over the rail, her crewmember poured wine into her cup.

"Great West Wind, grant us permission to use your mighty powers, ever sparing us the overwhelming scourge of your wild breath," the Ship's Master said.

Alorsha tossed the wine from her cup to the west.

The small group moved through the gathered crewmembers to the eastern side of the ship.

"Great East Wind," Master Eztevo said, "grant us permission to use your mighty powers, ever sparing us the overwhelming scourge of your mighty breath." The crewmember filled her cup, and she tossed her wine to the east.

Last, at the south side of the ship, the Ship's Master said, "Great South Wind, grant us permission to use your mighty powers, ever sparing us the overwhelming scourge of your scalding breath." Alorsha's crewmember filled her cup, and she faced south from the stern and tossed the wine to the south.

Then everyone aboard filled their cups and lifted them high for the toast that closed out the ceremony.

"To the *Deliberia!*" they shouted.

"It suits," Master Eztevo told Alorsha as they joined the rest of the crew for the celebration that traditionally followed the ceremony.

~ ~ ~

The next morning, Master Eztevo and Alorsha oversaw the loading of a few additional provisions for the anticipated journey. They included a couple of crates of chickens and a basket with two new cats, a brown striped one and another black and white one that looked almost like a twin of Stormy, one of the ship's cats already residing on the *Deliberia*.

The Ship's Master grinned at Alorsha's astonished expression. "We've got room for the chickens, and a few of the crew already know how to care for them. The eggs'll be welcome, and if we're sailing long enough, we can have some roasted chicken eventually, too. The cats are of a completely different line from ours and from each other, so that'll help with breeding our ship's cats, if we choose. I've named this one Cattitude." She pointed to the brown striped cat. "And the other is Purrocious."

The last crewmember to board carried a crate filled with those distinctive blue jars.

Alorsha leaned close to the Ship's Master. "Looks like you bought all the powder that the town's healers and herbalists had."

"Aye, and a couple of towns further along the coast,

too. Don't know how long we'll be out there, and we want to have enough be certain we won't be overrun with chicks, kittens, and toddlers."

Alorsha could only nod agreement.

~ ~ ~

Close to a week after the *Deliberia* sailed away from that town into the open water, Alorsha discovered the knack for creating the passage. Instead of trying to copy Devrand's method, she found a way to use her technique of drawing forth a plant's magic to draw forth the combined other-magic and taiawood magic in the ship.

She used her mage ring as a sort of focus and managed to open a passage for the *Deliberia*.

~ ~ ~

Alorsha caught her balance as exhaustion washed over her and the world around her gained color and bits of detail. Grayness surrounded them, like they had sailed into a strange, stormy fog bank. Winds howled, so the grayness was more likely rain and tossed seawater than real fog. The wind tore at her hair and whipped it into her eyes as she sank to the deck, sat on her heels, and took a steadying breath. *Hope the rough part's over.* She suspected she might be deluding herself. *No matter.* It was done and had left her bone-tired, as deep magic often did.

Their new location came into focus around the ship as the haze of fatigue cleared from her vision and she looked around. Well, somewhat into focus. *Some side effect of the magic? Or the passage, perhaps.* Not much to see yet with the storm.

Through the gloom, Alorsha spotted a bright spot overhead that must be the sun, although a different color from what she knew. *So, this isn't someplace far away in our own world. We must truly have come to another world.* The bright spot, more orange than the sun she knew, vanished as gusts of wind whipped the clouds around and tossed the ship. She levered herself to her feet, staggered the couple of steps to the rail and clutched it.

With the murky weather, she could not tell much about the water they sailed. Although it smelled much like the seas they had sailed back home.

Master Eztevo joined her at the rail and clutched it like she did. "What now, lass? With those random gusts, we're not going to get much use from the sails. At least while they continue. But once the weather clears, we can pick a direction. Or even before, if we know which way to go. We can row for a time." She glanced at Alorsha. "So, which way?"

Alorsha stared out into the swirling gloom as she tried to sense anything through the faint link to Jarthan, and Devrand.

"They feel closer than they did before," she said after several minutes. "So, I believe we've come to the right place."

"But?"

Alorsha sighed. "But... I can't tell a direction." She stared at the waves and let her thoughts wander.

"Let me try a few things. I'll come up with something," she told Master Eztevo after a time, and returned to her previous spot near one of the masts.

She knelt, placed both hands flat on the deck at her sides, and dove into the ship's magic to look for inspiration.

Sometime later, she was not sure how long, she became aware that someone stood near her.

She looked up, and the man, one of the new crewmembers, bowed to her. "Honored Mage, Master Eztevo's asking if you have a heading for us. The storm's begun to lift."

Alorsha looked around. *Yes, definitely brighter now.*

"Please tell her I need just a little more time and then I

should know."

The man bowed and hurried off.

Alorsha levered herself to her feet and studied her mage ring. A dim red glow swirled within the stone and grew brighter under her regard. She nodded; she was learning. *The other-magic in the ship sufficed to open the passage and bring us to this new place. But the other-magic in the ring is where the link to Jarthan and Devrand resides.*

She stretched her hand out in front of her, braced her feet against the motion of the heaving and swaying ship, and concentrated on the magic within the stone in the ring, drawing its strength forth. *Nothing that way.* She turned slightly, still concentrating.

After she had turned in a slow, complete circle, she recognized what to look for, realized what the slight change in the feel of the link meant. She also decided that she would have to find a better way to work this wayfinding magic. Her arm ached something fierce.

Rubbing her upper arm, she wobbled across the deck to Master Eztevo, who acknowledged her with a nod.

"Got something for me?"

"Yes. We need to head that general direction." Alorsha pointed to the right of the direction the bow of the ship pointed.

"On it, lass." And Master Eztevo was away, shouting out orders and sending crewmembers running.

Alorsha fought her way aft to her cabin, there to finish settling things for her solitary occupation of it and wait out the rest of the storm.

~ ~ ~

Hours later, as Alorsha worked on some potions and creams that she believed might be useful to have, a knock came on the outer door.

"Come."

Master Eztevo entered, bowed, and closed the door

behind her.

"We're well on our way," she said. "No sight of any land, yet, but we've got a steady breeze now to help."

"That's good news. My thanks."

When Master Eztevo remained standing there, Alorsha gave her a quizzical look.

"What is it?"

"May I speak freely, Honored Mage?"

"Of course." Alorsha waved a hand at one of the other chairs at the table. "Please sit. Why so formal all of a sudden?"

"I've had some thoughts I believe you must hear. Also, although Mage Devrand first hired me, us, you are, now, the only owner of the ship still here. It makes this a rather unique situation."

"Please, Master Eztevo. Say what's on your mind. And I'm Alorsha when we have no need for formality, such as when we are in discussion with just us two."

Master Eztevo nodded. "Then I'm Saevalde, please."

She watched as Alorsha finished one of her concoctions, one she could not just leave in the middle, and shifted in her chair.

"Have you any battle experience?" Saevalde asked as Alorsha packed away the rest of the components for another day.

Alorsha gave her a sharp look. "No. But I expect you know that. Home has been at peace, with no armed squabbles pretty much my whole life."

Saevalde nodded. "Then no weapons training, either?"

Alorsha shook her head. "Not to speak of. I came from a very small village. I learned to chase off the rare predator from our flocks but nothing beyond that. I can use the sling, but haven't done so in years."

"And your type of magic isn't for the fighting, is it?"

"No. It can help others, strengthen armor and weapons, help keep the fever from wounds, a few other things."

Saevalde nodded again.

"Here are my thoughts," she said after she studied Alorsha for a few minutes. "While we sailed at home in familiar waters, I saw no need. But now we have no knowledge of what we sail into. So first, you need to learn a weapon, or two. You won't be very good, likely, for a good long while. We have no idea of how long it'll be before we can catch Devrand. We should look to defense in case we encounter hostile people along the way."

Alorsha nodded. "I can see that. What weapons?"

Saevalde studied her again. "You've used the sling... how's your accuracy?"

"Pretty good, when I'd kept in practice."

"I'd say resume practicing that to start. Gives you something right away, and at range. Some sort of knife or short sword for if anyone gets close. Maybe the bow, if your sight is that good at range."

"We have all these weapons?"

Saevalde grinned. "That's what I added to our stores before we left. The best of the weapons the town had. Best to be prepared when sailing strange waters."

"They don't get much stranger," Alorsha said.

"That they don't. Which leads to my next thought. We have a good crew. Trustworthy. But you're all alone in here now, and you won't be good at defending yourself for a time."

Alorsha looked at her with narrowed eyes. "What are you getting at?"

Saevalde shifted in her seat. "You're vulnerable here." She waved a hand around at Alorsha's two rooms. "Perhaps you should take a room below instead."

Alorsha tilted her head and considered.

"I see your point, but I'd prefer not to work with the plants and potions in a room below-deck. At times, I need fresh air for my workings. But...." She raised a hand to forestall Saevalde's objection.

"But, how about this?" she continued. "I don't need

the two rooms for just me. Help me move this small table into my inner room and shift some things around in there, and you take this outer room. Maybe we get a large table in here, too, for meetings. You should have had these rooms from the start, anyway."

Saevalde waved that off with a slight smile. "Where I sleep isn't a concern. I've dozed at the wheel often enough." She winked at her, then sobered. "You won't mind me in your outer room?"

"It'll be your room," Alorsha said. "We'll bring your things in here and move mine in there."

Saevalde scrutinized her expression. "It's a good solution. I can guard you when I'm here. And I'll see about getting you a lock for your door. You should lock it whenever you're in there."

Alorsha grinned. "Yes, sir."

Saevalde grinned back at her. "Sorry, I do sound like my da used to with me and my sisters. But still, lass. Be mindful of your safety and defense, now. We can't trust that we sail safe places anymore."

Alorsha nodded.

~ ~ ~

They worked together to shift the furnishings around, with little need for conversation. When it came time to move the heavier pieces, Saevalde called in a couple more crewmembers to help, while Alorsha guided them. Before long, they had transformed both rooms.

"Are the crew set for their needs?" Alorsha asked as they rested at the rail and peered into the haze that lingered from the storm.

"For now. It wouldn't hurt if we find a port to see about getting a few luxuries."

At Alorsha's raised eyebrows, she shrugged. "This might turn into a long journey, lass."

Alorsha nodded. "I'd hope not, but you're right." She

glanced back at the normal bustle of the crew.

"What do you think about arranging weapons work for all of us? Not just me."

Saevalde nodded. "A good notion. I'll see to it."

Alorsha gave her a sidelong look. "You'd already thought to do that, hadn't you?"

"Aye. But it's good to come from you, lass." She stared the way they sailed. "Are we still on the right heading?"

Alorsha stepped back from the rail. "I should check." She was nearly drained, but this needed to be done.

As before she extended her arm and turned the circle to sense the faint link to Jarthan. When she stopped and opened her eyes, her extended arm now pointed a little to the right of the bow again. But her arm wavered back and forth, the motion none of her doing. She exchanged a look with Saevalde.

"A slight adjustment," she said. After Saevalde acknowledged that, she lowered her arm with a sigh. *Now it really hurts.*

Alorsha joined Saevalde at the wheel. "Do we have any metal workers among—no, wait. That wouldn't be practical on a ship, would it? How about woodworkers? Someone who can carve? I have an idea to make this easier on me." She rubbed her sore arm.

Saevalde gave her a long look. "Lass, why don't you go talk with them. Find out yourself. You don't need to go through me. You ought to get to know your crew and give them a chance to know you. We could all be together a long while." She squeezed her shoulder. "They're all good people, I wouldn't let any problem-makers join us. But I wager they're a mite confused and worried."

Alorsha dropped her head. "You're right. I should've already been doing that."

"Don't let it be worrying you, lass. You're new to this and you've had some things on your mind."

Still rubbing her arm, Alorsha started with the crew on deck. She stayed out of the way of their duties, but learned names and some about them, and tried to answer their questions the best she could.

It took time, and for several days she struggled to connect names to the right people, but soon the crew acted more comfortable around her and seemed to consider her one of them more than some aloof leader who handed out decrees. Saevalde also introduced her to Sonne Vernandos, a strong-looking woman close to the Ship's Master's age, with sun-lightened hair and brown skin. The woman stood a little taller than Master Eztevo and had been a warrior before she joined the crew. Saevalde recommended that Sonne take on the duties and responsibilities of Ship's Captain and take charge of the weapons work for Alorsha and the crew, if Alorsha agreed. Which she did.

Alorsha and Saevalde arranged for the newly appointed Ship's Captain to move into Saevalde's old cabin, as better fitting Sonne's new position aboard ship.

As the days passed and they sailed, Alorsha felt certain that seeing her dripping with sweat, fumbling with the unfamiliar activity of learning to use a sword, went a long way to endearing her to the crew. It seemed all of them were better than she, but none worked harder. She found she enjoyed the concentration required when sparring, the need to focus and ignore other concerns. It gave her moments of freedom from her fears for Jarthan and of what Devrand might do.

She found several among the crew who loved to carve, one of whom, Grabe, had carved jewelry before and worked with exotic woods. And Grabe had no more than the minimal spark of magic, which should keep him safe.

So, when Grabe did not have other duties, he helped her solve her problem of working the wayfinding magic to determine their direction of travel without pain.

Based on ideas Alorsha shared with him, Grabe created a small frame to fit around the narrow, coppery metal rim that encircled the stone in her mage ring. He used one of the smallest taiawood scraps to make it. She let him decorate it however he wished, but as he worked on the carvings, she linked the other-magic wisp in her ring to the magic in the small piece of wood and worked to draw the magics' strength into a use for locating.

When Grabe completed the carving, Alorsha fitted her ring into the hole he had left for it in the center. It snapped into place, and the stone glowed briefly.

"My thanks," she said. "It couldn't have been better made."

Grabe smiled in pleasure, bowed, and left for his other duties.

Alorsha removed the chain she still wore, with the King's disk pendant that hung from it, and strung the small carved frame-with-ring on it.

She climbed up on deck—they had worked below this past day as they traveled through a chilly rain—and moved to the middle of the deck. For the moment, the rain had decreased to a fine, cold mist. She shivered but did not plan to be there long, so did not go grab a cloak. Saevalde joined her.

"Now we see if it worked," Alorsha told her. Saevalde nodded.

Alorsha extended her arm and let the chain and pendants dangle from her fingers, with the lightest touch to the magic in the ring. The pendant swayed back and forth, then inscribed a circle.

Saevalde glanced at her, and she shook her head. "I'm not making it move."

It spun several times. Then the chain jerked straight out and nearly pulled from Alorsha's grasp. It held that way, parallel to the deck, and swayed back and forth to inscribe an arc that pointed roughly the same way the bow pointed.

She nodded at Saevalde. "Now the old way." She gathered in the chain and snapped the ring out of its frame. She placed it back on the thumb of her left hand and performed her arm-extended spin. She ended facing the same direction.

"Great. I believe we can trust it. I'll still double-check for a while."

Saevalde nodded. "Can you get any idea at all of distance?"

"I'm sorry, no. But we've got to come to land at some point. Devrand had no ship, and we know he stepped through the passage to a field."

Saevalde nodded.

Alorsha returned the ring to its frame and placed the chain around her neck.

CHAPTER 14

As one day of sailing blended into another, the crew grew better acquainted with each other and began to form into a kind of floating village. Despite the inevitable squabbles, Saevalde informed Alorsha this was a good thing.

The crew also turned to Alorsha for her help and judgement on things that happened, much as if she held the position of headwoman of their unique village. Just a day after Grabe finished the carving for Alorsha, a knock on her door disturbed her long after the evening meal.

Alorsha set aside the book she had been trying to read, too distracted by thoughts of Jarthan to make much headway, and minced across the cold floor in stockinged feet to open her door.

"Sorry to bother you so late, Honored Mage," said one of the crew who ran messages throughout the ship. The young woman shuffled her feet and would not meet Alorsha's gaze. "Master Eztevo sent me to get you. Said your presence is needed right away on deck."

"Of course." Alorsha grabbed a cloak against the cool night air, slipped on some soft shoes, and followed the messenger.

As she descended the stairs to the main central deck, she observed the tableau before her.

Saevalde stood with her legs braced wide and her arms crossed. Her whole manner radiated stern disapproval. Captain Vernandos faced her and gripped the arms of a young man in front of her. When Alorsha got a good look at his face, she frowned. *Haven't seen him before.*

"What's this?" She stopped next to Saevalde.

"Found him hiding in the hold," Captain Vernandos said.

"Stowaway," Master Eztevo muttered.

Alorsha studied the man, skinny and with a gaunt look to him. *Looks around my own age.* Fine dust coated his black hair and black-brown skin, and his scruffy clothing looked nothing like what any of the crew wore. When he looked at her, she saw that his eyes were as dark as her own.

"Please don't send me back, Honored Mage," he said. "They're after me."

"Who?" Alorsha said.

"The authorities back in that town, I'd wager," Saevalde said. "Pretty sure I saw him with the other wharf-rats there. A thieving bunch, but mostly just after enough to eat. Didn't even suspect he'd stolen aboard."

The man grinned at that. "I'm the best at that."

Saevalde frowned and exchanged glances with Captain Vernandos, who nodded.

"What's your name, lad?" Saevalde said.

"Parl Smas."

Saevalde nodded. "If we weren't to send you back, what good will come of it for us?"

He looked from one to another of them, hope in his expression. "Like I said, I'm good at sneaking around. I could do that for you. Just don't send me back."

"We're not going back, lad," Saevalde said. "At least not yet." She glanced at Captain Vernandos, who shrugged and released the man's arms.

"Don't know how much use any sneaking around will be," the Ship's Captain said. "But I expect we can put you to work here. If you agree, Honored Mage."

Alorsha scrutinized the man's hopeful expression, then looked from Saevalde to Captain Vernandos. "If you two think so, I've no objections."

The man's grin transformed his whole face. "My thanks, Honored Mage, Master, and Captain."

The Captain clapped a hand on his shoulder and turned him toward the hatch that led below. "See that you express your thanks with your actions, too. Now let's get you settled in."

Alorsha and Saevalde watched the two walk away.

"Is this wise?" Alorsha murmured. "He's not one of your carefully selected crewmembers."

"As I said, lass, most of the wharf-rats are just looking for a good meal, and a chance. This one's found his. And who can say, mayhap some sneaking might be doing us some good at some point.

With a nod, Alorsha returned to her own pursuits.

~ ~ ~

Another day, several days after Parl joined the crew, the cook called Alorsha below decks soon after dawn to help when his new helper got hold of the wrong dried herbs from the stash and ruined the day's soup. After the helper's one taste of the bitter concoction and several trips to the head to empty his stomach, the man had certainly learned the difference between the herbs he had grabbed and those he should have used. Alorsha exchanged wry looks with the cook, with a slight smile, as she handed the helper some different dried herbs to make a tea that would settle his stomach.

"You know what to do from this point," she said to the cook.

"Of course." The cook turned to his remorseful helper.

"You'll toss the soup overboard. It's unsalvageable. Then you'll give the pots a good scrubbing while you recite for me which herbs are for cooking. Until you can list them letter perfect."

Alorsha smiled to herself as she returned to the main deck.

~ ~ ~

For two full weeks, they sailed the sea with no sign of land. Alorsha worked the wayfinding magic twice each day, and Saevalde rigged a pole to attach to the rigging to hang the pendant, so she need not still hold it outstretched. Otherwise, Alorsha worked with her potions and elixirs and weapons-work. It became clear that she would likely excel at the bow, at least at the distances they could practice aboard ship. She struggled with the sword but continued to make progress.

They traveled in mist or a true fog most of the time, interspersed with rain. The rare moments of sun drew any idle crewmembers to the deck to enjoy the warmth. But mostly, cold and dampness enveloped the ship.

From time to time, Alorsha reached out to see what, if anything, she could sense of the magic in this world. She had never before sensed the magic in the seas or rain. But it seemed worth a try. When the fog was at its thickest, she did sense a hint of the world's magic. It felt nothing like the other-magic she had grown accustomed to, which meant the other-magic she and Devrand and Jarthan had called up had probably not come from this world, but some other. *So why did Devrand's passage lead to this world?* With no way to find an answer, she set that aside for another time.

This world's magic also felt nothing like her native magic. But once she discovered its sense, she found that a bit of it seeped into all of them. Not enough to alarm her, but enough to pique her curiosity. So, she watched and monitored.

All it seemed to do was blend with any magics anyone already had—and the others had at most a very little—and perhaps increase the magic's strength a tad. It also sank into the taiawood, spread throughout the ship, and pooled within it.

Finally, one day about midday, one of the lookouts called out a sighting of land. Any crewmembers not tied to other duties crowded to the rails to try to spot it. Of course, those on deck saw nothing for a long time, but the crewmembers in the rigging called down information as they saw it. The biggest news was that they approached an archipelago. And they saw ships there.

In the time left before they met whoever lived there, Alorsha realized that they would need to talk with the people there. There was no reason to assume they spoke anything that resembled the same language. *But how...?*

Remembering the world's magic that had seeped into everyone, into the ship, she reached out—through the ship, as it was strongest there—and found light links to everyone aboard. Time spent on the *Deliberia* must be linking them all together. *Is that a good thing?* The idea of it unsettled her to some extent, but she set that thought aside for some other time. After a quick glance up—*is that a ship approaching*—she sank into the magic and tried to give it a pull and twist, an inclination toward communication. She hoped it would work.

She ran into her cabin to change into clothes more suitable for a first meeting with people of another land.

~ ~ ~

The *Deliberia* dwarfed the other ship that drew alongside it. Master Eztevo and Captain Vernandos stood together at the rail, near the rope ladder a crewmember lowered to the smaller ship. Alorsha joined them and took her place between them. For a moment, she felt small and lost, but she reminded herself she ranked among the most accomplished coppice-mages of her homeland. She had already crossed to a new world, had brought a ship and many people safely with her. *I can handle meeting complete strangers in their completely strange world.*

Two people climbed onto the deck, a man and woman. Alorsha studied them with interest. Stockier than she was, they both stood a little shorter than she did and looked to have some strength in their bodies. Both wore blue-green trousers gathered at their ankles and long, sleeveless tunics of a lighter blue. Both had long hair, pulled back and tied at the napes of their necks. Their skin was a brown darker than Alorsha's skin, and their hair so light it looked almost white. Both had eyes as dark as Alorsha's own.

Master Eztevo and Captain Vernandos bowed to the newcomers, and Alorsha inclined her head as one would greet equals in her own land.

The strangers exchanged a look and bowed in return, the motion clumsy. Alorsha wondered how they usually greeted people, since this did not seem to be their way. *Seems promising that they attempted to match our people's custom.*

"Welcome aboard the *Deliberia*," Master Eztevo said.

The newcomers shared glances and the man spoke, saying something Alorsha could not understand. Master Eztevo gave her a worried look. *It didn't work? We can't speak with each other.*

Alorsha rested one hand on the ship's rail and reached into the magic of the taiawood. The man said something else, and she latched onto the sounds to further impress the magic with the need to communicate. A faint shiver ran through her, and the man's words became clear.

"—saying?" he said.

Alorsha nodded to Master Eztevo.

"My apologies. I welcomed you to the *Deliberia*," the Ship's Master said. "Do my words now make sense?"

The newcomers again exchanged glances. They shot looks at Alorsha before they returned their attention to

Master Eztevo.

"Many thanks to you," the man spoke. Alorsha found his accent strange, but she understood him. She caught the slight nod that Master Eztevo directed to her, to acknowledge the success of her magical working.

Master Eztevo introduced Alorsha, herself, and Captain Vernandos. Alorsha said nothing when Master Eztevo did not mention that Alorsha was a mage. *Maybe to exercise caution with strangers and keep potentially key information close. Or at least uncertain.*

"I am Alaylu," the man introduced himself in turn. "And this is Ioli. We are the Speakers for the Kayamo Archipelago. May we ask of you what your purpose is in coming to us? Yours is the first ship ever to come to us from the north. We'd not believed that there were any lands there, and we've not seen your ship's like before."

Master Eztevo gestured in the direction of her cabin. "Would you care to sit while we talk, perhaps take some refreshment? We can prepare a spot for us in short order."

The two Speakers exchanged looks and cautiously agreed.

Master Eztevo sent a couple of crewmembers running for food and drink and corralled a couple more to help prepare a spot in her room. As Saevalde passed her on her way to oversee the preparations, Alorsha leaned close. "Take extra chairs from my cabin," she suggested.

Saevalde nodded.

Alorsha turned to the newcomers and noticed Captain Vernandos standing stiffly nearby and looking uncomfortable. *Means it's up to me.*

So, she engaged the Speakers with light talk about traveling long distances on the seas and discussed the fogs and rains, which she learned were the norm for this area this time of year, although they mentioned an unusual storm that they experienced a couple of weeks earlier. As she spoke, Alorsha made small comments also to the Captain, who started to act more at ease and joined in some.

It felt odd to speak a different language, while it still seemed like her own. *Odd too that our speech, and theirs, sounds so formal. Must be something with the magic so that we can speak with each other. Might have to see if I can tweak it so we don't all sound so stiff.*

After Master Eztevo returned, they followed her to her cabin, where Alorsha saw that the bed had been shifted further to the side, with a sheet hung as a partition to hide it. That change left a large space for the table and chairs. A crewmember followed them in and placed a platter of bread, cheeses, and dried fruits and a jug of wine on the table, along with plates and mugs.

Alorsha watched the Speakers take small bites, at first, of the food, then grab more of the foods that appealed to them. When everyone had settled and had a chance to sample the food and wine, Ioli leaned toward Alorsha.

"As we said, we've not seen a ship like yours before. Do you come to trade?"

"The *Deliberia* is unique even where we're from," Alorsha said. "And our main purpose is not trade—"

"Although we'd welcome any, if all are agreed," Master Eztevo broke in.

Alorsha nodded. "Yes, we're certainly open to it. But our actual purpose is one less enjoyable. We seek two men from our homeland."

"We've not seen any strangers," Alaylu said. "I'm sorry we cannot offer help there."

"They are fugitives from your land's rule of law?" Ioli said.

"One is, yes. The man with him accompanies him against his will," Alorsha said. "You've seen no strangers, but have you perhaps heard from others of newcomers? Strangers dressed much like us? Or do you know of a place that grows many orange flowers that look like this?" She ducked into her cabin to grab a sketch that she had made of the scene she had seen though Devrand's passage. She brought it back to the table and set it before the Speakers.

Alaylu looked at the sketch and passed it to Ioli.

She studied the sketch, then looked sharply at Alorsha.

"You perhaps are touched by the spirits, can hear them speak?" she asked.

Alorsha looked at Master Eztevo, and at Captain Vernandos, who both shrugged.

"I don't understand what you're asking," Alorsha said.

The two Speakers exchanged glances again.

"This," Ioli said. She leaned over Alorsha's sketch and studied it more intently. As she concentrated on it, the flowers rose from the paper and took on life and substance. Something brushed along Alorsha's arms. It raised the fine hairs there. Ioli looked up at Alorsha.

"I see," Alorsha said. "I cannot do anything like that. But yes, something like what you describe as being touched by the spirits. I've seen the place I drew without ever having been there. Do you know of it?"

"Ships from many days' sailing to the south have brought us, from time to time, some of these flowers to trade," Ioli said. "They are good for making dye and also smell sweet."

"So, we can at least send you a direction that might help," Alaylu said.

Ioli's conjured images sank back into the picture in front of her and she returned the sketch to Alorsha.

"Perhaps you would welcome walking on land for a time before you continue?" Alaylu said. "We can extend guest-invite to you and your people."

Alorsha looked to Master Eztevo uncertain what to say as her desire to hurry after Jarthan warred with her awareness of the crew's needs.

"We'd all be the happier for a day or so off the ship," Master Eztevo said. "But we can't tarry long."

The two Speakers rose, and Ioli stuffed a last piece of dried fruit in her mouth, with a grin for Alorsha. Both Speakers bowed to the Varoians and looked more comfortable that time with the gesture.

"Our thanks for the hospitality," Alaylu said. "We'll go prepare for your visit. Please follow at your leisure. Although, you'll need to use your small boats to reach shore. Our harbor was not intended for a ship this size."

They saw the Speakers back to their small ship and watched as they sailed back toward the island chain.

"What are your thoughts," Saevalde asked Captain Vernandos.

The woman never took her eyes off the islanders' boat. "We still need to watch ourselves, but they seem no more than they appear. I'd advise reasonable caution but see no reason to reject their offer." She turned to Alorsha and Saevalde with a grin. "Better warn everyone to beware of different customs. Be unfortunate to lose crewmembers to some unusual rule of law, as they put it."

~ ~ ~

The people of the *Deliberia* spent two full days with the islanders. A few minor misunderstandings occurred, but nothing that everyone involved could not resolve with little difficulty.

Alorsha learned that fish comprised the main portion of the islanders' food and arranged for them to deliver a few barrels to the *Deliberia*. In turn, getting some dried fruits from the *Deliberia* delighted the islanders, such things being a rare luxury for them. Some of the crew made trades of their own for things they wanted. Grabe's carvings were popular, enough so that he even used them to make some trades for others in the crew to get some things.

"Let me know when you need more wood for your carvings," Alorsha told him. "We'll be sure to get some."

He grinned and nodded and returned to his bargaining.

Alorsha also told the rest of the crew to be sure to obtain materials for any crafts or trades they could do aboard. She would cover the cost or arrange the trade for them.

After they left the islands, the crew acted much more relaxed and positive about the journey and tackled their duties with more enthusiasm than before. Jokes flew back and forth with some frequency, and everyone smiled more often, even Alorsha.

Alaylu had pointed them in the direction of the lands with the flowers, and Alorsha later verified the direction with her wayfinding magic. They coincided.

Although they faced another two weeks or so of sailing, according to the islanders, they set off with less trepidation than when they had first set sail for this other world.

CHAPTER 15

While they sailed to the land of the orange flowers, Alorsha spent a good portion of her time investigating some plants she had gotten from the islanders. As with the plants from home, she sensed a magic within them. But the world's magic was proving difficult to grasp well enough to be able to draw out and strengthen it within the plants, as she was used to doing. She struggled for several days but found her concentration grew less the more she fought to work with the magic.

With that undertaking apparently stymied, she turned her attention to her chervynai and returned to her studies of its magic. *Did the magic in this different world affect it?* After several hours she could not say that it had. But she could not say that it had *not* either. The chervynai's magic remained strong, the plant filled with it, as usual, but she had yet to draw it forth into any specific use.

She groaned as she stretched the stiffness from her body. *Not learning anything here. Should probably focus on something else.*

So, she abandoned her room in favor of the fresh air

on deck and spent most of the rest of the days of travel working on her weapons skills. During that time, she noticeably improved with the sling and bow, and continued to make some progress with the sword. She noticed that the crew seemed to also spend extra time on their weapons skills during those days and increased their focus on other preparations.

A couple of days shy of the expected two weeks, the lookout atop the tallest mast called out a land sighting not long after dawn. "It looks very orange," she added. "Even accounting for the morning light."

When she also informed them that it looked large, Alorsha climbed up to see for herself. It looked much bigger than the islands they had previously seen, maybe even as large as their own homeland.

They dropped anchor a distance from the shore later that day and took one of the ship's small tenders in closer and drew ashore near the mouth of a river.

Master Eztevo and Captain Vernandos had insisted that Alorsha take with her those of the crew who were best at weapons, aside from the Captain herself. So three others accompanied her: Kluir Reez, a young man around Alorsha's age with nearly white hair with just a hint of brown to it, brown skin, and gray-brown eyes; Hali Arithi, an energetic woman with blue-gray eyes, browned skin, and yellow-brown hair that she wore most often gathered up into a knot at the back of her head; and Parl Smas, the sneaky stowaway. Alorsha carried a bow and sling, and her sword, just in case.

~ ~ ~

From the shore, the small group saw the edges of the fields of brilliant orange flowers, but the trek to reach them took some time. No easy way there presented itself, so they climbed and scrabbled their way up a steep dirt rise to the higher plains. Once there, though, the sight that greeted them drew them to a stop.

"Remarkable," Alorsha murmured.

The flowers stretched away from them, inland, all the way to what looked like a forest in the distance. The flowers stood taller than Alorsha had expected, reaching her knees. Her companions fanned out around her, staying within a pace or so, and looked around.

"One moment," Alorsha told them.

She brushed a finger across one of the flowers and reached toward its magic.

The magic reached for her, too. It enveloped her in warmth and what felt like welcome. Something prompted her to look up and she saw a creature that seemed pure light hovering before her. About as tall as the length of her hand, it glowed the same color as the flowers. In outline, it was roughly human-shaped, but Alorsha could not see any details in its brilliance.

It brushed her cheek, and she felt the world's magic much clearer than before. She sensed all the nuances of the magic in the flowers. But more than that, she sensed potentials when combined with other plants that she caught glimpses of in the magic, plants that she had never seen before.

She became aware that someone was speaking to her and pulled her attention from the flowers' magic. "Yes?"

Kluir directed her attention to the right, across the field. "Looks like a village over there. Shall we head there?"

Alorsha looked around. No way to tell if this was the same field that Devrand had dragged Jarthan to. There could be many others on this island. Or even elsewhere.

She nodded. "We'll at least start there and see what there is to find out."

It took them almost an hour to cross the field to the village. They took care to avoid any damage to the plants and so moved slower than they might have otherwise. As they approached, they saw that several adults had come

143

out to meet them.

These people differed from the islanders they had met previously. The people of this village, at least those they saw then, were very pale of skin, with hair that ranged from pale yellow to an orange-gold. They had elders with them, white of hair and bent. Even so, they stood slightly taller than Alorsha.

As they approached, Alorsha and her companions kept their hands away from the weapons they carried, hoping to convey their desire to avoid conflict.

"Welcome, strangers," one older man greeted them when they got close enough. "What brings you traipsing through our crop?"

Alorsha smiled to herself. The magic to speak with people in this world still worked, even away from the ship. "Our apologies," she said, with a slight bow to the elder. "We saw no other way to reach your village from our ship."

"You have a boat out there? Why didn't you just sail around the headland to our wee harbor back there?" The man waved an arm in the general direction of the other side of the village.

"We're new to your lands and didn't know it was there," Alorsha said.

"Why don't we talk in the hall instead of out here in the hot sun?" one of the women suggested.

Alorsha exchanged glances with her companions. The sun did not feel hot to her. But she nodded.

The small group of villagers led them down the main street to a large building at the other end. Inside, it was furnished with benches aligned one behind the other, with a long table with chairs on a slight raised portion of the floor before them. The villagers led them to the table.

Alorsha sat, but her companions arranged themselves behind and around her, still keeping watch.

"You asked what's brought us here," Alorsha said, after they had all run through introductions, during which she learned the elderly man who spoke most was Mantorol. "First, I did wish to see your flowers. I'd heard of them from some islanders we encountered in our journey. They are remarkable."

That drew smiles from the villagers.

"And second?" Mantorol asked her.

"Second to see if you might have seen, or heard of, any other newcomers recently. We seek two of our countrymen."

The villagers exchanged looks.

"There was that happening over Umastac Town's way," a woman named Fiafas said. "Remember, Peddler Nuana told us."

Mantorol nodded. "Yeah, he told the tale right well. Those two men. One rather rude and overweening, and the other seemed in a daze. Ill perhaps."

Alorsha shared a worried look with her companions. When she turned back to the villagers, she described Devrand and Jarthan, and what they had worn the last time she had seen them.

Mantorol nodded. "Sounds like the way the peddler described them, 'cept for the clothes, but those're easy enough to change. Could be they're your fellows. Problem is, this all happened back near a month gone. No telling where they could be now."

Alorsha frowned. *That's not good.* "Peddler Nuana didn't say anything more about them? Maybe he, or someone, overheard them talking about their plans?"

"No, seems they weren't very talkative, least the way he told it. Umastac Town's a port town. Easiest way there is to sail that way." Mantorol indicated a direction opposite the one he had indicated for his village's harbor.

"Less than a day's sailing, if your boat is fast," one of the others added.

Alorsha rose. "Our thanks for the news. Is there a better path than through your crop to take us back to where our boat is?"

"I'll show it to you." Mantorol glanced back at the others as he led Alorsha and her companions out the door. Alorsha also glanced back but could not tell what he might have communicated to them. Several waved hands in farewell and she gave them a slight bow in return.

Mantorol led them back along the street and to the left near the edge of the village. After several paces, he stopped at a slight trail in the wild grasses.

"Follow this." He waved an arm to the right. "It'll take you around and out toward the shore. You should find your boat easily enough."

"Again, our thanks," Alorsha said.

When the town was almost out of sight, Mantorol's voice came to them faintly. "Watch yourselves. There's something chancy about one of the men you seek, the darker-haired one."

Alorsha waved back at him to indicate that they had heard, and they continued along the path. After they no longer saw Mantorol, Alorsha collected some of the different plants they passed and tucked them in the bag she carried slung crosswise from one shoulder.

The trail took them along the edge of the fields.

"Oh, I meant to ask if I might have a couple of the flowers," Alorsha said as they walked.

"Shall I run back to the village and ask?" Parl said. "Won't take long."

Alorsha shook her head. "My thanks, but I fear losing even more time." She picked two of the flowers and left two gold pieces standing upright in the dirt next to the plant. *Hope that's sufficient payment.* "Let's go."

Back aboard the *Deliberia*, Alorsha checked the direction the villagers had indicated for Devrand and Jarthan. Her wayfinding magic agreed that was the way to go, so they set sail.

As the villagers had indicated, less than a day later they came to Umastac Town, a large town, well situated at what looked like a natural harbor. Although no ship the size of theirs docked there, Saevalde judged the harbor adequate for the *Deliberia* and they docked at the pier closest to the sea.

This time, Master Eztevo and Captain Vernandos accompanied Alorsha ashore, at least for the first visit. A self-important official met them before they even stepped off the pier and explained the rules of the harbor and docking fees. Alorsha paid enough for a week and the official gave her a palm-sized chit, which she handed to Saevalde. Then the official hurried off before they could ask anything of him.

"How are you thinking to handle this?" Saevalde asked Alorsha.

She shrugged and watched the people on the docks as she tried to get a feel for the place. "I'm not sure. Maybe start by just looking around and listening, see if anything catches my attention."

Saevalde nodded. "I'll send a few small groups into town to buy or barter for a few things and keep their ears open, too."

"I'd like for you to take your three companions with you again," Captain Vernandos told Alorsha. "I see a few weapons about, so it seems prudent."

Alorsha nodded her agreement. "Just please make sure everyone knows that if they spot Devrand or Jarthan, they shouldn't go near them. They'll need to tell me where and when, but don't get too close. I don't trust what Devrand might do."

Both Saevalde and the Ship's Captain nodded.

"Don't worry about that, lass. None of the rest of us has the magic to have any chance against either of them," Saevalde said.

They returned to the *Deliberia* to gather the groups to go into town and assign tasks. Alorsha checked again with her pendant and verified that the town lay in the same direction as Devrand and Jarthan. She could not tell if they were in the town, but at least the direction was good. She slipped the pendant around her neck, tucked it into her tunic, and grabbed a few of her elixirs and potions to take along, on the off chance that there might be something to barter for.

Alorsha and her three companions drew a few curious looks as they crossed the docks and headed into town, but no one seemed overly interested in them. As Captain Vernandos had mentioned, some people went armed, enough of them that they did not look out of place.

The town's brick-paved roads formed a grid pattern. Alorsha spotted a few animals being ridden: large, stocky birds, with long necks and legs. They stood taller than the tallest person she knew, and behaved tame and trained. The ones she spotted that stood tied to a pole outside some kind of tavern seemed docile enough.

Hali nodded toward the tavern. "Stop in there?"

"Perhaps later," Alorsha said. "The villagers had word of our people from a peddler. Let's try to find some kind of market, or some shops, and see what we might learn there."

Before long, they found a market square. It looked like most of the people were setting up for the day. Alorsha and her companions wandered through and perused the various goods offered for sale, mostly produce. Again, they drew some curious looks. But Alorsha saw a variety of people in the town, and a variety of clothing types, so she and her companions did not stand out too much.

While the market held much of interest for sale, they did not hear anything that might be about Devrand and Jarthan.

"Shops, next?" Parl asked when they had finished their circuit of the market.

"Let's try them," Alorsha said. "And if there aren't too many ears to hear, we can start asking questions, I think. I doubt Devrand's aware we're after them, but I'd like to keep it that way, if possible." The others nodded their understanding.

The shops flanked the streets that radiated from the market square, so they had a short walk to look there.

Again, the variety of goods was wide, and intriguing. A couple of Alorsha's companions picked up a few things. But the cautious questions that they asked of the shopkeepers led them no nearer to the men they sought.

Until the jewelry shop.

Inside, Alorsha looked around and admired the various pieces and the unique stones used in some of them. Off to the side, two of her companions joked together about buying some of the pieces for various friends.

When she came to the counter at the back of the shop, Alorsha sensed a sudden interest from the older woman seated there. Alorsha gave her a friendly nod.

"Welcome, m'dear," the woman said. "Let me know if you and friends wish to try on any of the pieces."

"My thanks," Alorsha said. The woman's attention dropped to her hands.

"What is it?" Alorsha said.

"Just admiring your rings," the woman said. "Not a custom I'd seen before, until the two men visited, and now you. Your rings look to match the two that one young man wore."

Alorsha glanced at her hands, at the rings she wore, one on the third finger of each hand, which matched the rings Jarthan wore in the same fashion.

"When were the men here?" she asked. "And do you know where they went after here?"

"A couple ten-days ago," the woman said. "The one with rings like yours was quiet and looked unwell. His companion was brusque, almost rude. I don't know why they visited my shop. They didn't buy anything or even seem particularly interested, although the dark-haired man looked closely at the pieces with the stones."

"They *are* beautiful," Alorsha said. "Is there something special about the stones?"

"I wouldn't say so. Although some of the stones are

reputed to help those the spirits favor."

Alorsha looked up sharply. "Did the dark-haired man seem interested in those."

The woman nodded. "That he did."

Alorsha stared toward those pieces and reached out with her magic but sensed nothing special from the stones. They did not seem to hold the magic like the plants she knew. *Or perhaps I just can't sense it since they aren't plants.*

She turned back to the shopkeeper. "Did they say anything about where they might be headed next?"

"No. But as they left, I saw that they headed that way down the street." She pointed to the left. "There are a number of inns that way. Perhaps they stayed at one and the people there can tell you more."

Alorsha gathered her companions with a look. "My thanks," she said to the woman. Hali paused to buy a bracelet and joined the others outside.

Alorsha looked toward the inns, then up at the sky, as she tried to judge how long they had been in town.

"I can run back and tell Captain Vernandos and Master Eztevo what we know so far," Parl offered. "Then meet with you all again."

Alorsha looked a question at the others, who both nodded.

"Yes, please," she told Parl. "We'll wait for you at one of the inns, so look for us there."

Parl nodded and headed back toward the docks.

Alorsha and the others headed to the inns, to see what they might learn there.

The street the shopkeeper had directed them to held four inns, two on either side of the street. The first two they tried had no knowledge of the two men.

"Yes, they were here," the innkeeper at the third inn said as he tidied his common room. "I remember them well. The one so quiet and the other acting like he thought he was some lord."

The innkeeper faced Alorsha, hands on his hips. "We

agreed to a certain amount for lodging, but after they'd gone, I had no payment in my box. Though I put it there myself. Can you tell me what that's about?"

Alorsha sighed. "I'm not sure, but it's possible that the lordly-acting man somehow made you believe you had payment, when really you didn't."

The innkeeper frowned at that. "'Tis wrong to use the spirit's gifts so. But yes, I can see that." He gave her a suspicious look. "And you're friends of theirs?"

Alorsha shook her head. "I'm trying to catch up to them. The lordly-acting man has taken the other with him unwillingly."

The innkeeper looked her over. "You're a slight one, to be going after two."

Alorsha smiled. "I have companions." She nodded toward Hali and Kluir. "I have other resources, too."

The innkeeper nodded. "You've got the confidence to prove your words. I wish you fortune in this. I overheard the lordly one mention Palilen. That's where those who best hear the spirits gather to teach and learn. I fear he means ill to those there but have no proof."

Alorsha nodded. "I'd fear that, too. Where is this Palilen? Do you have a map?"

"I don't. But down the street you'll find Rahaer's place. Likely he's got a map that will show you. Palilen's not a secret, just not a place that most go."

"My thanks."

He nodded. "You take care. I didn't like the look in that man's eyes when he mentioned the place."

"I will."

Alorsha left Hali at the inn to inform Parl of her whereabouts if he returned before she did, and she and Kluir hurried to Rahaer's.

At Rahaer's, they found a map that showed both the coastline all around the island and the major places on land.

Palilen was located to their south, still in the direction

Alorsha's pendant had indicated from the ship. Judging by the map, it was perhaps a day's walk away from a port to its north.

Alorsha took the map back to the inn and met Hali and Parl as they came out the door to join her. Together, they all returned to the *Deliberia* to share what they had learned.

~ ~ ~

Sailing with some speed, the *Deliberia* reached the port just two days later. It was small, and looked too shallow for the ship, so Alorsha went ashore in one of their tenders. This time Master Eztevo and Captain Vernandos accompanied her along with her three, all of them armed. Alorsha carried a selection of potions that she hoped she would not have to use, but that might be needed in a confrontation with Devrand.

The town that the port belonged to was also small, but they had some of the riding animals that the Varoians could use for the journey inland.

"They're called oriches," the stablemaster told them. "It's common practice for a traveler to Palilen to purchase the use of an orich for the journey. You return them to me when you come back." He included a pack of feed for the oriches. "They'll be happier with that rather than just the forage along the way."

So, the six Varoians set out. With the oriches, they expected to decrease their travel time by a third and so estimated they would arrive a little before sundown.

~ ~ ~

The journey was pleasant, although Alorsha's dread of seeing Devrand again when they arrived marred any enjoyment she might normally have taken in traveling. She had checked his direction through the wayfinding magic; they headed the right way. She hoped, and doubted at the same time, that he would still be there.

Both Parl and Hali complained before too long of the riding, neither of them accustomed to it, and Captain Vernandos shared tips with them to ease their discomfort. They did not stop to eat when they got hungry but just ate as they rode. As the sky darkened toward night, they topped a small rise and regarded the valley that contained Palilen.

It was nothing like Alorsha had expected. In the center of the valley stood seven upright stones, larger than any stones they had yet seen in this world. They formed a rough circle. Alorsha estimated the stones stood a couple of paces high. The stones glowed, their light faint in the twilight, a pink-orange color that had nothing to do with the sunset.

A collection of modest wooden houses surrounded the stones, set back from them a pace or more. As Alorsha and her companions watched, people came from the houses to stand in a ring around the stones. Then Alorsha spotted two others who approached from the darkness further out. She pointed them out to her companions and urged her mount down the hill.

No one looked at them as they approached. The two figures who came from the darkness reached the middle of the circle before the Varoians could dismount. The stones glowed brighter and Alorsha spotted some light creatures like she had seen in the field several days before. They seemed agitated. The light illuminated the two figures in the center of the circle: Devrand and Jarthan. Devrand stood tall, while Jarthan crouched at his side.

Devrand's gaze fell on her.

"Alorsha?" He sounded surprised. "How'd you follow? Have you come, too, to gain more magics?"

Alorsha looked at the people around the stones. All had a dazed, unaware look to them. As did Jarthan.

The light creatures swirled around Alorsha and brushed against her. Judging by Devrand's expression, he could not see them. From them, Alorsha picked up distress and an image of a web that touched all the people save her and her companions. The strings of the web image all led to Devrand's hand, the one on which he wore his mage ring.

"Let them go, Devrand" Alorsha said. "Let Jarthan go."

Devrand shook his head. "I can see you'll always be nothing but a flower-mage." He pulled on the magic of everyone in his web. Jarthan moaned. The others collapsed to the ground and the light creatures vanished.

"Go home, Alorsha," Devrand said. "Take off your rings and forget Jarthan. Find someone else and live your little life in some little village, surrounded by all the pretty flowers."

"No." Alorsha pulled out a vial and flung it at Devrand's feet, where it smashed and released a magic-laced vapor. She sent another after the first. Devrand coughed, and clasped Jarthan's shoulder with his free hand. Jarthan swept a hand out and raised a thin wall between them and the vapor. The wall resembled the boxes he had made before. Devrand's grip tightened and Jarthan brought the wall crashing down to bury the vials and their mist.

"Jarthan, hear me! Fight him!" Alorsha shouted.

Jarthan slowly turned toward her, his eyes unfocused. His mouth formed the shape of her name.

"No," Devrand shouted. Jarthan's attention snapped back to Devrand. "I need him, his magic, *all* their magics."

Alorsha started forward and almost fell. A rock-like substance wrapped her feet and ankles and held her in place, her companions also.

She pulled out a different vial and splashed its contents on the magic-made bindings. They began to smoke and dissolve, but far too slowly. She wrenched against them, to no effect.

"See," Devrand yelled. "His magic is now mine. These others', as well."

The small light-creatures became visible, swarmed the Varoians and crashed against them, blinding them with their numbers. Alorsha crouched and tried to protect her face with her arms. *Can't think of any potions that'll help with this.*

"Jarthan," she called out.

All she heard was an ugly laugh from Devrand. "No use, Alorsha. Go home. Go back to your flower-picking life."

An inrush of magic streamed past her as Devrand pulled all in the area to himself, pulled magic from the people sprawled on the ground. Alorsha grabbed the flask she had carried on her belt and swallowed a mouthful of its bitter contents. His pull on her magic ceased, cut off. *At least that works.*

She looked up and squinted against the light-creatures that still swarmed, but no longer crashed into her.

The oval, the passage to another world, took shape next to Devrand. It expanded, large enough for him to fit through.

Alorsha tried to fling herself forward, but the magic bindings at her ankles still held and she fell flat. She raised her head in time to see Devrand step through the passage into a place that looked heavy with strange trees.

"Jarthan!" she called.

He flicked an anguished glance back at her and followed Devrand through. The passage snapped shut.

~ ~ ~

Alorsha freed herself from the magic-made shackles as they fell apart after the passage closed. She and the other Varoians moved among the downed people to see what they might do for them. None were badly hurt, mostly bruises from falling. But all still seemed dazed and uncertain.

Kluir found a well between a couple of the small

houses and pulled up water that they shared out among the reviving people. A few sips of water, and a brief time to get their bearings, and they looked better. Those who had recovered enough helped tend to the others and get them back to their houses.

When all but one had returned to their homes, Alorsha turned to the one older woman who seemed in charge of the place and who had remained with them.

Alorsha bowed low to her. "I'm so very sorry for what happened here."

The woman patted Alorsha's arm. "It's not any of your doing. And I saw that the spirits accepted your presence. Before that man interfered. The apologizing isn't yours."

Alorsha indicated the houses around them. "I hope they'll recover, and recover their magics... uh, their connection to the spirits, in time."

The woman nodded. "I'll care for them and hope that it's so."

"Do you know... were the spirits hurt?" Alorsha voiced a fear she had not wanted to consider.

The woman gazed toward the standing stones for a long moment. "I don't see any near right now, but I've yet to see anything hurt them directly. I expect they've just left for a time to replenish themselves, too. They also can need such a thing."

Alorsha smiled in relief. "I'm glad to hear that. I worried that he'd killed them."

The woman smiled in return and shook her head in denial of such a thing. "You pursue him? To the new place he's invaded?"

Alorsha glanced at her companions, who all nodded.

"We do," she said.

CHAPTER 16

FROM ALORSHA'S JOURNAL

World after world, chasing Devrand and his magic hunger, ever entangled in this hunt, stealing closer to catching him. Too often *not* stealing closer.

After that first world, we split the cabin aboard ship that had been Devrand's into three for the three warriors who became guards for me. That rewarded them for their extra duties and responsibility with larger cabins. At the same time, it put them close to my own cabin, should something happen that they needed to reach me without delay.

Devrand gathered magic to himself as time passed, and it seemed my own magics lagged behind what he could do, although I grew able to sense from a distance, through my ring, when he drew magic from the world. So, I followed after. And I and the *Deliberia* picked up bits of different magics from the different worlds.

We in our little ship-village grew closer. Weapons-work continued, and we all grew much more proficient with those weapons we carried. Every chance we had, we stopped ashore to practice longer ranges with the bows than we could manage aboard even our large ship.

I insisted that all aboard learn to swim, if they had not already known how. Saevalde grumbled at me at that, as one of the ones who had never learned.

We were fortunate in that the first many worlds into which we ventured showed us neutral faces at worst. Still, we prepared to defend ourselves, should the need arise. I worked hard to create new concoctions that might help counter Devrand's growing magics.

And we continued to follow.

~ ~ ~

Alorsha stumbled toward the small cluster of lights that she hoped meant a friendly village. She had hated to leave the others, but she alone was still able to walk any distance, even at a stumble, after the bandits had attacked.

She came to the outskirts of the village, larger than she had first thought. Quiet blanketed it, but night had not advanced so far that all lights were out. A quick look did not show her any building that looked like an inn, so she just knocked on the door of the first house she came to that had a light inside.

After no answer, she knocked again, more insistently. "Hello?" she called. "My friends and I need help."

She heard what sounded like a bar slide across the inside of the door. It opened a crack and a circular metal tube pointed through the crack at her. She saw a man's face beyond the tube, his hair and eyes brown, and his skin a little darker than her own. She had no idea what the tube might be, but his expression seemed to indicate it was some sort of weapon. She took a step back.

"Please, can you help? Or someone? We were attacked on the road."

The door opened wider, and the man looked her over.

"Not safe to travel the roads at night, you should know that," he said.

"We're newcomers here. Can you, or someone, help please?"

The man studied her a moment longer, then tucked the tube into his belt. It seemed to have a grip of sorts attached at an angle at one end of the tube. Without asking her to enter, he ducked back inside and returned with a sword buckled at his hip. He glanced at hers, with a quick nod.

"Come. We'll get Voitsek's wagon and one of the medicos and get your folk. How far down the road are they?"

She felt small next to him, when he came out the door: the top of her head only reached his shoulder. She had not noticed during the attack if others in this land stood as tall. If so, she resigned herself to feeling small, and therefore even younger than her almost score and eight years. He wore his brown hair long, in two plaits that hung over his shoulders, and she guessed he had likely seen a few years more than a score and ten. He wore a tunic and trousers, as she did, but his tunic reached longer than hers, to below his knees, with slits up the sides.

"Not too far," she said. "I'm the only one able to walk more than a couple of steps, and it took me about an hour to get here."

He looked her over again as he led her to another of the houses.

"You're injured, too. Might be that we can get to them in half the time it took you to get here. If not quicker."

Alorsha nodded. "I hope so. They're worse off than I am."

"We'll make haste. I'm called Mikolus Ludek."

"Alorsha Tavano." She scurried after him as his long strides sped him through the town.

At two different houses, Mikolus called out and people ran out to hitch a wagon, to go to Mikolus's house to secure it until he returned, and to climb into the wagon to travel with Alorsha and her benefactor.

"We have two medicos in town," Mikolus said with pride. "Most others make do with the one."

He climbed up to the seat to drive the wagon and helped her up next to him.

He set a fast pace, which meant the wagon bounced them around. Alorsha studied him as they went.

"Ask your question," he said after a time. "I can see that it pesters you."

With a seated bow, she pointed to the tube thing. "I take it that's a weapon of some sort?"

Mikolus glanced at it and gave her a surprised look. "That it is. Called a flintlock. It's new to you?"

"Yes."

"How is it you don't know of flintlocks?"

"I did say we're newcomers."

"That you did. You must be from quite a distance gone, then."

Alorsha nodded. "Yes, quite a distance."

"Just came in from the docks at Slarov, if you took this road?"

Alorsha nodded again.

"Did no one warn you of the road?"

"We didn't speak much with anyone."

He fell silent and observed her with quick sidelong looks.

"You do have a foreign look to you. I've not seen the likes of your clothes before, and your accent is strange. Someone should have warned you."

Alorsha shrugged. "We're hurt, but no one was killed. Except a couple of our attackers, I think. Also, we caught one."

Mikolus glanced at her. "Ah, that's good news. Might be it'll help."

The ride in the wagon to where she had left the others was uncomfortable. Alorsha ached and suspected she had several bruises. The cuts she had taken in the fight had been minor and had scabbed over on her walk. Still, they hurt too. She was relieved when the trip did turn out to be about half as long as hers the other way to the village.

She climbed down almost before the wagon stopped and waved to Parl and Hali, who both leaned against trees keeping watch. The villagers followed and helped tend to her companions. Mikolus checked the two dead attackers and moved to the third, who wriggled in his bonds.

Alorsha knelt near Kluir, who had been most wounded. She watched the healer—the medico as Mikolus had called him—clean and tend Kluir's wounds with poultices and clean bandages. She longed to touch the creams he used, to see if she could decipher the magics within, but she held back. Time enough for that later.

A touch on her shoulder made her jump and she looked up at Mikolus.

"You all must be favored of some luck god or other. Many brigands now carry flintlocks, but not these. You might not have survived if they had."

Alorsha nodded.

"There were just the four of you?"

"Yes."

He nodded and looked to his fellows. "Let's get them back to town. The live brigand, too. I'll return then for the other two."

Alorsha was no help for lifting her companions into the bed of the wagon, so she stayed out of the way and kept an eye on the brigand, who glared back at her. Although crowded, the wagon bed held her injured companions and the medico. Alorsha rode next to Mikolus again, and the other villagers surrounded the brigand and escorted him on foot behind the wagon. They kept to the walkers' pace and so took longer to return to the village.

When they arrived, what seemed like the whole village turned out to see to them. Someone threw a blanket around Alorsha's shoulders which she clutched close with a nod of thanks. She stayed out of everyone's way and watched the goings-on.

The medicos, a man and a woman, took charge of her injured companions and herded the volunteers who carried them to a house not far from Mikolus's. Several villagers, also with those flintlock weapons in their belts, surrounded the prisoner and took him to another building toward the center of the town. Two of those villagers took positions outside the building as the others hustled him inside. The medico who had ridden in the wagon called out that he would be with them soon. After he saw all Alorsha's companions into the house he had indicated, he hurried to the guarded building and inside. Alorsha headed toward the building where her companions were. Mikolus met her on the way there.

"You should let the medicos look at you, too," he said. "Your limp is worse."

She nodded. "I will. I just want to see my friends cared for first. They took the brunt of the attack."

"Did the brigands say anything when they attacked? Demand anything?"

Alorsha shook her head. "They just charged at us out of the trees at the side of the road. I think that three ran, after we fought back, maybe also injured."

He nodded and opened the door for her. "Rest. We can talk again."

Inside, the other medico, a woman who introduced herself as Eranthia, guided Alorsha into a back room, helped her clean up, and tended to her wounds. Eranthia clucked over a large bruise on Alorsha's thigh, her expression worried, but told her she did not believe the bone was bruised. She helped Alorsha into a warm, loose gown. At the touch of the ointments on her skin, Alorsha indulged her curiosity and reached toward the magic within. Healing magic, without a doubt, and strong. If she sensed correctly, minerals held the magic rather than plants as she was used to.

Eranthia smiled at her when she looked up from her testing of the magic.

"You work too in poultices and potions?"

Alorsha smiled back. "Potions, anyway. Yes. But I have next to no talent with the healing ones, such as this. Mine serve other purposes."

The woman nodded. "Your homeland's then far removed from our ways. Someplace that doesn't work with the earth-essences."

"Plants, for me," Alorsha said. "Although it seems I can at least touch the magics in these minerals, too. Something I'd not known before. I've certainly not worked with such before."

"Perhaps, if you stay a time, we can share some knowledge."

Alorsha nodded and yawned. "My apologies."

"No need," Eranthia said. "The healing creams tend to make one sleepy, even without a battle and a lot of walking before." She grinned at Alorsha. "The sleepiness isn't by chance, as the patient can benefit from rest to help with healing. Come."

She helped Alorsha back to the front room, which held several beds. Looking around, Alorsha realized that what had seemed a small house from the outside was in truth a narrow but deep building that extended far back from the large front room. Eranthia took her to a bed near her companions and helped settle her in it.

"Sleep all you need," she told Alorsha. She shuttered all but one lantern and moved to a chair at the other end of the room.

~ ~ ~

Alorsha woke to unfamiliar bird song and needed a minute to remember where she was and what had happened. She saw that her companions still slept. Perhaps it was earlier than she thought. No one else was in the room.

She rose, pleased to feel only mostly stiff. Although

that bruised leg still ached, but not as much as she would have expected. She found her clothes piled on a small table next to her bed and changed into them, much more comfortable in the tunic and trousers than the gown. In stocking feet, she padded to the bedsides of her companions and checked on them. All three slept and looked free of pain.

She grabbed the rest of her belongings, sword belt, boots, pouches, and cross-body bag, and eased out the door. Two villagers with those flintlock weapons still guarded the building that held the prisoner, although different people from before. With a quick nod for them, she hopped awkwardly to pull on her boots, hoping that she did not make too much noise.

A chuckle nearby drew her attention, and she looked up after she finished with her boots.

"You could've just sat down," Mikolus said with a smile.

Alorsha looked at the dirt beneath her feet and back up at him. "I could have."

He chuckled again. "The medicos tell me your people are healing well but will likely sleep the day. They'd prefer that they have that chance at sleep, if you can stay in town."

She nodded, aware of his gaze on her as she buckled on her belt. She settled her pouches and cross-body bag, with a questioning look for him.

He turned away from her gaze and rubbed the back of his neck. "Sorry," he muttered. "I've traveled these lands a bit but haven't met the likes of you and your friends before. So similar in some ways, and yet very different in others."

She nodded at the flintlock weapon in his belt. "And yet those brigands didn't carry any of those, but swords much as we do."

He nodded. "True enough. We found traces of the others, the ones who fled. Our tracker says your count is right. Three. But she lost the trail a distance out."

Alorsha nodded, unsure where this was going.

"Walk with me?" Mikolus asked.

She nodded and kept pace with him as they strolled through the village, with apparently no particular destination in mind.

"As you might have figured out," Mikolus said, "I'm in charge of keeping our village safe. Along with others." He nodded at the two who guarded the brigand's prison. "What you've told me so far fits all I've seen, but I'd like to know more."

She nodded. "Fair enough. You're concerned we might mean trouble for your town. I'd hope not. I intend no trouble. But we come here seeking two men who would also be strangers to you, not from any lands you know. One of them could be great trouble. The other he's dragged with him, an unwilling traveler."

"You're the first strangers that we've seen who are clearly not from our lands, or any we've heard of. Would one of the men be of auburn hair, with unusual blue-green eyes, who stands perhaps a half-head taller than you? And the other man about the same height, green-eyed, with yellow-brown hair and skin much lighter than yours?"

Alorsha stopped to face him. "Yes. You've had word of them?"

"In a manner of speaking. Our brigand friend, and his fellows, were hired by such an auburn-haired man accompanied by the other. Their instructions were to stop a woman, and her companions, who followed. The brigand said the man didn't specify how to stop those who followed him." At her look of dismay, he clasped her shoulder in support.

"With this news, I'm of the mind that while you're in our lands, perhaps you'll want to consider getting yourselves some flintlocks, and some learning of them."

Alorsha nodded and shuddered at the thought of Devrand's apparent hostility toward her.

"We were once friends," she murmured.

Mikolus gave her shoulder another squeeze. "That can mean the worst kind of enemy, if it comes to that."

Alorsha nodded again. "So, it seems you're right. About the flintlocks. Where can we get ourselves some, and someone who'll teach us their use?"

"We have none to spare in town, so we'll have to go to the next town over, for you to get some. But I can start with your teaching right away, if you like. The same for your friends, as soon as the medicos say they're recovered enough."

CHAPTER 17

Alorsha's companions recovered well from their injuries, although several days passed before the medicos let them do much more than rest. In that time, Alorsha returned to the *Deliberia* and told Saevalde what had happened and discussed the flintlocks with her and Captain Vernandos. Mikolus insisted he accompany her against the chance that the rest of the brigands still sought to stop her.

Both Master Eztevo and Captain Vernandos returned with her to the town. On the way back, Mikolus began teaching all three of them about the flintlocks and how to use them. Of the three, Alorsha had the best eye and surprised Mikolus with her accuracy even as she was just learning.

To keep from fretting at the delay in following Jarthan and Devrand, Alorsha tried to fill her days in the town with practice with flintlocks and work with the medicos to exchange knowledge about potions and elixirs and such. But she still worried.

What was Devrand doing? Did he continue to gather magics to himself as he had been so far? Or did he have something else in mind, now? *Will he send more people after me?*

But Eranthia was a good teacher and Alorsha spent long, useful afternoons together with her during which she learned a lot about the magic in the minerals and how to draw it out to best use, usually to strengthen metals. It was similar to what she did with plants, but different enough that it felt strange, her attempts clumsy and ineffectual, more often than not. It did become easier the more she worked at it.

By the time she and her companions were ready to venture to the next town to see about getting flintlocks, she was able to reliably sense the magics in most of the minerals, although able to draw out the magics of only a few and only somewhat. Doing so also gave her a severe headache most of the time when she managed it. The minerals that worked best for the healing creams were ones she could barely sense and could not draw out at all.

But she found a few metals with magics that she could draw forth. The magics seemed such that weapons made from those metals might be better than normal. Maybe they could find someone in the next town to shape weapons for them.

As they prepared to leave soon after dawn two weeks after they arrived at the town, Mikolus joined them.

"I'll come along with you," he said, with a grin. "I can help make sure you get quality flintlocks at a reasonable cost."

Eranthia also approached. "I'd like to join you as well. I've a desire to journey."

Alorsha gave both a long look, then nodded. "You both are certainly welcome."

"The next town, Ulask, lies a long day away by foot," Mikolus said as they set out.

They traveled slower than Alorsha would have liked, and so spent an uneasy night camped at the edge of the road. They set watches, but all was quiet. No brigands made an appearance, as Alorsha had half-feared.

They arrived at Ulask midmorning. It was larger than either Yauntla—Mikolus's town—or Slarov, and obviously a center of trade. Mikolus led them to a street where several gunsmiths had their shops and introduced them. He guided them through each shop and pointed out the qualities they should look for when choosing a flintlock. He also exchanged good-natured barbs with the smiths and purchased for himself some of the metal balls the flintlocks shot.

Alorsha watched and listened but let Captain Vernandos take the lead on the purchases. After they finished, they carried noticeably fewer gold coins, but they had fifteen flintlocks for the *Deliberia* crew.

When they discussed how to divide up to spread out through the town to see about any word of Devrand, and see what supplies they could obtain, Parl elected to stay behind to learn as much as he could about how the gunsmiths made the flintlocks and their metal balls. Mikolus recommended a good inn as a place to meet.

Alorsha accompanied Saevalde and the Captain while Mikolus and Eranthia took Kluir and Hali to see about refreshing their supplies.

"This change in Devrand is disturbing," Saevalde said in a low voice as the three of them ambled along a row of shops and scanned the various goods offered for sale.

"I expect he was trying to warn us off," Alorsha said.

"But those brigands seemed to have attacked in earnest, far beyond a simple warning," Captain Vernandos said.

"I won't leave off the hunt," Alorsha said.

"Aye, lass, of course," Saevalde said. "So, we should be taking the time again to improve our capabilities as much as we can. Am I correct that you've been working on some new magics toward that end?"

Alorsha smiled. "Yes, for some weapons, I think."

"So, we see if any of these weapon-smiths can make us

better weapons that include your magics, maybe also some armors, if we can manage it."

Alorsha looked at her companions, who gave her determined looks in return. She nodded. "Yes, I've been too complacent. Too trusting on our past friendship. It seems we must expect the worst from Devrand, now. So, let's get us the best prepared we can."

With a brisk nod, Saevalde said, "I'll see if there's a port nearer to this place and we'll bring the *Deliberia* in close for the time we'll need to spend here."

"Give the crew time ashore, too," Alorsha said. "In rotation. Perhaps with things we can barter, including these things I've discovered with the metals magics, we can get all of us better weapons."

~ ~ ~

A few days later, the *Deliberia* docked at Ulask, which they had found boasted a large, deep harbor, and members of the crew took turns ashore. Alorsha stayed ashore at the inn Mikolus had recommended and worked with various smiths first to show that her magics improved their metals, then to improve as much of the metal as she could each day, in exchange for those smiths to provide her crew with some new swords and arrowheads of the better metals.

After she saw the results of Alorsha's efforts, Saevalde brought over the old weapons from the *Deliberia* to be improved or reforged. So, for a time, the *Deliberia* and its people became resident guests in Ulask.

Alorsha left the searching out of armor to Captain Vernandos. The other woman surprised her when she returned with some stiff vests that looked like some kind of leather.

"These are already as effective as the ring shirts I'd thought to get," she told Alorsha. "And they're lighter to wear. They'll be even better after you've had a chance to treat them with those concoctions of yours. Here, try one."

The Captain helped Alorsha into one of the vests, which she found easier to move in than she expected. But when she tucked her ring pendant down the neck, it pressed against her chest under the tight garment. It also made an obvious and uncomfortable lump, which defeated the purpose of hiding it under her clothes.

"Get as many as you can," she told Captain Vernandos as she returned the vest. "Take them to the ship, please. I'll work on them there."

The Captain nodded her agreement and left to make the arrangements. Alorsha followed her partway and turned aside at a jewel-smith's shop.

Inside she showed the woman there her ring-pendant.

"With the whole ring in the frame, it's too lumpy," she told the woman. "Is there something that can be done to make it lie flatter while still letting me wear it as a ring, too, when I choose?"

The woman turned the pendant over and around, and smiled. "Not too difficult. The stone and its setting are what snap into the pendant. I can simply separate them from the ring's band and put a small bit of magnetic metal on the back of the setting and in your ring. They'll hold the setting on, when you want to wear it as a ring, and you just pull them apart to put the setting in the pendant frame when you want to wear it that way."

Alorsha matched her smile. "Perfect. How soon can you do that?"

"I've the time this afternoon. You can leave the ring here and come back before the evening meal."

Alorsha shook her head. "I'll stay while you work on it. I'll not be separated from that ring."

The woman looked surprised, but then nodded. "Certainly."

They bargained for the cost. Alorsha handed over the coins and watched as the woman worked. Before the evening meal, she left the shop well pleased, with the plain band of her coppery mage ring back on her left thumb, now boasting a tiny gray disk – the magnet. She wore the mage ring's erythros stone in its setting—with a tiny magnet on the back—snapped into the pendant's frame, where it lay flat under her shirt.

~ ~ ~

Although exhausted most days from coaxing the magics forth from the metals, Alorsha tried to spend some leisure time with various crewmembers. Mikolus and Eranthia often lingered nearby. So, one afternoon, she cornered them.

"Join me?" She indicated a nearby tavern.

The two exchanged looks and headed toward the tavern.

"I told you we should've just approached her directly," Mikolus murmured to Eranthia.

Alorsha led the way to a table at the back of the tavern and waited until they each had a drink.

"Approached me about what?" she asked the two. "I didn't get the impression that either of you was shy."

Mikolus chuckled and Eranthia shook her head.

"Not shy," Mikolus said. "But not knowing your land's customs, we were trying to see what we could figure out by watching."

"And?" Alorsha prompted. *Where is this going?*

"We'd like to take ship with you," Eranthia said in a rush.

"We'd swear to your service," Mikolus said, "but we cannot see how your people regard such a thing. Whether you do that."

Alorsha looked from one to the other. From their expressions, they were serious.

"What of Yauntla?"

"I came there about a year ago," Mikolus said, "to help them better defend themselves, much as I've been helping your people. I've stayed longer than I intended. The townsfolk are well defended now. They no longer need me there. I'm restless and it's time to move on, as I always do. I've no true ties there and your people intrigue me."

Alorsha looked at Eranthia. "Mine is a similar tale, although I've been there much longer. But Yarmil is an excellent medico, and now confident enough to teach others. I also have no strong ties there."

Alorsha studied them. "We can use your skills aboard. But there are things both of you must know."

She told them of their travels from world to world, that they had not yet seen the same world twice, and more about why they traveled.

"We're like a village," Alorsha said. "Just in one ship. I can't promise that you'd ever return here, to your lands. For my part, you're certainly welcome. But the decision isn't mine alone."

The two nodded.

"I've no ties here, as I said," Mikolus said. "No family left anywhere in these lands, or any others. I do wish to go with you, and not returning wouldn't vex me."

"It's the same for me," Eranthia said. "If we're welcome."

Alorsha finished her drink. "Come to the *Deliberia* after the evening meal, then. Meet with Master Eztevo and Captain Vernandos about this, and we'll see."

~ ~ ~

After they met with the two townsfolk, Master Eztevo and Captain Vernandos both welcomed them to join the *Deliberia*'s crew.

"A word?" Captain Vernandos said and guided Alorsha away from the group.

"What is it?"

"With Mikolus coming aboard, I'd like to resign my position to him and stay here in this land. I've spoken with

Master Eztevo, who now should have no concerns since Mikolus will do well as Ship's Captain. But, of course, I needed to speak with you."

Alorsha nodded. "Of course, if you wish to leave the *Deliberia*, I wish you all the best. You do realize that this place will likely be your home from now on. I don't know if we can ever return here."

"I do understand that." The Ship's Captain gave her a low bow. "Thank you."

Alorsha returned the bow. "And I thank you. You've served the *Deliberia*, and me, with honor and excellence. Master Eztevo will ensure you're set for starting over in your new home."

Then Mikolus and Eranthia approached, and Captain Vernandos dropped back. The two newcomers dropped to one knee before Alorsha.

"We'd swear to you after our customs," Mikolus said. "If that's acceptable?"

Alorsha looked to Saevalde, who shrugged.

"I suppose. But I'm not a member of any kind of nobility, or anything like that."

"In our lands, wizards are always of rank, no matter their birth circumstances," Eranthia said.

"And you're clearly the Lady ruler of your 'town' *Deliberia*," Mikolus added, with a smile.

"Very well, I concede your points," Alorsha said. "How does this work?"

Mikolus held his right hand out to her. "Just take my hand and hear my oath."

She clasped his hand in hers.

"I, Mikolus Ludek, do this day swear to the lady Alorsha Tavano to serve her aboard the *Deliberia* to the best of my ability for as long as she shall desire my service."

He bowed his head to touch his forehead to her hand. He stepped back, while Eranthia spoke her oath, similar to Mikolus's.

"My thanks," Alorsha said, when both had finished. "For my part, I welcome you to the *Deliberia*. Your service here will be valued and should you one day find a place you'd rather stay than with the *Deliberia*, you of course may go, with all good wishes."

And so, the *Deliberia* lost one crewmember but gained two.

~ ~ ~

The next morning, uneasiness disturbed Alorsha's sleep. She slipped out of bed and looked out the window from her inn room. It was just past dawn and the day looked to be cloudy, maybe even with rain. But she sensed something.

She opened the window and sank into the half-trance she used to draw out deep magics. A light breeze blew in her face. A hint of smoke came to her, like the remembered smell of burning wood rather than actual smoke. The magics felt disturbed, torn somehow.

She pulled out her pendant and stepped to the middle of her room. The pendant snapped to make its arc in the direction from which the breeze came, the same direction it had every day they had stayed at the town. But now magics that tasted of this world flowed through the pendant into her. They filled her with a sensation of alarm and urgency.

She dressed and gathered her things. They would just have to collect whatever weapons and armor were ready today. Time to go.

CHAPTER 18

Mikolus's knowledge of the area helped them find the fastest sea route to a landing near the place they would likely find Devrand. Eranthia had mentioned a center of magic, a place where some of the land's magic pooled somehow, off to the east of Ulask, and Alorsha's pendant seemed to point to its location as they sailed close.

They dropped anchor in a cove and took two small tenders to the shore. Many more of the crew had wanted to accompany her than would fit. They had been incensed when they learned that Devrand had set the brigands on her.

Alorsha bowed to everyone's requests in that both tenders were full, and all the crewmembers carried weapons. She won the argument about who would travel inland with her, though. As few as possible to expose to the possible danger. So, Mikolus and Eranthia joined her and her usual three for the journey. The others held the approach to the boats secure and kept the boats ready.

Alorsha set a ground-covering pace and they pushed to reach the magic center by nightfall.

They almost made it. Sundown caught them just at the edge of the forest that Eranthia said surrounded the center.

Mikolus took the lead. "I've some woodland experience."

He led them along faint paths as they traveled deeper into the trees. Alorsha jumped at every little sound they made, and the sounds they heard that they did not make.

After a long hour during which they tried to avoid tripping in the dimming light, Mikolus brought them to a halt at some bushes.

"Beyond should be the center Eranthia spoke of," he told them.

Alorsha held out her pendant and it pointed straight through the bushes. She nodded and spoke softly.

"I don't want him to discover too soon that all of you are here, if we can avoid it. So please stay hidden as long as possible. We're in the midst of a lot of plants, my specialty. It's my hope that we can end this mad hunt here."

"I'll wait here," Eranthia said. "I hope we won't need my skills, but I'm ready if we do." She pulled a flintlock out of her bag and checked it over.

Mikolus looked to the other crewmembers. "We'll spread out to both sides, close enough to see you. Wait a couple of minutes before you step out."

Alorsha nodded.

"Should you even go out there?" Hali said. "His magic has topped yours before."

"Other times, we've almost had him," Alorsha said. "I've some new tricks. Also, this." She ran a hand over the new armored vest she wore. "Now, go."

She waited a count of a hundred, then made her way closer, taking care to keep her steps quiet. As she moved, she reached out to the plants nearby and touched their magics. She wove herself into their magics and the magic of this area. She sensed the center that Eranthia had described but avoided that. Even at the edges of it, she perceived an imbalance. *Devrand, likely.*

She paused at the edge of the plant life, within the shadowed branches but able to see into the large clearing in front of her. Faint moonlight filtered into the clearing and gave her enough light to see but left everything washed of color.

Ahead, Devrand and Jarthan stood in the center, Devrand barefoot, with his arms spread wide and his eyes closed. Jarthan knelt at his side, slumped, with both hands flat on the ground. Alorsha strung her bow, for later if needed, and reached through the grasses—their roots were all entwined and connected—and urged them to grow.

They did and rapidly reached Devrand's knees and wrapped around them. They grew around Jarthan, too, but did not entwine him.

"Alorsha." Devrand's eyes snapped open, and he looked her direction.

She took a small step while she kept close to the bushes, as the grasses still grew and entwined. A tremor of fear shot through her as Devrand appeared unconcerned about her attack. He glanced at Jarthan, who stood and turned toward her.

"Let him go!" Alorsha said.

Devrand shook his head and turned to call behind him. "Come."

From the forest behind him stumbled several people, all with dazed expressions. Through the grasses they trod, Alorsha discerned that these were this world's equivalent of the master-mages of her world. Devrand had drained most of their magics. Light flared from around Devrand's feet, and he laughed as it burned away Alorsha's grasses. Then it shot out toward her.

She grew the branches of the bushes nearby into a shield in front of her. The light burned through it but did not touch her. She grew the roots from the ground at Devrand's feet, stretched them long and increased their thickness to wrap him. He fought them with splashes of the light, then fire from Jarthan. Still, they grew.

Then Alorsha felt him pull. The mages with him dropped to the ground and he linked to the magic center beneath his feet. Fire blasted out around him, followed by a concussive wave that knocked Jarthan over and threw her back into the bushes. She heard one flintlock and the twangs of bowstrings. She scrambled back to her feet.

"Wait," she called as she waited for her eyesight to clear. She felt Devrand pull the magic center, and he tried to reach through their faint link to pull her magic, too. When she squelched that, she sensed him reach beyond her.

"You brought the *Aiokta?*" He sounded astonished.

"It's the *Deliberia*, now," Alorsha snarled and grew layers of plants between them while she harried him even more. She used the plants closest to him as she tried to break his concentration.

Her vision finally cleared from the fire's bright flash, and she squinted through her plants. Neither Jarthan nor Devrand had been hit by any of the weapons.

Time to try mine.

Alorsha picked out one special arrow, the arrowhead a metal of this land. She dipped the arrowhead into a vial she carried, the elixir within designed to interfere with a person's ability to draw upon their magic. *Hopefully.*

She nocked the arrow, drew and sighted, and released the string. The arrow flew true, into Devrand's thigh. He cried out and lost his hold on the magics as he fell. A wild wind raged through the clearing. Alorsha struggled to stand against it.

"Jarthan," she called and tried to reach out to him through their link with her magic. She struggled to move, eyes squinted against the wind. Jarthan turned toward her.

Are his eyes clearing?

"Jarthan!"

With a curse, Devrand flung a hand out toward her and again pulled on the center's magic, drawing the last of it to himself. Something slammed into Alorsha and threw her back. The bushes broke her fall but left her scratched and bloodied. She hauled herself out of the bushes and stumbled back toward the clearing in time to see the thin line of the passage shrink and vanish.

Devrand and Jarthan were gone again.

Cursing to herself, she tottered forward as fast as she could and reached for a taste of the magic from the land Devrand had fled to. She dropped to her knees at the center and felt the faintest echo of the magic different from this world's. She grabbed for it and pulled it to her, so she would be able to follow with the *Deliberia*. Then she sat back, wearied, and gazed at the devastation around her.

The ground had been scoured clear of plants in the entire clearing. The plants at the edge had been stripped of leaves, many uprooted, and some small fires smoldered there. The mages that Devrand had controlled lay unmoving.

Alorsha's companions joined her. She waved Eranthia to check the mages and allowed her to treat her when the medico shook her head over the others.

Mikolus agreed with Eranthia's assessment and dropped to the ground next to Alorsha. After they checked the vicinity, the other three joined them.

"I was sure I hit him." Mikolus cleaned his flintlock in preparation for reloading it.

"He raised one of those magic-made shields at the last minute," Parl said. "But Alorsha got him." He waved a hand at the blood on the ground where Devrand had stood.

"But the magics in the elixir didn't work fast enough." Alorsha winced as Eranthia pulled a large splinter from her arm and wrapped the wound. "He still stole magics, and this time he killed." She contemplated the downed mages, her expression one of sorrow.

The others nodded, somber. Alorsha surveyed them, all scratched and bloody as she was, but alive.

"Did you see where he went this time?" Kluir asked.

"I got the taste of its magic. Enough so the *Deliberia* can take us."

She looked back at the bodies, then at Mikolus. "What are the rites? They deserve them."

He nodded. "I'll take care of them while Eranthia finishes with you. Burial would be best for this location. Can you...?" He waved a hand vaguely toward the ground.

Alorsha nodded. "I believe I can help."

Holding up one hand, she stopped Eranthia's ministrations. "Just a moment."

Alorsha placed both hands flat on the ground next to her and reached for any roots that remained. She found enough and grew them to pull aside the dirt and create a large hole near the mages' bodies.

Eranthia caught her as she slumped, dazed and close to unconscious. "Enough," the medico said.

"That's good." Mikolus took the others with him, and they laid out the bodies in a row in the bottom of the hole, arms folded on their chests and their faces covered. They scooped the disturbed dirt back atop them, handing off the job to one another as Eranthia finished with Alorsha and tended to them in turn.

Alorsha lay where Eranthia had left her, aware of what the others did but without the energy to get up and help. She reviewed her memory of the battle. How might she have saved the mages? Was she responsible for their deaths? Had she pushed Devrand to that extreme? Made him kill?

After a time, she became aware of the faintest hint of the magics beneath her. At least he had not drained the magic center permanently. *But all that magic....*

A touch on her arm woke her. Eranthia leaned close and scrutinized her face. "They're done. We should return to the ship."

Alorsha nodded and Eranthia helped her to her feet. She looked back at the mounded dirt.

Mikolus moved to block her view, with a stern look for her. "I know what that expression means," he said. "This wasn't your doing. The responsibility lies directly on this Devrand. You remember that."

"If I hadn't attacked—"

"Look at me."

She raised her eyes to his.

"Don't take his evils on yourself," Mikolus told her. "That way lies madness. I see what he is, what you're trying to do. It almost worked. Your Jarthan almost broke free. So, we keep at it, you with your magics, us with whatever we can contribute. And we *will* prevail. You hear my words?"

She nodded and tried to give him a smile.

"So, we regroup and heal and go see this next world."

After she nodded again, he led the way back to the *Deliberia.*

Chapter 19

From Alorsha's Journal

Once, and only once, during a prolonged period of sailing toward Devrand's location, I decided to try to open a passage back to the previous world. To learn how or even if I could. What a debacle!

When I drew on the previous world's magic in the ship, gray wisps shot up from the deck and engulfed the ship, although only I saw them. A storm blew up out of nowhere and sent the ship plunging and spinning, cracking timbers, and throwing everyone around. After I released the magic, the tumult vanished, but left us sick well into the next day and with injuries to care for and repairs to make. And I hadn't even managed the beginnings of the passage.

As the *Deliberia* gathered magics from world after world, the sails changed to take on a gray-red tone that looked like blood in some lights. Some of the crew muttered at this, at first, but after they saw the awe the ship received in world after world, they looked on her colors with satisfaction.

Unfortunately, about a year into this strange voyage, hostility met us in one of those worlds, not awe. We escaped, but with several wounded and the *Deliberia* damaged. We lost Eranthia to her injuries.

I still miss her, her gentle instruction in healing magics—although I'd clearly never have managed them— her smile, the delight she took in each new world.

Her death shouldn't have happened.

But from that same world, I gained an apprentice: Gyasi K'rond. Out of the horrific destruction of his home and heinous personal tragedy for him.

I wish…. I should have found some way to prevent it.

Mikolus still viewed those with magic as of high rank and so he insisted we divide his cabin to give half to Gya.

Strange to think *I* have an apprentice. *Jarthan's* the real master-mage. With the strength of his magic, *he* should have had the apprenticing of Gya. I try to instruct him as well as Jarthan would've. For Gya's sake, I hope I at least come close.

Not all around us was grim, though. During our travels, Saevalde officiated several times at the simple ceremony that recognized life-partners. Two ceremonies most closely affected me. The first was Hali and Remdor's ceremony, in which I stood up with Hali and Remdor had Mikolus stand up with him. The second was Parl and Flenar's ceremony. I stood up with Parl and Kluir stood up with Flenar. All the life-partner ceremonies provided welcome joyous interludes for our floating town.

~ ~ ~

The disorientation—quickly gone—the wind, the ship unsteady underfoot, all of these had become common and familiar for the passage between worlds. *But is that snow?*

Alorsha shivered in the sudden cold and peered into the whirling gray-white chaos that was all she saw. A jolt threw her back from the rail and hard onto the deck, which was icing over.

She scrambled to her feet and tried to look over the rail. *Did we hit something?* Nothing to see with the storm raging. She heard Mikolus's voice boom through the tearing wind but could not make out his words.

Her feet grew numb as she edged along the rail toward the aft part of the ship and her cabin. She gripped the rail as she moved for stability against the wind and iciness underfoot. Dealing with whatever had happened, and connecting to this world's magic, too, would have to wait until she had shelter or was properly attired.

She slid more than stepped down the ladder to the main deck and scurried along the rail again.

A dark shape loomed in the storm and Mikolus stood before her, a cloak held out to her. He shouted something, but she still could not make out what he said. Then he pointed to her feet, still bare as usual for aboard ship. She noticed he wore his boots. *Probably grabbed them to come get me as he also usually went barefoot. As most do aboard, at least when the weather isn't doing* this.

He whipped the cloak around her, lifted her in his arms, and tucked the cloak around her feet in the process. It was long enough to cover her completely. *Must be one of his.*

He fought the wind to get her to her cabin. She helped open the outer door and they blew into Saevalde's cabin on a blast of freezing air. After Mikolus set her back on her feet, Alorsha hobbled to the nearest chair and tucked up her feet. Saevalde jumped up from a cocoon of blankets on one chair and fought the door shut behind them, then tossed Mikolus a blanket.

Alorsha winced as her frozen feet warmed. She wished they had found a healer to travel with them. Since Eranthia had been killed, they had been without one. She turned her thoughts from that useless desire, at least for now, and to the matter at hand.

"Did everyone get inside? And did we actually hit something? I couldn't see."

"Everyone's sheltered," Mikolus said.

"Couldn't see, as you said, but it feels like we've run aground." Saevalde tossed Mikolus a second blanket and tucked herself back in her own. "We'll be waiting for the storm to subside some before we can get any idea of what we have to deal with."

Alorsha frowned as the howling of the wind dominated the room. The view through the windows showed gray-white swirls. She closed her eyes and reached out to the *Deliberia's* magic to check for any damage. She found some strain in the wood supports in the forward lowest storerooms, but nothing bad enough that it needed immediate attention. No leaks threatened.

She opened her eyes again and shared what she had discovered with the others.

"Seems so odd that this is the first time we've come into a new world with a storm like this one. With snow. In all the passages we've done." Alorsha pulled the cloak tighter. "Should have planned to have extra-warm clothing, just in case. Better get that, first chance we get."

Both Saevalde and Mikolus nodded.

"Might be we can make some of it," Mikolus said. "The weavers have some cloth set by."

All three stared out the windows for a time at the snowstorm that raged outside. Alorsha shivered again. "Is it getting colder?"

Mikolus stood. "I'll go see if the cooks have any warmed bricks to spare. He frowned at the storm and buckled his blankets to himself. Then he plunged out into it, slamming the door behind him to ensure it stayed shut.

Alorsha jumped to her feet as the door slammed and grabbed her stockings and boots from her own room. "Another thing I can't believe I didn't think of before," she muttered as she put them on and knelt next to the mast that rose through the center of the cabin.

"What are you about, lass?"

Alorsha placed both hands flat on the floor and drew

on the *Deliberia*'s magic. "We should have a way to get to the lower decks without the need to go outside all the time. Since we use this side of the cabin for meetings anyway, I'm opening a hatch here so we can make that access. After the storm's done, I'll do the same at the forward compartments. It'll mean we have to rearrange some, but the benefit should be worth it."

Saevalde joined her but stood far enough away to give her plenty of room. "Coming down in the passage just below us will work well enough, but the decks below that will take more work."

Alorsha grinned. "It's not like we haven't made similar changes before."

"Aye, true. What help can I be?"

"I won't need any for this part. But if you can get some of the crew to construct the ladder later, that'll be a great help."

"I'll do that. But for now...." She returned to her blanket cocoon and bundled up again.

With a nod and another grin, Alorsha turned back to her task. She placed both hands flat on the floor and closed her eyes to better visualize the hatch she wanted to make. She sank into the *Deliberia*'s magic and shaped the square hatch in her mind's eye. The wood beneath her hands followed what she pictured.

A slight hint of another's magic, and an impression of query from a cabin below and nearby, told her that Gya had noticed her actions. *Good. His skills've come along nicely since he joined us nearly a year past. His help'll be valuable.*

She sensed it when he joined her in the ship's magic. Felt like he might be at the mast where it ran through the deck, right below her.

Together they shaped the hatch. When the piece separated from the surrounding deck, it fell below and Gya and Kluir caught it.

Alorsha leaned to look through the square hole. With the mast situated at one edge, it should be a simple matter to tack steps to it, or a ladder, for access.

"I plan to carry this through to the next deck, too," she told the two men as they looked up at her. "Once we can get to the stores without getting blown away by going outside, we'll need more taiawood, and some hinges to finish this."

Saevalde helped Alorsha reclaim the hatch cover when the men passed it back to them.

"Shall I do the same here?" Gya looked up at Alorsha as he stood beneath the hole in the ceiling of the hallway that bordered his cabin, and Mikolus's, Kluir's, and Parl and Flenar's. Hali's cabin stood empty as she had moved into a different compartment below-decks with Remdor, her life-partner of more than half a year. *Have to see about expanding theirs, too,* Alorsha reminded herself. *With their first child due to arrive before too much longer.*

Alorsha nodded her assent to Gya's query. "But start with a small hole to let those below know what you're doing, since it will go directly into their compartments. We'll have to fix that, of course. But later."

With nothing else to do while they waited out the storm, Alorsha reached through the ship's magic to connect to the world's. She found it, faint and slippery, and settled in a chair to work at a better grasp on it.

At some point, Mikolus returned in a blast of frigid air from the door. He set a warmed brick at her feet, but otherwise did not disturb her. She was aware of his voice, and Saevalde's, but ignored them as she chased the world's magic.

She focused so on her task that it took a couple of repetitions of her name to alert her that they spoke to her. She pulled away from the world's magic, perplexed at its elusiveness, with a quizzical look for the others.

"The storm's eased, lass," Saevalde said. "Coming to see what we ran into?"

With a nod, Alorsha returned the cloak and blankets to their respective owners. After she grabbed her warmest cloak from her own room and put it on, she followed Saevalde and Mikolus out onto the deck.

The wind had subsided. Snow still fell, but the bitter cold had eased to leave them feeling merely frigid. The deck sloped toward the stern which made the walk to the bow a challenge with ice underfoot. Some crewmembers already checked the ropes and sails for damage. Saevalde barked some additional instructions to them as she and Alorsha and Mikolus passed.

At the rail at the bow, the three leaned over to see what they had hit and looked around. Land was near, but not close enough that Alorsha would have expected shallows. The murky water obscured what lay beneath its surface.

"Sand," was Saevalde's assessment. "Sandbar or shallows, can't tell from here."

Alorsha peered at the land. "No sign of any buildings, town, or settlement, at least from here. Can we free ourselves?"

Saevalde frowned. "Have to look into it some more. Get closer in one of our tenders."

"I'll take another over there and see what there is to see." Mikolus indicated the land just visible in the haze.

Alorsha nodded. "The magic's strange here. Well, stranger than we've seen before. I can tell it's there but can't pull on it yet. After I determine the direction to Devrand and make any repairs that the *Deliberia* needs, Gya and I'll work on that. But if you encounter anyone over there, you'll not be able to talk with them through the *Deliberia*'s magic. Can't do that yet."

Gya joined her as Saevalde and Mikolus left to their tasks. He leaned over the rail and frowned at the ship's predicament, then gazed off into the distance and his frown deepened.

"Problem?" Alorsha said.

"Somewhat. Well, perhaps. But maybe not too bad."

"So why the troubled expression?"

Gya shrugged. "I've been trying for months now to

record the sigils I used to work magic with. In case I might find a way to use them again. But I'm sure I keep forgetting lines of them. At least I *think* I'm forgetting them. Something doesn't look right. And when I look back at earlier ones I drew, they don't look right. But I was certain they were close when I drew them." He rubbed the back of his neck with one hand and with his other scratched at the pale-yellow close-cut beard that stood out against his dark brown skin. "I don't want to lose them."

"Why didn't you say something before?"

Gya shrugged. "I wanted to do this myself. I was sure I could. But now...."

"Maybe step back from your project for a short time, then return."

"I worry that I'll forget even more if I don't get them all drawn as fast as I can. I'm afraid to be away from it for too long."

Alorsha considered that while she crossed the deck to the rigging. Gya kept pace with her. "I might have an idea or two to help, possible combinations of some plants' magics," Alorsha said. "But let me look into them further first before we try anything."

"My thanks." He shivered. "I'm heading back inside."

Alorsha nodded and watched Gya until he disappeared through one of the hatches on deck and down the steps, headed below-decks. *Hope I can produce something to help.* While he had taken to the plant magic well enough, he still seemed somewhat lost without the magic he knew best, his native sigil magic.

With a small sigh, Alorsha turned her attention to her wayfinding. The wayfinding magic she used seemed unaffected by the world's strange magic. The pendant's arc pointed roughly toward the land. Mikolus passed as it did so and noted the direction with a nod before he climbed over the rail and down to the tender that waited for him. Three other crewmembers followed him – all of them well armed.

After she saw Mikolus off, Alorsha found Gya again, in the depths of the ship.

"I tried touching this world's magic as you've shown me," Gya told her as he climbed down a ladder after her. "But it almost seems it's tied up elsewhere."

"Tied up. Yes, it does seem like that, doesn't it? After we've strengthened the *Deliberia* below and finished our changes to her for the indoor ladders, we'll look into it further. I don't see an immediate need. No one out there to talk to yet."

In the hold, Alorsha and Gya moved as far forward as they could. They skirted a couple of upset ship's cats, various displaced barrels and bundles of goods that had been knocked loose when the ship stopped so unexpectedly, and the crewmembers who worked to return order to the chaos. Most of those crewmembers shuttled the goods further toward the stern. *Probably something to do with helping to free the ship.*

Alorsha found a clear space at the hull and beckoned Gya over. "You take the lead. See if the *Deliberia*'s sustained any damage and fix it."

With a nod, Gya placed both hands on the hull and closed his eyes. Alorsha placed a hand atop one of his to follow along and help, if he needed any. Like she would have, he reached into the ship's magic and followed it throughout to look for any holes or weaknesses from running aground. When he found a few weaknesses, he worked with the ship's magic to strengthen those areas.

After he finished, he gave Alorsha a questioning look.

She smiled. "Excellent work. Your grasp of the magic does you credit. Now, let's get those accesses finished and people's rooms fixed around them."

That work took them several hours, interrupted only by a meal and some further attempts to reach the world's magic.

As Alorsha finished the final pieces of a new wall to accommodate the new access to the upper decks, a sense of welcome shivered through the *Deliberia's* magic, followed by a curious caution.

"Mikolus must have returned," she said.

Gya nodded. He fitted the last piece into place and twined it with the rest of the wall through magic. "Some visitors, too, I think. From the feel of the *Deliberia*."

"Indeed. We're done, here. We'll let these two," she gestured to the waiting crewmembers, "get their room back in order. Come on."

Alorsha brushed wood dust from her hands as she led the way back to the main deck.

There she found a continuing bustle of clean-up after the storm and two strangers standing with Mikolus near the rail. Alorsha studied the newcomers as she and Gya approached.

The two, a man and a woman, stood close to each other, both bundled in fur clothing. *Looks warm.* They were both older, from what Alorsha saw, their faces heavily weathered, brown, and wrinkled. The man's hair and mustache were half white, while some completely white hair peeked from the woman's hood. But their smiles as Alorsha and Gya joined them were wide and delighted.

The woman said something, but Alorsha could not understand her. Mikolus spoke to the woman, and Alorsha could not understand him, either.

"Mikolus?"

He grinned at her and nodded toward the newcomers. They each held out something in one hand, which Alorsha and Gya both took — a small carving of glinting curves and swirls, of some kind of lightweight metal, flat and no longer than the joint of one finger.

The woman raised her empty hand to her mouth, blew on her fingertips, and touched them to her lips. She nodded toward Alorsha and Gya.

After they exchanged glances, the two imitated her motions, with the small carving balanced on their fingertips. Alorsha felt a whisper of magic.

"There, that should be better," the woman said.

Alorsha smiled. "These contain your magic?" She returned the small carving.

"In a sense," the man said. "The creation of such charms brings the magic to them." He tucked the charm Gya handed him into a pouch at his waist. It jingled, implying he had others within. The woman matched his actions.

"I'm called Naltha Bashiad. And he, my spouse, is called Taesen Bashiad." The newcomers each held out a hand, palm up.

With a glance at Mikolus, Alorsha tentatively reached out with her own hand as she introduced herself. With a smile, Naltha clasped Alorsha's wrist with her extended hand and gave it a slight squeeze before she released it. Taesen repeated the gesture. Both repeated it again with Gya when he introduced himself.

"Let's get out of the cold." Alorsha led the way to the meeting room that formed half of Saevalde's cabin. The Ship's Master met them there, with some food and drink already on the table.

After the newcomers handed Saevalde a charm to use, they all made introductions. Taesen and Naltha peeled off the thick fur gloves they wore as they took seats at the table.

When her hands brushed the wood of the table, Naltha startled, then placed both hands flat on the surface. "A unique vessel you've got here. A different magic." She reached for the food and drink.

After they each got something to eat and drink, Naltha leaned on the table. "Your Mikolus told us of your trouble—"

"And we see for ourselves," Taesen interjected.

"How did you come to run aground here? Surely your lookouts would have seen the shallows from afar. Or your ship's magic, perhaps. Can't tell what it might be capable of but it's clearly not from around here."

Alorsha glanced at Mikolus, who gave her a slight shake of his head. Her decision, then.

"True, under normal conditions the lookouts would have given warning," Alorsha said. "But when we sailed here, into your world as I suspect you've guessed, we found ourselves in the midst of the storm. We could see nothing ahead and so ran aground before we even realized the danger. Can you help?"

Naltha and Taesen exchanged glances.

"Not as strong as a guess," Naltha said. "More just a wondering if it was possible. If it was possibly true."

"Our world," Taesen muttered. "So, the old stories *were* more than just tales."

"The old stories?" Saevalde leaned closer, interest clear in her expression.

"Indeed," Taesen said. "We have many tales the storytellers share about people who travel to and from other worlds, worlds apart from this one where we live. Different."

"But we never imagined we'd live to see the truth of the stories." Naltha shared another look with Taesen. "Too bad they all left and will never know."

At the quizzical expressions they received, Taesen elaborated. "It's been a bad year, with the last few not much better. Cold that has lingered far too long for the crops to thrive. So, everyone packed and headed away, to the warmer lands."

"But you stayed?" Gya said.

"Just we two. Unable to walk that far and unlikely to make it anyway. Better to let the young folks have that much more food to see them through. And with the new crop of healers we trained, they no longer needed us."

He shrugged at the horrified expressions he received. "It's our way."

"Healers," Saevalde repeated, with a significant look directed at Alorsha. "You're both healers?"

"We are," Naltha said.

"Why not come with us," Gya said.

"We'd welcome your skills. We've been too long without healers of our own," Alorsha said.

"You'd take us with you?" Naltha said.

"Do you plan to go to yet another world?" Taesen said, his expression at the same time apprehensive and eager.

"We're not going anywhere right now," Mikolus pointed out. "We won't, either, unless we can get free of the sandbar."

"You've just the one ship?" Naltha asked.

"Aye," Saevalde confirmed.

"And we need to get free. We aren't the only ones who've come from another world," Gya said.

Both Naltha and Taesen nodded. "The two young men. Dev and Jarth, they named themselves. After the use of the conversing charm, of course," Taesen said. "They're scouts for you then?"

Gya shook his head.

"You've seen them? Met them?" Alorsha leaned toward the healers. "How long ago?"

"A week, perhaps," Naltha said.

"We're so close." Alorsha jumped to her feet and paced the small area around the table. "Are they still nearby?"

Taesen shrugged. "Unlikely. They were in some hurry."

"Especially since they stole fully half our charms," Naltha grumbled.

"They... what?" Alorsha peered at the healers.

Naltha nodded. "We hosted them, honored guest right. Two nights they stayed with us, and gathered things left behind that they could use."

"Warm clothes, mainly," Taesen said. "You should do the same."

Naltha held up a hand to forestall any further talk of that. "Yes, yes. But the third morning when we woke, they had gone. The charms we kept in the box by the door had gone, too."

Alorsha frowned. "The charms. He's after the magic in

them."

"Needs it, I'd say," Gya added.

"We need to get free so we can go after him," Alorsha said.

Saevalde nodded. "Working on that, lass. But our attempts so far have been no good. Even with shifting our load sternward and with the most rowers we can manage hard at work aboard and in tenders roped to the *Deliberia*, we've not reversed off the sand. Next, we'll offload as much as we can into the tenders. Maybe lighten the *Deliberia* enough to make a difference."

"High tide is a few hours off," Naltha said.

Saevalde nodded. "That'd be a help, too. Might be making the difference."

"If not," Taesen said. "A spring tide's not many days off. Surely you can wait until then to avoid damage to your ship from ill-advised attempts when the conditions aren't the best possible."

"I'd prefer to not wait, but not at the cost of damage to the *Deliberia*." Alorsha turned to the healers. "Perhaps we can catch Dev and Jarth. Would you show us where they headed?"

Taesen frowned. "We can show you their path, but they are long gone."

"They were hearty, like the others who left. They'll have covered much ground." Naltha stood. "But still, you can see for yourselves. And gather warmer clothes, too, from what the others left behind." She nodded to Taesen, who also stood.

"I'll show you around," he said.

"I'll stay here for the time being, if that's agreeable. My knees hurt something fierce this day." Naltha looked from Saevalde to Alorsha.

"Of course," Alorsha said.

"I'll make the preparations," Mikolus said and left.

"Before we go, may I see one of those conversing charms again," Alorsha said. "With your permission, I'd like to try something that I hope will let all of my people be able to speak with you."

With a nod, Naltha pulled out the small charm again and handed it over. "Try whatever you like. Although it's not got much magic left for now."

"Gya." Alorsha beckoned him close and together they touched the magic in the charm before Alorsha looked back at the two healers.

"It should be enough." She placed the charm on the floor at her feet and knelt to touch it with the thumb upon which she wore her mage ring. Gya joined her and likewise touched it with a finger. Alorsha reached out to the magic in the *Deliberia* and that in the charm—and Gya followed along—and drew them to each other.

The charm's magic flowed into the ship and joined its magic to spread out and touch all the crewmembers aboard.

With a nod of satisfaction, Alorsha returned the charm. "I'm afraid it took the rest of its magic. But it's now part of the *Deliberia* and will allow everyone to converse with you."

"The magic will return," Naltha said. "It only needs to sit idle for several hours to draw in some ambient magic again." She waved a hand in the air.

With that accomplished, Alorsha and Gya turned their attention to gathering what they would take with them ashore while Saevalde took Naltha to find a crewmember to show her as much of the ship as the older woman's aching knees would allow. Taesen returned to enjoying the rest of the food still on the table while he waited for the others to be ready to go ashore.

CHAPTER 20

Mikolus included in the group headed ashore only himself, Parl, Alorsha, Gya, and Taesen. Mikolus, Parl, and Gya rowed the tender. On the way to the shore, Taesen told them more about the dwindling crops, the cold that had encroached the last few years, and the hard decision for the villagers to leave their ancestral homes.

"We used to be a trade center for the area," Taesen said with pride. "Hence the use of the conversing charms. All our charms were much in demand and both Naltha and I can make new charms. We can also renew the magic in any that became depleted. Not everyone could do that."

He grinned and pulled a partially completed charm from his pouch and held it up. "The process of making new charms is called 'chip-carving'. We use a small knife to remove small chips of the material from the flat charm, which creates these facets that sparkle in the light." Taesen then demonstrated the chip-carving on the charm, which he put away when they reached the shore.

A short walk took them around the curve of a low hill to the village, a small collection of low rounded buildings made from rough tan stone. Taesen led them to a building roughly in the middle of the others, limping as he walked.

"Can't you do anything for that?" Gya indicted the healer's limping gait.

"Gya!" Alorsha glared at her apprentice.

"It's a valid question," Taesen said as he led them inside. "Your answer is: only to a point. Age brings some things that even the best healer cannot cure or heal. Merely relieve." He grabbed a walking stick that leaned against the wall and grinned. "Many things are best helped by a good walking stick. This way."

Back outside, Taesen led them to the far side of the village, to what looked like a path or road that ran into the foothills under the snow.

"Those two would have gone that way." Taesen pointed toward the hills and the mountains beyond them. "Before this storm came. So, any traces they might have left will be buried. Not that you can get through the mountains now anyway. This most recent storm will have closed the path behind them. I'm sorry to have to tell you so."

Alorsha scanned the visible portions of the supposed path. *No reason to doubt the healer's words.* "Where were they headed?"

"They didn't say. In fact, that Jarth didn't say much of anything at all. But Dev seemed eager to find the rest of the villagers."

"Can we sail to where the villagers headed?" Gya asked.

Alorsha shivered in a sudden gust of wind and Taesen turned back to the village. "Perhaps. But let's get you and your people those warmer clothes. We'll get back to your nice ship—on which I'm sure Naltha has already chosen a place for us—and we'll see what might be done."

Although few buildings made up the village, fewer than the village in which Alorsha had spent her childhood, they found a good number of furs and fur clothing that had been left behind. From the villagers' need to avoid being overburdened in their journey, Taesen explained. Taesen also pulled additional charms from various hiding spots within his own dwelling.

"We gathered any that the others had left behind. So, that Dev left with fewer than half what the village still held of charms." Taesen grinned at that. He gathered a few things he and Naltha wanted from their home.

All the goods they brought back filled the tender and then some. Alorsha and Taesen both clutched bundles to themselves to try to keep them out of the way for the others to row the little boat. Even so, the rowers worked around bundles piled around them, too.

Alorsha settled into the warmth of the furs that sat atop and surrounded her. *These will be welcome aboard.* The swish of the oars in the water soothed her and she drifted in a dreamy languor.

A stab of magic jolted her from her peace and sent her to her feet, spilling furs everywhere. Parl and Mikolus had weapons in hand before she even sorted what she had felt.

"We're too late." A wail tinged her words.

"What is it?" Concern filled Gya's expression.

"Devrand?" Mikolus offered.

Alorsha nodded. "He's gone already. I didn't even feel him gather the magic." She fought against the panic that twisted her insides. *I can't lose Jarthan! But how am I to follow them into the next world this time? He opened the portal so far away.* She twisted her mage ring on her thumb as she tried to get her thoughts in order. *This can't be the end of it.*

Oh, my ring!

She dropped back onto her seat and grabbed the furs she had scattered. "We have to get back to the *Deliberia*. Without delay. I might still be able to get a sense of where they've gone, but it'll fade as time passes."

With nods, Parl and Mikolus returned to their rowing, pushing hard.

Gya, however, placed both hands on the side of the tender and reached into the wood's magic. "Some extra help, I hope," he said. "Something I've wanted to try."

After a moment, the tender's speed increased, and it seemed almost to slide across the water. Alorsha shot a questioning look at her apprentice.

"Made the hull smoother." Gya shrugged. "It seems to have helped, but I expect it won't last long." He stretched and grabbed his oars again. "Takes a bit out of a person, too. Don't know if we can use it for the whole ship."

He turned his attention to helping row. "While the magic holds," he said when she raised her eyebrows at his actions.

Back at the ship, Alorsha scrambled up the ladder without waiting for any help with her bundles. She just hauled them with her. When she reached the deck, she dropped them at her feet and stepped to the side as she turned her mage ring around, so the stone was on the inside. She grasped the ship's rail with both hands and made sure the stone pressed against the wood. When Gya made a motion to join her, to try to help, she waved him off.

"A moment. This is specific to the magic we three shared," she told him. "I don't know that you can help. So please wait. For now."

With a nod, he backed away and helped sort the furs and clothing. He kept an eye on her, though, ready to help.

With a smile of acknowledgement for him, Alorsha closed her eyes to sink her awareness into the ring's magic, the magic she had shared with Devrand and Jarthan, bolstered by the ship's magic.

Hope this'll work. I can't lose him!

Too long it seemed, she reached and searched, stretched out through the magic in her ring and looked for the connection to Devrand, to Jarthan. Long, long, and too far.

Then a spark. A hint.

Straining, she grasped at it and willed it to come to her. Dark wisps lifted from her ring, from the stone there, and from where her hands grasped the rail. The wisps stretched out into the frigid air and faded from sight, reaching.

A flimsy wisp streaked toward the ship from the direction the two men had supposedly gone. It twisted around Alorsha and plunged into the faint wisps already around her. They all then slid back into her ring and into the ship.

With a gasp, she opened her eyes. Her legs buckled beneath her, and she slid to the deck, Gya and Mikolus were beside her in an instant.

"I'm fine." She half-heartedly waved them off, but they did not budge. "Really. It was just harder than I expected."

"Did you get it?" Gya asked.

"A faint hint, yes. But enough, I think." She smiled. "We *will* be able to follow. As soon as we get off the cursed sandbar."

~ ~ ~

High tide came and went and still they remained trapped on the sandbar. With little further to do to free the ship until the promised spring tide arrived in three days, Mikolus took several crewmembers with him to gather all they could find of use from the village and made certain they had not missed anything that Naltha and Taesen wished to bring with them.

The rest of the crew worked at any needed repairs and amused themselves with their individual crafting pursuits and some spontaneous contests and games.

The second morning after they grounded on the sandbar, Alorsha sought out Gya. She found him settled on the deck in a spot sheltered from the wind. He held a book in his lap and was drawing something on a scrap paper atop the book, his pen scratching across the paper. A closed ink bottle sat on the deck by his side. When her shadow crossed his paper, he looked up.

"A book of sigils drawn from my less-than-complete memory," he said in response to her questioning look. "And these are attempts at two sigils I've thought might do something when combined into a new one. Some possibilities. If I can figure out a way to activate their magic." He drew more swirls and lines as he spoke.

"Whoever first figured out the kri-stone and sigil magic of my homeland must have done so without anything to guide them. So, with even my half-memories of actual sigils, I have to be in a better position than they would have been. Right?"

Alorsha drew a breath to speak, and stopped when he held up a hand to ask her to wait. "Something's there," he murmured. "This last sigil's almost right. But what's missing? I know something is. But together...."

He added one more swirl.

A whiff of the tingle of magic that Gya had described feeling when he had drawn a sigil correctly brushed Alorsha. Then it slipped away.

Gya groaned and grinned at the same time. "So close."

"What is it you're so close to?" Alorsha asked.

"What if I can combine that 'turnaround' sigil with the one that would trap someone for a time, maybe 'turnaround' might change the trap magic to a freeing magic. Maybe something to free us from the sand without having to wait another couple of days for that tide."

"I'd welcome that."

"*If* I could get it to work. I've tried everything I've thought of to draw the sigils and perhaps get more than a hint of magic. I've drawn with sticks, twigs, stems, petals, and crushed versions of each, from the many different plants that you've collected. I even tried to use flour from the kitchen stores to draw a sigil. Cook was *not* happy about that."

Alorsha chuckled.

"I just can't get anything to work," Gya muttered. "I can feel it, the edge of the magic. But there's still something not quite right with the two sigils I think I need. I can't try to combine them if they're not right to begin with. What am I missing?"

"Have you tried to use any of the oddments from my chervynai?"

"I've not been able to truly grasp that plant's magic," Gya admitted. "I don't know what it would do. Anyway, I thought those were rare and so you've been saving them."

"It's true I save the plant's oddments. But this might be one time it's worth it to try to use them. But first, I've an idea of something else to try."

Gya gave her a quizzical look as she ran back to her cabin. When she returned, he focused on the small jar she held out.

"Something that occurred to me. This ointment helps provide focus and clarity of thought."

Gya took the jar and opened it. Inside, a small bit of pale-green semitransparent salve clung to the side of the jar.

"Can you make more?"

Alorsha shook her head. "That's the last of it. The plants I used came from another world and I've used all their parts now."

Gya replaced the lid. "Then we should save this for something important." He held the jar out to Alorsha.

She placed her hand atop the jar and pushed it back toward him. "This is important. Especially if it helps you retrieve the sigils from your memory. Even more so if those sigils can help free the *Deliberia*."

Gya opened the jar again. "So, what do I do?"

"First, make sure you're comfortable. Any discomfort might distract you."

Gya set aside his book and writing materials and shifted his legs to a more comfortable position. Alorsha sat next to him.

"Here's how this works. You'll close your eyes and put the ointment on your eyelids and a touch on each temple.

I'll take the jar when you're done. Then you'll imagine that you are drawing the sigil like you used to, with the kri-stone powders. Go through the motions, whether here on the deck or in the air in front of you. Try to be *in* your memory of drawing it, like it's not a memory but something you're doing right now."

"That's it?"

She nodded and smiled. "That's it."

"How long will it last?"

"Long enough for what you need. Don't be concerned about that."

With a slight nod, Gya followed her directions. He vaguely noticed when she lifted the jar from his hand but had already immersed himself in the memory. His hand cupped the kri-stone powder as he had so many times. With a measured pace, he drew the trap sigil on the deck, taking care to form each line and swirl just so.

Ah, that's the one he'd had wrong.

Gya finished drawing that sigil and turned his attention to the other. By the time he had completed that one, he had identified three line-swirls that he had misremembered. But now he saw them clearly.

He opened his eyes, surprised to see no sigil drawn on the deck in front of him. It had felt that real.

"Did it work?"

Gya grinned. "Oh, yes. I recall them as if I had just drawn them with kri-stone."

"Good. Next try drawing the combination you've been working on. But use this." She took a small pot from a crewmember who hovered at her side before she dismissed him.

Gya peered into the pot she handed him. Inside was a reddish dust, much the consistency of pepper.

"Crushed chervynai petals and seeds," Alorsha told him. "Draw with this like you would if you used your kri-stone powders. Reach out to the chervynai's magic, the *Deliberia*'s magic too, while you do that."

With a doubtful expression, Gya did as she instructed.

When he finished connecting the last swirl of his combined sigil, the usual tingle of the magic danced across his skin. It flared, settled, and flared again.

The ship shifted, the motion slight but noticeable. Gya shared a look with Alorsha and could not contain his grin.

The magic flared yet again... and every knot on the deck came undone. Everything that had been tied came loose and dropped ropes and sails and people's hair.

With a groan of its timbers, the *Deliberia* settled back into the sand.

Gya met Alorsha's gaze with a pained, sheepish expression and winced as she worked to contain laughter. Then he abandoned his attempt to stay serious and joined her merriment.

"Not what I'd intended," he gasped when his mirth faded. "And it still didn't work."

"Perhaps not at what you'd hoped. But who knows, that might come in handy sometime. Return as much of the powder as you can gather to its pot and take it back to my cabin, please. And draw those two sigils and the new one in your book while they're fresh in your memory. After that, better help us get everything tied back up again."

With a rueful sigh, Gya turned to his assigned tasks.

~ ~ ~

That afternoon, Alorsha sequestered herself with Grabe, the crewmember who had made the pendant frame for her, to have him create a ring for Gya. *It's high time he has his own mage ring.*

In her room, after the evening meal and into the night, she prepared the ring for him, connecting its magic to the *Deliberia*'s magics. She emerged the morning that the spring tide was due and sought out Gya, finding him where he leaned on the rail at the stern.

"Is it time?" he greeted her.

"Not yet. Taesen and Naltha say we'll see the tide about midday. But I'm not here about that. I've got this for you. I should've done this sooner. By your skill level, you've certainly long ago earned it. If you'd like to have a ceremony to receive it, we can do that."

She held out a carved taiawood ring. "A mage ring for you. A custom of my people, as I've mentioned."

Gya took it and turned it over and around, examining it. "I can feel magic in it."

Alorsha grinned. "It gives you a concrete connection to the *Deliberia* and her magic, much as my ring does. I judge you're somewhere between a craft-mage and an artisan-mage in your skill with magic, as my people determine those levels, but I've made it more of a true mage ring rather than a student ring, which means artisan-mage level and on the left thumb as I wear mine."

Gya considered that. "Maybe sometime soon. But I still feel more craft-mage level."

Alorsha smiled. "Then it goes on the first finger of your right hand. Would you like to have a ceremony to mark officially receiving it?"

Gya grinned and shook his head. "Thank you, but no. This is just fine." He slipped the ring on his finger and held out his hand to admire it.

"Congratulations," Alorsha said. "Your next task, when you return to your learning, is to learn to work with and through the ring."

"Wonderful, more work," Gya muttered, but smiled.

Alorsha smiled in return and left him there admiring his new ring.

~ ~ ~

When the spring tide arrived at midday, the *Deliberia* finally won free of the sand. And in the midst of another howling snowstorm, Alorsha took them to the next world.

Chapter 21

From Alorsha's Journal

More worlds. More chasing the man who used to be a friend. I just wish....

No, I'll not do this.

At least I learned that I didn't have to be able to see Devrand open his passages to get a sense of the magic.

Many of the worlds we've visited have been amazing and beautiful. And we've managed to curb Devrand's damage to them several times now. Others, we were lucky, and he rushed through with little impact. If I could only manage to catch up to him....

I'd never imagined that on this odd journey we'd use the *Deliberia*'s unique magic to save an entire society by bringing them to a new world. But that's exactly what we've done.

~ ~ ~

In a rare moment of calm, Alorsha watched the little girl crawl as fast as her arms and legs would take her. Hali and Remdor, her parents, followed right behind her, harried expressions on their faces as she unerringly headed for the port rail. Again.

Alorsha had long since narrowed the gaps between all the rails' balusters. Still Hali and Remdor grabbed their first-born before she reached the rail and carried her back to the middle of the deck to the others: the children of the society the *Deliberia* had rescued.

"Hope the scouts have found a place for these people," Alorsha murmured as she watched three of the children make a dash for the starboard rail. "All these children won't stay well contained much longer, I'd say."

"I expect most of us, and them, are ready for less-crowded living again. Helps that we can get them on the deck now that the storm's subsided," Gya said.

Alorsha nodded. "That was the longest storm yet, but I suppose we were due for another bad one."

Gya shrugged. He came alert as one of the children reached the rail and started jumping and yelling. Alorsha followed his gaze. One of the warriors of the people they had rescued hauled himself over the rail, having climbed the rope ladder from one of the tenders below. Alorsha smiled to herself as Gya leaned that direction, interest clear in his expression when Shyvoan Naivaschld, a red-haired, brown-eyed warrior of that same society, pulled herself onto the deck. Crewmembers of the *Deliberia* followed those two and Mikolus climbed up last.

He looked around until he spotted Alorsha, then gave her a slight nod.

"Looks like they've found a spot," she told Gya and hurried from her vantage on the aft deck to the main deck to greet the returning scouts.

A crowd gathered around the scouts, Shyvoan's people, the 'denizens' as Shyvoan and her fellow warriors called them. When Gya joined Alorsha, he and Shyvoan exchanged shy smiles.

Mikolus and Alorsha stepped to one side away from the denizens who peppered their warriors with questions.

Gya followed.

"It's not what we had expected to find," Mikolus told her. "Still, might be it'll work for them, if they're willing. Inland there are several deserted villages."

"Devrand?" Alorsha said.

Mikolus shook his head. "No. Beyond those empty dwellings, we found a village with a few people who still lived there. They told us a mortal sickness swept through there some five years ago. Wiped out those villages and many others in their land. They assured us the sickness was long gone – no signs of it since. They also told us that these denizens would be welcome to move into any of the empty villages. They'd welcome having neighbors again."

Alorsha frowned. "If the denizens are interested in these villages, I'd feel better if our healers visited first to make sure this sickness isn't lingering somehow. I'd not see these people face that after all they've already dealt with, if we can prevent it."

"I can take them there any time," Mikolus said. "Will you come?"

Alorsha shook her head. "If it's to be their home, the denizens must decide. They need no opinion from me. But I do hope this finally is the place for them."

Mikolus grinned. "Ready to have your ship back?" He kept his voice soft, for her ears only.

Alorsha nodded as she looked at the gathered denizens and spotted several pockets of intense discussions among them, especially where Shyvoan stood some distance away from the others clearly arguing with her sister. Or rather, her sister seemed to be ranting at her about something. Much as she had at least once a week the several months they had been aboard.

Alorsha indicated the sisters with a tilt of her head, drawing both Gya's and Mikolus's attention to them. The three watched as the sisters' altercation grew even more heated.

"Might be Shyvoan could use a friendly presence,"

Mikolus said.

Needing no further urging, Gya headed that direction.

"Is that wise?" Alorsha watched Gya interrupt the unpleasantness. Shyvoan's sister stomped off in a huff while Shyvoan and Gya shuffled their feet and seemed to be trying to decide what to say to each other.

"Maybe not," Mikolus said. "Still, just a small nudge."

"Hm. Well, I can see it might help her to know she has an option, if she doesn't want to endure her sister's vitriol any longer. Though I'll make certain she understands we can't return to places we've been before. That's valuable information for such a decision."

With a nod, Mikolus headed back to the crowd. "I'll get ready for the next trip. That assumes they decide others want to see the place."

Alorsha smiled. "I'd imagine they will. I'll tell Naltha and Taesen to prepare for a brief excursion off the ship, that we need their expertise to make sure that sickness truly is gone."

~ ~ ~

A tap at the door to her cabin later that evening pulled Alorsha from her contemplation of a plant that seemed to have a hidden magic that she could not yet pull to the surface. With a slight sigh, she set it aside.

"I'm here, come in," she called.

The door opened and Hali peeked around the edge. She entered, her manner hesitant, when Alorsha beckoned her in.

What's this? Hali's not the hesitant, peeking type.

Alorsha waved Hali to one of the few chairs not covered in plant bits. "Is there a problem?"

"Ah, no. Not really. I just hate to do this."

Alorsha gave her a questioning look. "And what is it you're doing?"

Hali sighed. "Remdor and I have been talking about

this for a while. Especially since there have been other children around.... Well, we think we should stay with these denizens. When they pick out a new place to live. I'm so sorry, but we expect it'll be best for our family."

Alorsha nodded. "Being with other families, other children would be a good thing. I'm not surprised."

"You're not?"

Alorsha smiled and shook her head. "I've seen how you two have struggled to care for your daughter and keep her safe aboard the ship. Even with everything we've all tried to do to make that easier. So, no, I'm not surprised. But if you'd decided the other way, decided to stay with us, we'd have continued to try to make it the best place we could for little Viyeva."

Alorsha's smile dimmed. "I can't say I'm not going to miss you, though."

Hali tried to smile but struggled with it. "I'll miss you, too. Something fierce." She jumped to her feet and clasped Alorsha's hands to pull her close and into a strong hug.

Alorsha squawked in surprise and returned the embrace. "You're going to make me cry."

"Then it won't be just me."

They both laughed a little through their tears before they parted again.

"You've talked with the denizens' leaders, then?"

Hali shook her head as she swiped the back of her hand across her eyes. "Wanted to talk with you, first. But I'm sure they'll be agreeable. I'll head there next."

She turned back at the door. "From what I've heard, it sounds like some of their warriors might want to stay with the *Deliberia*. Maybe one of them can fill my place."

"Maybe take over the position for you," Alorsha said. "But I'm sure not fill your place."

Hali waved off that comment, but smiled her thanks as she closed the door behind her.

Alorsha sank into the closest chair and stared at the door. She wrapped her arms around her middle as she tried to squeeze away the hollowness that filled her at the thought that in just a few days she'd never see her friend again.

I can't just let my friend go forever. Have to find a way for the Deliberia *to return to the worlds we've already passed through. There* has *to be some way to do that.*

A twinge in the magic from her ring alerted her to Devrand's actions. In a sudden surge, he gathered magic and opened the way into another world. No time for her to catch him.

She reached through her ring, through the *Deliberia's* magic to get the sense of where he headed, so the ship could follow. He and Jarthan stepped into the new world, and she sensed the passage snap shut behind them.

Now to just get the denizens into their new homes and take the Deliberia *after him again.*

~ ~ ~

After two days of frantic preparations and repeated visits to the town the denizens had chosen for their new home, they were at last ready to depart the *Deliberia.* The mood as they waited to board one of the ship's tenders was overall festive, with a few solemn pockets as friends bid each other farewell. While most of the denizens had chosen to leave, a few had decided to stay, to travel with the *Deliberia.* And a few from the *Deliberia* had decided to stay with the denizens in their new village, with their welcome, including Hali and her family.

Alorsha spotted Shyvoan and the members of her squad in a cluster off to one side, saying their farewells. Of the four, only Shyvoan had decided to stay with the *Deliberia. A tough decision for all of them.*

From some comments that Alorsha had overheard, they had worked together a long time and become close friends. *Another reason to find a way to return to previous worlds.*

Alorsha stayed out of the way of the preparations and

leave-takings and only helped guide wayward children who ran around with the excitement of the change. After she returned one small offender to her grandfather, Hali approached her, and Shyvoan trailed behind her.

"All ready?" Alorsha asked her former guard.

Hali nodded. "And we thank you for the seeds. I hope they'll grow here."

"I drew some of this world's magic into them, so they should."

"Wonderful! A piece of home to stay with us." Hali's expression tried to crumble, but she fought back the sadness as she caught Alorsha in a quick hug.

"Be careful. And when you catch him, make sure he gets what's due him."

Alorsha nodded. "My thanks for everything. For keeping me safe and putting up with me."

Hali ducked her head. "Same here. Try to be happy. When you can."

Alorsha nodded again.

Another hug and Hali jogged back to where Remdor waited with their daughter. Then it was their turn to climb down to the tender. A last wave and they were gone, headed for their new home.

Shyvoan shuffled her feet, reminding Alorsha that she still stood there.

"So, bodyguard?" the warrior said.

A chuckle came from behind Alorsha.

"Bodyguard," Mikolus said. "Sometimes minder." Alorsha made a face at him over her shoulder and shrugged.

"Co-conspirator, at times," Mikolus continued. "I've seen you in our weapons-work sessions. Interested in taking that position?"

Shyvoan looked from Alorsha to Mikolus and back. "So, he's offering me the position?" she said to Alorsha.

With a grin, Alorsha nodded. "Strictly speaking, you work for him. And I trust his assessments. You've already met Parl and Kluir? You'd be working with them."

Shyvoan nodded. "We can work together. And yes, I'd like to take that position."

"You do know that we've not yet been able to return to a place we've been before," Alorsha said. "We might not ever manage that. You wouldn't ever see your relatives again."

Shyvoan frowned but nodded. "I know. They've all but eliminated me from their lives already. For a long time, now. I've said my good-byes and wished them well. I can live with the likelihood that I won't see them again."

"Well, then. Welcome!" Alorsha smiled at her.

"Let's get you settled in and moved into your new cabin – the one that you're entitled to with your new standing aboard ship." Mikolus led Shyvoan off.

Alorsha turned her attention to preparations for the *Deliberia* to follow Devrand again. When the crewmembers returned after they saw the denizens settled in their new town, she opened the passage to the next world.

CHAPTER 22

FROM ALORSHA'S JOURNAL

Shyvoan has fit well with my small group of guards. While I still miss Hali, I enjoy Shyvoan's company – her wit, the unique way she views things. I think she's growing happy with her new life with us aboard the *Deliberia*.

She hasn't carried her dragon-scale infused blade since Devrand used it to kill a dragon in her world. While I've not felt magic from the weapon, I do have the sense that it's tied to the "luck" her friends among her own people had mentioned. Could that luck help us catch Devrand? Wonder if the sword has to be with us when we get close to him. Maybe I can persuade her as we continue our journey....

~ ~ ~

Alorsha dropped to the deck to escape the heavy metal ball that sailed her direction after it ripped through the mainsail. It narrowly missed her as it hit the rail and fell into the sea, taking pieces of the rail with it.

"I think they're after the ship," a crewmember yelled.

"They can't have it," Alorsha yelled back. She flinched

at the roar from the other ship—a ship nearly the size of the *Deliberia*—that meant another of those balls headed for them. That one flew across the deck, not much higher than their heads, and splashed into the sea on the other side.

"They've got another ship coming behind them," Mikolus said from Alorsha's left. "If they wished, I expect they could sink us with those oversized flintlocks, or whatever they are. And our ballistae aren't discouraging them at all. Might be we should stop trying to run before they get serious with those weapons of theirs."

Alorsha looked at Saevalde, who nodded. "I think we need to let them aboard and talk."

"If they wanted that, why did they shoot those things at us first?" Alorsha demanded. "We're not the ones who started this."

"Let's just finish it, lass," Saevalde said. "We're running low on provisions, so perhaps we can steer this into a way to solve that problem. Then be on about our business, I'm hoping."

"Better than facing the destruction of the *Deliberia*," Mikolus added.

Alorsha fumed but could not argue with that.

So, she moved out of the way and watched as Saevalde barked the orders that brought the *Deliberia* to a standstill in the water. As the other ships came alongside, flanking them, and hooked ropes across to hold the ships together, she drew in what magic of this world she could from the air and sea and meshed it with the taiawood. *At least we'll be able to talk with these people.*

From the ship to their starboard a man in ornamented clothes hailed them. Alorsha, Master Eztevo and Captain Ludek strode to that railing.

"Could this be Devrand's doing?" Saevalde said before they reached the railing, her voice quiet.

Alorsha shrugged. "I'm undecided whether to hope so or hope not."

"What ship and what port?" the stranger demanded

when they got close enough for speech.

"This is the *Deliberia*, from Varoia, a long way from here," Master Eztevo said. "What of you? Why do you attack us?"

The stranger glanced at some other men who stood behind him on the deck of his ship and turned back again.

"You sail in sovereign waters. Do you not have the charts?"

Saevalde shook her head and spread her hands wide. "As I said, we're from *far* away. We don't know your sovereign waters nor your customs. Can we make peace of this?"

Gya stepped up beside Alorsha as Saevalde spoke. "What do you need me to do?" he murmured.

"Continue to draw the world's magic to the *Deliberia* as much as you can," Alorsha said. "Otherwise, avoid attracting attention to yourself."

Gya nodded and headed back toward the ladder that led below decks. He sat on the deck beside the opening and closed his eyes to follow her instructions.

"We'll take you with us to straighten this out," the man on the other ship answered Saevalde.

The Ship's Master looked to Alorsha.

"I suppose we must," Alorsha said in a low voice, with a shrug.

"Agreed," Saevalde told the stranger, who nodded and ordered his crew to unhook the ropes that bound the ships together.

"We'll sail one in front of you and one behind," he told Saevalde. "We have cannons that can shoot both forward and aft, so you'll still be under our guns."

"We'll cause no problems," Saevalde assured him and ordered the crew to be ready to follow the other ship when it moved.

Alorsha crossed the deck to the opposite railing and looked over the damage. While the strangers' ships maneuvered into position and had no clear view of her actions, she reached into the *Deliberia's* magic and called the broken pieces of wood from the water to her. *Not leaving any of that special wood to float around if I can help it.* A crewmember helped her get the sodden wood below decks.

~ ~ ~

The *Deliberia* sailed between the other two ships and matched their speed with no difficulty. Still, it was late in the day when those on deck spotted the land they headed for. The other ships lit lanterns along their rails as twilight engulfed them. Saevalde had the *Deliberia's* crew follow their example.

Alorsha estimated they arrived at the harbor near midnight. The largest harbor she had yet seen, it swarmed with watercraft of all shapes and sizes, even at that late hour. But the *Deliberia* and her escorts were the largest of any there.

From the ship in front of them came the faint voice of the man who had spoken before.

"Follow, and dock between," he instructed.

Alorsha looked to Saevalde, who nodded. "Should be deep enough where they head. I suggest you take the measure of Devrand's direction before we get any closer, so we know where we stand on that, at least."

Alorsha fed her pendant the little magic it required and watched as it pointed toward the city dimly visible up the hills from the harbor. Saevalde saw and nodded, her expression grim. "They could be working with him, then. We'll be on guard."

They docked toward one side of the harbor, at some distance from the access to the city above. They waited and watched the crews of the ships to either side as they settled their ships in for a stay at dock and many people left both ships. Half of them set off for the city and the rest came to stand on the dock by the *Deliberia*.

Saevalde lowered the gangplank, and headed down when one of the men below waved her forward.

Alorsha followed, with Mikolus behind her. All those who waited for them carried a flintlock or two tucked in their belts, and they all dressed much alike. *Some kind of uniform?*

"We don't wish to offer discourtesy," the man who had spoken to them earlier said when they set foot on the dock. "However, it's a difficult time for our land just now. We ask to see your ship, to see that you are what you say."

Saevalde looked to Alorsha.

"I see no problem with showing you our ship," Alorsha told the man. "With an escort, of course. Speaking of courtesies, may we know your names?"

"Of course, Lady," the man straightened. He clicked the heels of his boots together and inclined his head to her. "I am Oyuchim, Captain of these two ships of the fleet." He introduced the others in his group. Alorsha introduced herself and Saevalde and Mikolus.

"With your leave, I would come aboard with my two officers, while the rest remain here," Captain Oyuchim said to Alorsha, but his eyes also strayed to Saevalde and Mikolus, perhaps unsure whose permission he needed. Alorsha clarified that she was the *Deliberia's* owner, with Saevalde the Ship's Master and Mikolus the Ship's Captain. Then she led the way aboard.

Saevalde took over and led the strangers through the ship. She left out no part of the ship and kept a close eye on their visitors. Alorsha and Mikolus tagged along, although as the tour stretched longer, Alorsha had trouble keeping her eyes open. Still, she stayed with them until they all returned to the top of the gangplank for the strangers to return ashore.

Captain Oyuchim performed his heel-click and bow again. "Thank you, Lady. We won't disturb you further tonight, but we ask that everyone remain aboard until tomorrow."

Alorsha nodded and watched them walk down the gangplank. They set guards at the bottom and spaced along the pier.

When it became clear that was to be all for the night, she headed toward her cabin. "I'm for bed," she told the others. "But wake me, if there's need."

~ ~ ~

A clash of swords woke Alorsha, setting her heart racing. Then she realized it was just the morning weapons-work on deck. Surprising how much of the noise came to her cabin, even with Saevalde's between hers and the deck. She had not meant to sleep so late but felt much better for the rest.

As she strolled out on deck, a group of crewmembers just finished their weapons-work. She circled around them and leaned on the rail near the gangplank. Different guards stood on the dock this morning. One nodded to her and sent one of the others running toward the town. With a sigh, she retreated to her cabin to find something fancier to wear. She expected they would soon meet with someone in charge. *Have to find something not too warm. Already hot and not yet even midmorning.*

When she returned on deck, she spotted Saevalde and Mikolus to one side talking with Gya and her usual three guards.

"Hello, the *Deliberia*," came a woman's voice from the dock.

Alorsha crossed the deck to the top of the gangplank. "Good morning," she called out.

The woman did the heel-click and head nod that seemed to be a salute of sorts with these people. She wore the same sort of attire as the guards along the dock, although fancier.

"Prince Falshinku requests the pleasure of a meeting with you," the woman said. "Please accompany me."

"One moment." Alorsha turned away from the rail.

"At least they're still being polite. Mostly," Mikolus murmured.

"Don't be trusting them," Saevalde said. "They did attack us."

"We should be able to assure them we're not whatever they seem to think. Then we can replenish our supplies and be on our way," Alorsha said.

"Should you be one of the ones to go?" Gya said.

Alorsha gave a firm nod. "From what we've seen, they seem very formal. I doubt this prince would meet with anyone else from the ship. You need to stay aboard, Gya." She held up a hand to forestall his objections. "After me, you've got the most magic and knowledge of its use of anyone on the *Deliberia*. If needed, we'll be able to coordinate the magic. Continue pulling this world's magic into the *Deliberia*, as much as you can. Mikolus, you also stay aboard. I trust the ship's safety to you and Saevalde while we're gone." Alorsha waved a hand at her three guards.

Both Gya and Saevalde frowned at her words but nodded.

"You're not taking any of your concoctions?" Mikolus said and tapped the shoulder from which she usually hung her cross-body bag.

Alorsha shook her head. "My supplies are limited, and I can't think of any of the ones I've already made that will likely help, even if this meeting goes badly." She glanced at the town. "Looks like a lot of the place is made of wood. I'll find other plants. I can manage something if I have to."

Mikolus frowned too. "Watch yourself."

Alorsha nodded. "You, also. I don't trust this veneer of courtesy."

Mikolus nodded agreement as Alorsha and her three guards headed to the gangplank.

The uniformed woman scrutinized Alorsha and her companions while they descended to the dock and seemed to note all the weapons they carried. She made no mention of them, however.

Again the salute, directed at Alorsha. "I am Mongom, Lady Tavano. It's my pleasure to escort you to the prince's inn."

"My thanks," Alorsha said.

Mongom led them along the dock. As they walked, several guards fell in behind them, which increased their numbers to exceed that of Alorsha's small group. One of them took a place at Mongom's side, close, like he guarded her, too. Mongom led them into the city at a brisk pace, and uphill, until they were well above the harbor. Alorsha paused to look back.

"The view from the upper city is spectacular," Mongom said at her shoulder. "Prince Falshinku prefers the inns on this level for that reason, among others."

"We're meeting with a prince in an inn?" Parl muttered.

"The prince owns most of the buildings on this level of his city," Mongom said. "And he prefers to conduct business away from his private residence."

The man at Mongon's side nudged her and tilted his head away from the view. She frowned, and turned her head so that man could not see the expression. "We must continue. Please...." Mongon gestured back to the city and upward. "The inn is near the top of this level."

Alorsha nodded and again followed her.

Their destination became obvious as they drew closer: a large building with two guards who flanked its door. While they approached, Alorsha counted seven of the uniformed people scattered about the street plus the two at the door. Mongom stepped between them with a nod and led everyone into the common room, which held only the innkeeper, wiping some tables, before they crowded in. Mongom exchanged nods with the innkeeper.

The man who clung to Mongom's side nudged her again and she gave him a curt nod. She pulled her flintlock from her belt and laid it on a table, followed by her sword-belt.

"Please leave your weapons here." She gestured to the table as the other guards also disarmed themselves. "Only a select few are allowed to go armed in the prince's presence."

Alorsha exchanged uncertain looks with her fellows and shrugged. *Outnumbered. And there are those cannons on the ships to consider. Nothing to do at this point but see this through.*

She placed her weapons on the table with the others. *Good thing I didn't bring any of my concoctions. Wouldn't do to leave them sitting out in a strange place.*

The others from the *Deliberia* followed her lead and placed their weapons with hers, Shyvoan the most reluctant and eyeing the guards all the while.

"Thank you," Mongom said. "Davaj and Hathu here will guard them during the meeting."

With the man still at her side, she led them up two flights of stairs to a short hallway, again guarded by two in that uniform. She knocked on the door between them, opened it, and gestured Alorsha and her companions within.

Inside, they found a mostly empty room, with a rectangular table placed in the center, and chairs around it, enough for all of them. At one end of the table sat a youngish man, perhaps a few years older than Alorsha's score and ten, with brown hair and eyes, and golden-brown skin much like Alorsha's.

Next to him sat an older woman, with gray-blond hair, light skin, and pale blue eyes. Behind her stood a girl of perhaps ten years, with skin and eyes that matched the woman's, and hair that showed what the woman's likely looked like in her youth.

The man rose and bowed to Alorsha.

"My Lady, thank you for coming to meet with me. I am Prince Falshinku, and this is Seer Bilguon. Please, be seated. Mongom, bring the refreshments."

Alorsha returned his bow and made her own

introductions as she took a seat at the opposite end of the table, with her companions seated at either side, Kluir on her left, and Shyvoan and Parl on her right. That arrangement left two seats open between her people and the prince on the one side and one seat empty next to Seer Bilguon on the other.

Under the unwavering gaze of her own guard, Mongom placed cups before everyone and two jars full of a pale golden liquid in the center of the table. She and her shadow then left the room, closing the door behind them.

The girl took one of the jars and filled the prince's cup. With a slight smile for Alorsha, she took the other jar and filled Seer Bilguon's cup. She placed the cup in the seer's hand, wrapped the woman's fingers around it, and let go after the woman nodded to her. It was then that Alorsha saw that the seer was blind.

Prince Falshinku waved a hand at the jars. "Please, help yourselves."

Once everyone had some of the drink, he lifted his cup, tapped the bottom once on the table, and raised it in front of him. The seer did likewise. The *Deliberia* crewmembers followed their example, after they exchanged quick, confused looks.

The prince smiled. "It's our custom to raise a toast to new beginnings. So, here's to meeting new peoples and coming to profitable agreements between us." He drank from his cup.

"New beginnings," the seer said, and also drank.

Alorsha and the others sipped their drinks, then looked to their host to see what came next.

The prince set his cup in front of him and folded his hands on the table. "I cannot express how pleased I am that my people came upon your ship and brought you here. You're most welcome, and we have much to discuss. I believe you'll find your stay here can be very rewarding."

"What is it that we have to discuss?" Alorsha said.

"Why, your commission here, of course, Lady Tavano.

We're prepared to compensate you munificently for your talents."

Alorsha sat back, nonplussed. *What's this?* "Perhaps you should share with me what you think it is I can do for you?"

Prince Falshinku smiled at her and sipped his drink. "Of course, Lady Alorsha. May I call you that?"

Alorsha shrugged.

"We've seen that your magic works much differently from our magic here." He nodded at Seer Bilguon. "Seers in our lands are the people here who use magic. They're not extraordinarily common but are particularly valued subjects. They provide us with information, knowledge of things we might not be able to learn otherwise."

"I have Seen you," Seer Bilguon said and turned toward Alorsha. "I've Seen that your magics, such as you place in your ship, might help us prevail against our adversaries."

Alorsha hid behind a sip of her drink. *This doesn't sound good.* "Such things have taken me many years to accomplish. They're draining and somewhat unreliable. I've not come here to stay."

"What's a few years? We who are young have plenty of time," Prince Falshinku said with a chuckle. "And, as I mentioned before, you'll be abundantly compensated for your time and efforts."

"I cannot stay that long," Alorsha said. "I seek two of our countrymen. I follow them and cannot let them get years away from me."

Prince Falshinku studied her, his expression thoughtful. "Why do you seek these men? Are you agents of your liege that you hunt them?"

"What does it matter why we seek them? We cannot delay so long. We just ask to continue on our way."

"To our enemies? Is that where you'd go?"

"Not at all. We are not involved in your conflicts and wish to keep it that way. We only wish to continue our journey."

With a quick look to Alorsha, Kluir spoke up. "Your highness, would you please tell us exactly what it is you expect we can do for you? What is it you want from us?"

Prince Falshinku gave Kluir a pensive look. "Seer Bilguon has seen your lady take stored magics and impress them into the very structure of your ship to strengthen it and, from the results we've seen, offer it some defense. The cannonballs my people shot at you were perfectly aimed to hit your deck, yet none of them did."

Alorsha shared a look with her companions. *Interesting.*

The prince continued. "She'll work such magics on the ships we're building now. And if such a thing is possible for personal armor, that, too. Also, any magics she can mesh with our weaponry. We're a wealthy land and can offer much in exchange for this service, including the gratitude of our people and my father, the King."

"I'm no shipwright, but I do have some idea of how long it takes to build ships," Alorsha said. "I can't stay here that long. We must be on our way."

Prince Falshinku stood. "And I cannot allow such an action, which could take you to our enemies. Mongom!"

Alorsha and her companions stood also, her companions taking defensive stances around her, as he shouted for Mongom again.

The door swung open and Mongom stumbled inside like she had been pushed, her expression a scowl that vanished as she regained her balance. Several of the uniformed people poured into the room behind her and surrounded the *Deliberia* crewmembers, fists clenched and expressions grim.

Alorsha's companions looked to her, and she stopped them with a gesture. *Too many to fight.*

The prince smiled at Alorsha. "You'll partake of my hospitality here while you reconsider my offer. It would be a true shame for me to have to take more extreme measures to ensure your compliance. I'm sure you'll soon see wisdom. Mongom, show them to their rooms."

As the prince's people herded her and her companions out the door, Alorsha turned back. "Your highness, don't keep me from my journey."

He waved a dismissive hand, and Mongom closed the door.

CHAPTER 23

The guards escorted the *Deliberia* crewmembers to two rooms on that same floor and locked Kluir and Parl in one room, Alorsha and Shyvoan in the room next to it.

After the door closed behind them, Shyvoan prowled around the room, checking the door, walls, corners, and floor, opening the shutters of the window in the wall opposite the door to peer out. She looked behind and under the large bed that sat to one side of the window along the adjacent wall.

While she was so occupied, Alorsha checked the drawers in a small table that sat between the head of the bed and the window and the matching table that sat against the wall next to the door. Both drawers held nothing.

She brushed a hand against the wooden wall. *Very faint magic there.* The wood of the building must have been cut many years ago. Even plants cut long before usually still held a small spark of magic - something she could probably work with.

Alorsha sank into one of two plush chairs that

occupied the half of the room opposite the bed. A small round table sat between them and the wall behind them held pegs, at Alorsha's eye-level. Alorsha leaned back and glared at the door through slit eyes, idly noting the two chamber pots that sat in the corner, behind the door when it opened.

Did this seer truly *see my magics somehow?* Alorsha had only gathered magics of the world. While she *had* used that to allow them to talk with these people, she had not done anything obvious.

"I don't see an immediate way out of here," Shyvoan said. "There are even guards below our window. We'll need to come up with something."

Alorsha nodded absently, pondering the conversation with the prince. Someone who watched her while she gathered magic for conversing should not have been able to discover that she used magic. *Well, I did* call the pieces of the ship from the water before that. But that's not what the seer talked about. Quite the coincidence that this seer saw me at just the right time, whenever that was, to figure out that I'm a mage.

"Oh."

"What is it?" Shyvoan said in a low voice, with a questioning look.

Alorsha motioned her close. "What they told us this seer saw…. That happened back in my world."

"Can magics see into other worlds?"

"I wouldn't have thought so. The only way we've ever seen into another world is through one of those passages when it was open. I'm sure I'd have noticed one of those back when we sailed the *Deliberia* in the seas of my home."

"Devrand?"

Alorsha nodded. "I suspect he's somehow put the notion in the seer's head or shared that information with her, doubtless planning just such a delay for us."

"That Mongom didn't seem too happy with things," Shyvoan murmured.

"I noticed that, too." Alorsha kept her voice as soft.

"Maybe something there to help us."

Shyvoan crossed to the door and leaned against it to hold it closed against any surprise guests.

"Check the direction?" she whispered.

Alorsha nodded and pulled out her pendant. A moment's concentration on the wayfinding magic and the pendant swung straight out and pointed inland to her right. She replaced the pendant around her neck and tucked it in her neckline as she returned to the chair.

Shyvoan pulled the second chair closer to Alorsha's and settled into it. "The city doesn't lie on a straight line between the *Deliberia* and Devrand," she said.

"He still could've come through here. With no idea how far away he is, he could've been here just a day or two ago."

Shyvoan nodded.

Alorsha gazed toward the open window. "I suppose I *can* help this prince with some simpler, quicker magics. The *Deliberia* needs resupplying, and now repairs, too. So, we'd have to stop somewhere anyway, why not here? But not for the whole time it'll take to build his ships."

"And we need to figure out a way to get away if he turns as stubborn about the whole thing as seems likely."

Alorsha nodded. "Yes, that too."

"Better get a start on that, then," Shyvoan said. She left her seat and crawled across the bed to the corner of the common wall with Kluir's and Parl's room that was away from the door.

"What do you have in mind?" Alorsha said.

Shyvoan grinned. "You'll see."

She sat on the edge of the bed and tapped on the wall next to her. Alorsha could tell the tapping held some sort of rhythm, but it changed periodically.

When Shyvoan paused, Alorsha heard faint taps from the other side of the wall.

"A code Mikolus had us learn, just in case," Shyvoan explained. "I told them to have someone watch their door.

And they ask, 'What now?'"

"I should learn that code, too. Tell them that I'm working on the 'what now'. They need to see what they can come up with, too. And tell them I'll be linking the magic of the wall between us, and the rooms' floors and ceilings. I don't yet know to what end, but maybe we can use it."

Alorsha waited while Shyvoan conveyed all that and told her that she had told the men that they would talk more later.

Alorsha then traded places with Shyvoan and placed both hands on the wall. She reached into the wood, seeking the spark of magic within.

The faint magic had lost any inclination it might have had toward a particular function and only retained a kind of connection magic. Alorsha drew on it and strengthened it, linking neighboring planks to each other, much as she had done years ago for the *Deliberia*.

Fatigue and a headache stopped her after she connected the magics throughout the wood wall between the two rooms and the floors of both rooms.

She plopped down in one of the chairs and wiped sweat from her eyes. *Rest, then see about doing the same for the ceilings and maybe more walls.*

When Shyvoan gave her a concerned look, she just smiled and leaned back and closed her eyes.

At a knock on their door, Alorsha glared that direction while Shyvoan moved to the door and spoke with someone outside when it opened. She leaned back to look at Alorsha over a shoulder. "The prince wishes to speak with you again."

Alorsha sighed and nodded as she straightened her hair and wiped her hands on her trousers to dry them. *Hope the recent magical exertion won't be noticeable.* "He can come in."

Shyvoan gave her an odd grin and opened the door wider to reveal only Mongom standing outside, along with two guards flanking the door. "He wants you to return to that meeting room," Shyvoan told Alorsha.

Alorsha matched Shyvoan's grin. *Time to enter into the game in earnest.* Fortunately, Saevalde had instructed her in such matters some time ago, should she ever need it.

"His highness wishes to see me, not I him," Alorsha said. "We're not his subjects. If he wishes to talk, he's welcome to visit me here at a decent hour."

Shyvoan stepped back behind the door, where the prince's people could not see her as she stifled laughter.

After a surprised look for Alorsha, Mongom gave her that salute of theirs. *Is that a hint of admiration in the woman's expression?*

"Also, the walk from our ship was vigorous," Alorsha said. "We're not accustomed to such warmth as your weather here. Please bring us and our companions next door adequate water with which to refresh ourselves."

Mongom nodded to one of the guards and he ran off. "I'll convey your message to his highness," she said.

As she closed the door, Alorsha caught the hint of a grin on Mongom's face before she turned away.

Minutes later, someone tapped at the door. It opened as Shyvoan reached it and a boy stepped into the room, clutching a pitcher in each hand, and balancing a large bowl and two mugs in his arms. Shyvoan took the pitchers while the boy set the bowl and mugs on the table beside the door. He took cloths that he carried draped over one shoulder and placed them next to the bowl, then ran back out the door. A guard closed it behind him.

Shyvoan set one pitcher next to the bowl. "Warmed water. Slightly."

She set the other pitcher on the small table by the bed and moved the mugs there, too. "And some cool water."

Alorsha and Shyvoan took turns with the cloths and warmed water to wipe their faces and hands. They drank some of the cool water, a welcome refreshment. Shyvoan then settled in a chair, leaned back, and closed her eyes.

Alorsha fluffed her hair away from her neck and

headed to the window, wishing she had brought a tie for her hair. She leaned on the windowsill to give an impression of idly watching the goings-on in the town below. She slipped her pendant from its hiding place and wrapped one hand around it.

With half-closed eyes, she reached into the magic in the stone, and through it, to its connection to the magic in the *Deliberia*.

The world's magic tried to intrude, and she blocked it away the best she could. Best to avoid working with any magics the seers might also use.

She brushed the *Deliberia*'s magics and wove her way into them. The magics felt clear from any influences from anyone or anything other than herself and Gya.

She touched on that defense that had kept the cannonballs from the *Deliberia*'s decks. While not something she had specifically arranged, it was well done. Maybe a result of her general defensive weavings.

She nudged more magics to that, to strengthen it, and looked through the magics to see what she might learn of what was happening on her ship.

The rest of the crew were all still there, and both Saevalde and Mikolus hurried about, keeping close to the prince's people who swarmed the ship. It seemed the prince's people continued to search, but for what, she could not tell. They had taken nothing from the ship. She sensed that Gya had added more of the world's magic to the ship.

"Alorsha?"

Alorsha came back to herself to a touch on her arm.

"They brought us some food." Shyvoan indicated a platter that now sat where the water bowl had.

"How long was I…?"

"More than an hour. Anything useful?" Shyvoan began to eat.

Alorsha joined her. "Not yet. They're searching the ship again, it looks like."

"Wonder what for."

Alorsha shrugged and continued with her meal.

A couple of hours after the food had arrived, the boy returned with two new pitchers, one of fresh, cool water and the other with that same drink from that morning.

After the boy left, Alorsha sat on the bed and leaned against the wall shared with the room Kluir and Parl occupied. Refreshed from the food, she reached out to the magics in the ceilings of the two rooms and worked on linking them.

It took her longer than before. *Probably should have rested more.*

No one disturbed them the rest of that dull afternoon and they filled some time with word games with each other. From time to time, Shyvoan checked with the men next door through the tapped code. They were as listless as Alorsha and Shyvoan and had not thought of a way out yet.

Late afternoon, Alorsha and Shyvoan slumped at the table and sipped some of the pale golden drink while the silence stretched.

"Your sword," Alorsha said eventually.

Shyvoan winced but gestured for Alorsha to continue.

"Don't mistake me," Alorsha said. "I'm glad you didn't bring it with you this time. But isn't it special? Worth carrying? That Ezei called it 'gift-scales', didn't he?"

Shyvoan nodded and smiled at the mention of the steadfast hob back in the world she had come from.

"Yah, the blade was infused with dragon scales, somehow. And passed down in my family. My fellow warriors believed it helped bring us good luck." She clenched her hands and turned her gaze to the floor. "But Devrand murdered that poor dragon with it. How can I carry it after that? With that taint on it?"

"Is it tainted? I've felt nothing like that from it, no magical taint. *You* didn't use it against the dragon. And Ezei returned it to you. Would he have done that if it carried a taint from someone else's actions with it?"

Shyvoan shrugged. "Perhaps not. Do you feel any magic from it at all?"

Alorsha frowned. "Not in the way I normally sense magic. It's not a plant so I don't feel much of anything from it. Except for a sense of... value? Worth? I'm not sure how to describe it. Something special, anyway. And it belongs with you. Don't let Devrand take that from you. He's taken so much already."

Shyvoan glanced at her and away again. "Perhaps." She finished her drink and moved back to the wall shared with the other room. "I'll think on what you've said."

Alorsha nodded and also finished her drink. "Time to bother the men again? See if they're awake?"

Shyvoan grinned and tapped again on the wall. After she exchanged various sequences of taps with those on the other side, she looked over her shoulder at Alorsha. "Parl wants to know if you can make a hole in the wall. Like when you and Gya made those new hatches on the *Deliberia*."

Alorsha considered that. "The wood might be too removed from when it lived to respond well to such a working. But it's worth a try."

Shyvoan passed along what Alorsha had said and listened to the response.

"He says he understands, and hopes it'll work."

So, Alorsha set to work at a spot near the floor and behind the foot of the bed. Her task progressed slowly as her previous magic work that day had drained her enough that she had trouble holding her concentration. She created a crack no wider than the width of her finger before she needed to stop and rest again from working the magic.

The boy brought an evening meal not long before sundown, along with a lantern that contained enough oil in it for a couple of hours. He returned a couple of hours later to clear away the remains of the meal, take the lantern, and leave two pitchers of the cool water and new mugs for them.

After a few whispered words through the crack in the wall, augmented by a tapped exchange—nothing new for the men either—Alorsha and Shyvoan settled in for the night. Shyvoan stayed awake first to watch while Alorsha slept, and they switched places after a few hours.

CHAPTER 24

Just after dawn the next morning, the boy returned with the bowl, cloths, and pitchers of water. Mongom accompanied him, with a bundle of something in her arms. Alorsha self-consciously tried to smooth her tangled hair in the face of Mongom's precise appearance so early. Shyvoan hauled herself from the bed, yawning, and moved to a chair.

A younger boy ran in behind Mongom, with two new chamber pots. He exchanged them for the old ones and ran off. Alorsha felt sorry for him, having such a duty. After the other boy set out all he carried, as before, he ran back out the door.

While Alorsha's attention had been on the boys' actions, Mongom had flipped the covers up on the bed and spread out what she had carried, a variety of clothing in muted colors. She set two combs on the table by the bed.

"These are for you to keep," she said. "Courtesy of his highness. He decided that you must want a change today. I'll return with his highness shortly."

Alorsha peered at the other woman. *Is that contempt I hear when she says 'his highness'?* Mongom met her gaze with a bland expression. She gave Alorsha her salute and left, closing the door behind her.

Shyvoan moved to the crack in the wall to the neighboring room. "Sounds like they're getting the same," she reported.

Alorsha looked over the clothes Mongom had brought. "At least they're maintaining the politeness and consideration façade for us. Pick out what you like."

The two women chose similar pieces, long tunics with no sleeves, which reached their ankles and had slits that ran almost to their waists, and light trousers. Alorsha was pleased to find deep pockets in the sides of the trousers. After she washed, she slipped into the pleasantly soft new clothes. The clothes also carried a light scent of some mild perfume. She bundled the previous day's clothes into a ball at the end of the bed. Shyvoan placed her bundle of clothes next to it.

They gathered the last few pieces that lay on the bed, four additional tunic-and-trouser sets, with tunics of varying lengths, along with two long coats similar in style to the uniforms the prince's people wore. The pegs on the opposite wall served to hang the clothes.

After a quick bit of wayfinding magic to check Devrand's direction—still inland to her right—Alorsha looked out the window. She scanned the *Deliberia*. All looked well there. Still a guard in the street below. They exchanged nods.

With only a light knock for warning, their door opened, and Prince Falshinku swept inside. Mongom followed him, carrying a platter of food. She in turn was followed by an armed guard. The older boy darted in behind them with two pitchers, which Shyvoan took. The boy grabbed the used wash things and ran back out the door. The guard positioned himself in a corner of the room, from which he watched everyone.

As Alorsha settled into one of the chairs, Mongom placed the tray of food on the table between the two chairs, first sliding plates out from where she had carried them beneath. The boy returned with new cups and took the used ones away.

During all this activity, the prince peered around the room, then grabbed the other chair and set it before Alorsha's, too close. Alorsha recognized this tactic and gave him a small smile as he sat, his knees a finger's width from touching hers. She waited and watched him.

Mongom handed out plates of food. Alorsha tasted her meal and continued to watch the prince but said nothing. He fidgeted under her gaze and cleared his throat.

"I'm aware that it's still early this morning," he said. "But we should speak again."

Alorsha widened her smile. "I do have some questions for you. Or perhaps they're better asked of your seer."

The prince took a bite of his food and washed it down with a gulp from the cup Mongom handed him. "I'll try to satisfy your curiosity," he said.

Alorsha nodded. "I find your seer's magic interesting. It's unlike any I've encountered before. How does it work?"

"Ah, no one is quite certain," Prince Falshinku said. "From what I've learned of such things, the seers can see events that are happening as if they stood right there."

"So, they see things as they happen right then? Just maybe somewhere far away?"

He nodded. "Yes. I've also heard that some catch glimpses of the future. Although, they say, those visions are murkier, unclear. Sometimes they even see two different, contradictory visions."

"Intriguing." Alorsha looked away from him to give him the impression that she was lost in thought. Then she looked back. "Do they also see things that have happened in the past? Is it possible to see events from years ago?"

The prince shook his head. "I've not heard of any seer

with such an ability."

"Ah. So, they can choose somewhere to look, and they can see whatever's going on there?"

He shook his head again. "They don't choose what or where, although Seer Bilguon has told me she can hold a desire for certain sights while she uses the magic and sometimes it cooperates and shows her things related to what she hopes to see. But predominantly, the visions just come to them. Whenever."

"Oh. Interesting." Alorsha ate some more of her food and kept her gaze on Prince Falshinku.

He leaned close and placed a hand on her knee. "But if there's something you need to know, something current or even future, as part of your compensation for using your magics for me, I can certainly have my seer see what she can learn for you."

She looked at his hand a brief time, then up at him with a bland expression. After a moment, he removed his hand.

"Haven't I told you that I can't stay long, can't do as you want?" she said.

"I'm certain that I can change your mind." he said, his expression earnest.

She smiled to herself at his tactics but kept her thoughts from showing in her expression. "My thanks for the nice clothes."

He looked startled at her change of topic, but quickly recovered. "I was certain you'd like them. I can provide many more. Fancier even, if that's your pleasure. Or jewelry. I noticed your rings. They're charming, but I can give you superior ones, if that's what you'd like."

Alorsha tilted her head, her expression pensive. "My ship is in need of fresh provisions."

Prince Falshinku sat back with a frown. "I see. I imagine I might see to that. But those won't be needed for a long time. Your people can stay here in town, too."

"Ah." She let the silence stretch out while she ate and drank.

Prince Falshinku ate another few bites but seemed to be having trouble concentrating on his meal. He kept giving her questioning looks.

"I estimate that it will need a couple of days or so to provision the *Deliberia*," Alorsha said. "In that time, as compensation, I can see about magics that might be of use to you. But I cannot do that from a room in an inn, no matter how nice it is."

She gave him a steady look.

"I see. I'll consider necessary arrangements." He rose. "Please enjoy the rest of your meal." He handed his plate to Mongom, and they left, the guard following.

Alorsha and Shyvoan finished their meals, and Alorsha tapped on their door. When it opened, she greeted the two guards outside with a smile. "Do you suppose we could have some flowers? Like in a vase or jar? This room is woefully drab. I wouldn't imagine that Prince Falshinku would object."

The two guards exchanged looks.

"We can pass along your request, Lady," said one and sent his fellow off down the hall.

"My thanks."

The guard closed and locked the door again.

"Flowers, is it?" Shyvoan grinned at Alorsha.

Alorsha shrugged. "Might as well see if I can figure out something while we're stuck here." She kept her voice low. "As I don't yet see any way out."

Perhaps an hour later, the younger boy knocked on their door and entered with two pitchers that held a variety of flowers. "Them's wildflowers from my mum's garden," he said and set the pitchers on the table.

"Please tell your mum we thank her and appreciate them," Alorsha said. "They're lovely and really brighten the room."

The boy grinned at her. "Yes, Lady, I'll tell her. She'll be that happy to hear it." He grabbed the plates and platter from breakfast and ran off.

Alorsha spent the morning learning the magics in the different flowers. None of the flowers by themselves offered anything particularly encouraging, but a combination of some of them with others' leaves showed some promise. Shyvoan alternated watching her with dozing and chatting with the men through the crack.

After they finished the midday meal they had been provided, Alorsha set Shyvoan to pulling certain petals and leaves from the flowers. "You can pull the wilted ones. That way it won't be obvious. We just want to keep the flowers looking their best, after all."

Shyvoan smiled at that. "Of course. I'll just do that for all of them."

While Shyvoan busied herself with that project, Alorsha took specific petals and leaves to the table by the bed, along with one of the new, clean mugs that had come with their meal. She poured water in the mug and dropped in the petals and leaves.

"Works better with heat," she muttered, and sighed at herself.

She took the mug to the other side of the window where a sliver of sunshine shone into the room. She propped the mug on the sill in the sun and leaned there herself. *Just a bored lady watching the town with my drink at hand.*

She reached out to the warmth from the sun and concentrated it into the water until the cup grew hot. Then she took it back to the table and sat.

Shyvoan joined her. "Do you want these other leaves and petals?"

Alorsha glanced at the small pile on the table by the door. "Please save out several of each kind but toss the most wilted into the chamber pots to support our story, should anyone even ask or notice."

Shyvoan nodded and returned to her task.

Alorsha sat on the edge of the bed and rested her fingertips along the edge of the mug. Now how to crush the plants in the water without her usual tools? She could try to do it with her magic, but her talents did not lie in that area. *Not sure I can even manage it. So, what to use? Shoe? Well, maybe on a plate, but too large for the mug. My ring? No, best to avoid mixing in other magics for now....*

Oh, of course.

She pulled off the pendant from the Varoian king. *The metal disk'll work well enough.* She used it to crush the plants in the hot water, while she reached within them to draw out their magics and blend them. Soon she had the plants and water mixed to the consistency she wanted. She set aside the pendant to clean later, poured more water into the mug, and swirled the contents to blend everything.

"I'll just clean that." Shyvoan took the pendant and the pitcher of water to the corner, rinsed the pendant, and let the residue of Alorsha's workings fall into one of the chamber pots. She returned the pendant to Alorsha who put it back on.

"So, what have we got there?" Shyvoan kept her voice low as she indicated the mug.

Alorsha smiled. "Something useful, I hope. Help me test it?"

"What does it do?"

"I need to keep that from you, at first, please, so I can make sure it actually works. But it won't harm you."

"What do *I* do, then?"

"Lift the mug and inhale the aroma. Don't drink."

Shyvoan did as Alorsha instructed, with a questioning look.

"Now show me the steps to that country dance the crew enjoyed a couple of weeks ago," Alorsha said.

"What?"

"Dance," Alorsha said.

"I'd rather not." Shyvoan set the mug aside. "I hate that dance."

"Hm," Alorsha said.

"What?"

"Let's try one other thing."

Shyvoan nodded, with a perplexed expression.

"You don't sing either, do you?" Alorsha said as she dipped her fingertips in the liquid in the mug.

Shyvoan laughed. "You've heard me. Croaking frogs with no sense of music sound better."

Alorsha smiled and swiped her damp fingers across Shyvoan's bare arm. "Sing softly," she said.

Shyvoan stared at her. "Are you sure you want that?"

Alorsha frowned. "You don't feel that you must sing?"

Shyvoan shook her head. "I'm supposed to?"

"It's supposed to make the other person do as they're told." Alorsha stared into the mug. "One more test. You try on me."

"Is that a good idea?"

"I need to know. Maybe it works if someone without magic uses it."

"Oh, of course."

Shyvoan tentatively dipped the tips of her fingers in the liquid, touched Alorsha's arm, and told her to jump up and down.

After a couple of minutes, Alorsha shrugged. "Well, so much for that one. I'll see if I can come up with something that *does* work."

Their captors left them to themselves for the most part, aside from the expected meal and water deliveries. Alorsha attempted a few more concoctions, then spent some time widening the crack in the wall. The magic was faint enough though, that she only managed to double the crack's width before she developed a headache that compelled her to stop for a time.

Shyvoan prowled around the room again, trying to figure a way out and then debated through the crack with Kluir and Parl about whether they could just fight their way out somehow, not knowing what other guards were in the building.

The evening meal arrived a short time before sundown, this time with a lantern full of oil. Alorsha and Shyvoan had just finished eating when someone knocked at the door, and it opened, revealing Seer Bilguon and the girl.

Alorsha offered them some food and drink, both of which they declined. But the seer did sit in the chair Alorsha offered next, and the girl stood nearby.

The seer turned toward Alorsha, her expression mild.

Alorsha gave her a slight smile and shared it with the girl when she remembered the seer's blindness. "Did Prince Falshinku send you to convince me of the necessity to delay my pursuits to accommodate his?" she asked.

Seer Bilguon smiled at that. "No, indeed. I bring you a message from the man you seek. He bids you take the prince's generous offer and forget Jarthan."

Alorsha and Shyvoan exchanged glances.

"How do you know this? How do you know the man I seek?" Alorsha said.

"I had the misfortune to cross his path just a few days ago. North of this city. He... did something... with his magics. Took my Sight from me. He told me what to tell Prince Falshinku. What to say about you. He promised to return my magic if I did as he said. Since then, he has talked to me, from a distance, wherever he is. Earlier today, he told me the message I've just given you."

Alorsha considered this. "Do you know anything of his plans? Or where he is now?"

"He's looking for something, but I don't know what," Seer Bilguon said. "As to where he is, only in a general sense. He's a few days' ride to the northeast. But he's still on the move."

"Did you see... did he have another man with him?" Alorsha said.

Seer Bilguon shook her head with a sorrowful expression. "He did not have anyone with him when I encountered him."

Alorsha shared a worried look with Shyvoan and received a reassuring pat on the arm.

"Is this all you have for us, then?" Shyvoan said.

Seer Bilguon nodded. "Little enough, I'm aware. One other thing… the prince is used to getting his way. And he's trying to win favor over his siblings with their father. Watch out for him. He's been pleasant so far, but that's unlikely to continue. And might change at any time."

She made her way to the door. In passing, she brushed the flowers in one pitcher with the back of her hand. She paused and fingered the petals first of a red flower then a blue one. "I remember these. So delightful. These two feature in many old tales and legends. They're said to have magic for the one who knows how to find it." She winked. "But you know how legends are. The petals are edible, too."

As she and the girl left, the boy returned. He cleared away the meal and brought them fresh water and mugs.

"Interesting," Shyvoan said, after the boy had gone. "Do you think Devrand can use these seeing magics of hers?"

"Possibly. He does seem able to use the magics he takes. At least somewhat. I hope Jarthan's all right." Alorsha pulled out the pendant with her mage-ring's erythros stone and reached to the magic within the stone to the link to Jarthan. She smiled when she touched it. She could not tell his condition through it, but he was alive, and in this world. Maybe she should alter the magic in her ring-pendant to concentrate more on the link to Jarthan rather than to Devrand. If she could. *Something to do soon as I have time. If I find Jarthan, and Devrand's nowhere around, that would be wonderful.*

She met Shyvoan's concerned look. "He's alive and in this world."

Shyvoan smiled. "Good news, then."

Alorsha nodded. "Now if this prince will just visit again. Hold on."

She tapped on the door and when the guard outside unlocked and opened it, she asked, "Would it be possible to speak with the prince this evening?"

Both guards who flanked the door shook their heads.

"His highness is occupied of an evening," the one to the left of the door said.

"He'll probably speak with you again tomorrow morning," the other added and closed the door.

"Sounds like we've got the evening to ourselves," Alorsha told Shyvoan. She grabbed the pitcher with the flowers that the seer had pointed out and moved it to the table by the bed. She positioned the lit lamp nearby.

"Can I help at all?" Shyvoan said.

Alorsha smiled. "I'm sorry, this all must be very dull for you. Certainly you can help, and not just to test things."

Shyvoan grinned. "I'd be grateful for that."

With Shyvoan's help, Alorsha retrieved the rather wilted petals of those two flowers from the drawer and crushed them, working to draw out their magics. As she squashed the petals together, she sensed a change in the magic, a faint indication that when combined, their magics became something different. Once they had crushed the petals into a gooey mush on the table, Alorsha scraped them into the mug that Shyvoan brought her. She added some water and swirled it around.

"Well... will you look at this," she held the mug out for Shyvoan to see.

"Uh, I'm not sure what I'm supposed to see."

Alorsha grinned. She pointed to the purplish remnants of the petals on the table then to the liquid in the mug, which looked like nothing other than plain water.

"Oh."

Alorsha sniffed at the mug. "Smells a little like vanilla." She tilted it to take a sip.

"Should you do that?" Shyvoan said in alarm. "Can we trust her?"

Alorsha lowered the mug without having sipped yet. "I can feel poisonous plants, so I've already checked them. It's fine." She grinned at Shyvoan again. "And no, I'm not blindly trusting her. Still, this needs testing."

"Isn't that my job?" Shyvoan gave Alorsha a mock indignant look.

Alorsha held out the mug. "Then here. But take the smallest sip to begin with."

Shyvoan took the mug and sniffed it as Alorsha had. "It *is* vanilla. Hope it tastes as good." She took a small sip. "Gah! No, it doesn't taste good at all."

After they sat in silence for a few minutes, Shyvoan said, "Does that lantern seem too bright?"

Alorsha partially shuttered the lantern. "Better?"

When Shyvoan nodded, Alorsha said, "Now look at me."

"What? What is it?"

"I wish we had a mirror in here. Your pupils are huge. Let's try something."

Alorsha shuttered the lantern to block out all its light.

Shyvoan's mouth dropped open. "Amazing. I can see just as if it was day. Am I speaking too loud? And what's that smell? What *is* this magic?"

Alorsha grinned. "The best I can describe them, the red flower's magic is enrichment, and the blue's is receptivity."

Shyvoan nodded and stepped to the window to look out. "I believe I can smell the food the guard at the end of the street is eating. Incredible. I can definitely see some use for this. Although it's not going to free us from these rooms."

She sat again. "That's with just one sip. Should I try another?"

"In a bit," Alorsha said. "Best not to push it. How do you feel?"

Shyvoan shrugged. "Fine. My mouth tastes something awful, but otherwise I feel normal. If you don't count the seeing, hearing, and smelling."

"Good. Let's wait, still, and see what this does."

Alorsha nudged open one shutter on the lantern to give her just enough light to work by. Shyvoan leaned back in her chair, and eventually dozed, while Alorsha tried other mixes of leaves and flowers. One combination would make a wonderful perfume, with nothing else special about it. The rest just made gloppy messes that Alorsha dumped into the chamber pots.

While she worked, Alorsha kept an eye on Shyvoan, and woke her after about half an hour.

"How do you feel?" she asked.

Shyvoan shrugged. "Still fine. I think the effects have begun to fade, though."

Alorsha nodded. "Your pupils are certainly smaller. Would you be willing to try two more sips?"

Shyvoan nodded. After the second sip, her pupils expanded until they engulfed the color in her eyes. She squinted against the little light from the mostly shuttered lantern.

"Shyvoan?" Alorsha whispered.

Shyvoan winced. "Ah, even that's too loud," she whispered back. "And the smells. I think I can smell everything from the entire city. It's too much." She scurried to the bed, buried herself in the bedding, and covered her head.

Alorsha patted her shoulder. "My thanks, and I'm sorry about that."

"At least we learned it only needs one sip," came Shyvoan's muffled voice from beneath the bedding.

Alorsha laughed softly. "Or significant dilution, yes. Rest now under there and I'll check on you soon. But let me know right away if you feel any ill effects."

"I will."

Alorsha returned to her tests with the leaves and petals. The concoction Shyvoan had tested might help them avoid any pursuit once they got away from these rooms, but she would like to discover other useful combinations, if she could.

"Is this what Jarthan would do?" Shyvoan asked some time later. "Test your potions and such?"

"Yes. And I'd help him test things, too."

"Must be chancy to be a mage, then."

"Early on, I *did* by chance make Jarthan sick a couple of times. But after those mishaps, we never tested anything until we made sure nothing would be harmful." She laughed a little and sighed.

"You must miss him terribly."

Alorsha nodded even though Shyvoan could not see her. "Sometimes I dream that I wake to him next to me and all this—" She waved an arm around, although Shyvoan would not see that gesture either. "All this is just a dream."

"We'll get him," Shyvoan said. "We'll get Jarthan back and get that Devrand!"

Alorsha agreed. "Although sometimes, anymore, I don't care so much about getting Devrand. As long as we can at least stop him from doing all the harm he's doing and Jarthan comes back to me safe."

They fell silent as Alorsha continued to work. After another half-hour, she checked on Shyvoan, who dozed again. She opened her eyes when Alorsha shifted the bedding and squinted at her.

"Less intense now?" Alorsha said.

Shyvoan nodded. "Back to about what it was with just the one sip. So, it *is* wearing off."

"Seems the level that's tolerable lasts for about half an hour," Alorsha said. "We can work with that. Still feel normal?"

"Yah. But tired."

"Stay there, then. I'll wake you in a few hours for your watch. I'm going to work a little longer to see if I can make anything of these others, then clean up." Alorsha indicated the petal-covered table next to the bed then grabbed the mug with the enhanced-senses potion. "No place to keep this away from the prince and his people," she muttered and poured the remnants into one of the chamber pots.

With a smile for Shyvoan, she added, "Just have to make more when we're ready for it."

CHAPTER 25

Anticipating the prince's likely visit, Shyvoan and Alorsha woke early to get ready. Alorsha checked Devrand's direction—still the same—and the two women each changed into one of the other sets of new clothes.

Pince Falshinku again visited them with breakfast. Mongom accompanied the prince and attended them. The armed guard again stood in the corner to watch everything. Prince Falshinku spent most of the meal watching Alorsha, so she spent the time mostly ignoring him. Mongom glowered at the prince behind his back.

"After our meal, I've arranged for a visit to the shops that make some of our weapons and armor," he said as Alorsha finished eating. "Will you need any tools or materials from your ship to help with your magics?"

Alorsha shrugged. "I'll have to see. Could be, but maybe not."

Falshinku scowled at her vague answer, but let it pass. He offered her his arm. She lightly grasped it, and he escorted her from the room. Shyvoan followed close behind, with Mongom and the armed guard following her.

As they traversed the halls and stairs of the inn, Alorsha counted guards to herself. *The two outside our doors, plus one guard for each flight of stairs and four in the common room. And those are the ones I see. Not going to be easy to get away.*

They left the inn, and its two guards who flanked the door, and headed to a lower level of the city. Alorsha spotted guards standing at regular intervals along the way. *Sneaking away somehow doesn't look likely.*

Mongom nodded to each guard as they passed.

Several minutes of walking brought them to a section of the city that had been set off from the rest by a low wall about as tall as Alorsha. The guards who stood along the wall saluted the prince when the small group passed through the gate.

Within, Alorsha saw several different areas of activity, most of which seemed centered around smithing of some sort. Stone buildings comprised most of the structures in the area, but several tents stood nearby, too.

"Please, look around all you like," Prince Falshinku told her.

Followed by the others in their small party, Alorsha wandered the walled compound, which turned out to have only the one gate. *No slipping away from here.*

Artisans worked on all sorts of weapons and armor, from swords to flintlocks, and chain and some kind of plate armor. At each building, she paused to see what she might learn of the magic in the metals, but she could not reach any magic in any of them.

She shook her head at Falshinku after each try, and he frowned. The expression deepened with each failed try.

"Magics in metals have never been a strong area for me," she told him, and he sighed.

She looked then to the tents. The people within constructed arrows and bows. *Can maybe do something with those.* But one different tent intrigued her. The several people within worked with some kind of fabric.

Prince Falshinku moved up next to her. "You've found

our great secret. We've learned that this fabric, when properly constructed into a long vest, can help keep a flintlock wound from being fatal. Please, look closer. I wish for you to improve on this, in particular."

Alorsha approached a table where some of the cloth lay. She touched it and reached for its magic, already sensing that it was made from some sort of plant fiber. She found that the fabric did indeed resist puncturing, which would include impact from flintlock-balls. And its magic had the potential to improve that resistance.

"Do you have one of those vests completed?" she said.

Prince Falshinku waved an arm, and a man scurried from the other side of the tent with a vest. Alorsha examined it and noted how the cloth had been layered to make the completed piece. She reached out to see if she could still touch the cloth's magic. She found it with a little more trouble than with the unused cloth and looked up at Prince Falshinku.

"I can see what I can do with this."

"Excellent. What do you need?"

"A chair would be welcome, as it will likely take me a while. And some water to drink."

Before long, she was set up in a chair at a small table near one wall of the tent, with a pitcher of water and a mug at hand. She tried to ignore the stares she received from everyone except Shyvoan and sank into the cloth's magic.

Sometime later, she looked up. "How long?" she choked out of a dry throat.

"Well over an hour." Shyvoan handed her a mug of water.

Alorsha nodded and gulped the drink. She held out the vest to the prince.

"I've magicked all I can for this one," she said. "I suggest you test it and see what you think of the results."

Prince Falshinku grabbed the vest and shouted orders to prepare the practice yard on the other side of the compound. He herded the small group there.

A straw-filled sack shaped roughly like a person perched in the center of the yard. At one end, several paces from the sack, a man stood with a selection of flintlocks on a bale of straw next to him. A woman hurried to the dummy and fitted the vest around it, then stepped out of the way.

Everyone stood grouped behind the gunman to watch. He lifted the flintlocks one after another and fired them at the target. One misfired, but the others hit.

After the gunman finished, the prince ran to examine the vest. He looked back at Alorsha with a huge grin.

"Amazing! Better than I could've hoped. Come see."

Alorsha and the others joined him. Clear blemishes on the vest marked where the flintlock-balls had impacted, but no holes punctured it. The prince stripped the vest from the dummy and examined the areas where the flintlock-balls had hit. Shallow dents marred the dummy at those points, almost imperceptible. And no other damage.

The prince's people all spoke at once as they exclaimed over the success and discussed finishing more vests.

The prince drew Alorsha and Shyvoan aside. "I'll let them figure all this out while I show you my ships."

He turned to Mongom. "We're going to the shipyard overlook now."

"Of course, your highness." She led the way out of the compound and waved two guards to follow them.

Alorsha again spotted numerous guards on the way, all of them alert and armed with both sword and flintlock. *Won't be slipping away here, either.* Alorsha also caught glimpses of the *Deliberia* along the way, but not long enough to see what might be going on there.

Several minutes of walking brought them to the edge of that level of the city, to an open area walled off from a steep drop to the side of the harbor furthest from the *Deliberia*. Below them lay the shipyards.

The activity there was even greater than in the

compound they had just left. Alorsha counted ten ships, all in various stages of construction. As far as she could tell with her limited experience, none looked closer to completion than about a year. That assumed their construction techniques resembled those used for the *Deliberia*'s.

She shook her head. "I could work some on what's already there and the parts already assembled," she told Prince Falshinku. "But I simply cannot stay until these are completed. I haven't got that time."

With a slight smile, Falshinku said, "We'll see about that. For the rest of today at least, work on more of those vests. They'll have gathered some more for you, all ready for our return there. Mongom will stay with you to make sure you're taken care of."

"And what of my companions?" Alorsha said.

"They're hale and fine in their room." With a nod to Mongom and the guard who shadowed her, he headed off a different direction with the other two guards who had accompanied them to the overlook.

"Please," Mongom said. "This way."

As they walked, Alorsha caught several sidelong glances from Mongom.

"What is it?" she said after the fifth or sixth glance.

Mongom looked around. "Later."

Alorsha and Shyvoan exchanged a look. *Interesting.*

Back at the compound, Mongom indicated they should go to a large table in the tent with the cloth armorers. Piles of vests already covered the table.

Alorsha looked around and spotted several tables that held uncut cloth. She waved a hand at them. "I work better, and a bit faster, with materials before they've been made into something. So how about I start with the uncut cloth and work my way to the finished vests after."

Mongom shrugged. "Sounds fine to me. I'll check with the head armorer. Wait here."

She spoke with a woman on the other side of the tent

who glowered over the shoulders of the people who worked on the vests.

Shyvoan sidled close to Alorsha as they both watched Mongom. "I don't see a way out from here right now," she said in a low voice. "Too many of the prince's people around and we'd be too obvious."

Alorsha nodded. "Agreed. And when we leave, we *all* leave at the same time. I'll not leave anyone where the prince can get to them. Also, I'd like to make more of that concoction—" She paused. "Here comes Mongom."

"However you want to do this is fine," Mongom said as she joined them. "Let's move the chairs over to the uncut cloth and you can get started."

Alorsha worked the rest of the morning to draw forth the magic of the cloth. Mongom focused her attention on Alorsha the first hour or so, but then seemed to lose interest as Alorsha just stared at the cloth and slid it through her hands to stare at a different part.

Alorsha got through about half the cloth there before the midday meal. For the afternoon, Mongom moved the cloth to the first table, displacing the vests piled there. She told them it was to be more out of the way.

After they settled at the table to the side, Mongom leaned close.

"I know you and Seer Bilguon spoke," she said in a low voice.

"Oh?" Alorsha looked up from the cloth.

Mongom nodded. "She's my grand-aunt. Chimeg, the girl with her, is a cousin. Few know that, now including you two. My aunt finally told me about that man taking her magic. I don't know why she didn't say anything before."

Alorsha gave the woman's uniform a pointed look, and returned her gaze to her face, with a questioning expression.

"Ah, yes," Mongom said. "There's that. But the more I'm around the prince, the more I learn of his dealings, the more any loyalty I might have felt slips away. For him to have one of our family in service brings him prestige and he holds the rest of my family, like your friends, to ensure my continued service. I've learned this is his way."

Alorsha turned her gaze back to the cloth, to appear to be hard at work again. "You could be saying all this on his orders."

"True," Mongom admitted and leaned even closer and acted as if they spoke of the fabric Alorsha held.

"You should know... the story of an enemy is a lie," she said. "All this. Prince Falshinku is desperate to prove himself to the king, over his siblings, and I suspect he might be preparing to start a war to further his ambitions."

"So, what do you propose?" Alorsha said.

"I think we can help each other. The only way I can think to prove I'm not acting under the prince's orders is to help you get away, maybe help you somehow get to that man who stole Aunt Bilguon's magics. And you could help me. Maybe you can get him to release her magics, give them back. She's lost without them. Maybe you could help free the rest of our family, too."

"Makes sense," Alorsha said. "I wouldn't mind having some of these vests for the *Deliberia*."

Mongom chuckled. "Another thing to add in." She raised her voice back to a more normal volume. "I'll just get some water for the afternoon. These tents can get hot." And she left.

"Think we can trust her?" Shyvoan said.

"Possibly. We'll take what help we can get."

"But keep our eyes open," Shyvoan added.

Alorsha worked on the fabric all afternoon and she finished working the rest of the cloth as the others in the tent secured everything for the night. She stumbled as she tried to stand, and Shyvoan caught her.

"You're exhausted," Mongom said as she rejoined them.

"She didn't exaggerate when she told the prince that this magic is draining," Shyvoan said.

"Let's get you back to the inn," Mongom said, "so you can rest.

She sent a runner ahead to get a carriage and she and Shyvoan helped Alorsha from the compound. The carriage waited just outside the entrance, and they piled in.

Alorsha leaned back with a sigh and closed her eyes. "If I'm going to be in that tent for a while, I'm going to need a few more comforts."

"I'll see to it," Mongom said.

"And I'd like to see my companions," Alorsha said.

"I'll try to persuade the prince to let that happen," Mongom said.

Back at the inn, Mongom led Alorsha and Shyvoan first to a storeroom off the kitchen. Within sat two bathtubs, already filled with warm water. Two guards flanked the door, outside the room.

"I thought you might need this," Mongom said. "I'll be back with towels and a change of clothes."

Alorsha and Shyvoan enjoyed the unexpected luxury and were ready when Mongom returned. Alorsha kept her pendant tucked in her hand while Mongom grabbed their dirty clothes and left them the clean ones.

After she dressed, Alorsha hid her pendant again beneath the neckline of her shirt. Mongom returned and escorted them upstairs to their room, where the evening meal awaited them. Their other sets of clothes hung from hooks, clean, and the bed had been changed. The flowers in their pitchers looked untouched.

Alorsha devoured her meal then, refreshed, pulled more petals and leaves from the flowers. As she laid out the flower petals, Shyvoan placed a small, stoppered bottle on the table.

"Something to help, to hold that potion," she said.

Alorsha opened the bottle. It carried the faint scent of some kind of spice. "From the kitchen? It's perfect. My thanks."

Shyvoan nodded and grinned. "Something I can do

beyond testing your concoctions. But shouldn't you rest?"

"I really want to see what other concoctions I might be able to create. And make more of that enhanced-senses potion, now that I've got a place to keep it." She waved a hand at the small bottle.

"Well, then, I'm going to get some sleep. Do wake me when you're ready to catch some sleep."

Alorsha nodded, already back to work on the potion. Before she crawled into the bed, Shyvoan exchanged a few words with the men held next door, letting them know about Mongom and the seer.

"They're making themselves a little crazy trying to figure out a way to overpower their guards and get us all back to the ship," Shyvoan said after she finished talking with the men. "But they agree with seeing what we might work out with Mongom. And otherwise, they're still fine." Then she stretched out on the bed and slept.

Alorsha worked a few hours to fill the bottle with the potion. For a hiding place for it, she coerced the wood in the bedpost to open enough to create a small hole into which she placed the small, stoppered bottle. She then smoothed the wood closed to leave no visible trace of what she had done.

After that, she worked on a different concoction, one that became a thick cream. To contain it, she tore a strip off a leftover washing cloth. She bundled the cream inside it and tucked the small bundle into her pocket. Then she cleaned up the remnants of her work.

When that task was completed to her satisfaction, she woke Shyvoan to take a turn at watch. With a sigh, Alorsha stretched out on the bed to get a little sleep in the few hours remaining until sunrise.

CHAPTER 26

In the morning, Alorsha's wayfinding magic still showed Devrand's location as inland to her right. She and Shyvoan enjoyed a peaceful couple of hours only interrupted once by the boy bringing their food.

They finished their breakfast with no princely visit, but he arrived after the boy cleared the remnants of their meal. Prince Falshinku did not enter the room, just stood in the doorway.

"Today you work on the ships," he greeted them. Then he peered at Alorsha. "Although, you look like you need more rest to be at your best. This afternoon, then."

Alorsha and Shyvoan exchanged glances. "We want to see our companions, to speak with them," Alorsha said.

"I'll consider it. But you must rest more now," the prince said and left.

About midmorning, their captors allowed the men to join Alorsha and Shyvoan in their room. While crowded, Alorsha welcomed the chance to see that everyone was, in fact, well. They exchanged news, what little news they had, and discussed Mongom and Seer Bilguon in low voices, without reaching any conclusions. After an hour, the guards took the men back to their room and Alorsha settled in to rest some more, after which she worked again to widen the crack in the wall.

Prince Falshinku visited again during their midday meal and brought Mongom and the other guard with him.

"You look much better than earlier," he observed.

Alorsha nodded. "Seeing my companions was a great relief. Why not send them back to the *Deliberia*? You don't need them here."

"Oh, but I do," Prince Falshinku said. "Their presence ensures that you won't consider doing anything foolish and detrimental to our agreement."

Alorsha laughed. "At best we've had a contradictory conversation punctuated by many non-agreements."

"You're delightful," the prince said. "This afternoon you shall work on the ships. The sooner you start, the sooner you can finish. Perhaps you'll even do something to hurry along the building process."

"It doesn't work that way," Alorsha said with a frown.

Prince Falshinku shrugged. "We'll see about that. But now you'll excuse me, I have other matters that require my attention this day."

He told Mongom, "Stay and attend to anything they might need to ensure the Lady Alorsha is fit for her work." Then he left.

"We'd best head out," Mongom said. She grabbed some cheese from their tray and escorted them from the building, her guard following a few paces behind.

"I'll work on the vests some more," Alorsha told Mongom in a low voice. "Not his ships."

Mongom nodded. "I believe we can accommodate that."

She stepped closer to the other two women. "He means to keep you here indefinitely. All of you. But so far, he hasn't been able to remove any of the others from the *Deliberia*. You've got good people on that ship. So, it's just you four that we need to get out.

"I know where he holds my family. They're not in the city, but rather in a small town further along the coast." She tilted her head to indicate the direction—roughly the same as what Alorsha's wayfinding magic indicated for Devrand's location.

"You should know that the prince is growing impatient," Mongom continued as they walked. "He's been polite and has restrained his less-savory impulses, but that won't last. He's determined to keep you here and won't let anything stop him from achieving that. In the past, he's been willing to use any brutality, any barbarity to get what he's required. I doubt he'll hesitate now. So, we need to get you out of here soon, a couple of days, at most. Have you made plans?"

We? Alorsha studied her a long time before she answered. "I have some ideas. They can fit into any action we take as needed. But before we go too far, we *do* need some provisions for the ship."

"I've been working on that. I've managed to have some food taken to your ship, as well as a few of the vests. And we've sent ahead to make arrangements for food at that town I mentioned."

"We? Who else is in on this?"

"No one else. Just me and my aunt. As a seer she has some standing and so can go pretty much wherever she wants. She's already well on her way to that town. By ship, we can be there in a day or so."

"Won't that be an obvious place to go? With your family held there?"

"No one knows that I know they're there."

Alorsha scrutinized the other woman's expression. Mongom seemed to believe it. Not so sure herself, Alorsha left her misgivings unvoiced.

All conversation ceased when they reached the weapons and armor compound. The rest of the day passed much like the previous day. More fabric awaited Alorsha's magic work, which took her most of the afternoon. She spent the rest of the time working on the vests.

As sundown colored the sky, Mongom returned for Alorsha and Shyvoan and took them back to the inn and their evening meal. There Mongom left them to themselves.

After they finished eating and the boy had removed the remnants, Shyvoan darted to the shared wall to tell the men what was going on.

"I've got another concoction to test," Alorsha told her when she finished.

With a grin, Shyvoan plopped in a chair. "Another awful drink?"

Alorsha matched her grin. "No, just this." She opened the bundle that contained the cream and held it out to Shyvoan.

"A little on a finger, then please smell it."

"Smell it?"

Alorsha nodded.

With a shrug, Shyvoan did as she requested. After she inhaled the scent of the cream, she slumped in her chair, staring the direction of the window, her gaze unfocused.

Alorsha wiped the cream from the other woman's finger and tried to catch her attention. When she failed to, she sat in the other chair to wait out the effects.

Close to a quarter-hour later, Shyvoan turned toward Alorsha, her motion languid. "Wha…?"

"It's just one of my concoctions," Alorsha told her. "We'll wait until it wears off, and then we'll get some sleep."

With a silly grin, Shyvoan nodded. "Dreamy," she muttered. And so that became the name of that cream.

~ ~ ~

The sound of someone saying her name penetrated Alorsha's strange dreams of streamers of fabrics that chased after her demanding that she decorate them with flowers.

"Alorsha, we need to go." That was Shyvoan's whisper.

With some difficulty, Alorsha pulled herself free of the lingering remnants of sleep and back to the moonlit inn room.

"What's happened? How late is it?" She kept her voice as quiet as Shyvoan's.

"A little past midnight. And nothing's happened. Yet. But we must go this night, so Mongom says. Falshinku's pet harrier, as she called him, will arrive in the morning. He'll be set upon us, your companions, to force you to do what the prince requires."

Not yet completely awake, Alorsha nevertheless grabbed the flowers from the pitchers and tied them into a small bundle in one of the tunics. "Mongom was here? What about the guards?" She waved a hand at the door, and at the window.

"Mongom just left. She told me she's our guard in the street below and warned that she can't send the other guards to other duties, the guards that are outside our doors, at the stairs, and in the common room. So, we might need to consider a different way out. She said she believed in us."

Alorsha snorted. Shyvoan grinned and, with a wink, leaned close to the narrow hole in the wall. "Are you two ready?"

Alorsha moved to the window and did not hear the answer. But she did come face to face with Parl's grin.

"You could've warned me!" She jumped back and tried not to make any noise that would draw the guards.

Parl only smiled and climbed through the window. "We can't all go that way." He waved an arm toward the window. "I can manage the climb, but there's not nearly enough grips for the rest of you."

"Kluir's got an idea," Shyvoan said. "It needs you, Alorsha."

Parl nodded. "And we'll still need something to help us down the outside, if Kluir's plan works." Parl pulled the bedding from the bed.

Alorsha leaned close to crack. "Tell me," she instructed Kluir.

"Can you widen the crack and make an opening in the floor at the same spot?" he whispered. "Big enough for us to slip through?"

Alorsha considered the idea. "None of us is very big," she said. "But it might make some noise. Though not enough for the guards in the stairs and common room to hear. I think. Just the ones outside our doors."

"Maybe use that dreamy cream on them," Shyvoan said.

"Do it."

"I'll act as her backup, if she needs any," Parl said.

Alorsha nodded as Shyvoan grabbed the small bundle that contained the cream and smeared some on one hand, holding it away from her face so she could not smell it. Shyvoan pushed Parl back behind the door to hide him and tapped on it to get the guards' attention.

When one opened the door, she slipped out around it. Parl lurked behind the door, ready to go to her aid.

Alorsha knelt next to the end of the bed. She placed one hand on the wall next to the crack and the other flat on the floor there. She reached into the wood, to the minimal magic there, and pulled apart the lower part of the wall and the near section of the floor along the seams between planks, working to make it wide enough for them to drop through. She widened the split in the wall at the same time.

Shyvoan stumbled back into the room before Alorsha made much progress and leaned against Parl with a dazed expression.

"The guards are taken care of for now," Parl whispered. "Shyvoan here got a good whiff of that stuff, though. I hope she'll be back with us soon."

Alorsha nodded and glared at the minimal openings. "This is too slow."

"Can you weaken the wood, then?" Kluir said from the other side of the wall. "Maybe enough that we can break it apart."

"It *is* old enough," Alorsha said. "That'll probably be faster, and it'll take less magic from me too."

She reached into the minimal magic again. Much like when she grew a plant, she tugged the magic toward an increase in the age of the wood around the holes. As she did so, the wood grew more brittle.

Once she judged it was brittle enough, she reached through the magical connections that she had made earlier throughout the two rooms and expanded both rooms' doors and doorframes to jam the doors shut.

When she finished, she drew back from the wall. "See if that's enough."

Parl shifted the dazed Shyvoan to Alorsha's care. Together with Kluir, he tugged at the edges of the two holes. They tore off pieces of wood until they made the holes big enough, with more noise than when Alorsha had worked to magic the openings bigger.

"Quickly now, Parl, Kluir, drop down first," Alorsha said. "I'll help Shyvoan down to you and follow."

With a nod, Parl wriggled his way through the split to the room below, empty fortunately. He dragged bedding with him. Kluir followed right after, dragging more bedding from their room. Alorsha guided Shyvoan to the hole and helped her into the room below. She next dropped her small bundle of flowers down to Kluir. Then Alorsha retrieved the bottle with the senses potion from its hiding place in the bedpost, grabbed a mug from the table, and followed.

Kluir and Parl ripped the sheets into strips and tied them end to end while Alorsha guided Shyvoan to a chair against the wall near the window. Alorsha then dashed to the room's door and sank into the minimal magic there to jam the door as she had in the rooms above them. She returned to the window, eased open the shutter, and peered out.

"I see Mongom," she whispered to the others. "And no one else."

"Almost ready," Kluir said.

Alorsha nodded and tied her small bundle to Shyvoan's waist with a strip from the bedding. She then poured the senses potion into the mug, stoppered the bottle, and tucked it in her pocket. "Everyone take a sip, just one. It enhances sight, hearing, and sense of smell."

Parl grinned. "Nice."

"Shyvoan, too?" Kluir said when he took the mug from Parl.

Alorsha shook her head and took the mug after he had sipped from it. "Better not to mix the concoctions. I've not tested them that way."

She drank the last sip and returned to the window. *Good. No one other than Mongom, still.*

"How will we get Shyvoan down?" Alorsha whispered as she peered into the other woman's face in the dim moonlight that came from the window. Shyvoan remained expressionless, although she did glance at the movements of the others in the room. She still clutched the bundle in her hand that contained the dreamy cream.

Alorsha took care to not breathe in its vapor as she pulled the bundle from Shyvoan's hand and tucked it into the pocket with the small bottle. "How'd this happen?"

"The second guard got suspicious and turned enough that she got a whiff of it too," Parl said. He tightened a last knot around the bedpost as Kluir carried the rest of the makeshift rope to the window.

"I can climb down without the rope," Parl said. "Then you two lower Shyvoan to me and follow behind. Use the rope to help you."

Alorsha nodded her agreement and secured the rope around Shyvoan, with Kluir's help.

Parl clambered over the windowsill and was gone down the side of the building.

Kluir and Alorsha lowered Shyvoan to where Parl waited. After he had her safe and freed from the makeshift rope, Kluir climbed down, followed by Alorsha.

"Do we care if they find this?" Kluir tugged on the rope.

"No. Let's go," Alorsha said.

Kluir helped Shyvoan stay upright as they scurried away from the inn, heading toward the harbor. Mongom joined them before they had gone too far.

"This way is fastest." She led them away from the more obvious main streets and into a series of small side streets, traveling consistently downhill. She hurried them through the city and gave them no chance for conversation as she guided them around several pairs of guards out walking in the night. None of them told her that they heard the guards long before she led them around them. When they reached the long road that led to the harbor, she stopped in the shadows of the last large building there.

"There are still guards at your ship," Mongom told them. "No good way to approach it without being seen."

"Leave that to me," Parl said with a grin. "Still have some of that dreamy cream?"

Alorsha pulled it from her pocket and handed it over.

"Back in no time, then." Parl slipped around the building and vanished into the night.

Mongom inspected Shyvoan, who looked better, but not entirely aware yet. "Is that what happened to her?"

Alorsha nodded. "Parl won't be long. Can we get closer, so we need little time to get to our ship?"

Mongom looked around, and waved a hand toward some low buildings with wide open areas between them that ran along the street toward the harbor. She glanced at the moon and clouds above.

"Perhaps. We'll have to be more careful even than we have been and hope the clouds cooperate."

So, they jogged from shadow to shadow when the clouds dimmed the moonlight, drawing ever closer to the harbor, pausing when the moon shone brighter. They had covered perhaps three-quarters of the distance when Parl returned.

"It's clear, now. I also got the guards on the other ships that were most likely to notice anything our direction. And I alerted the *Deliberia* that we need to leave."

"Let's go, then."

They scurried the rest of the way to the harbor and along the docks to the *Deliberia*.

As they approached, three figures at the ship's rail extended the gangplank. Alorsha and the others ran up it.

"Set sail," Alorsha said when she gained the deck.

With a nod, Saevalde gave the orders, and the ship began moving even before crewmembers had wrangled the gangplank completely aboard.

Gya and Alorsha glanced at each other and took places at the rail. Together, they reached through the ship's magic to the water to raise fog to blanket the harbor and their escape.

Alorsha looked up as shouts of alarm pierced the murk, but the fog had grown thick enough that no one should be able to spot them.

"Keep it thick between us and them," Alorsha instructed Gya. "But thinned ahead so Saevalde can steer us."

Gya nodded, his focus still in the magic, as Alorsha turned to Mongom. "Please guide Saevalde to this village of yours." After the woman headed to the aft deck where the Ship's Master stood, Alorsha eased Shyvoan to her feet.

"Let's get you to your cabin and see what we can do about clearing that concoction."

Shyvoan murmured something unintelligible but went along with Alorsha without complaint as the others scattered to various tasks to get them safely away.

CHAPTER 27

The two tenders moved with little sound through the nighttime sea. Behind them, the *Deliberia* sat dark and awaited their return. Alorsha and Gya rode with Mikolus in one tender, while Mongom rode with Parl, Kluir, and Shyvoan in the other. Shyvoan carried her heirloom sword this time as they headed ashore. Gya whispered to her, asking about it.

"I decided to bring it along this time, in case my friends were right that the sword is somehow part of my so-called "luck" that I bring to my companions. Maybe it might help. I've a feeling we could use some luck here," she told him with a shrug.

They reached the modest bay around which nestled the town that Mongom had directed them to. The small group pulled the boats onto the narrow sand beach and crouched next to them to look for any signs of late-night movement.

"Where do they hold your family?" Mikolus whispered to Mongom.

"A house on the inland side of the village, from my information." Mongom pointed a little to the right.

"Was Bilguon going to meet us?" Alorsha said.

"That was the plan."

"We'll head toward the house and watch for her on the way," Mikolus said and suited action to words.

As they drew closer, Alorsha studied the small town. Somewhat bigger than the village she had called home, this town clearly centered around fishing. Many well-used boats were secured around the small bay, with nets and poles visible in them. An aroma of smoked fish hung in the air. All was dark and quiet. Forest surrounded the village on the inland side and isolated it from the rest of the land and the road beyond that Mongom had told them Bilguon would take to get there.

Alorsha saw nothing to alarm her. *And yet....*

"Shouldn't there be some guards?" Gya whispered. "If they're holding people here."

"Stay alert." Mikolus whispered also.

Motion at the edge of the trees caught Alorsha's attention. She shared a look with Mikolus, who nodded and headed that direction. At the same time, he waved to the others to stay back. Mongom ignored him and followed close behind.

Alorsha crouched near some bushes and readied her bow. Gya joined her and dug through his bag of potions and other concoctions. Parl, Kluir, and Shyvoan eased off to the sides, drew their swords, and held them out of sight so they would not catch the dim moonlight.

As Alorsha watched, Mikolus strode toward the motion they had seen, not hiding his approach. Two figures stepped out to meet him.

"It's Bilguon and Chimeg," Alorsha murmured, and the others moved forward at Mikolus's come hither gesture.

"Something's wrong," Gya said when they got closer.

Alorsha nodded. She could not see Mongom's face, but both Bilguon and Chimeg wore expressions of worry and sadness. Chimeg clung to Bilguon's hand.

"You're sure?" Mongom's voice broke as she spoke.

Bilguon nodded. "My friend saw it. She took us to where they buried them."

Alorsha and Gya shared stricken looks.

"Your whole family?" Alorsha said in a low voice.

Mongom did not turn to look at her.

Bilguon and the girl both shook their heads. "We three are left," the seer said. "Word is a few others managed to escape and ran."

"We shouldn't linger," Mikolus murmured.

"Did you get those supplies?" Mongom asked her aunt.

The older woman shook her head again. "The prince's folk have left little enough in the town. Didn't seem right to make that even less." She turned toward Alorsha. "I hope you can understand."

Sudden rustling in the surrounding forest put them all on their guard. Parl crouched and slipped into the shadows just as several people stepped out of the foliage, all with flintlocks pointed at Alorsha and her companions.

"I'm so sorry," Bilguon murmured as two of the newcomers pulled her and Chimeg back from the others. "My friend had no choice but to tell, and I also had no choice." She turned toward Chimeg, her expression anguished.

"Hand over your weapons," one of the newcomers said.

Alorsha counted six opponents. She met Mikolus's gaze, and they exchanged slight nods.

"Now!" Mikolus shouted.

Alorsha and the others from the *Deliberia* dropped to the ground and rolled toward their opponent's feet. Shyvoan pulled Mongom down with her. Gya threw a small jar from his pouch at the ground, where it shattered. Liquid oozed out and a thick fog rose from it to obscure the area.

Shouts and the roar of flintlocks followed.

Searing pain sliced across Alorsha's side as she rolled behind the newcomers. The fog expanded and hid her.

She lay on the ground. *Where are the others?* She did not dare cry out for fear she would attract the wrong people.

She had a potion that would help....

Trying to get it from her pocket sent pain slicing through her and her vision darkened momentarily.

Grunts and exclamations and other sounds of fighting drifted through the gloom around her. Someone's feet came close to her face but moved off again. She did not recognize the boots.

The fog grew thicker and the moonlight—dim to begin with—faded, especially around the edges of her vision.

No....

Panting from the pain, she pushed herself off the ground, but only reached hands and knees. Her side burned and screamed at her.

Have to get back to the Deliberia.... *Maybe something in the plants can help....*

She reached for the magic in the plants beneath her hands. *Something there.* A glimmer. But when she tried to grasp it, pain clutched her and yanked her from the magic. She took a shuddering breath as tears stung her eyes.

Then Shyvoan and Gya were there. Gya dug in his bag and pulled out a concoction. He splashed the jar's contents on her side and the pain receded a little.

"We need to go," Alorsha mumbled.

With nods, Gya and Shyvoan helped her to her feet and supported her from either side. Shyvoan handed her a bundled cloth.

"Press that on the wound. Focus on that. Let us worry about getting you back to the tender."

Alorsha did as Shyvoan directed and the three of them stumbled away from the village. Alorsha squinted against the darkness that again tried to engulf her. Other figures hurried to the two tenders ahead of them.

Looks like everyone's here.

They reached the small boat, and many hands helped her climb in. She collapsed partway along one of the benches and leaned against someone who steadied her.

"Hurry." That was Shyvoan.

"Anyone else hurt?" Alorsha tried to ask. *Did they hear me?*

"What did she say?" That was Gya's voice.

"Scrapes, bruises, and a few cuts," Shyvoan murmured in Alorsha's ear. "You've outdone us all there."

Alorsha chuckled and gasped at the renewed pain.

"Sorry," Shyvoan said and wrapped an arm around her shoulder. "Won't do that to you again. We'll be back to the *Deliberia* soon."

Alorsha drifted. The motion of the tender on the water both soothed and irritated her. Then hands helped her up the ladder to the *Deliberia's* deck and to her own cabin, where Taesen and Naltha took charge of her.

"The others?" Alorsha whispered around the pain.

"Everyone made it back," Taesen said. "Minor injuries."

"And we've two new passengers," Naltha said. "But don't fret about any of that right now."

She placed a cool hand on Alorsha's forehead. Alorsha felt the small charm the healer pressed there, then peace and darkness took her away.

~ ~ ~

Magic swirled in shades-of-gray, twists, and tangles.

Need to see something. Need to See! Random openings before. Trying to get close enough… somehow find the way.

Dark wisps roiled, seeking the way. They tugged and directed, forced, and guided.

Dark wisps flashed across blue-green eyes.

Must draw the magic to See. Find the way to finish.

Alorsha lurched upright, her hand clutched around her ring-pendant tightly enough to hurt.

She'd connected somehow with Devrand. And she might better grasp what he was after.

"Oh, quite the start you've given me." Naltha stood at the side of Alorsha's bed and placed a hand on her shoulder. "What is it? Are you still in pain?"

Alorsha struggled to focus on the healer's concerned face, still caught in the vision or dream or whatever it had been. *Certainly something more than just a dream.*

"How long was I out?"

"Several hours. You're healing nicely. The charm is working well, but you'll be stiff and ache for a while. I'd not recommend doing anything too strenuous yet."

Alorsha nodded. She opened her hand and found that the edges of her pendant had sliced into her skin from her tight grip.

Naltha clucked her tongue at her. "I'll tend to that, too."

"It'll wait just a bit. Please call for Mikolus, Saevalde, Gya, Kluir, Shyvoan and Parl. I need to talk to them. Then you can see to this." Alorsha raised her hand and let the pendant fall back to hang from its chain around her neck.

When Naltha headed out to the deck to send word for everyone to gather, Alorsha scooted in the bed to lean her back against the pillows and headboard, wincing at the blossoming ache in her side. She rested her injured hand palm-up in her lap and pondered the images and impressions from the dream-vision.

Naltha returned, Mikolus and Saevalde trailing her. She sat on the edge of Alorsha's bed, cleaned and wrapped her injured hand, and tucked a small charm into the wrapping.

"The others will be here soon," Mikolus said. "Did you want to see the seer and her family, too?"

Alorsha shook her head. "Not yet. But they're well?"

Saevalde nodded. "Aye, lass. You had the worst of it."

"And lucky the ball didn't do much more than tear a stripe across your side," Naltha said.

Mikolus nodded agreement.

"Any pursuit?" Alorsha stretched to look out the window near the bed but subsided at a warning pang from her side. By the light from the window, she judged it was early morning.

"Nay," Saevalde said. "Gya called up that fog and we sailed well away before light. We're following the last heading you gave us."

Alorsha nodded. "I'll have to check that soon." She glanced at Naltha, who shrugged.

"After your meeting here, if you can walk unaided, I don't see why you can't do that small bit of magic. But no more than that for a day, at least."

"As you say."

Naltha gathered her supplies and moved to the side of the room to make way for the others who entered. When everyone filed in, Alorsha examined them for injury. As Saevalde had said, they were all far less damaged than she was. Scrapes and bruises, on their way to being healed from the care of the ship's healers, and a black eye for Kluir.

He grinned at her when he noticed her gaze on him. "Didn't duck fast enough." He hauled a chair close to the bed, after he relocated the plants and plant bits that sat there. The others did likewise.

Alorsha waited until the others had all assured themselves of her continued health and expected recovery before she spoke.

"Naltha, that was a magical sleep you had me in, wasn't it? I think I remember you placed a charm on my forehead."

The healer nodded. "Yes. The better to help you heal. Also, to keep you still while we worked on your injury." She grinned at Alorsha.

"I saw something while in the grasp of that magic," Alorsha said. "I've not experienced anything like it before. A sort of vision, dreamlike but I know it wasn't a dream. I believe I caught glimpses of Devrand's plans."

At the others' surprised exclamations, Alorsha raised a hand. "Wait. Maybe 'plans' is too strong a word. But I know some things now. He needs the seer's magic to see the way. That came through clearly. I think it's the way to where he's been going all these years."

"He's not known where he's been headed all this time?" Saevalde's express was incredulous.

Alorsha shrugged. "It *has* seemed rather random. But then I've never known why he's doing this. Gathering magic and traveling world to world. But in the dream-vision, I saw wisps of gray. A magic I've seen before."

She told them then—those who had not heard the whole story—about what had transpired with her, Jarthan, Devrand, and the wisps.

"I remember seeing something like that wrapped around his hand," Shyvoan said.

Gya nodded. "I saw something similar swirling around him."

"So we're knowing why he wants the seer's magic, but is there a way to stop him from taking it?" Saevalde said.

"I know of no way other than just stopping him," Alorsha said. "Maybe that magical sleep if we can get to him. I did get an impression that he feels he's close to having what he needs 'to finish', whatever he means by that."

"Maybe the end of the chase," Parl murmured.

"But what lies at that point?" Kluir said.

"So, you've not yet felt him gather the magic to himself here?" Gya said.

Alorsha shook her head. "At least not like he has before. He's gathering some. But very little so far."

"Could mean we've time yet," Saevalde said.

With a nod, Alorsha scooted toward the edge of the bed. "I'll just confirm our direction." She met Naltha's gaze. "Then rest again to finish healing."

With a curt nod for her, the healer headed out the door. "I'll return to check on you again soon."

The others stood, pulled their chairs away from the bed, and returned them to the various spots around the room, taking care to avoid disturbing Alorsha's plants.

Shyvoan grabbed a wrap from Alorsha's clothes chest and draped it around the other woman's shoulders. "Will you truly walk all the way out to the mast to work the magic?"

Alorsha grinned as she eased her legs over the edge of the bed. She paused to catch her breath against the sudden stab of pain and shook her head. "Apparently not. I'll do it the old way right here."

With extra care, she pushed herself to her feet while Shyvoan hovered nearby, ready to offer support.

After she stood, and felt steady enough, Alorsha pulled the chain with the erythros pendant from around her neck and held out her arm to work the wayfinding magic.

When the pendant settled into its horizontal arc, a narrow one centered a bit starboard of the direction they currently sailed, Saevalde grabbed Alorsha's compass and a piece of paper and marked out the direction. With a nod, she left to alter their course.

Shyvoan helped Alorsha the two steps back to her bed and got her settled in again.

"What of Mongom and her family?" Alorsha said.

Mikolus frowned. "Both Mongom and Bilguon are certain they know where the others would run. They'd like to sail further from the prince and hope to get closer to the place they expect they'll find the rest of their family."

"Are they returning then to stay with us?" Alorsha squirmed around to a more comfortable position.

Mikolus shook his head. "They've already spoken of making their way on land on their own. Both Mongom and Bilguon seem confident they'll be able to manage. They're settled in a compartment for now, but requested we drop them off in a village not too much further along. I believe it's even on our way, or at least close to it."

Alorsha nodded and Mikolus and the others headed out the door, with promises to return later to see if she needed anything.

She closed her eyes against the morning light, planning to rest just a little longer, and sank back into sleep.

~ ~ ~

Alorsha startled awake some time later, sensing Devrand drawing a massive amount of magic to himself to open the way to the next world.

She grabbed her ring-pendant and dove into its magic to catch where he was headed. She also caught a sense of purpose from him.

This latest destination was *not* a random one.

Chapter 28

From Alorsha's Journal

I grow weary. It's hard to tell how long it's truly been. The chase. How long have I followed this insane path, this ceaseless hunt? Seeing so many different worlds, different suns and moons, sometimes there for mere days. How to accurately track the time?

Best I can tell, I'm approaching my thirty-first year. So that means around three or four years on the move. Chasing a magical madman.

Feels like a lot longer.

I would expect that *he* must be getting weary too.

He's grown stronger with each world, his magic more potent. Mine has, too, I think. Maybe. But not to the same extent. But why does he gather magic to himself? What's his end purpose?

I'm ready for an end to this mad hunt. Is he? These last several worlds he's been so focused in the magic, with a sense that the end is getting closer. But what end is he leading us to?

~ ~ ~

Alorsha pulled herself upright and looked around to assess the ship's condition. That crossing had been the roughest yet. She shared a look with Gya, who had helped with the portal, as he had the last many months, learning the magic. He winced but gave her a slight nod.

So he was fine, then.

The ship still spun slowly in the remnants of the wind-whipped whirlpool the gale of the crossing had created. The ship showed few signs of damage and that only minor, but several other crewmembers pulled themselves up from the deck. Saevalde tottered to her and Gya, walking as if uncertain of her footing.

"Are you injured?" she said. "Any idea what happened?"

"We're fine." Alorsha tried to rub the ache from one elbow. "And no idea. Give me a minute."

With a nod to Gya who had slumped to sit on the deck, looking somewhat ill, she hobbled to the port rail, as unsteady as Saevalde had been. She felt as if they still rode rough seas, but the water had calmed, and the deck barely rocked.

She looked out over the water, gray with a slight tint of blue, dark, and foreboding. The sky seemed hazy, gray too, and the sunlight weak, with a hint of a reddish cast. She could not see any land.

She reached out, through the *Deliberia*'s magic, to see what she might make of this new world's magic. After a moment, she drew back, and turned to Saevalde with a frown.

"What is it, lass?"

"The magic's very strange. A sense of heaviness without strength, and sluggish. I'm not sure I'll be able to draw some into the ship to help us talk with any people we meet here."

Saevalde frowned. "That's not sounding good. Perhaps

you'd best check the direction."

Alorsha nodded and stepped to the rigging that held the pole for her wayfinding magic. She slipped the chain from her neck and onto the pole and reached out with her magic to brush the magic in the stone from her mage ring. No movement, although she did sense the link to Jarthan and Devrand.

She pulled on the world's magic from the air and added some of the *Deliberia*'s magic to help. Slower than it ever had before, the pendant swayed, then circled. After several minutes, it snapped out straight to port. It dipped toward the deck, then snapped out that direction again.

Alorsha and Saevalde exchanged looks. Saevalde shook her head. "I'm not liking this at all. I'd wager Mikolus will want everyone to keep their weapons close at hand."

Alorsha nodded and retrieved her pendant. She crossed the deck to the starboard rail and looked into the water. She reached with her magic through the *Deliberia*'s magic and into the water. Maybe she could reach some plants on the sea floor to give her a better idea of the magic in this place.

The land underwater was too far for her to reach, but she did notice some sparks of magic in the water.

Plants? They didn't seem to be. Might they be sea creatures? She'd never been able to feel the magic in creatures before.

Every bit of magic she spotted felt feeble and sluggish. Dulled. Gray like the sky and water.

What's going on with the magic in this world?

~ ~ ~

The *Deliberia* sailed through a gray-blue sea that seemed endless. Well, not truly sailed, as they had yet to catch even the hint of a breeze in the sails. The crewmembers took turns at the oars, except for the two healers, the oldest among the crew.

While the sun never broke through what seemed a

persistent cloud cover, the air was warm enough, with a musty damp feel to it. Alorsha breathed it in with some relief after she finished her turn below at the oars. She wiped the sweat from her face and the back of her neck and peered ahead. Gya joined her.

"Still that same direction?"

Alorsha nodded. "As of this morning's wayfinding. Any progress with this world's magic?"

Gya frowned. "Maybe. I'm not sure. I still feel those sparks of magic in the water that you noticed the first day. It might sound crazy, but I'm not sure they're alive."

"Rocks? Or crystals like your original magic?"

Gya shook his head. "That's not what I mean. I mean maybe some sort of creatures, sea life, which *used* to be alive. But aren't now. But still have magic somehow. And I think the magic's all connected. More so than we've seen in any of the other worlds."

Alorsha stared at him as she considered that. "I've never encountered something dead that held onto its magic."

With a troubled expression, Gya said, "I'm not sure they're truly dead."

"Who's not truly dead?" Shyvoan asked from behind them.

Gya greeted her with a big grin. Alorsha nodded to her and filled her in on what they had been discussing.

"Sounds like the scary stories we used to tell each other as children," Shyvoan said. "About magic that takes over people who had died and makes them do things. Their bodies anyway." She looked from Gya to Alorsha. "You know. The undead?"

"We had nothing like that in the world I come from," Alorsha said.

Gya shook his head. "Me neither. Not even rumors of such things."

Shyvoan waved a hand in the air. "I'm not saying we had them in my home world, either. They were tales told by older children to younger ones to see how much they could scare them. Just stories. No one ever encountered anything like that."

"Wonder where the stories came from," Gya murmured.

Shyvoan shrugged. "Imagination." Her expression grew thoughtful. "Or maybe a nugget of truth from the past. My people came from another world to that world where I grew up, so we learned. Maybe in that other world, such stories were real."

Alorsha nodded. "Could be possible. But did the stories ever talk about such things being in the sea?"

Shyvoan shook her head. "No. They told only of people and always took place on the land."

Alorsha frowned. "Wonder how there might be something like that here. If that's what they are." She peered at the nearly smooth sea around the ship.

"I could be wrong about them," Gya said. "I'm guessing at the 'sea life' part because the magic doesn't feel like plant magic."

"Yes, I noticed that, too," Alorsha said. "I'll look again in a bit. Maybe both of us. And perhaps I've got a potion to help." With nods to Gya and Shyvoan, she headed toward her cabin. She glanced back at the two and saw they had edged closer and seemed deep in conversation. When Gya laughed at something Shyvoan said, Alorsha smiled to herself.

Good. At least they weren't talking about the 'undead', as Shyvoan had labeled them.

And wonderful to see them take time to themselves.

~ ~ ~

Side by side, Gya and Alorsha leaned against the starboard rail, their fingers wrapped around the top, the edges of their hands and arms touching. Alorsha led the way through the *Deliberia*'s magic and into the water that surrounded the ship.

Gya's magic brushed hers as it traveled alongside into the murky depths.

He's much improved at this.

Alorsha reached out through her magic, through the *Deliberia*'s magic, into the water. The sea floor was closer than it had been when they arrived in this world. *But no plants anywhere down there.*

She reached out wide then, through the water all around the ship. Sparks of magic here and there, but when she focused her attention on one it vanished. Gya's magic joined hers, as he returned from his own search, and together they repeated the search.

A sensation of cold brushed Alorsha, not the cold of deep water, but something else. She could not define it though, even to herself. Eyes closed to focus better, she reached and sought those sparks again.

One there.

They drew close to the spark. Definitely magic and just as definitely not plant-magic. So, while Alorsha could tell it was there, it eluded her grasp. She also could not determine what it was part of, whether a creature, living or not, or an object. There was no seeing it, in the usual sense, going through the magic like that. Still, Alorsha thought the sparks were various shades of purple.

As she studied the spark they had approached, the thinnest ribbon of bright gold flashed from it and stretched away from it in the same direction they headed. The flash left an afterimage that faded back into darkness. A moment later the spark vanished also.

A gasp next to her ear yanked Alorsha back to herself on the *Deliberia*. Gya crouched next to her and fought for breath. Shyvoan knelt behind him and rubbed his back.

Alorsha suppressed a laugh. "I've told you that you don't need to hold your breath when we do that sort of thing. We're not really underwater."

Gya waved a hand in the air and managed to speak as

he slowed his desperate breathing. "I know. I know. I just can't seem to help myself."

Alorsha did chuckle then. "Enough times of doing this and maybe you'll remember," she teased.

Gya nodded and managed a chuckle himself. "Maybe. I'll not wager on that, though."

When his breathing returned to a more normal rhythm, Shyvoan helped him to his feet. "Any success this time?" She leaned back against the rail next to Gya.

Gya shared a look with Alorsha. "Maybe?" He drew the word out.

"I don't know that I'd say success. Something new, though," Alorsha said and looked to Gya. "Did you see that thin ribbon of magic that extended away from the spark?"

"I did. Might that be Devrand gathering magic?"

Alorsha reached into the magic in her ring-pendant and shrugged. "It might be. Especially since it stretched the direction we're headed, toward where my wayfinding indicated he is. But I don't feel him drawing magic to himself." She frowned.

"So still no idea what the sparks are?" Shyvoan said.

Both Alorsha and Gya shook their heads.

"Don't get a good sense for them," Gya said.

"They appear and vanish, apparently randomly," Alorsha added. "But we'll keep trying. Maybe something will change, or we'll get some inspiration that will reveal more to us."

Shyvoan scrunched her nose but nodded. "Maybe. Well, my turn soon at the oars." She shared a smile with Gya and headed below.

Gya winced. "My turn again soon, too. I don't look forward to it."

"I'm doubt anyone aboard would say otherwise. But I've an idea for a different combination of some of those plants from our last few worlds. Let's see if we can come up with something to help." Alorsha headed to her cabin with Gya on her heels.

~ ~ ~

Days passed, of too-calm waters and too-weak breezes to send the *Deliberia* where she needed to go. No sea birds flew in sight. The gray sky and sea changed little. They just grew brighter during the daytime and faded into darkness during the nighttime. A brighter spot at night hinted at a moon, but it did little to illuminate the nights. And still no sight of land. Not even a small island.

The *Deliberia* crewmembers kept to their usual routine, with the added burden of rowing, but their animation dwindled. Attempts to fish resulted in no catches, so the meals developed a sameness to them. Fortunately, they carried plenty of stores, so they had no worries that they would run low on food, just variety.

Close to three weeks into their voyage in this world, Alorsha and Gya discovered a combination of plants that showed promise for helping with the matter of the ship's speed. Just one problem with it....

Alorsha waited on the ship's raised foredeck and brushed the *Deliberia*'s magic to follow Gya's progress. Gya and Shyvoan ran through the ship's passageways. He clutched a small metal pot wrapped in many layers of cloth. She ran ahead of him.

"Clear the way," she shouted at a crewmember who emerged from a side passage. The startled man jumped back as the two charged past him.

Gya almost trod on Shyvoan's heels as she rounded a corner. "Almost there," she told him.

"Might make it this time," he panted.

They dashed around another corner, up the stairs, and onto the main portion of the deck. They raced to the raised deck at the bow and up those stairs, where Alorsha stepped out of their way.

Gya nearly fell over in his haste as he placed the pot on

the deck by Alorsha's feet and removed the lid. He squeaked in pain and dropped the lid on the deck as he burned his hand.

Alorsha peered inside the pot and smiled. "Still boiling!" She pulled the cork from a small vial of pink liquid, poured it into the pot and—careful to touch only the cloth that wrapped the pot—tipped the pot over on the deck so the contents poured out.

She and Gya knelt to place their hands on the deck. They dove into the ship's magic and drew the magic of the spilled liquid into the wood even faster than the *Deliberia* normally did.

Kluir, Mikolus and Parl joined Shyvoan. All four stood back and waited to see if it worked.

"Now?" Saevalde called from the raised deck at the stern, where she stood near the wheel.

"Doesn't look like yet," Parl called back to her.

Alorsha tried to ignore the shouts and focused on the magic as she spread the potion throughout the ship, concentrating it in the hull. When it was as dispersed as it would get, and evenly spread, she sat back.

"Tell them now," she called to Saevalde, who in turn shouted down to the ship's interior where others would relay the message to the rowers.

Alorsha felt the ship move again as the rowers worked at the oars. The *Deliberia* picked up speed and Alorsha looked aft at Saevalde to see her reaction.

As the ship's speed increased and approached what they usually saw with a brisk tailwind, Saevalde grinned, and her expression grew wider.

"Think that's got it, lass."

With a smile and a wave, Alorsha turned back to the overturned pot.

"It absolutely must be boiling?" Mikolus said.

"Afraid so." Gya gave his burned hand a rueful look while Alorsha gingerly righted the pot, using the cloth to protect her hands.

"How many times is that now with the burns?" Kluir asked.

Gya shrugged. "It's not always my fault."

Shyvoan snorted. "Have to get you some good gloves and *make* you wear them."

Alorsha nodded agreement. "First, let's get that burn eased. Then, Gya, see one of the leatherworkers about some leather gloves. I assume they'll have to make them to fit, so once they've got your hand-size figured out, let's get back to work on that potion. I want the components as combined as possible—except for these last steps, of course—and in reserve, for when the effects wear off."

After Gya and Shyvoan left to find the healers, Mikolus drew Alorsha off to the side away from the crewmembers at work. Kluir and Parl followed.

"We've got some uneasiness making its way through the crew," Mikolus said. "Saevalde's managed to sooth it for now...."

"Isn't this close to the longest we've ever gone before we've found land, or at least some people to talk to?" Parl broke in. "Are we sure there even *is* any land in this world to find? Or people?"

Alorsha nodded. "It's true this time is unlike any before. But this potion will help."

"It increases the *Deliberia's* speed?" Kluir said.

"Not directly. What it does it make the ship move more smoothly through the water. Makes the water drag on the hull less so the ship is easier to propel with rowing, and that results in greater speed."

Kluir nodded his understanding.

"I can't say we're sure of anything in this world," Alorsha told Parl. "But we know that Devrand's here and that direction, roughly." She pointed the way the ship headed. "We know that always before he was on land. He's never taken a boat of his own through into another world. So that implies that there *is* land here, somewhere that way."

"Or he's on a boat *this* time," Parl muttered.

Alorsha smiled. "Or he's on a boat this time," she repeated. "Somewhere. But still, that direction."

"He's still not drawing the magic to him?" Kluir said.

"He's not. Although the sparks Gya and I have seen in the water seem to have ribbons of magic that extend that direction, there's no feel to the magic at all that Devrand's gathering it."

"Something strange going on here," Kluir muttered.

"Yes, and I've a feeling that Devrand's certainly part of it somehow. Tied into it. But it doesn't feel like he's actually *doing* anything. Not controlling or instigating anything."

"So far," Mikolus muttered.

Parl stared at her, his eyes wide. "Are you saying there's someone else in charge? Someone who's done all this?" He waved a hand at the lifeless gray around them.

Alorsha shrugged. "I've felt nothing strong enough or definitive enough to say anything like someone's 'in charge'. Just that there's something else going on here. Strange, as Kluir said. At least Gya and I have been able to draw some of this world's magic into the *Deliberia*. Very little and very slowly."

Kluir pointedly scanned the empty water and horizon around them. "Doesn't look like too much of a problem. I don't see anyone to talk to anytime soon."

"True," Mikolus murmured.

Alorsha nodded her agreement. "Even so, I'd at least like to have some connection to this world's magic. Makes it easier to sense when Devrand *does* do something. Might also give us some help in countering him."

Mikolus grabbed the cooling pot in its cloth wrapping. "I'll return this to the kitchen."

"We'll come, too," Parl said.

Kluir chuckled. "Hoping to get some of those sweet breads when they're hot out of the oven?"

Parl grinned. "You know it."

After she watched the three men head below, Alorsha turned to stare out at the gray water.

With so little magic in this world, what does that mean for Devrand? Might he be stuck here, now? Can I finally catch him and get Jarthan?

Are we going to be stuck here?

Devrand always seems to have a plan, but what's he thinking coming to this place?

CHAPTER 29

Shouts that land had been sighted drew Alorsha's attention from the magic within the mixture she stirred in the small pot on her table. But she had reached a crucial point. She could not go see just yet.

A whisper of magic from across her cabin drew her attention next. Her chervynai had been dormant for some weeks—its usual pattern—the leaves the usual rich green, but no stalk with the single large flower. As she watched, its stalk grew from the ball bush of its foliage. It always bloomed at the same speed as when she had first grown it.

Atop the stalk, the bud formed, then opened into the familiar dark-red flower with its gold-edged petals.

A matching zing of magic from the mixture in front of her reminded Alorsha of the task at hand. She carried the mixture with her, and continued to stir it, as she crossed the room to the chervynai. She plucked a single petal from the flower and dropped it into her mixture, nudging it beneath the surface. She placed the bowl on the shelf that ran beneath the window and positioned it so it would be in the dim light for a while.

Only then did she run out the door to see what the yelling on deck was about.

Alorsha sidled through what looked to be most of the ship's crew. She found Shyvoan and Gya leaning against the rail at the ship's bow and joined them.

"How long ago did the lookout spot it?" She peered into the grayness. No sign of the land yet from their vantage point on the deck.

"Not long enough to be seeing it yet from here," Saevalde said as she and Mikolus joined them. "Lookout reports a low, darker smudge on the horizon."

Shyvoan frowned. "So, it might not be land at all?"

"Might be it's a storm," Mikolus said.

Saevalde nodded. "We'll keep watch and let everyone know when we know." She moved back into the crowd and shooed crewmembers back to their duties.

Alorsha worked the wayfinding magic from the pole in the rigging. She usually only checked in the mornings. *But another look won't hurt.* Still the pendant pointed the direction they sailed and formed only the smallest arc.

He's moving around much less than usual. Wonder what that means.

With a shrug for her thoughts, she returned to her cabin to finalize the concoctions that she believed might be most useful when they confronted Devrand. Maybe, with this world having so little magic, they'd manage to catch and stop the man at last.

~ ~ ~

Some hours later, someone tapped at Alorsha's door. With some effort she drew herself from the plants' magic and glanced out one of the room's windows.

Good, still light at least. Haven't worked the whole day away this time. At least not entirely.

She stood and stretched away the stiffness from sitting so long.

"Come," she said when the knocking repeated.

The door opened and Gya peered around it. "I came by earlier, but you were too absorbed in the magic. We can see the darker smudge from the deck now. Did you want to take a look? Lookout still thinks it's land, but very flat."

With a nod, Alorsha eased through her messy work area and followed Gya to the raised foredeck. Saevalde stood there peering through her spyglass, Shyvoan next to her. When Alorsha and Gya joined them at the rail, Saevalde handed the spyglass to Alorsha.

"Not much to see, even through the glass," Saevalde said.

Alorsha took a look, then handed the spyglass to Gya.

"Dirt and maybe some rocks?" Alorsha said.

Saevalde nodded. "That's what it's looking like to me, too."

"More grayness, too," Shyvoan added. "Just a different tone."

"Maybe it's sand," Gya murmured and offered the spyglass to Shyvoan, who held up a hand and shook her head.

"Might be." Saevalde shrugged as Gya returned her spyglass.

"No plants," Alorsha muttered. "That might make this harder."

Saevalde gave her shoulder a light pat.

"What's that?" Gya said and drew their attention to port.

Alorsha, Saevalde, and Shyvoan peered the direction he indicated.

"Some kind of haze?" Shyvoan ventured. "True fog, maybe?"

"Seems too dark a color for that." Saevalde peered through her spyglass again.

"It's moving, but there's no breeze," Shyvoan said.

Could it be? "Can I borrow that again?" Alorsha reached for the spyglass.

"It kind of looks like those wisps of the *Deliberia's* magic," Gya said.

"There are more now," Shyvoan said.

Alorsha looked through the spyglass a long time in silence after Saevalde handed it over. Then she sighed.

"What is it, lass?"

She returned Saevalde's spyglass. "I've seen the like of those wisps before." She turned to Gya. "They're not the *Deliberia's* magic, but that magic the ship absorbed near the start of this journey. Remember, I told you of that."

Gya nodded. "The ones I've seen from the ship are more reddish. Because they've blended with the taiawood magic?"

"Yes. But those...." Alorsha waved a hand at the distant wisps. "I don't know what they're doing here. Unless.... Could this be the place they came from originally?"

They exchanged glances.

"Is this then where he's been headed all this time?" Saevalde said.

Alorsha watched as the distant wisps flowed from the water's edge onto the land and headed inland. "If it is, that means we might be within sight of the end of this whole business. One way or another. I've things to see to." She headed back to her cabin. "Please let me know when we reach the shore," she called back over a shoulder.

"I'll tell Mikolus about this and about what we suspect," Shyvoan said and headed below decks.

Gya and Saevalde exchanged looks.

"Feeling ready for this, lad?" Saevalde said.

"I think so. Yes. I've learned so much from Alorsha. I can be a strong support for whatever magic she decides to work."

"Good lad. I'll leave you to it, then." She headed back to the wheel at the stern.

Gya leaned on the rail and watched the distant wisps. Could they have been the sparks he and Alorsha had seen underwater? So, did that make the gold ribbons somehow Devrand's draw on the magic made visible? *So many questions.*

With a sigh, Gya let his awareness slip into the *Deliberia*'s magic. If they were to have a last confrontation with Devrand, he needed to be ready to take the ship away if Alorsha was too drained magically to do it herself after she got Jarthan back. She had taken Gya through all the *Deliberia*'s magic workings several times already. While he had not yet taken the ship to another world by himself, he felt ready to do so.

Hope it won't come to that, though.

~ ~ ~

The *Deliberia* reached the shore later that night. A strip of shallow water rimmed the shoreline. Saevalde managed to maneuver the ship close enough for those on deck to get a sense of the land, even in the darkness of night slightly lit from some moonlight that filtered through the ever-present clouds overhead.

Alorsha followed Gya to the rail after he came to get her as she had requested. She stifled a yawn. She had been nearly asleep when Gya had knocked at her cabin door.

"Not much to be seeing, lass," Saevalde greeted her.

Alorsha peered at the nearby shoreline, flat and mostly featureless. Dark dirt or sand with larger rocks scattered about. It extended as far as she could see.

"No sign of any threats," Mikolus reported as he lowered the spyglass. He handed it to Saevalde. "Still, I plan to increase the watches for the rest of the night."

"So, we'll drop anchor here?" Gya said.

"We'll back off again from the shore first, but aye," Saevalde said. "For the rest of the night, anyway. Tomorrow we can sail along the shore if we like when we can see better."

Alorsha nodded. "I'd like to see this in the daylight,

such as it is. Any further sightings of the wisps?"

"I've seen a few random flashes of those gold ribbons, heading off the same way we saw the wisps earlier," Gya said. "Nothing closer, and nothing headed toward us."

"Good enough then, for now. Morning will be soon enough to consider our options." Alorsha looked from Saevalde to Mikolus. "But inform me right away if anything changes during the night. Even if it seems trivial."

After they agreed, she returned to her cabin.

~ ~ ~

The morning light revealed nothing new on the land. Alorsha enjoyed a slice of warm bread while she contemplated the view. Her wayfinding earlier had indicated inland and somewhat to port.

Those wisps were on the port side.

The land she saw stretched out to the horizon ahead of the ship. *So, a good-sized island, at least.*

The dark ground rose a few feet, at most, above the sea's surface. Nowhere did it rise any higher and no plants grew anywhere in sight. Just the dark dirt or sand close to the water, and numerous rocks of close to the same color.

She gazed to port but saw no wisps in the morning light.

Does the shore curve over there? Maybe there's a bay that'll let us get even closer in.

She pointed it out to Saevalde when the other woman joined her.

"Aye, lass. I'd thought to be taking a look there if you'd no objections."

"Agreed. Those wisps were somewhere that direction. And now my wayfinding shows Devrand also to port, but inland."

"Then that's the next step." Saevalde left to get the ship underway again.

Alorsha remained at the rail as the ship turned to port

and skirted the coast. She kept her attention mainly on the land but noticed Mikolus stationing several warriors with bows along the ship's rails. She accepted her own bow and a quiver of arrows with a slight nod when Gya brought them to her.

"Don't know what we'll use them against, but Mikolus is happier with us ready with ranged weaponry," Gya muttered.

Alorsha chuckled. "And you're prepared with some ranged magic, right?"

With a short snort of a laugh, Gya said, "For what it's worth. I've not seen those magic-ribbons yet today."

"Nor have I."

After they rounded the curve of the land and spotted a small cove that lay beyond, Alorsha worked her wayfinding magic again. The pendant pointed inland with a slight waver.

Still nothing different to see that direction, though. Only the near-black sand, dirt, and rocks. Nothing grew and nothing moved. Nothing broke the plane of the horizon.

As the motion of the ship slowed, Saevalde joined them. "Put to shore here or keep sailing to see if we can find a landing further inland?"

Alorsha gazed into the distance. "Let's at least sail the rest of this day, following the coastline, and see what we see. We can reassess the decision this evening."

"Aye, we'll be doing that, then."

~ ~ ~

Except for the shape of the shoreline, the land did not change throughout the day. Whenever Alorsha worked her wayfinding magic, the direction always indicated inland, with only a small arc.

They discovered several other small bays and some sandbars, but still no sign of anything alive. The best they could judge, the land did seem to curve ever so gradually, perhaps to form an island in the end. But it was so gradual, Saevalde estimated it might take days, at best, to circumnavigate it, assuming it kept to the same rough curve.

When sundown approached, Alorsha instructed Saevalde to drop anchor some distance out from the latest bay. She then gathered the group who had over the course of the journey become the informal ruling council for the floating town that was the *Deliberia*. They met in the room next to Saevalde's cabin and took seats around the large table there. Shyvoan, Kluir, and Parl entered carrying large plates of food, along with smaller plates and utensils.

Alorsha raised an eyebrow at them.

"Got to eat the evening meal sometime," Parl said as the three placed the plates on the shelf that sat beneath the room's windows. "Might as well do it while we figure out our attack."

Taesen and Naltha followed behind the three warriors, bringing jugs of wine and mugs. The healers placed them at either end of the line of plates of food. They filled smaller plates for themselves and took seats together in the middle of one of the longer sides of the table.

"I don't know that I'd call it an attack." Alorsha fixed a plate for herself and took a seat at one end of the table.

Mikolus plopped another two wine jugs next to the plates on the shelf. "We should look at it that way." After he filled a plate for himself, he took one of the seats along the side, next to Alorsha.

The others also fixed plates and settled at the table. Gya took the other seat at the side next to Alorsha and the others filled in the rest of the seats. Saevalde took the end opposite Alorsha.

"I think he's got the right of it," Shyvoan said after everyone had eaten some. She pointed her fork at Mikolus, then speared a piece of meat from her plate. "We shouldn't wait to see what Devrand's doing or going to do."

"I might still be able to convince him…." Alorsha's voice trailed off.

Saevalde sighed. "Lass, you know he's not the boy you knew before. The one the both of us originally sailed with."

"We've got to be ready to stop him right away," Gya said. "Keep him from doing *anything*. Or at least anything more."

"I know. Really, I do." Alorsha stared at her plate. "I'd truly prefer that we find some way to incapacitate him. And then can take him back home."

Silence descended on the room.

"Home?" Saevalde said. "Is that even possible? After what happened that time we tried to return to a previous world."

Alorsha nodded and sipped her wine. "I've been working on that. Delving into the *Deliberia*'s magic. I *think* I might have it figured out."

"We could go back anytime now?" Parl said.

Alorsha shook her head. "No. If we tried right now, I'm sure it would be just like before. But I suspect that the wisps of magic belong here. That they came from here and somehow have wanted to come back here. I expect if there's some way to remove them from the *Deliberia* and leave them here, the ship would be free to travel elsewhere. The magic to go to other worlds is set in the taiawood now. So, the wisps shouldn't be needed to make it work."

Everyone exchanged looks.

"That would be a wonder," Saevalde said. "To be able to decide ourselves where to go."

Murmurs of agreement circled the table.

"But first, Devrand," Mikolus said. "Is it these wisps that magically tie you and Devrand and Jarthan all to each other?"

"In part, from what I've perceived through the magic," Alorsha said. "We *are* tied together elseways, too. But the wisps seem integral to our ability to follow Devrand to the various worlds."

"So, wisps and Devrand to take care of," Kluir said.

"But what's Devrand been doing all this time here," Parl said. "From what you've seen with the wayfinding, he's moved little."

"Of a certain there don't seem to be the people to have to talk to or work with or around," Taesen pointed out.

"Plenty of time to set a trap," Shyvoan said.

"Aye, I'd be wagering that's what he's been up to." Saevalde gave a decisive nod. "Especially if these wisps are from here and he's got that stronger connection to them that you'd told us about when you shared how this all started."

"Even if so, there seems little to do about any trap he's set for us," Naltha murmured.

"Except spring it," Gya said.

"Surprise him somehow," Parl said.

"Alorsha, have you and Gya worked some new magics?" Kluir said.

Alorsha nodded. "Some. Mostly variations on things I, or we, have done before. But improved, I hope. And better ways to implement them."

"Better how?" Shyvoan looked from Gya to Alorsha.

Gya grinned. "In one case, we've managed to concentrate that distraction scent, the so-called dreamy cream that we used before, into a powdery concoction. Put it into a small jar. So just break the jar near him to affect him. Throw it to the ground at his feet and the stuff will burst out when the jar breaks."

"Won't be able to use local plants against him," Mikolus pointed out.

Alorsha grimaced. "True. At least, not unless he's somewhere where some plants grow."

"Not likely," Gya mumbled. "He's learned about that trick."

Alorsha nodded. "Agreed. Still, I'll bring some seeds along, too. I can grow some plants quickly for use, if needed."

"Do you need more time to prepare?" Mikolus asked.

"Not more than just a little bit tonight to gather everything together." Alorsha looked around at the others. "We'll leave the ship in the morning."

Mikolus and the other three warriors exchanged glances.

"We can pull everything together to leave early and still get some good rest," Shyvoan said. "We've already half prepared as it is. Just need to figure out how much food and water to carry."

"So then, who'll be going with you?" Saevalde said.

Mikolus answered her. "I will. Alorsha's three and Gya, too." He looked at the two healers. "I'd like one of you, too, if you're up to it."

The healers exchanged looks with each other.

"Neither of us can travel fast or for long before we need to rest. We might slow you too much," Naltha said.

"Understood," Mikolus nodded. "But we need to have a healer with us. We can make accommodations."

Kluir, Parl, and Shyvoan exchanged glances.

Parl broke into a grin. "We can modify a cart we've got in the hold to carry one of you. It won't take too long. The ground, at least as far as we can see, isn't *too* rough. We can take turns pulling it."

"Like those small, two-wheeled open carriages we saw in that one world. The ones that a single person pulled along," Gya said.

Alorsha nodded. "Right. What did they call them?"

"It was 'tilbry', wasn't it?" Shyvoan said.

"You can get one ready for morning?" Alorsha asked Parl, who nodded.

"Then I should go," Naltha said. "I'm lighter than Taesen." She shared a grin with her husband. "And I'm the better at throwing. I can throw those jars for you."

She and Taesen clasped hands. "She's well-practiced at throwing things," Taesen said with a chuckle. "She's right.

She should be the healer to accompany you."

"Sounds like it's settled," Alorsha said. "Seven of us to go."

"And don't be worrying about us here on the *Deliberia*," Saevalde said. "If that Devrand's plans any sort of trickiness, we'll be ready for him."

Mikolus nodded. "Double up on the watches and everyone keep weapons at hand while we're gone."

Saevalde nodded.

"We've got some special jars to leave with you, too," Alorsha said. "When they break, flames shoot out."

"Hope we're taking some of those with us, too," Kluir said.

Gya grinned. "Oh, we are. We definitely are."

On that note, they finished their meal and separated to deal with their individual preparations then get what sleep they could.

CHAPTER 30

"Looks like we've got a bit of a trek." From the deck of the *Deliberia*, Gya gazed into the distance, across the expanse of land. The ship had not been able to get close enough for the group to go ashore directly, so crewmembers ferried them the short distance in the ship's tenders.

"Coming through," Parl's voice accompanied the rumbled of wheels across the deck as he and Kluir pulled the tilbry to the opening in the rail.

"I hope it'll hold together," Shyvoan murmured in Gya's ear.

Gya nodded and studied the little carriage while Kluir and Parl attached ropes that would let them lower it to the tender that waited below. The thing was not much more than a couple of boards that formed a seat, attached to two large wheels, with two poles that extended forward to allow someone to pull it.

Gya grimaced. *Doesn't look very comfortable. But at least it's got a backrest.*

"Maybe we should put together some kind of cushion."

Alorsha joined Shyvoan and Gya. Together the three watched Kluir and Parl wrestle the tilbry over the side and down to the tender.

Shyvoan shook her head. "No need. I saw Naltha stuff a couple of pillows into a pack. I believe she's set."

Alorsha nodded absently, her gaze on the horizon.

Gya and Shyvoan followed the direction of her gaze.

"I worry what he's got planned," Alorsha murmured.

Shyvoan nodded. "He's got to know we're coming, right?"

"Should we take more people with us?" Gya said.

Alorsha shook her head. "I doubt more would help. And I prefer to leave a good number of potential defenders with the *Deliberia*. In case Dev somehow gets past us." One of the crewmembers called to her. With a pat on Gya's shoulder she headed to the rail in answer to the call.

"Would he go after the *Deliberia*?" Shyvoan did not turn from her scrutiny of the land.

Gya shrugged. "He hasn't before in the time I've sailed with her. Not before that, either, from what I've heard. Why would he need to? He's been able to go from world to world without the ship."

Shyvoan nodded and turned to look back over the ship. She stiffened. "Another of those wisps," she murmured.

Gya looked where she indicated. A thin, reddish, smoky wisp lifted from the deck of the ship. It stretched out the direction they intended to travel, the direction Alorsha had pointed out from her wayfinding magic. The wisp hovered, a murky line in the air. Then it streaked away and vanished in the distance.

Gya turned to alert Alorsha and met her gaze. She nodded. She had seen it. She turned back to urge the crewmembers to greater speed. Shyvoan and Gya grabbed the packs that sat on the deck and joined Alorsha at the rail.

After everyone—and everything—going on the journey

reached the shore, they sorted themselves out. With little time lost, they checked flintlocks, bows, and swords, and shifted the contents of the packs for the best ease of carrying.

Gya gave Shyvoan a questioning look as she pulled her dragon-scale infused blade in its scabbard from her pack and buckled it on, which gave her a sword at each hip.

She met his gaze and shrugged. "I can't continue to blame a perfectly good sword for what Devrand used it for. And Alorsha's wound from that flintlock a few worlds back could have been so much worse than it had been. If I hadn't brought my sword along that time…. Anyway, if it *is* part of the 'luck', I'd like to encourage as much of that as possible."

She smiled and turned away to rearrange some things in a pack.

Naltha pulled two flattened pillows from a bag and situated them as cushions for the seat and backrest before she climbed onto the tilbry's short bench. She settled her two packs of necessities tight at her sides and grinned at the others.

"I'm set here. Shall we give this cart a try?"

Kluir swung his pack on his back and handed his other pack to Parl. "I'll pull first. Parl, follow please and watch for anything we need to tighten or fix."

With a nod, the younger man took his place behind the tilbry, with his two packs and Kluir's second.

"Are we ready then?" Alorsha asked.

After agreement all around, she and Mikolus both waved to the ship and turned away after Saevalde waved back. Alorsha paused to watch another wisp from the *Deliberia* float off the direction they intended to go. She headed after it as she hitched the pack on her back to a more comfortable position. The others fell into a rough line behind her, with Mikolus pacing to her left.

The ground sloped upward from the shore, but the slope was gradual. Kluir assured Naltha that pulling the tilbry was no problem the several times she asked as they climbed the slope. At the top, they paused for Parl to secure something on the tilbry that had jostled loose over the pebbly ground. Kluir helped while the others spread out a few steps to look around.

The slight elevation provided no more of a view than what they had seen from the ship. Mostly flat, dark, dry dirt and a multitude of pebbles of the same color, with a few larger rocks here and there.

"And still no plants," Alorsha murmured.

Mikolus took a sip from his waterskin. "At least it's not overly warm. With no shade, this would be brutal otherwise."

"More wisps," Gya said.

Everyone turned to watch the several wisps flow the direction they themselves headed. Most of the wisps were gray, but three were the reddish color that marked the ones from the *Deliberia*.

"Is he purposefully drawing them in or doing something that attracts them?" Gya wondered.

"I can't tell for sure," Alorsha said. "Best guess, it's something that attracts them. If he was drawing them in, I'd feel something like when he gathers magic. But I've not felt that."

"That's got it," Parl announced and straightened from his work on the tilbry.

"On ahead then," Alorsha said.

The hours passed as they continued their journey, and they lost sight of the ship behind them. They paused from time to time to switch off tilbry-pulling duty as none of them was accustomed to that sort of work.

Around mid-day, with the brightest spot of the sky overhead, they stopped to rest and eat, after they first cleared an area of the larger pebbles to let them sit in relative comfort. No one seemed inclined to talk and they finished their meal before long. While the others repacked the few things they had not eaten, Alorsha worked the wayfinding magic. When they set out again, they adjusted their heading to match the direction the magic had indicated.

As they traveled, the scenery remained unchanged and the ground underfoot mostly flat, with the random larger rocks to stumble over or guide the tilbry around. The afternoon wore on and a stupor crept over everyone as they trudged across the monotonous terrain.

A sting across the back of his left hand yanked Gya from his gray daze. He jerked to the side, away from the sensation, and nearly knocked Shyvoan off her feet. One of those gray wisps flowed past. *Must've been that.*

Shyvoan steadied him with a hand on his shoulder, her other held a drawn sword. "Are you all right?"

Gya examined the darkened line that crossed the back of his hand. "I think so." The others paused and gathered around.

"Looks like we don't want those wisps to touch us," Shyvoan said, her tone wry.

Naltha climbed down from her seat and held a hand out to Gya. "Let me take a look."

"It's not bad," Gya protested. "Not even a scratch. More like a bruise, if anything."

"Still," Naltha insisted and took his hand when he relented.

After a few minutes of silence while she examined the injury, the healer glanced at Alorsha. "Please look at this, too," she said.

With a puzzled frown, Alorsha stepped close and brushed her hand across the mark on Gya's hand.

Both women reacted at the same time and jumped away from each other with almost identical exclamations of pain. The warriors of the group also jumped back and scanned their surroundings, each with a weapon ready.

"What happened?" Gya demanded. "What is it?"

"A part of the wisp lies under the skin," Naltha said. "I can wrap the hand with one of the healing charms, but I don't know that it will be helpful."

"I've seen something like this before," Alorsha said. "But it was Devrand who pulled the other-magic splinter from the afflicted boy."

Gya closed his eyes to concentrate on the magic. *Yes, there.* A touch of different magic in his hand, which resembled what he felt from the *Deliberia*. *But not quite the same*

"Can you try anyway?" Shyvoan edged closer to clasp Gya's unaffected hand.

"I can try," Alorsha said.

"Do we really need to do anything?" Gya said at the same time.

Alorsha considered that. "With the boy, it was an actual object, a long splinter that was infused with the other-magic. It seemed to act with some purpose and caused the boy a lot of pain. I don't know what leaving it might do."

"This only stings some," Gya said. "And maybe if I carry it, I can use it somehow when we face Devrand. The *Deliberia* carries this magic after all and has suffered no ill effects from it."

"You're not a taiawood ship." Shyvoan shook the hand she held. He grinned at her.

"Let me at least investigate it for a while," Gya said to Alorsha. "If it gets worse or tries to crawl up my arm or something, I'll help you yank the thing out."

With a dubious expression, Alorsha agreed. "I'll keep an eye on you, though."

Shyvoan seconded her statement and released his hand after another shake.

With glances at Gya's injury that were as dubious as Alorsha's, the others resumed their places. They sheathed their swords, and again they walked.

The sliver of magic he carried in his hand drew Gya's attention to it. He reached toward the magic and tried to touch it as Alorsha had taught him to touch the magic in plants, while he still kept at least some of his attention on the surroundings.

The magic felt little like that in the *Deliberia*. Rather it had a slippery feel to it and Gya could find no particular purpose or inclination in it, as he found in plants' magics.

While he felt little from the wisp fragment other than its strange magic, he did notice that he better perceived other wisps nearby. A glance around, however, showed him nothing flowing past. But he sensed them there. They swarmed around the group, and all headed the same direction.

Daring greatly, he sank into the wisp's magic. He pulled gently on it and looked around again.

This time he saw tiny wisps all around them, and beyond. They streamed in the same direction. But unlike the wisp that had stung his hand, these seemed to avoid coming too close to any of them. He looked beyond the diaphanous wisps near them and saw larger ones nearly at the limits of his vision. They too flowed the same direction. Some wisps curled around themselves and changed until they vaguely resembled people.

As he watched, he discerned more and more of those, many almost invisible in the gray surroundings. One paused in its forward motion and turned what resembled a head toward Gya. The swirling smoky head transformed and gained features he recognized with no difficulty. It seemed Devrand stared right at him.

With a cry, Gya stumbled away. His concentration dissolved and all he had seen vanished back into the gray surroundings. A sharp headache hit behind his eyes, and he sank to his knees and held his head.

The others immediately surrounded him, and their voices added to his agony – until Alorsha shushed them and sent them back a few steps. Naltha knelt next to him and placed a cool hand on his forehead to hold one of her healing charms against the skin there.

Alorsha crouched in front of him. "Tell me."

He shared all that he had seen.

"Does that mean Devrand now knows where we are?" Shyvoan gave Gya a concerned look when met her gaze.

"Might be that he does," Mikolus said. "Though it wouldn't be surprising if he knew already."

"Not exactly any way to hide and sneak up on him here," Parl murmured and waved a hand at the open expanse around them.

"Did it help?" Naltha asked Gya as she sat back and took the charm away.

Gya cautiously raised his head and looked around, surprised to see that in the time he had been occupied with the magic, short as it had felt, they had moved into evening, judging by the ambient light.

"Much better," he told Naltha, with a slight smile.

Shyvoan plopped down next to him, with a hard stare for Alorsha. "So, let's get this wisp magic out of him."

"We can just set our camp here, such as it'll be," Kluir said.

Alorsha nodded. "Naltha, please stay nearby, just in case." She shooed Shyvoan off to help Kluir and gave Gya a questioning look.

He answered with a shrug. "I could keep it a while longer, so we can see what those tiny wisps and the people-like shapes do," he suggested.

Alorsha considered that. "I'm uncertain that it's worth the risk. Not counting the *Deliberia* and my mage ring's erythros stone—special cases, I expect you'll agree— everything else that I've seen come into such close contact with this other-magic has come to destruction and ruin."

"*You* haven't," Gya pointed out. "And honestly Devrand hasn't, nor your Jarthan."

Alorsha frowned. "True. And I don't know why. So, I'll defer to you for now."

Gya nodded. "My thanks. I'll be sure to let you know instantly if something happens that means we must try to remove it immediately."

Alorsha grinned. "See that you do." She left him and

headed to help the others.

Gya and Naltha exchanged looks.

"Is the pain gone? From your head and your hand?" the healer said.

"For the most part. My head now feels sort of fuzzy. The hand still stings, but not as much as at first."

Naltha studied him a moment. "Good enough, then. For now. But as with Alorsha, get me immediately if that changes for the worst."

"I will."

"Good." She levered herself to her feet. "For now, rest and drink some water. The others can get the camp set without you this time."

With a nod, Gya pulled a skin of water from his pack and sipped it while he watched the others set up the camp. They had a cold camp that night, but Alorsha surprised them with a small pot of herbs that, when she dribbled a few drops of water into it, grew warm enough to heat the food they had brought with them. That raised their spirits as they cleared areas of the ubiquitous rocks to provide reasonable places to sleep.

They set watches for the night so that two people would be awake at any given time. Gya offered to help, but Naltha nixed that idea.

"While you've got a strange magic to deal with, you'll not short yourself on rest," she told him.

Shyvoan gave him an emphatic nod of agreement when his gaze happened to meet hers.

So Gya settled on his bedding, as did the others— except for Mikolus and Kluir, who took first watch—and they passed around a skin of wine. When Gya took a drink from the skin he choked and coughed at the sharp flavor.

Parl laughed. "True, it's not the best homemade. But it travels better than the better ones we've got aboard.

"Probably doesn't get finished on its travels, either," Gya muttered. His comment drew chuckles from the others.

Gya laid back and listened as the others tossed around guesses about what they would find Devrand up to.

He watched the clouds above, backlit from the moon. They changed shape, unhurried, and drifted with unfelt winds. Where he lay, the air was still.

Funny that they never seem to thin or thicken. He missed seeing the sun and moon. *And stars. And the ground's so dusty and gritty. What happened that it's like this?*

Slowly, the clouds above stretched, elongated, and formed streaks that pointed the direction they headed, the direction he had seen the wisps and the people-shapes going.

Something tugged at him. Magic pulled at him, urged him to travel with the wisps, the clouds, the shapes. Seemingly of its own accord, his left arm rose from his blankets, stretched out toward the horizon hidden in the dark.

He rose, too, and tossed his bedding back behind him. *That's the way to go.* He saw well enough in the dim moonlight. He needed to go there. Soon everything would be made right.

More and more of the wisps appeared. They streamed past him and urged him along with them. Other shapes formed in the gloom. Hints of structures. Buildings.

Whispers brushed him, faint voices that spoke of wonder and bliss... of knowing what was needed... of commanding all magic.

"Gya?"

Why can't I go there? Something tugged at him, holding him back.

"Gya!"

Shapes coalesced and he saw....

Magic touched him, familiar. It flowed from something cool pressed against his right temple. Another magic lingered beyond, also familiar.

Gya opened his eyes and looked at the wisp in his left hand. It had stretched to reach up his arm almost to his elbow. "I think the time's come to get this thing out of my hand."

Shyvoan tugged on his right arm. "Then let's get back to our camp.

Gya shook his head to clear his vision of the wisps and figures and looked around. Shyvoan and Alorsha stood with him, the three of them several hundred paces from the camp. He shook his head again.

"That was strange."

"Back to the camp," Alorsha urged as she continued to hold one of Naltha's charms against Gya's temple. She grabbed Gya's hand and brought it to the charm. "You hold this."

With a nod, Gya complied and the three of them returned to where the others waited. From the light, Gya judged it to be near dawn. But he'd been walking in the night right until Shyvoan's voice had brought him back to himself. *Interesting.*

When they returned to the camp, Naltha bustled to him and took charge of the charm. She added another that she clutched against his upper arm, beyond the reach of the wisp. She led him back to his bedding and pulled him down to sit, her grip stronger than he had expected.

Alorsha and Shyvoan sat next to them.

"Was it Devrand again?" Alorsha said.

Gya shook his head. "At least, not directly, I believe. I just felt a pull to go that direction. With the wisps. And I saw many more of them, even in the darkness. It felt like he's definitely attracting them, but they seemed willing. Complaisant with the whole thing. I sensed something about making something right."

Alorsha frowned. "Any idea what?"

Gya shook his head. "Mostly the feeling. But I did see some things. Maybe what happened here."

"Tell us after we get this splinter of magic out of your hand and arm," Shyvoan said.

Alorsha nodded. "It's time. If the wisps are working

with Devrand, we don't want that kind of connection to you."

"Who knows what he'd do with it," Shyvoan said.

Gya nodded. "I don't need to be convinced now. I'd rather not wander off again. Let's get rid of the thing. What do we do?"

"I'm afraid it's going to be trying different things," Alorsha said. "I have hopes that we won't have to do too much to get it out. This might take your help, too, Naltha."

"Will we need to cut it out?" Shyvoan brushed a hand across the hilt of the dagger she carried on her belt.

Gya shuddered. "I hope not."

"Agreed," Alorsha said. "But it's possible it could come to that."

Naltha patted Gya's shoulder then Shyvoan's. "This will take magic, I expect dears." With a smile, she took Shyvoan's hand and placed it in Gya's. "Your moral support will be your first offering. You both just hold on there. If we need the blade, you'll be right here for it."

"Best you lie down," Alorsha told Gya. "Harder for you to walk off on us, if this has you trying to do that again."

Gya stretched out atop his bedding and Shyvoan shifted to sit on his right side, their hands still clasped. Naltha took a position by Gya's left shoulder while Alorsha knelt next to his left hand.

Gya shuddered again, which drew concerned looks from the three women.

He shrugged. "It's tugging. Also, I'm getting these shivers from it."

Alorsha frowned. "We'll get to this, then. Gya, brush the wisp's magic, if you can without getting caught in it, and push it away. I'll pull on it at the same time and hopefully this will work. Everyone ready?"

After the others nodded, Alorsha closed her eyes and clasped Gya's fingers, below the wisp. "Now, Gya."

Gya also closed his eyes as he reached out to the magic in the wisp. He brushed it, as directed, and tried to push it away from him. He felt Alorsha pull on it as she drew it at the same time, not too dissimilar to drawing the magic out in a plant.

Tension built in the wisp. It thinned and lengthened.

Gya felt a tugging on something within himself and worked to block the wisp from whatever it tried to do while he continued to push against it.

A thin tendril slid from the back of his hand, something he felt rather than saw since he still had his eyes closed. It paused, still connected to him, split into two tendrils, and lashed out toward the nearby magics, toward Alorsha and Naltha.

With a cry of warning, Gya clasped the wisp's magic and tried to throw himself back from both Alorsha and Naltha – hard to do while he lay prone. At the same time, Shyvoan also cried out a warning and sliced at the wisps with her sword—one she had gotten from the ship's stores—sprawling across Gya in the process.

Alorsha and Naltha fell back from the others as the sword passed through the wisps without any apparent effect. Gya scuttled further away and yanked the wisp back. With a spike of pain that ran up his arm and into his shoulder, the wisp again withdrew under his skin.

Mikolus, Kluir and Parl rushed to assure themselves that no one had been injured and that they did not need to defend from an attack. Trembling in reaction, Gya eased back to the bedding.

"A surprise, but Gya contained the wisp," Alorsha assured the concerned warriors who hovered around the group on the ground.

With a nod of acknowledgment, Mikolus set Kluir and Parl to watch around them and he joined Shyvoan to guard the mages more closely.

Naltha placed a hand, which held one of her charms, on Gya's forehead and his trembling ceased as the pain vanished.

"Well," he said.

Alorsha sighed. "I'm sorry, I should have anticipated that. It didn't occur to me that this wisp would react that way, although I've seen that type of reaction before. It was a physical splinter that time, but it's clear it must have had something like this wisp in it."

"Don't blame yourself," Gya said. "Now we know."

Alorsha nodded. "Last time I saw this done, pulling this magic from someone, we had something to catch the wisp. A box to put it in...." Her voice trailed off.

Shyvoan looked around their meagre camp. "Maybe pilfer some pieces from the tilbry to make a box?"

Alorsha studied the little carriage. "Using taiawood would work, I think, but taking even just a few pieces from the tilbry might make it unusable."

"Maybe my ring?" Gya said. "It's also taiawood."

Alorsha's expression turned thoughtful. "We already know the wood can contain wisps," she murmured. "That should work."

"But won't it still try to get to Gya?" Shyvoan said. "Try to make him follow the others?"

Gya grinned. "The *Deliberia's* never had that problem, but I'll just keep the ring in a pocket unless I need its magic." He pulled off his taiawood ring and held it out to Shyvoan.

"That'll work?" Shyvoan looked from Gya to Alorsha and back.

Alorsha nodded. "And as you've no magic, please hold the ring for this. As we've seen, the wisps are attracted to other magic and so you'll have nothing to worry about. Although, maybe set your heirloom sword aside for a moment."

After Shyvoan drew her dragon-scale infused sword and set it on the ground several paces away, Alorsha positioned Shyvoan's hand, in which she held Gya's ring, within a handspan of the wisp in Gya's arm, then looked to the healer. "Ready?"

Naltha nodded and Alorsha turned to Gya. "As before, Gya, push the wisp from you. I'll pull on it at the same time and this time drag it to the ring."

Mikolus shifted closer and held his sword ready. At Gya's glance, he shrugged. "Might not make a difference, but best to be prepared." Gya nodded and glanced at Alorsha, who had already closed her eyes.

"Whenever you're ready, Gya," she said.

This time Gya kept his eyes open. He focused on the mark on his hand and again touched the wisp's magic. It tried to wriggle away from him, but he grasped it and worked to push it away from him. Bit by bit, the end of the wisp furthest up his arm slid back toward his hand. The wisp grew thicker again as it bunched into a shorter space. The process was not without pain and Gya grimaced as it increased as he pushed the wisp further.

A welcome easing of the pain came from one of Naltha's charms where she pressed it against the shoulder of the arm with the wisp. Gya pushed harder against the wisp and sensed Alorsha's pull grow stronger.

The wisp bunched under the skin on the back of his hand and formed an ugly knot there. A hint of it oozed out of his skin and reached toward the ring that Shyvoan held close. But with that motion, the wisp yanked on something within Gya's hand and caused it to contort into a desiccated claw, accompanied by sudden agony that tore a scream from him.

"You have to stop!" Shyvoan said.

"No," Gya countered. "Almost there…."

With a last push against the wisp, channeling his desperation and his fear, too, Gya lurched back as the wisp tore free of his hand and plunged into the ring. The force of it knocked both Alorsha and Shyvoan to the ground.

Naltha slapped a wadded bandage on the back of Gya's hand and pressed it there. Alorsha and Shyvoan both sat up and they all looked at Gya's ring. The red-brown taiawood had darkened and a hint of the wisp hung around its edges.

Shyvoan held it out at arm's length, angled away from Alorsha, Gya, and Naltha, but her attention was on Gya, her expression concerned.

While she worked on Gya's hand, Naltha glanced at Shyvoan. "Maybe better take that thing further away. Don't want it to get back to him."

Mikolus grabbed a narrow bandage from Naltha's pack nearby and strung it through the ring, wrapped it around it, and knotted it to hold it secure, with no part of the ring visible. He tucked it in a pocket. "I'll hold onto this for now."

"But I'll want it back when Naltha's done what she can," Gya said, his voice little louder than a whisper.

"We'll see about that in a bit," Alorsha said as she pulled Shyvoan to her feet. "Do you need anything from us, Naltha?"

"Another waterskin is all."

Mikolus grabbed one and handed it to the healer then headed back to his watching duties.

Alorsha drew Shyvoan away. "Let's give them room."

Shyvoan reluctantly agreed. After she returned her sword to its scabbard, she pulled together some food for a morning meal to distract herself from constantly looking to Gya and Naltha.

CHAPTER 31

Naltha worked her healing on Gya's hand for close to an hour. When she finished, he slept, and she joined the others where they sat nearby. Alorsha handed her some food and a cup of the sharp wine.

Unable to restrain herself any longer, Shyvoan blurted, "How is he?" as Naltha took her last bite of food.

Naltha swallowed and washed the bite down with a hefty drink, then patted Shyvoan's hand. "He's in no pain and the sleep is natural. I managed to mitigate some of what the wisp did to his hand, but not all of it. While it might improve in time, I doubt he'll regain full use of it."

"There's nothing more you can do?" Alorsha said.

Naltha shook her head. "That wisp all but gutted his hand from the inside, as it pulled on his magic, I suspect. This is the best outcome after that. He'll need to rest today, as will I. But we should be ready to continue tomorrow."

Alorsha gave Mikolus a questioning look.

He nodded. "We can do that. Since we won't be moving, though, I recommend we stay low to the ground while we're here. Less visible from a distance. Although I do want to do some scouting, too."

Alorsha nodded in turn. "Set watches for the day. Otherwise, rest too. And I'll take the ring now."

"Are you sure it's safe?" Shyvoan asked.

A slight smile touched Alorsha's lips. "I wouldn't call it safe. But it *is* contained. And if I've got it and something changes, I'll be able to react that much faster."

Mikolus pulled the bundle from his pocket and handed it over. "If swords can help at all, you'll let us know."

Alorsha did smile then. "Of course."

With a nod to her, Mikolus sent Parl off the direction they had been traveling. Parl stayed low to the ground as he went. Alorsha lost sight of him before too long. She set herself to watch back the way they had come and to the sides, while Kluir watched the direction Parl had gone, and to the sides too. Mikolus and Shyvoan dozed nearby.

Not half an hour had passed when Parl returned at a jog and waved Kluir and Alorsha to join him. "Something ahead. A lump on the ground, larger than any of the rocks we've seen so far. Wasn't there last night," he told them.

Kluir woke Mikolus and Shyvoan.

Alorsha and Shyvoan took defensive stances by Naltha and Gya, while Parl led the other two warriors off again. The women's wait was short as the others hurried back before long, Parl and Kluir supporting someone between them.

Alorsha's expression became a mix of hope and fear, as they approached then sank to the ground at the edge of the camp.

"Jarthan?" Alorsha dropped her bow and ran the few steps to what Shyvoan saw was a man crumpled on the ground. He looked little like Shyvoan remembered, much thinner and with a withered look that resembled Gya's hand. His clothes were thin, with many tears and holes. He was unshaven, for many days it looked like, and his gold-brown hair hung long, shaggy, in his eyes.

Alorsha gathered him into her arms and after a moment he wrapped his arms around her and buried his face in the crook of her neck.

Mikolus woke Naltha who grabbed her charms and patted Alorsha's shoulder to get her attention.

"Let me see what I can do for him," the healer said.

With a nod, Alorsha scooted away, but still clasped his hand. Naltha held a charm against Jarthan's upper arm and closed her eyes.

Jarthan looked at the people who surrounded them, with a slight smile for Kluir and more of one for Shyvoan. He exchanged nods with Mikolus, who introduced himself, Parl and Naltha, and the still-sleeping Gya.

"I remember you," Jarthan said to Shyvoan, his voice weak.

Shyvoan smiled back. "And I you, of course. How did you escape him?"

Jarthan's gaze returned to Alorsha. "I didn't. He sent me away. He said he has all he needs from me."

"And what's that?" Mikolus said.

"The magic," Alorsha said.

"Your magic to make things out of nothing?" Shyvoan said. "Right?"

Jarthan nodded. "He's used it to make the passages to the various worlds. Tied in with the other-magic of these wisps." Jarthan waved an arm at the area around them.

"Has he taken it all somehow?" Alorsha said.

"Nearly all," Naltha said as she opened her eyes.

Jarthan nodded. "I've a little. About what I had when we first discovered my magic." He sighed and slumped.

Naltha sat back with a sigh. "I've done all I can for now. What will do you best now is some food and a long rest."

Jarthan nodded. "I welcome both. But rest first."

With Kluir and Parl again supporting him, Jarthan stumbled the few steps to the bedding Alorsha guided them to, her own. Jarthan's eyes drifted closed moments after he stretched out there.

Alorsha shared a worried look with Naltha while the others returned to their previous pursuits, Shyvoan checked on Gya before she settled again herself.

"How is he truly?" Alorsha asked Naltha while she helped the older woman settle again for her rest.

Naltha frowned. "Your fellow's been drained of his magic over and over until he can no longer regain most of it. That might not ever change now. He's also weak and exhausted, but those we can help with."

Alorsha nodded. "My thanks. I'll let you sleep."

She took her place again to watch the surroundings, but her gaze often drifted back to Jarthan. *He's so thin. And he shook so when I held him. I can't lose him now that I just got him back.*

She wiped away the tears that threatened. *But at least I do have him back. We'll figure everything else out from here.*

~ ~ ~

The group spent the gray day in their small camp with no further scouting trips after Parl returned from his aborted one. Everyone except Gya, Jarthan, and Naltha took a turn or two at watch and otherwise rested or honed weapons to pass the time.

Shyvoan and Alorsha both checked on Gya at intervals throughout the day, while the others watched from a distance. Gya seemed to be sleeping peacefully, his left hand wrapped in bandages that obscured its condition, with the telltale lumps of several charms tucked in the bandages. He stirred little throughout that long day, only to roll over in his sleep.

Alorsha spent most of her time otherwise at Jarthan's side and watched over his fitful sleep. At one point he thrashed about while still asleep. Rather than being soothed when she clasped his arm in a gentle grip, he sat up with a cry and looked around wildly before he apparently realized where he was. With a sheepish look for her, he fell right back asleep.

Naltha, too, slept the day away. But while she rose at dusk, and Jarthan woke then too, Gya slept on.

"He'll be fine," Naltha told Shyvoan and patted her arm as she sat next to her to eat the evening meal. "It's good for him to sleep this long after that strain. It wore on his body and his magic, so this is normal recovering."

Shyvoan nodded. "But his hand...."

"An undeniable shame, that. But we all bear the scars of our trials, don't we? Some are just more obvious." She looked at Jarthan and nodded approval as he ate eagerly.

"I suppose." Shyvoan said.

Gya woke as the others were finishing the meal and took a place next to Shyvoan, with a smile for her. He accepted some food and ate with almost as much enthusiasm as Jarthan.

After Jarthan finished his meal, and disregarding those around them, he pulled Alorsha to him into a long, deep kiss.

They broke apart when Parl cleared his throat, Alorsha's cheeks darker than usual and Jarthan's flushed pink. He looked at Parl.

"I missed her."

Parl nodded and chuckled.

Jarthan and Alorsha settled close together, drinks in hand. He kept one arm around her shoulders. "You do know that *he* knows you're coming," he said as he gazed around at the group.

"Not surprised," Kluir said.

"Did he deliberately send you to us?" Mikolus said.

Jarthan shrugged. "Not that I'm aware of. Best I can tell, he's released all the control he had over me." He looked at Alorsha. "But he mentioned that he welcomed your presence here to complete this."

"Complete what?" Parl asked. "Do you know where he's going next?"

"He doesn't plan to go anywhere else. He's been headed here on this whole journey. Something to do with the other-magic, the wisps. I don't know what. Bringing them all back here, maybe. Whatever it is, since he wants you, my love, I say we deny him. Just leave him here. He's mad. Maybe he always was...."

Alorsha frowned as she considered that.

"I might have something to add about what he's doing," Gya said. He glanced at Shyvoan then Alorsha. "When the wisp took me off on that little walk, I saw some things. I think I said something about that?"

Alorsha nodded.

"I've been trying to figure them out," Gya continued. "I believe I saw some of what happened here."

He frowned. "Although 'saw' isn't the best way to put it. It's more that I got impressions from the wisps than anything I actually saw. Something about the people who lived here. They drew all the magic together, everyone's magic, giving no one the choice whether to contribute or not. The leaders decided they alone knew what was best for everyone and pulled the magic to do something that would make everything perfect for everyone. That's the impression I got. But whatever they did had completely the opposite effect. The magic escaped their control, such as it was, and swept their world. It destroyed everything and everyone."

"And so, this world is the devastation we see. The wisps all that's left," Shyvoan murmured. "So *should* we just leave him here?"

"It would be a sort of justice, I suppose," Gya said into the thoughtful silence. "To leave him here with nothing. Seems I've got my answer about why he did what he did. At least all the answer I expect I'll get."

"But can we?" Kluir said. "Leave, I mean."

"Why not?" Jarthan said.

Alorsha sighed. "We've not been able to return to any of the worlds we've been to before. With you saying he's doing something with the wisps, I have to wonder. Maybe they're why. The wisps are in the *Deliberia*. Just as they're in our rings – remember when they went there?"

Jarthan scowled. "What if we can get them out, leave them here, too?"

"That could work," Gya said. He smiled at Jarthan. "Alorsha took me on as apprentice and has taught me how to open the passage with the *Deliberia*'s magic. When I've done that, I've sensed the magics of the other worlds lingering in the ship. If we didn't have to work against something that drew us here, we should be able to go back to those other worlds that we've visited."

"Maybe there'd be a way to go to new worlds, too," Shyvoan said.

They fell silent after that, as they finished their drinks.

The group split the night watches much as they had the daytime ones. Morning found them eager to be on their way again. Shyvoan woke surprisingly refreshed and immediately looked to Gya.

He already sat eating, one-handed, while Naltha rewrapped his other hand. With a toothy grin, Gya acknowledged Shyvoan's attention on him. "Looks like I'll be right-handed now."

Shyvoan's gaze dropped to his injured hand. The skin was its normal color, but the hand looked wasted, nothing more than skin and bones. He did move his fingers some as Naltha wrapped a thin bandage around his palm to cover the angry wound on the back of his hand. She slipped a new charm under the wrappings.

He sighed. "Much better. Thank you."

"Of course." The healer patted his shoulder as she rose. "After today, will see a big improvement in that wound."

Gya nodded his agreement.

Naltha tended to Jarthan next and made a makeshift pendant with a charm for him. She draped it around his neck before she moved off to finish packing.

Shyvoan clasped Gya's hand to help him to his feet. "All set?"

"Mostly. But I wasn't joking about the handedness. I might have to learn how to write all over again." He gave her a mock frown to invite her sympathy, but it morphed into a teasing grin.

She bumped his shoulder with hers and grinned back at him. "Not getting me with that. I know you can draw those sigils almost as well with your right hand. So, at worst, just a little extra practice doing it that way. If you even need to draw any of them."

Kluir grabbed Gya's pack as he passed. "Naltha says we'll take care of this for today," he said.

With everything packed again, they gathered around the tilbry.

"Well, if we're leaving, shouldn't we be getting to it?" Naltha said.

"But to continue after Devrand or return to the *Deliberia?*" Kluir said.

Alorsha looked around while she considered those options.

"Can we just leave?" she said. "I'd planned to take him back to our world, if at all possible."

"As your apprentice said, leaving him here with all this nothingness could be considered a form of justice," Jarthan said.

Shyvoan had been watching the wisps nearby, and something else drew her attention. "What's that?"

"Alorsha!" Mikolus said at the same time, facing the opposite direction.

His voice overrode Shyvoan's, and everyone looked where he indicated.

On the horizon a cloud of sorts had gathered. As they watched, it surged toward them, streaks of dark gray and red that writhed together within it. Shyvoan estimated it hovered less than a pace above the ground and stretched perhaps two paces from side to side. From their vantage, it formed a rough circle. From time to time, flashes of light illuminated it from inside.

"Down," Alorsha shouted and dropped prone. The others followed her example and the cloud flowed above them, headed the same direction as everything else.

Shyvoan rolled over to watch it as it passed above them. While it had looked circular from the front, from beneath it stretched back the direction it had come looking much like the wisps around them. Just much bigger.

It grew thinner as it passed but did not dissipate entirely.

Jarthan's frantic voice caught Shyvoan's attention. "What are you doing?"

Alorsha had risen to her knees and extended one hand toward the wisp-cloud above them, her fingers reaching within just a bit. The next instant she groaned and sank back to the ground.

Everyone scrambled to her, but she levered herself up on her elbows, with a frantic look for Jarthan.

"That's from the ship."

She scrambled to the side to get out from under the wisp-cloud and the others followed.

"He's not just pulling the wisps; he's pulling the other-magic that the *Deliberia* absorbed before we ever took passage to the first world," she told them. "He's taken our choice from us. We have to stop him. That magic's attached to the *Deliberia*'s own magic. He'll *not* take the magic of the ship!"

The crew, her people, depended on it. It belonged to them as much as to her.

She grabbed her bow and packs. "If he gets that, there'll be no magic for us to open a new passage. We'll be the ones left here with nothing."

CHAPTER 32

They again set out across the dark, dry plain. This time they followed the path of the cloud and traveled faster than they had before. Parl took the first turn pulling the tilbry and Alorsha and Mikolus led the way.

Shyvoan paced at Gya's side, her attention more on their surroundings than on him, although she did glance at him from time to time to make sure he took no further harm. As before, wisps flowed past them, headed the same direction they were. Most of them were gray, but Shyvoan spotted several of the reddish ones from the ship.

"Are there more wisps than before?" Kluir said near midday.

"I've been wondering that, too," Parl said.

"Might be we're getting close now," Mikolus said.

"Scout ahead again?" Shyvoan said.

"Yes, both you and Mikolus, please. Use this." Alorsha held out two small vials. "It's a concoction I made that lets one go unnoticed. Mikolus, you might remember it."

He nodded. "Wouldn't you rather save it until we get there?"

Alorsha shook her head. "This is the last of it. Just enough for two. Seems suited for scouting now, close enough to our destination, I suspect."

With nods, Shyvoan and Mikolus each took a vial.

Mikolus glanced at Alorsha. "I don't suppose you managed any improvement to the taste?"

"Unfortunately, not." Alorsha turned to Shyvoan. "It tastes truly awful and I'm sorry for that. The effects last about an hour."

Both warriors drank the concoction, with nearly identical grimaces and shudders, and set off ahead at a lope. They separated to cover more ground.

The others settled back to wait and pulled out some food and drink. Kluir and Parl kept watch even as they ate and drank but stayed near the others where they leaned against the tilbry. Naltha checked Gya's wound and rewrapped it. She handed Jarthan a second charm to string beside the first.

At Alorsha's questioning look, she nodded. "The charm's working, and Gya's hand's healing nicely. No change to the hand's gauntness, though."

"At least it doesn't hurt anymore," Gya said.

"Jarthan's doing better," Naltha added.

Jarthan nodded agreement.

The two scouts returned close to an hour after they left. After they grabbed some food and water, everyone hunkered together near the tilbry.

"The land's not as flat as it looks," Mikolus told them. "We jogged out about half an hour and discovered a large depression on the horizon out there. The land gradually slopes down to the upper edges of the basin, starting not too far from here."

"The wisps are definitely more numerous, and gathering closer together," Shyvoan said. "One guess where they're headed."

"So, you saw him there?" Gya said. "In that basin?"

Both Mikolus and Shyvoan shook their heads.

"Too many wisps gathered there, all twisting and turning," Mikolus said.

"From where we stopped, we couldn't see through them," Shyvoan added. "But that's where they're all headed. Looks like that cloud's there, too."

Alorsha looked around at the others. "While I've not yet felt him draw magic to himself in preparation for another passage, these wisps certainly have magic. Is everyone ready for this?"

The group exchanged glances.

"We don't know how far it is to Devrand, yet, but we've been lax to this point. Might be it's time to change that," Mikolus said.

He opened one of the packs he had brought and hauled out two of the stiff vests that Alorsha had treated with her concoctions, so they offered more protection, and protection against more things, than they seemed designed for at first glance. He handed one to Naltha and kept the other for himself, while everyone else pulled out their own from their packs.

"I didn't think to bring an extra," Mikolus said to Jarthan, his manner apologetic.

Jarthan shrugged. "Might be better if I stay behind anyway."

With a quick hug for him, Alorsha said, "We'll think of something."

Jarthan nodded but did not look convinced. "Might not matter," he muttered.

Shyvoan helped Gya into his vest when he was unable to tighten the lacings with just the one working hand. But at Alorsha's questioning look, he just smiled. "I'm ready for this. Let's finally get this bastard."

She nodded her agreement. "The vests now have some fire resistance on them," she told them. "A good thing since I've not been able to duplicate that fire-resistance concoction that I made back in your world, Gya. As with that other, though, it's short-lived, so if there's fire don't stay in it. They're also now almost impervious to piercing and slicing.

She dug in her pack and handed out various small jars and bottles. "These offer a variety of things that might be helpful. There's a pain-easing potion in the bottles with three ridges below the corks. This is the last of those so if you need any, try just a little at first to see if that's enough."

"I've got a salve to help ease pain, and my charms, of course," Naltha said. "But you'll need to get back to me as I plan to stay back from the conflict. And with that in mind...." She passed the vest that Mikolus had given her to Jarthan. "You take this. I suspect you'll get much closer than I will."

With a look at the others, who nodded, Jarthan put the vest on.

"The small brown jars hold the concoction that shoots out flames when the jar breaks. The jars are somewhat fragile, so don't grip them too hard." Alorsha handed one to each of them, except for Naltha, who got five. "Use them as you need."

Of the rest, she handed out one small jar of each type to each of them. "Small blue jar is the one that can cause distraction. Break it and the powder inside bursts out."

"I'm familiar with that one," Shyvoan said with a wry grin.

Alorsha nodded at her. "A variation on that. The small green one has something to help you keep going. A burst of energy. Drink that if you need it. I've got an extra of each, if needed and if you can get to me."

"If you get close, don't let him touch your skin," Jarthan spoke up.

"Right," Shyvoan said. "I remember that. He can influence you through touch."

"What of that elixir that's supposed to interfere with someone's ability to use their magic?" Parl said.

Alorsha frowned. "With all the variations I've tried, it's

never seemed effective enough against Devrand. I do have it with me, but I believe I'll put my trust in other magics, and arrows."

"What about against these?" Kluir waved a hand at the wisps that streamed by them. "Didn't you say they were magic? Or had magic?"

"Might be that elixir would help with them," Mikolus said.

Alorsha's expression became thoughtful. "It might. Easy enough to test. Just need a blade...."

Before she finished what she was saying, each of the warriors held a blade out to her for her to choose from. She grinned at them and chose Parl's sword. She pulled out the small jar that contained the elixir and a scrap of cloth. After she donned her leather gloves, she dipped a corner of the cloth into the elixir. The stuff clung to it, viscous and sticky. She carefully wiped the elixir along the edges of Parl's blade, both sides. That little amount was enough to coat those edges and give them a slight lustrous sheen. She returned the sword.

Parl took a step away from the group and swung at a nearby wisp. The sword passed through the middle and the wisp's reaction was both instant and gratifying. It split in two where the blade passed, and both pieces recoiled from the sword. At the same time, they each grew fainter and smaller. They rushed to rejoin, but the wisp that resulted from that action, much less cohesive, measured only half the size of the original.

"That's a success, then," Parl said.

"Next your special blade, Shyvoan," Alorsha said. She coated its edges and Shyvoan repeated Parl's actions. The wisp recoiled even faster, and when it reassembled, it was even smaller.

"See," Gya said. "There *is* something to that blade."

Shyvoan grinned.

Alorsha nodded. "We'll coat all our weapons, then." She passed the elixir and cloth to Mikolus. "Anyone with magic needs to keep from touching the stuff, but the rest of you needn't worry if you get some on your skin."

She grinned and pulled a round gray pot the size of her fist from her bag. "With this, I can give us fog. It won't last more than about a quarter hour, however."

Grins spread around the group.

"Long enough to get close enough without him knowing exactly where we're coming from," Kluir said.

Alorsha's grin matched the others'. "Gya you and I will draw on the *Deliberia*'s magic and see what we might accomplish with it, with its connection to the wisps. And one last thing...." She drew several small bags from her pack and handed them out. "These contain some oddments from my chervynai which will, at the very least, tend to enhance any magics I've a hand in. Use them if the potions and elixirs I've handed out need more magic to them. Otherwise, please hang onto them."

She and Mikolus exchanged looks.

"I'd prefer to be able to bring Devrand back to face justice," Alorsha said, "in whatever shape he's in. I suspect we'll end this here. Time to stop him."

Mikolus gave a decisive nod. "As she said. Check your weapons, be prepared to walk right in to conflict. We'll pause again near the basin if we're not already fighting him." He looked around at the others and met each person's gaze to impart confidence and resolve. Then everyone turned their attention to last-minute adjustments.

After Alorsha arranged her concoctions in her bag for easy access, and strung her bow, she stared the direction that the wisps headed.

Gya and Shyvoan finished their preparations and approached her.

"Alorsha?" Shyvoan tapped her arm.

"Is it Devrand?" Gya said.

Alorsha shook herself from her concentration. "No, nothing different there...." Her voice trailed off.

As Kluir and Parl helped Naltha settle again in the

tilbry, Mikolus joined the others. "A problem?"

"No. Not a problem," Alorsha said. "Have I forgotten something?"

"Doesn't seem like it," Shyvoan said.

"Might be this," Mikolus said and tapped Alorsha's pocket, the one in which she had placed Gya's bandage-wrapped ring.

Alorsha pulled out the bundle, considered it for a moment, and gestured to Gya, who reached out for his ring.

"But won't it just do that again?" Shyvoan waved at Gya's withered hand.

"I don't think so," Alorsha said. "Taiawood is good at holding other magic, including that one. It might give us an edge here. When we can see Devrand, use the ring to draw the magic, much as you draw it out in plants. You'll have the connection to the ship to help you and I'll work toward the same end. I believe we might be able to deny Devrand enough magic to keep him from opening another passage and running again, if he's so inclined."

Gya gave her a doubt-filled look but nodded. He tucked the ring into one of his own pockets.

"Makes sense to do that," he told Shyvoan. "In spite of practicing, I've never gotten very good with even simple weapons. The magic, though… *that* I can work."

With a long look for Alorsha and a supportive squeeze for her arm, Mikolus grabbed his packs. The others grasped theirs and they hurried across the barren land to the edge of the basin.

In the basin, wisps swirled and contorted into a cloud that resembled the one the other-magic from the *Deliberia* had formed. Within the swirling maelstrom, various colors flashed and briefly lit the mass at random intervals. But otherwise, they saw nothing within it.

They stopped just shy of the edge of the basin and shed anything they would not need in the anticipated confrontation. Naltha slipped out of the tilbry and settled on the ground next to it with her pack of charms and other healing supplies at her side. The others placed their packs around and under the tilbry.

"Ready?" Alorsha looked from one to another of them.

"I'm not sure what help I can be." Jarthan hunched down on the ground near the tilbry. "I should just stay here."

Alorsha clasped his hand, the one with the mage ring on his thumb, and held it up. "You still have this." She brushed a finger across the stone in the ring. "It's unchanged. Remember how we connected our magics with them. You can help through that."

Jarthan gave her a look full of doubt, then hung his head. "I don't know that I can," he muttered.

Alorsha clasped his other hand. "If not, that's fine. But stay with me?"

He lifted his gaze to meet hers and slowly nodded.

"We should all pair off," Mikolus said, "as we spread out and try to come at him from different directions."

"I'm with Gya." Shyvoan exchanged a smile with him.

"And I'll stay with Naltha," Parl said.

"Then you're with me," Mikolus said to Kluir, who nodded.

"Try to stay in sight," Alorsha told Gya. "So we can coordinate magics, if needed."

He nodded his agreement.

Mikolus told Alorsha, "We're ready for your fog, and we'll go."

Alorsha pulled out the gray pot, set it on the ground, knelt next to it and removed the lid. She held out a hand to Jarthan and her other hand to Gya. "Join me, please. Together we can extend the area and maybe get it to last longer, too."

After the two men clasped her hands, she closed her eyes and reached into the magic of the concoction in the pot. Gya and Jarthan closed their eyes, too.

Gya did not sense Jarthan's magic, but he reached out

with Alorsha to draw the fog out.

At first just light gray tendrils, fog puffed from the jar and expanded around them, thickest in the direction of the basin. After the last bit slipped from the jar, Alorsha opened her eyes.

"We've got about half an hour before it dissipates. Maybe a little longer," she said as she stood and drew the two men with her before she released Gya's hand. "It covers most of the edges of the basin right now."

"Then let's go," Mikolus said.

He and Kluir headed deeper into the murk and angled to the right.

"We'll go straight," Alorsha told Gya and Shyvoan. She exchanged nods with Parl, who drew his sword and took a defensive position near Naltha.

Alorsha drew Jarthan with her into the edges of the fog. Shyvoan and Gya paced them. They angled to the left and stayed just within sight.

Shyvoan kept a pace between her and Gya and kept him between her and Alorsha. They eased up to the edge of the basin and paused there when Alorsha and Jarthan did.

With the fog and wisps mixed, there was little to see in the basin. The flashes of light still occurred periodically and resembled colored lightning more than anything else.

"Gya, connect to the *Deliberia*'s magic. It's all around us now, and in your ring, so you shouldn't have any problem," Alorsha said.

Gya pulled his ring from its wrappings. After a moment of hesitation, he slipped it in place on the first finger of his right hand. After a few minutes of concentration, he nodded. "Got it."

"Good. Use it if you need."

Gya nodded again and Shyvoan met Alorsha's gaze. Then she and Gya headed down the slope of the basin when the others did.

The fog thickened, but the air did not have that moist

feel that usually accompanied it. Shyvoan started at a breath of air that brushed past her. She whirled, to find nothing there and met Gya's questioning gaze with a shrug before they continued.

The ground was no different from what they had crossed before and the slope was gentle, but they hiked a long time, longer than it seemed they should have, yet did not reach the bottom. The fog and wisps thickened further around them, and the light faded, except for the flashes which grew blinding as the darkness grew.

A tremor ran through the ground, and she caught Gya's hand to keep them both from falling. When it ended, they found themselves on a shelf of rock that stuck out from the basin's wall with no obvious way to go anywhere but possibly back up. Murk obscured the way ahead and further into the basin. It hid Alorsha and Jarthan too.

"Such wonderful gifts you've brought me," Devrand's voice cut through the gloom. A faint echo followed his words. "Your magic, your apprentice's, and this ship that has gathered the magic of worlds. You've even returned with our good friend Jarthan, with the little magic he can still bring me."

Shyvoan clasped Gya's hand, her grip tight, at the mention of his magic. Gya smiled grimly. "Not without a fight," he said in a low voice.

"Have to pinpoint his location in this," she said, her voice just as low.

"What do you want with the magic? What will it get you that you haven't got already?" Alorsha's voice sounded further away than Shyvoan would have guessed. She became aware of a low moaning sound that seemed to hover all around them. A hint of a breeze brushed past her.

"I'll make the magic mine and I'll have all that I should've had from the start. No longer need I be second and support to other mages."

Gya pointed to their left and down. "Sounds like he's that way."

Shyvoan nodded and eased over to the edge of their shelf to look for a way down.

"Look," Devrand shouted. "See the magic I've already gathered. Just envision what it'll be like when I've got it all!" Magic like lightning crackled through the fog and wisps.

Shyvoan sat on the side of the shelf with her legs over the edge. Her toes just touched ground, and it did not feel too steep. "This way I think."

"It won't be yours," Alorsha shouted, her voice almost obscured by the moans that had been steadily growing louder.

"What are you going to do?" Devrand taunted. "There aren't any plants here for you to twist to your needs."

Gya joined Shyvoan and together they eased off the shelf and continued down the basin's unseen slope.

"Hm, yes, I *had* noticed that." Alorsha's voice carried a heavy tone of sarcasm. "So, I brought something to help. You remember that flower of mine?"

A brilliant flash lit the area, red-gold in color and brighter than the colored lightning. Gya and Shyvoan caught hold of each other as the light momentarily blinded them and they slipped on the slope. Devrand cried out somewhere.

When her vision cleared, Shyvoan saw a myriad of red and gold sparkles hanging in the air. They moved slightly in the wake of the wisps' movements. They did nothing for visibility, but Gya grinned.

"The chervynai's magic," he said and closed his eyes. After a moment, his ring glowed a soft red. He opened his eyes and caught her in a quick embrace. "Now *that* will make a difference, I believe."

"Then let's get him," Shyvoan said, and they continued the way they had headed before.

"Alorsha, don't be a fool," Devrand's voice came from

somewhere ahead of them. "I can revive this world! We can. That's why the wisps came to us. Why they drew me, drew us, here. And they've promised so much in return."

A new light shone through the murk and the sparkles, an oval shape not far from Shyvoan and Gya. A light breeze came from that direction.

"He's opened a passage," Gya said.

Another one appeared somewhat behind them, and the breeze increased.

"What are you doing, Devrand?" Jarthan called.

Devrand laughed. "Just drawing the needed magic. With the ship, and in this place, I can draw the magic from all those worlds we journeyed through, bring it here. Give these people back their world and lives and they'll give me their adoration and magic. Why should those other worlds have the magic?"

"These really *are* people," Gya said to Shyvoan. "In spite of what I said earlier, I half thought I imagined what I discovered from the wisp."

She shrugged and pointed to another passage that formed in the murk. "I think I might have seen him over there." The wind increased and swirled around the basin. It carried the wisps and sparkles and fog with it.

"The wisps are the dead?" Alorsha called. "No magic has ever brought the dead back."

Devrand laughed again, the sound more than somewhat unhinged. "No one's had as much to work with as I will," he shrieked.

His tone calmed, his voice somehow carrying over the rising moans and wind. "What if you could go back home? I'll be able to do it. Use the magic from the worlds and get you back home."

"Home is gone," Alorsha shouted. "For me and for Jarthan. You cannot offer something that no longer exists."

More passages opened, encircling the basin, and providing additional light. Underfoot, the ground shook, and the images in the oval openings wavered. The wind gusted and roared in a rough circle, centered on the middle of the basin.

Shyvoan caught glimpses of the others and spotted a figure amidst the whirling wisps that could be Devrand.

Something tugged on Gya's magic, and he instinctively pulled back. He connected with the *Deliberia*'s magic that swirled all around. And with the chervynai's magic, too – something he had not fully accomplished before then. He grinned as the magic tingled in his arms and hands, even the withered hand.

Devrand pulled on it. He pulled back again, and some of Devrand's hold on it loosened.

A hoard of the wisps dove at Gya. They swarmed him and tried to wrap him, each touch pulling magic from him.

Then Shyvoan was there. With a ringing battle cry that echoed in the basin much as Devrand's voice had, she swung her heirloom sword around Gya. He felt the wind of its passage just a hand-width from him, but her precise slices missed him. The wisps broke apart, recoiled, and streamed away, seemingly unable to get away from Shyvoan's blade fast enough.

Across the basin, Gya spotted Mikolus and Kluir likewise slicing their way through wisps. Not as effectively as Shyvoan's blade did. Closer, Alorsha and Jarthan stood hand in hand. Gya saw, and felt, Alorsha's connection to the magic, and a whiff of magic that was Jarthan contributing what he could.

A nearby passage drew Gya's attention. Through the hole in the air, he saw a field of beautiful orange flowers shaken apart as the ground cracked and heaved. Broken. A huge wave washed across what was left.

"You've got to stop," Alorsha shouted.

"You're destroying those other worlds," Jarthan added.

The shaking of the ground underfoot grew worse and knocked everyone but Devrand off their feet. Alorsha struggled back upright to kneel on one knee and nocked an arrow to her bow. Jarthan stayed down and out of the way as she loosed two arrows in quick succession.

Through the magic, Gya saw the tendrils she used to help guide the arrows. The first arrow took Devrand in his upper arm and his cry held a mix of pain and anger. The second arrow was blown away as he raised a hand and yanked on the magic around them.

Mikolus and Kluir charged him from behind and were bowled over as he drew more magic from the other worlds and fed it into the vortex around himself.

From the edge of the basin, Naltha threw one of those fire pots. Her throw belied her appearance and arched high and far. The pot shattered at the base of one of the passages and flames surged up to obscure the oval. Devrand turned toward the fire, and it flowed away from the passage to engulf Mikolus and Kluir. The passage appeared unchanged. It still showed another world in upheaval, still wavering with the magic being drawn from there. Mikolus and Kluir escaped the flames, somewhat singed.

"The armor works," Shyvoan murmured.

As if they stood next to him, Gya clearly heard Alorsha's and Jarthan's voices. *Must be because we're connected through the magic.*

"We three started this together..." Jarthan said.

"Think it's going to take us together to finish it?" Alorsha said.

"Seems so."

"Then we'll just have to finish it our way, not his."

Alorsha and Jarthan braced themselves and each other against the howling chaos and they approached Devrand.

Another of the fire pots came from Naltha and broke in front of the two mages. It momentarily cleared the wisps from their path to allow them a few easier steps toward their destination.

Two of the blue pots arched out of the miasma from different directions and broke at Devrand's feet. They released a blue, powdery cloud that engulfed him.

"Please work, please work," Shyvoan chanted, her voice little more than a whisper, while she continued to slice wisps. Gya threw his own blue pot to break near the others.

Wind swept the cloud away from Devrand. He wobbled, looking dazed. He shook his head once, and again, and seemed to regain his senses.

Shyvoan cursed softly at the distraction-powder's failure.

Gya had lost sight of Mikolus and Kluir again, and the swirling wisps that surrounded Devrand made him almost impossible to see. Through the magic, Gya still saw the stream that came from the *Deliberia*, now colored only the red-brown of its taiawood, no longer containing any of the grayness from the wisps. He drew the ring from his finger and held it up. Devrand's storm drew the gray wisp from it.

With a smile, Gya again donned his ring and his connection to the *Deliberia*'s magic immediately grew stronger.

As Alorsha and Jarthan drew closer to Devrand, Alorsha paused and glanced over her shoulder at Gya. With a smile, she spoke one word.

"Untie."

Hand-clasped with Jarthan, she pushed toward Devrand again.

Gya frowned. *What does she...? Oh, she means that sigil.*

And he had the pouch of oddments from the chervynai plus what streamed all around him. But he'd not practiced drawing it with his non-dominant hand. *Can I?*

"I've got to stand still to work some magic," he told Shyvoan. "And I'll have to concentrate."

She nodded her understanding and attacked the few wisps that remained and seemed intent on reaching Gya.

"Anything else I can help with? For you to work the magic?" she said as she drove them off. She gulped the potion from her green bottle and followed that with a quick drink of water from her water skin.

Gya shook his head and drank from his own green bottle. "But they'll probably be back to try to stop me."

They both stumbled as the ground shook again underfoot.

"Seems that I'd better sit for this," Gya said. "Another of those at the wrong time could be bad."

With a quick look around, Gya led them to the side a few paces to a more level spot. The wisps and magic streamed around them, and the wind made the going a struggle, but they made it there.

Gya brushed some of the larger rocks away. He touched two fingers to the hilt of Shyvoan's sword and smiled at her.

"If that luck's a real thing, we need it now."

She smiled back as he sat. With a quick exchange of looks and nods, Shyvoan turned away to face whatever might come. The potion energized Gya, and he dove into the magic, blocking out all else around.

The *Deliberia*'s magic came to him, and the chervynai's magic followed. He set the open pouch of oddments in his withered hand. The plant's oddments came to him when he lifted his other hand and made the little gesture that used to draw the kri-stone powder to him.

He smoothed the ground in front of him and pulled the oddments there to draw the sigil. But an odd resistance made him pause. Without his volition, his hand was drawn up into the air in front of him. The sparkling oddments hovered around it. Like they waited on his actions. The wind calmed in that spot as he began to draw the sigil in the air.

Focused on making each line correct, each swirl accurate, Gya lost track of time. He vaguely noticed that Shyvoan again fought the wisps around him, but nothing beyond that even touched on his concentration. As each line formed, each swirl connected to another, the magic in the sigil grew, unlike any sigil he had drawn before.

A tremor reverberated through the magic when Alorsha and Jarthan reached Devrand. Gya felt Devrand in the magic, which momentarily disturbed his focus. *Can't let it. Back into the magic.*

Shyvoan felt like she had been fighting for hours. She sliced through another wisp that acted intent on reaching Gya and staggered as the ground shook. She felt little resistance as the sword sliced through the wisps. This was worse than when she first learned the sword. At least then, she'd had the brief respite when she struck the target.

Her muscles ached and protested the continued actions and the struggle to stay on her feet in the gale winds, Shyvoan attacked another group of wisps. *Hope Gya's magic is close to ready.*

Gya drew the last arc of the sigil, precisely placing the chervynai's oddments in a sweeping curve that encompassed half the sigil. The usual tingle of the magic pounced on him when he finished the curve. The sigil glowed and its light grew too bright to look at.

Gya closed his eyes, but still saw everything through the magic.

Alorsha and Jarthan stood with Devrand, their right hands clasped together between them. Their three mage rings glowed almost as brightly as the sigil and lit their faces. Devrand's expression was stunned, Alorsha's resolute, and Jarthan's resigned. Alorsha held her other hand out and slightly behind her, her fingertips in a stream of chervynai oddments and taiawood magic.

Devrand tried to seize control of the magic, but it twisted away from him. He tried to pull away from the others' clasp but seemed unable to break free.

Alorsha swept her hand in a half-circle. The chervynai oddments and taiawood magic followed her motion to form a star shape on the ground around the three mages, a star made from two squares, one rotated from the other. Jarthan made a similar gesture and not-quite-substantial candles formed at each corner of the star, red-gold flames alight atop them.

The winds stopped.

Everything stopped.

Wavers in the passages held frozen in an instant.

Ground crumbling, pieces suspended in the air.

Gya's ears rang in the sudden silence.

Jarthan stretched out his left hand, into the stream of oddments and taiawood magic. He joined with Alorsha's magic and together they drew the wisps from their mage rings, and from Devrand.

Devrand howled and all three mages dropped to their knees.

The wisps joined with the others and formed an angry cloud above the three.

Alorsha and Jarthan sent their magic into the stream of oddments, into the taiawood magic. Her ability to draw out the magic of the plants and his ability to make, both joined with the sigil's imperative to untie.

Alorsha's gaze met Gya's, and she nodded to him and smiled.

The sigil's magic exploded out, red-gold, the sigil stretching to an impossible size, taking the light with it, in a wave that flowed through the basin. The wisps shredded in the wave and dissipated as the magic that held them there unraveled.

Each passage the wave touched stabilized, stopped wavering, and magic flowed back through, freed from Devrand's grasp. Each passage oval shrank to the size of a pebble as its connection to Devrand was unmade. That pebble then flowed with the sigil's magic to the next passage. All those pebbles gathered together, and each added its glow to the group until they reached a last portal, which showed a burned-out stretch of land within its border.

The pebbles settled on the passage's edge, and it shrank, slower than the others had. As it did, it, the pebbles, and all the magics—sigil, chervynai, and taiawood—poured into the basin, charged the three mages in the center, and engulfed them.

Red magic burst forth, a gold-tinged circlet that blasted out from that center and bowled over everything in its path. It passed over the edges of the basin and continued outward.

After it passed, Gya rolled over to look to the center. Engulfed in a light almost too bright to look at, the three mages rose to their feet. Gya frowned at what he saw. They were almost impossible to distinguish in the bright light.

The oval light seemed to close around them.

Then it, and they, were gone.

CHAPTER 33

Shyvoan and Gya helped each other to their feet and stumbled to the center of the basin. Mikolus and Kluir met them there, and they all stared at what they found in the dirt. The star shape had fused into rock. It surrounded and centered upon three sets of footprints in the dirt.

Next to the footprints, tiny plants grew. Two little leaves for each poked through the dirt.

As they watched, the plants stretched upward, grew more leaves, and filled out into small bushes about a hand's length tall.

Shyvoan spun around. All across the basin, more of the plants grew, with stalks growing from the little bushes, topped by the deep red, gold-edged flowers that opened wide.

A light rain began to fall, watering the plants.

In wonder, they looked at the chervynai plants all around them, and exchanged looks with each other.

Gya brushed his fingers across the petals of one of the flowers. A brief flash sparked from them to his undamaged taiawood mage ring.

He straightened again. "We'd better get back."

He led the way toward Naltha and Parl, who awaited them at the basin's edge.

~ ~ ~

Gya and Shyvoan leaned on the *Deliberia*'s rail and looked over the land that stretched from the shoreline in front of them to the horizon.

Chervynai dotted the dark dirt and brought color and magic to the place. Gya easily perceived the plant's magic now, including Alorsha's plant that still sat in her cabin.

"Do you think they...?" Shyvoan broke the comfortable silence that had settled between them.

Gya shrugged. "At the end, that looked like a passage where they stood. They might have gone through. I just don't know. Although, we could go to that world to see."

Shyvoan shrugged. "I almost prefer the uncertainty. I can picture them home and everything turning out fine for Alorsha and Jarthan. And Devrand getting his due. Maybe that's enough. I don't know that I'd want to know otherwise."

Gya nodded.

"You're sure the magic to travel worlds is still in the ship?" Shyvoan said after another long silence. "Pretty as that is," she waved a hand at the chervynai field, "I don't particularly want to live in this world."

"I'm sure," Gya said. "I'll show you soon enough. We just need to determine where to go."

"Don't the others want to go back to their homes?"

Gya smiled. "I've overheard many of the crew talk about it. But most seemed to feel no sense of urgency. From what they've said, it did sound like there are some worlds some would like to revisit. And I sense the *Deliberia*'s magic will still let us travel to new worlds, if we wish. Although I don't know that we can steer, as such."

He turned away from the flowery scene to gaze into her

eyes. "But what of you? What do you want? You haven't said."

She laughed. "The *Deliberia* and travel both suit me fine. I also happen to be partial to the ship's master-mage, so I'd like to go where he's going."

He matched her chuckle. "I'm not sure I'd say 'master' yet. But that reminds me...."

He pulled his mage ring off the first finger of his right hand. "After all that, I've a feeling Alorsha would insist that I'm now an artisan-mage. So, I should wear the ring on my left thumb, although it's probably far too loose." Still, he slid it onto his thumb.

"Maybe I can get it adjusted...." Gya's voice trailed off.

He and Shyvoan watched in amazement as the taiawood ring shrank to fit Gya's desiccated thumb.

"That's handy," Shyvoan said with a soft chuckle.

"Very. And I'll just work toward becoming a master-mage at some point in the journey. In the meantime, though I can't imagine traveling anywhere without you. So, if you're truly willing to join me...."

He held his hand out to her, and she clasped it eagerly. "I am."

His smile grew wide. "Then it's time to get back to meet with the others and decide where we'll sail next."

~

Pronunciations

Aiokta – ay AHK tuh
Alaylu – uh LAY loo
Alorsha – uh LOHR shuh
Arithi – uh REE thee
Avorth – uh VOHRTH

Bashiad – bah SHEE uhd
Bilguon – BIHL goo uhn
Borysk – BOHR ihsk

Charnov – CHAHR nawf
chervynai – CHAYR vih nay
Chimeg – CHIH-mehg
Cothria – KAHTH ree uh

Davaj – DAH vahj
Deasa – DEE suh
Deliberia – dehl ih BAYR ee uh
Devrand – DEHV ruhnd

erythros – AYR ih throhs
Evka – EHV kuh
Eztevo – EHZ teh voh

Falshinku – FAHL shihn koo
Fiafas – fee AHF uhs
Flenar – FLEHN uhr

Grabe – GRAYB
Gramaire – GRAH mayr
Grigry – GRIH gree
Gya – G-EYE uh
Gyasi – G-EYE uh see

Hali – hah LEE
Hathu – HAH thoo

Horic – HOHR ihk

Ilyevano – ihl yeh VAH noh
Ioli – EE oh lee
Izmireva – ihz MEER ih vuh

Jarthan – JAHR thuhn

Kaimas – KAY muhs
Kayamo – kay YAH moh
Khagja – KAHG juh
Khagjayan – kahg JAY uhn
Kluir – KLOOR
K'rond – kuh ROND

Lorai – LOHR ay
Lovain – loh VAYN
Ludek – LOO dehk

Mantorol – mahn TOHR uhl
Mikolus – MIH koh luhss
Mongom – MAHN guhm

Naivaschld – NAY vuhs chuhld
Naltha – NAHL thuh
Nijole – nih JOHL
Nuana – noo AH nuh

Olza – OHL zuh
Olzanka – ohl ZAHN kuh
Oyuchim – OY oo chihm

Palilen – PAH lihl uhn
Parl – PAHRL
Pirkuo – peer KOO oh

Rahaer – rah HAYR
Raska – RAHS kuh

Ravnajor – RAHV nah zhohr
Reez – REEZ
Remdor – REHM duhr
Riovan – REE oh vahn

Saevalde – say VAHL deh
Shyvoan – shih VOHN
Slarov – SLAHR uhv
Smas – SMAHS
Sonne – SOH nuh
Sutoth – SOO tawth

Taesen – TAY sehn
taiawood – TAY uh wood
Tavano – tuh VAH noh
Tavaros – TAH vahr ohs
Thienas – THEE nahs
tilbry – TIHL bree

Ulask – OO luhsk
Umastac – oo MAHS tuhk

Varoia – vuh ROY uh
Varoian – vuh ROY uhn
Vernandos – VEHR nuhn dohs
Viyeva – vee YEH vuh
Voitsek – VOYT suhk

Wolshor – WOHL shohr

Yarmil – YAHR muhl
Yauntla – YAWNT luh

Zan – ZAHN
Zhivko – ZHIHV koh

~

TITLES BY S. LYNN HELTON

Wild Heritance fantasy series

Duplicity of Power
Power Awry
Power Redeemed

Trial Run (prequel novella)
Trial and Tribulation (prequel novella)

The Deliberia Chronicles fantasy trilogy

Crystalborne Sigils
Songborne Gates
A Galeborne Resolve

Author's Note

Thank you for reading my book. I hope you enjoyed it!

Please consider leaving an honest review on the book's
product page at your favorite online bookstore
and on Goodreads. Reviews from readers like you are
powerful and greatly help other readers
discover books they might enjoy.

-Lynn

About the Author

S. Lynn Helton lives in the foothills of the Rocky
Mountains, U.S.A., with her family and a couple of crazy
cats. Lynn enjoys camping and hiking, playing games,
crafting, reading (a lot) and, of course, writing.

Read more about her books on her website:
www.slynnhelton.com